AMERICAN ROSE

Also by Julia Markus

La Mora
A Patron of the Arts
Uncle

AMERICAN ROSE.

A NOVEL BY

JULIA MARKUS

BOSTON

HOUGHTON MIFFLIN COMPANY

1981

6/1981
gen'l.

Library of Congress Cataloging in Publication Data

Markus, Julia
American rose.

I. Title.
PS3563.A672A8   813'.54   80-20290
ISBN 0-395-30229-3

Printed in the United States of America

P 10 9 8 7 6 5 4 3 2

The author is grateful for permission to quote from the following:
Kaddish and Other Poems, by Allen Ginsberg. Copyright © 1961 by
Allen Ginsberg.
Lines from *Life Studies,* by Robert Lowell. Copyright © 1956, 1959 by
Robert Lowell. Reprinted by permission of Farrar, Straus & Giroux.
"Smoke Gets in Your Eyes"—Words by Otto Harbach. Copyright ©
1933 by T. B. Harms Company. Copyright Renewed. International
Copyright Secured. Used by Permission.
"Too Young"—original copyright © 1951 by Jefferson Music Co.;
copyright renewed 1979 by Aria Music Co.; music by Sidney Lippman,
lyrics by Sylvia Dee.
The poem "XII"—copyright © 1981 by Marjorie Markus Rice.

My special thanks to my friend Dr. Charles M. Timbrell, pianist and
scholar, who so generously and painstakingly advised me on the musical
sections of "Golden Girl."

For my mother, Ruth
and
In memory of my father, Morris

CONTENTS

The Addis Family

Before the turn of the century ROSE ADDIS, a fortune-teller, came to America from Alsace-Lorraine. ALSATIAN ROSE favored her youngest child and only son, CHARLES. Some of her luck rubbed off on him. He married ETTA, who convinced him to buy the butcher shop he worked in. Charles and Etta Addis became very rich. They had two children, HELEN and RAYMOND.

Helen was the light of her mother's eye. She was supposed to become a concert pianist, but that is not what happened. Raymond was the favorite of his grandmother Alsatian Rose, but he failed to inherit her luck. He went into the butcher business like his father and married ELLEN DIAMOND.

Ellen and Raymond Addis have two daughters. These are sisters born into a world very different from that of their forebears, yet they inherit a potion of old sorrows as well as a potion of magic and luck. The younger sister is named JANET. The older is Raymond's favorite, ROSE. AMERICAN ROSE.

GOLDEN GIRL

THE HOUSE on Clifton Avenue was a duplex. A wall split the grand staircase in two. Charles and Etta Addis bought the place in 1920 when they became rich, for very little money, and rented out the less interesting half.

Etta was the oldest of a large family; she had known what it was to be poor.

Her father was shot to death in Hartford, Connecticut, while collecting payments for Singer. Etta rode in a high, shining carriage.

Her mother moved to Jersey City and sold yard goods. Etta could count to ten in Yiddish, Italian, Polish, and Deutsch for the rest of her life.

Her mother then "married" an Englishman named Mordecai. *His* mother wore a shaytl, yet spoke like the old Queen. Mordecai put on a top hat and took Etta to the opera. He also beat her mother up and put the two children her mother bore him to work in the sweatshop at the back of his candy store.

Etta's mother died at home in agony. Etta was sixteen.

She took care of the family and wrapped packages in a box factory until she married Charles.

> *In Jersey City where I did dwell*
> *A butcher boy I loved so well,*
> *He took from me my heart away —*
> *Oh Joy! Oh Joy!*

Since Charles was younger than she, Etta lied about her age. That she had lied was an open secret in the family, but in time her real age became obscured.

Charles's mother, Rose Addis, was a French Jew, a beautiful widow originally from Alsace-Lorraine. She told fortunes (and gave abortions) in Jersey City. Etta always loved to hear her speak.

Charles was the apple of his mother's eye. Eventually Rose Addis died in his arms, of gangrene.

A man who has been able to reciprocate mother love is often a good man at home. Etta took care of her sisters and brothers, and Charles never complained once.

A man whose loving mother is a witch can be rubbed by luck. When Charles shot craps he often knew when he'd win big.

A man who has been able to *give* as well as receive mother love would have to be very short indeed to want to be Napoleon. And Charles was tall and lean.

Etta gave him the idea: Take the money you've won, add it to what I've saved, and buy the butcher shop. For a moment he was startled. Then he did it. That's how they became very, very rich.

Etta and Charles's daughter, Helen, was an infant when the meat market on Central Avenue became Addis. Their son, Raymond, was not yet born. They lived near the store over another store on the same block where Charles's mother told fortunes, Etta's stepfather ran a sweatshop, and her mother had once sold cloth to Italians, Poles, Germans, and Jews.

Every Sunday they ate at Charles's mother's place. Rose Addis had thick white hair, blue eyes shaped like the Lake of Nemi, skin transparent as the tissue paper gifts come wrapped in. She sat at the head of the table and presided.

Rose Addis had two daughters, one pretty, who liked to dance, the other plain, both mean with a penny and married to Germans. In Alsace-Lorraine these daughters would have been shipped to America — where they were, sitting with their goyisher husbands at their mother's table. The mother loved her son, Charles, too much to do anything but disregard her older daughters. She treated them as she did the world — as business to do right. When the pretty one's son was fourteen, Rose took him to the bank on Journal Square. "This is my grandson; I'm sure you can find *something* for him to do." The woman had $50,000 in her account. The boy got a job. *His* son roomed with the son of a Latin American dictator at Harvard and was invited to the palace between semesters.

Rose treated her daughter-in-law, Etta, correctly and told her fortune. Little Helen would someday have the world for her asking. Raymond would be a boy. When he was, Rose claimed success. She favored him. Perhaps life would have been different for Raymond if his grandmother hadn't developed diabetes. Once, on Central Avenue, when he was very young, he had a tantrum over candy. Raymond's sweet tooth from the beginning was insatiable. Rose Addis stuck her magnificent head out of the window, and in her grand voice, which hadn't a smattering of Yiddish but was washed with French, yelled, "Etta! Shame on you! Give the boy his chocolate!"

What a story this made in the years when to look at a baby you had to wear a mask, and grandparents were never allowed to take theirs off.

No. Etta never resented *her* mother-in-law. Her commands, her imperiousness, her grace. Some people shunned Rose Addis because of her Gentile sons-in-law, the pills she sold, the goyisher businessmen who consulted her cards. Let them talk — and stay besieged on Central Avenue. To Etta, the woman was a holiday. She admired majesty.

Beauty was magic for Etta. It transformed her brute of a stepfather with an aria. It reached beyond poverty and meanness and wretched death to a greater world. She remembered her uncles from the other side, with their red locks and beards and language that embarrassed her. They had to be taken to kosher markets in Hoboken — the butchers were fat men who wiped their bloody knives across aprons already streaked with filth. Charles's trayf shop was orderly and clean — he already needed two more boys. His mother foretold prosperity, but Etta could have told her that.

And their daughter, Helen, *would* have the world for the asking. The child's beauty and sensitivity were signs. Rose Addis didn't read blind. Before Helen could speak she could pick up a tune. And when Raymond was born . . .

By that time Charles and Etta only had Etta's full sister, Lilly, living with them; one of Etta's full brothers had married, one had gone west. Lilly was particularly pretty, not just pleasant-looking like Etta. She had Titian-red hair and chestnut eyes that slanted up from a long, lean face. Yet she wished she had thick hair like her sister's, which Etta could wear in one long dark braid to her waist.

Now like her sister, Lilly loved the opera, but her expectations were too grand. While the swell of music could carry Etta to eighth row center, it hurled Lilly onto the stage. In life that's where she found herself; everything happened to her. Even Etta's labor was her story. When she told it her voice rose to a song.

Lilly sat outside Etta's apartment at the top of the stairs with little Helen in her arms. Inside, her sister screamed. My God! was that what it was like to have a baby? It should never happen to her. On through the dark night went the terror, while Helen clung to her (and she to Helen) in fear. When the midwife opened the door to the morning light, Helen jumped from Lilly's arms. With her nails extended and her teeth exposed, the child hooked herself into the old midwife's leg and snarled like a dog. Lilly, stiff from the night's vigil, could hardly believe her light-tender eyes. "Helen!" she called, but there was no stopping her. The old lady yowled in pain, until Lilly with great effort loosed the furious child. So everything happened to Lilly the night that Raymond was born.

Of course it shouldn't have happened at all. Etta had sent them to her mother-in-law's, not to the top of the stairs. Yet to think of her little girl's love for her, in those tough weeks after Raymond's birth, stirred Etta's distant heart.

Who did Etta have to talk to? And she wasn't one to complain. She was over thirty, though she didn't admit to it. Her small frame was swollen by past pregnancy and by the sweet tooth she had just passed on. She felt all alone.

She went to her beautiful mother-in-law, who spread out the cards. Rose Addis looked at her with eyes like a lake — quiet on the surface, depths below. How many Ettas had she seen through the years?

Yet magic has its moments. Intuition overwhelmed the witch. Not a word of Raymond. Helen. Charles. Instead —

Suitcases

Music

Lawns . . . perhaps a meadow . . .

Silver

Extralong Life

circled round Etta's distress.

Etta's hand was taken firmly and held open, till sweat appeared on Rose's well-tended upper lip. "Everything in the cards is right here," Rose said, as her fingers traced the lines of Etta's palm. Then from across the table the woman grasped both of Etta's hands: "You have powers all your own!"

Twenty years later a more expensive witch doctor would make Etta recall that depression. He had the authority to dare ask her about sex. If the heaviness in her heart hadn't precluded it, she would have said to him: "You tell *me* about sex. You're a man. I'll tell you about lying in bed with my legs open, praying to God the best rubbers don't leak!" Instead she said slowly, slanting her eyes: "I'm not the patient." His look said, Worse for you. Much, much worse for her.

Let's go back to happier times. In 1920, the children were small, and the money was rolling in. When they were rich, they were no longer poor, and for Etta that was that. Poor people save, rich people spend. And how she spent. Usually successful people tell you of the horse that won, the job they got, the stock that doubled and split. The winnings shine, cry out for admiration, like all the beautiful things that Etta bought. But you can bet on torn tickets, waits in outer offices, tax losses. Not so with Etta's things. She had unerring taste.

The house came first. The statement of the theme. Five blocks down (at right angles) and one world away from the reservoir that ends Central Avenue. You'd have to go far to find a better house on a better block in Jersey City, and Etta saw it right away.

An enormous house. A concert grand fitted easily into the living room. Then Helen filled the rooms with scales and arpeggios, just as Etta filled them with beautiful things.

In those days things came by way of people who walked right up to your back door: poor people from foreign lands with skills and hope chests that crossed oceans; salesmen pathetically frayed and eager with wares worth money nobody had. Louie the linen man.

When they showed up at Etta Addis's door, they went away to eat a good dinner. Through her whole long life "bargain" was a dirty word — "Missus, my mother sent me for the three cents you owe. She's gotta buy milk for the children." Etta, age eleven, skilled at collecting for her mother at anybody's door.

Next door she rented to a young dentist and his wife. In his new office on the Avenue he put up a sign: "There's nothing a man can't make a little worse and sell a little cheaper. And he who considers price only is that man's lawful prey. — John Ruskin." Etta Addis too.

Blacks came to the door. Her backyard and front lawns were tended, her windows kept clean. Her screens put up in spring and dismantled in October. Her furniture polished to her instructions, her ivy plants washed with milk, her oriental rugs beaten out. Her own broad noodles, chicken soup, roasts of beef, and apple pies were served in the paneled dining room when she lifted the small oriental bell at her fingers and rang.

The opulence had a core, a dream. Helen was gifted. All through the twenties she sat at the piano and played. This was no ordinary Jersey City girl. The way she looked, the way she dressed, the soft way she smiled and spoke. This could be one of the Four Hundred. Golden girl.

Amid the luxurious bounty of Etta's kind of love there was a gash of vulnerability. The cold steel of mocking chance through all this blessed luck . . .

Now Charley loved broad noodles, and he liked them done just right. Within their limits, all his tastes were fine. He knew a good tailor once he had one, an excellent restaurant once he'd been. And his motherload of gentility found a home among new friends. Charley Addis, M.D., they kidded him on poker-playing nights. Just try to pick the Meat Dealer from the *licensed* butchers in the game.

When Charley was young, it was Rose Addis who served him broad noodles every Friday night. Making this kind of dough was tedious for a busy witch. So she cheated. One Friday morning, while Charley was at school, she went out and *bought* noodles. Charley came home to find the rolling board and pin on the table as usual, the bogus noodles sprinkled with flour sitting on the accustomed towel. He looked up at his mother petulantly and with disdain proclaimed: he'd never eat these noodles from the store.

Etta made him noodles with enthusiasm. She had an eye and an appetite, and was a wonderful cook. If Charley hadn't liked the food he liked, she'd have turned to haute cuisine. But he stopped short of sauces and disguises, so she cooked to perfection what he knew. The list was long; it was Raymond who cut it down. That boy hated liver and sweetbreads, mushrooms, fish with bones, any meat that ran red. He left the yolks of his eggs dry on his plate every morning and left the room when any cheese smelled like feet. Over the holidays he picked at one ball of the most sought-after gefilte fish in Jersey City. And he refused to have fresh chopped parsley sprinkled across his homemade chicken noodle soup. "What's wrong with you?" Etta would ask in her daily marathon to feed him. For him there was always dessert.

The accident happened when she was pregnant with Raymond, in the old apartment, where cooking wasn't such a delight. When she boiled her own water for clothes as well as for broad noodles, but this was a Friday night.

If she hadn't been so fat and clumsy in her pregnancy

If Helen hadn't been underfoot

If the noodles didn't have to be boiled *just* before serving

If Charles would have eaten them warmed up . . .

Then Helen wouldn't have been scalded. It could have been worse:

It could have been her face.

It could have killed her.

It was bad enough.

You forget physical pain when it's over, but never the scream of pain from a child you've just maimed. When Helen had one of her tantrums out of the blue, Etta heard echoes of that scream again. And she always heard it when she looked at Helen's neck.

There the blemish remained, spreading from the top of her chest. It faded some as Helen grew, but it had to be covered up.

Many years later, when Raymond knew he was about to die, when the white psoriasis that plagued him began to heal, he stared blank-eyed at the puffy, pink flesh around his elbow and remembered his sister's neck.

Are there accidents? That's a fifty-dollar-an-hour question. In the late thirties the Addises paid their dues. There *are* souls. There *is* destiny to be worked out in only one lifetime. And of malicious fate, carelessness, chaos, and the poltergeist, we can be sure.

Here was a custom-made hell for Etta, the ugly mark she had made on her daughter's neck. Can't replace it, can't match it, can't polish it away.

Except who, what owed Etta Addis anything? Who cooed at her cradle? What star shone at her birth? The love she had known had been that of a woman whose hard work had earned her a dead husband, a mean "husband," too many children, tough times, and a cancer to eat her to death.

"Poor you" was Etta's response to self-pity. Including her own.

In the luster of beautiful things she saw reflected the cold still point of her soul.

Black Friday came close to following Rose Addis's coffin to the grave. Charley lost her passbook on margin, and the bank stocks she left him turned to paper in his hands. While his sisters squeezed Rose's diamonds on their fingers, Charley saw the rest of the world grow poorer for his mother's death.

People didn't have much use for dentists, doctors, lawyers during the Depression, but on the whole they still ate meat. In a few years Charles was richer than before. Comparatively. During the twenties the Addises had joined the many who were affluent. Now the crowd thinned out.

Without his mother and with Etta, it was Charles's turn to feel alone.

His sisters recommended the cheap witch they were using. Charles tried her, but she couldn't compare.

She became his customer, though. Every once in a while he'd add a thick steak to her order and deliver himself. Things weren't going well at home.

That's putting it too directly. Making a statement out of the Addises' silent shifts. 1931. Etta blows Lilly to *Mourning Becomes Electra* the second time she gets good seats.

When Alice Brady turns her back to the audience, lifts the hem of her grand black skirts, and walks up the stairs of her colonial to her fate, tragedy is in the thrall of majesty. The sisters gasp. When things happen at home, Etta shrugs. That's life.

Charles slept through *Mourning* the first time Etta saw it, barely reviving for the dinner break. That world of fine feeling is barred to him, though he keeps quiet in his evening suit.

He is not introspective. He's a loving man, a lucky man, life fits him well. He married a sliver of a girl with dark hair and a strong will. The alchemy of her sex has turned her as plump as a German lady.

He is fascinated by the swollen breasts, the fat beneath the thighs and below the buttocks.

Don't touch!

She covers up now when he walks in the room.

She's asleep before he is, and when he wakes up, she's gone.

She was freer than he when they married. (He was her younger man — sssh!) She liked a good time as well as anyone. Better! Before she was married, boy could she dance!

But childbirth put a big dent in pleasure. Repetition of the sex act didn't bind the rift. Enter the will that said do and you'll be sorry . . . And life ripples down a new stream.

The women in Charles's life had always had powers. He had trusted his mother, though she could be devious with a rolling pin. She saw through souls with cards, crystal, and hunches, then pulled aside the curtain, walked into the kitchen, and did accounts.

As a man he trusted Etta's powers. She turned money into beauty; their teen-age daughter sat on the embroidered top of the piano bench and played.

Sure there were things he would have liked besides his mother's resurrection: warm sheets for cold sheets, Etta's stomach for her back, Helen enjoying the parties she played at, and Maxie out of the house. Yet he knew better than ever to tamper with Etta's magic at home.

He might have intuited his own resentment; he might have heard his anger when his voice rose. But he had a short temper to exorcise his self-awareness, and his allegiances, though varied, were clearcut.

It would take his heart being ripped out of his chest for him to wonder, Why?

But in those sweet years, when he and Etta fought, he could roll all dissatisfaction into a finale that cleansed his soul. In the tough voice that surfaced when he was white-hot he rasped: "Keep that fairy out of my hair!"

He meant Maxie. Maxie hadn't come to Clifton Avenue via the normal channel (the back door). Heralded by the chauffeur, Lionel, he appeared for an interview one cold winter day.

Through the flecks of falling snow, Etta saw the thin black figure breathe deep, exhale white, and walk up the powdered stairs. When he reached the inside portico, Etta opened the door to her side. Warmth suffused him. The affable woman, the maroon oriental, and the gleaming concert grand greeted his eyes. His surprise grudgingly turned to admiration.

When Charley arrived home that night he got a gentleman's gentleman straight from Central Park West: Maceo Maxwell back in Jersey City after his former gentleman jumped.

One week Charles endured it, then blew his top. Maxie was not to lay out his clothes, whiskbroom his shoulders, help him on with his coat.

Instead, Maxie did everything else.

One of his great successes was the party for Raymond's Bar Mitzvah. It could have been Fifth Avenue, the way the table was laid.

Hebrew lessons had been a repeated agony for Raymond, as endless as *Hänsel und Gretel* when his mother and sister refused to leave.

He played hooky, he bothered the rabbi, he cost his parents. But when he had to stand, with a look that said, see-what-I-can-do-if-I-want-to, he did a creditable job.

His mother, after all the tsimmes he had created, hardly acknowledged his success. Etta didn't nag much, she never kvetched. Anything he wanted, after a little insisting, he could have.

Yet certain things she demanded: a Bar Mitzvah — God help us, violin lessons — visits to the tailor, a fashionable summer camp.

Manners. Since Black Friday the affluent were finer types than before. Last summer the Addises had vacationed on Cape Cod. House guests of Judge Higgins and his wife. Gentile gentility, a clapboard house, charming inconveniences, precious objects *handed down*. Two couples on a wide green lawn. The men putting, the wives served tea. The crash of the sea. Four people brought close on the high dry land.

Raymond vied for mother love through pious spite. He reaped the method's reward. In her eyes, he could never do anything quite right.

Raymond was a dark-eyed, dark-haired boy. His thin frame stretched him. He broke his nose falling off a bike and it grew back Jewish.

Etta would one day mention to his wife's favorite aunt that he had never been sick before he married. Etta attributed his early bouts of breathlessness to the crooked nose he gave himself when he should have been in school.

Worse bouts helped him miss World War II. The doctors diagnosed asthma.

A specialist later thought he might have had undetected rheumatic fever as a child.

Before he died, Raymond also wondered if it hadn't been heart all along.

Heart. He had one. Questions too. The possibility of introspection in his eyes. A perfect sister. A fashionable mom. Culture, dark and durable as mahogany, all through the house.

On the day he became a man he stood among the crowd in the lush and scented house under Maxie's supervision, eating well-done white meat turkey, and joking above the Chopin with his friends.

"After the cake comes, let's get out of here."

"Sure, Ray."

But there wasn't any boy who didn't want to stay.

"Hey, Mom," he called, until she turned from her distraction, "where's the cake? We wanta get out of here and play."

Near the piano, Charles had his daughter build a crescendo. When everyone was quiet, he said, "Ray, I bet you in a few minutes you won't want to go *outside* to play."

"Wanta bet two fountain pens?"

"A twenty-dollar bill."

Raymond smiled at his father. Something was in the air. Etta walked to her husband's side.

"Leave it to Charles," she said and looked ambiguously at her sister Lilly. Her hand softly caressed the shiny edge of the piano.

"Before dessert?" Maxie whispered to her from behind. She turned and put her finger to her lips.

"Okay, I'll bet twenty dollars, Pop."

"Too easy. I'd be taking your money. Come on!" He went to his son and took his hand. "Helen" — he stretched out his other hand — "you come too."

"I've seen it," she said softly, lowering her head. She began a processional.

"Now all of Raymond's friends — come on guys — follow!"

They walked up the stairs, past the bedrooms. By God, his father was leading him up the second flight. Raymond's heart was beating in his ears.

"Go on, Ray, you first."

Raymond opened the door to the large attic. This is what he saw: a brand-new regulation pool table, bigger than a concert grand, with an acre of green felt across its top; two racks of cues already screwed to the wall, yellow chalk below, beads strung up.

The effect was similar to waking in Loreto in A.D. 1291 to find that the Holy House had just flown in.

Charles's sleight-of-hand — miracles made for young people. He loved the wonder he put in Raymond's eyes. His heart touched his children, later his grandchildren, like a magic wand. Look close and you see how the plain wooden stick pierces the sparkles. Be touched — and be awed by the silver tip.

Charley could give Raymond pleasure. He drew close to his son. Anything the boy wanted he could have.

"Let me come with you today, Pop."

"You've got school."

"I won't miss much."

Once won't hurt the boy.

Besides the delicious days of hooky, Charles often took Raymond with him on Saturday mornings. The day began early with the house of music at their backs.

On Central Avenue, Raymond could feel the loosening of his father's stride. The man would talk about the crap games, the numbers, the fortunetellers, the feuds between certain merchants with strange names, as dawn turned fog into a dusty Jersey day.

Charles stopped at the store over which his mother had lived. "Remember all the good times at Nana's?" He pulled his head back and looked up at his mother's front window — always a chance . . . Raymond watched the big Adam's apple bob in his father's throat.

Then they continued up the street to the Addis Meat Market. Here I am, his father seemed to be saying, as he carefully unlocked his own door. Underneath my mother-spawned gentility, away from *your* mother's widening cool grasp, I open the store, put on this white apron, take up this sharp cleaver, split meat.

He made up two special orders, before the day began, for Raymond to deliver to each of his aunts. No matter how bulky each bag might be, the bill was always a dollar and a half.

Raymond ate a bologna breakfast while the workers came in — eight butchers, two order boys on Saturdays, the cashier. The butchers kidded each other freely as they put on white coats. Their white hats said ADDIS — WHOLESALE — RETAIL on the sides.

By the time Raymond got each order delivered and paid a visit to each aunt, the store had crowded up. It looked as if half the world had just appeared at his mother's back door.

So many with accents and old coats to say just who they were.

His father was absorbed behind the counter, calling out orders to the men, slicing, pounding, chopping, wrapping, a bitchen this, a pezzetino that.

> *In Jersey City where I did dwell*
> *A butcher boy I loved so well . . .*

Charley, they called him. Maria, Sarah, Otto, he called back.

Raymond delivered his three dollars to the cashier, then slipped through the crowd. Behind the counter he hacked off more bologna for his lunch. His father came over and put an arm around him. "Pretty busy, hah?" Raymond heard a whisper, *Take a look.* Over the counter Raymond faced the crush.

See? Here they are, my customers, my people — as real as the sawdust on my wooden floor.

❧   ❧   ❧

Younger brother. Older sister. Ray was a boy who didn't think about tomorrow; Helen a young lady surrounded by order and light. They had a large room each. Ray would walk down the hall to the bathroom in his underwear; Helen in a high-necked robe.

When he teased her, she called him youngster.

When he snuck into her bedroom and frenched her bed, she emptied a bottle of blue-black ink on his head.

When he made a set of butcher hats out of the pages of her Bach toccatas, she bit him on the arm so hard, the sunken white marks slowly turned pink and almost bled.

He went to bed without dessert for upsetting his sister. She wandered downstairs until dawn.

They shared a tendency to oversleep in a household that would not tear them from their dreams. Helen woke up to her piano and played till the stars came out.

Raymond was packed off to his afternoon classes with a note from home.

Helen was the favorite. Who can argue with the gift of music and, most of the time, the composure of a queen? Raymond enjoyed the consolation of the underachiever — the secret knowledge that he was smarter than he seemed.

For example, every summer Etta made him take his violin with him. Every summer he "lost" it at camp. Three violins before she despaired of his carelessness. For all he knew, she never suspected a thing.

Why use his head? So he could play duets with his sister? He used his head to ward off any possibility of a musical ear. He was young; he used his head to get out of the house or up to the attic to play. Boys will be boys. Right?

Girls will be girls — except Etta wasn't raising an adornment. She was raising what she had before her eyes — a budding concert pianist.

Late afternoon. Helen is bent over the keyboard in the low shafts of light. Fine particles are suspended in the air. Etta sits in her deep chair at the end of a busy day. Her plump index finger noiselessly sweeps time on her fluted armrest. Her legs dangle. Her dreams drift into sound . . .

Maxie enters from the dining room and with a quiet pirouette he bends to the slow wistful call — of all he's not become.

Where's Raymond? In the attic or out playing ball. And Charley's just locking up the store.

"You just never know." Here's Lilly at the age of eighty-two, almost blind after a long life of seeing too much, speaking in her oracular, determined voice, which stirs the soul: "There was nothing wrong with Helen! There never was a sign. How my sister bore it, I'll never know."

There's an old Jewish expression. If everybody took their troubles and hung them on the washline, they'd grab back their own.

Lilly would.

HEIGHTS GIRL TRIUMPHS

Helen Addis daughter of Mr. and Mrs. Charles Addis of Clifton Avenue won the Etway New Jersey Piano Competition last night in the Newark Mosque before a music-loving crowd of hundreds who listened with bated breath to the three finalists including residents of Ridgeway and Hacketstown.

Miss Addis's playing of Grieg's Concerto won her a scholarship to the Juilliard School which was presented by Judge Arthur Higgins and a standing ovation from the crowd. She is the first finalist from Jersey City to the prestigious competition and the only one from Hudson County ever to have captured the coveted award.

"Thank you," she told the audience. "I don't deserve it."

"She is a most excellent student," contradicted Nicholas Pretorius formerly of St. Cecilia's Music School in Rome and now affiliated with the Newark Philharmonic.

With her becoming combination of beauty, modesty and talent, we can be assured we'll hear from Helen Addis, a Dickinson High School Senior, in years to come. Congratulations Helen!

Dear Helen,

As mayor of Jersey City and as a friend of your family it is my proud duty to congratulate you on your crowning achievement of having won the Tenth Annual Etway New Jersey Piano Competition.

How well I remember the beautiful music you played for me two short months ago when I had the honor of attending a party at your gracious parents', Charles and Etta's, lovely home.

Your achievement brings credit to your family and to your city. Best wishes for a rewarding future.

> Yours truly,
> Frank Hague
> Mayor

Until Helen went to college, life kept his top hat on. She trusted the expectation as fixed as the North Star in her mother's eyes. She accepted her father's doting, his absurd smile, his head ballooning over the raised piano top. Once a week she was rewarded for her intense concentration by the glint of satisfaction on Nicholas Pretorius's stern face.

Overly sensitive — she had her piano to feed her. At times apathetic — hours by the Victrola to steep. Bored and restless — Etta took her to opera and concerts. Outside contact — Pretorius, the dancing master of her soul.

Her father urged her to bring friends home. He insisted on surprise birthday parties at which all the guests got gifts. The gifts were embarrassing; they were like saying, Look, we're rich!

On the days she got to school she ate sandwiches and baked potatoes with girlfriends at Dickinson High School's huge lunch room. She was pretty, shy, soft-spoken. Elegant attributes in the days when teen-age girls hungered to grow up.

The girls talked too much of boys for Helen's taste. Accustomed to Pretorius, she wasn't interested in seniors. They talked about clothes; she liked clothes. But she remained reserved and tactful about what was on her back.

She inherited a best friend, Sheila Kaye, who told all her secrets to Helen. What did Helen have to share? Pretorius's delight that she was tackling the second movement of Schumann's Fantasy?

Helen was going to be a concert pianist. Sheila wasn't going to be anything at all. Helen gently steered around the anonymity of all her friends' fate.

She did have a secret she couldn't share and that her butterfly scarves couldn't hide. The mark from her breast to her neck. When she saw it, she looked into her own eyes.

She prayed God to take it away. He wouldn't be God if he did. In her bad moments she knew it was what she deserved.

It was bad to masturbate. She dug her fingers into the scar in spite.

"My God, leave it alone, Helen!" Etta would say when she saw it raw. "How do you expect it to fade if you keep at it like that?"

It.

It got infected. Dr. Cooper had to be called.

Helen socked him in the eye.

Etta was mortified. A friend of the family! Still . . . A young girl wouldn't want to be touched *there*.

She telephoned Charles at the store.

"You're kidding!"

"Is this a thing I'd joke about?" Before the words were out of her mouth his laughter tickled her ear. "Really, Charley!" She smiled into the phone.

"Don't worry, dear. I'll send Doc enough steak for *both* eyes!"

Raymond knocked at his sister's door and begged to be let in.

"All right. You may enter, child, for a moment," Helen condescended. She was lying in bed prettily, her head propped up on banks of pillows, a scarf covering the bandage on her neck.

"Did you give Doc a shiner? Did you *really* do it?"

"Yes I did."

"Wow! Just like that? How'd you do it? Come on, tell me!"

This incident might have joined Rose Addis's bogus noodles and Raymond's three violins. Instead, it became part of a different history.

History. Facts ossify, chance rots away.

With time enough and luck there are nose jobs, electrolysis — even skin grafts. Grown women deal with the marks of Cain.

Etta had brought Helen to Pretorius when the girl was eleven. Ashamed of how abundant her mother looked in his meager studio, Helen ran out. Pretorius found her huddled at the top of the stairs. "I had hoped you'd play for me," he said sternly.

Underneath she heard, Please little girl, please little girl, play!

She did. When she finished her practiced pieces, he asked for scales and arpeggios, four octaves. Then: "See if you can do this." He handed her the slow movement of a Mozart sonata . . .

Afterward he didn't say a word. Went to the anteroom and called her mother back in. He had expected bread and found hope.

"How serious are you about her piano, Mrs. Addis?"

"I want her to have the best."

"So she can be the best?"

"She has the talent, hasn't she?" Etta said, standing in the doorway, the light making her eyes and her accessories dance. "Even before she spoke, she sang."

He nodded. "She reminds me of . . . what I started out to be."

"Mr. Pretorius, I came to you because the women say you're the best."

"Yes, perhaps the best teacher. The best teacher for *her*. I don't accept everyone . . . a few I take for reasons of prudence . . . I wouldn't take your daughter without building toward a concert career. That means longer hours of practice, more discipline, competitions —"

"Spare no expense," Etta said simply.

"I won't, Mrs. Addis." Agreed.

Raymond would one day say to his own daughter, Rose, "There must have been something between Helen and that teacher. The Greek guy. We were jerks, we didn't see it then. Her off in Newark all the time. Never gave it one thought."

"What do you think happened?" Rose asked. When she and her father were alone, they could talk about her aunt.

"She liked him. Maybe they fooled around."

Raymond admitted to enjoying one musical in his life: *Roberta*.

> *They asked me how I knew*
> *My true love was true.*
> *I of course replied,*
> *Something here inside*
> *Cannot be denied . . .*

And once as a young man, trapped by Etta, fidgeting and bored before the curtain, he was struck by — and always remembered — the synopsis of *La Traviata*.

Rose doubted her father's surmise. But Raymond was in a mellow, confiding mood as he drove her to the airport — the way he could be with her. She kept quiet. Who needed his sudden shift, "Miss Know-it-all!" Her protestation. His follow-up, "Sure, sure. I'll-tell-him-when-he-comes-in."

Every Saturday through high school, Helen, who never wanted to rub the dried sleep from her eyes, was up at seven, running her bubble bath. She dressed soberly, ate lightly, warmed up for forty-five minutes, then took the Tube to Newark by ten.

Nicholas Pretorius was no lover. He was a slim man of medium height with thick black hair that rebelled against the care with which he combed it — a care that was echoed by his tight lips, dark suits, and well-manicured fingernails.

He had been a child prodigy, discovered right around his corner in Newark by the organist of the Greek Orthodox church. He was sent to New York once a week by church subscription to study with a favorite pupil of Liszt's. He won competitions, scholarships, and the one-year appointment to Santa Cecilia misrepresented in the newspaper.

He had talent — who doesn't? — and superb training — few do. He became excellent in a field that demands excellence. He thought he'd get somewhere because he was good.

Worse! He grew up to treat the world as if his achievement were his ticket. With the blunt idealism that can spawn out of a working-class home, he assumed he had only to flash his pass to get aboard. He treated the men he worked with as if they were violinists, flutists, conductors; audiences as if they were there to hear him play.

He ended up back in Newark. His widowed mother cooked his meals.

If they wanted Pretorius, they'd come to *him*. And they did! For lessons.

He was recommended in the music world — who knows how the rumor began? — as an excellent teacher.

Perhaps the world had the same trouble with him as he did with it — it never got him quite right.

"Pretorius? Sure I remember. Sort of a stiff to work with. But what integrity! No one I'd trust more to train a kid. He was quite a prodigy when he was young. Gave it all up to go home and take care of his mother. Eccentric little guy."

He took a job with the Newark school system that he never talked about — and he took it just in time. He would eke out a living through the Depression while many a musician starved.

What did Pretorius know of the morbid child in Helen that couldn't be burned away in the furnace of her art? What did he care? Helen for him was genius in its least accusing form — a pampered girl with servants in her house.

What did Helen know of the time bomb of middle age that had left Pretorius with tatters in his hands? How could she have understood his failure? He had lost the world; if she had known that, she'd have considered it the world's loss.

Raymond was wrong. No Roberta. No Camille. They never fooled around. Nothing happened.

They ripped from each other and then shared what a prize student and a tasking master can — the best of each other. A narrow and ruthless embrace.

Etta never worried about Pretorius. She brought street knowledge to Clifton Avenue, where she kept sex all hushed up. One look and she knew Pretorius wouldn't bother Helen. A few words and she liked Maxie all the same.

She wanted what was nice and knew what wasn't. She kept quiet and kept certain things from the living room. Just as Charley kept certain things from home.

Raymond responded to his parents' truce with human nature — he had an instinct for balance and order all of his life. When he acted like a dope — often — *he* knew he was wrong. For example:

"He couldn't have been fourteen years old, honest." Etta recollecting. "He was with a group of his friends across the street from the school. I don't remember why I passed by. 'Raymond,' I said. He turned round and saw me. His eyes grew to circles. I swear he went dead-white. There I am, his mother, there he is, with a cigarette stuck in his mouth. 'That's all right, Raymond. Just be careful,' I told him. He looked so shocked. He could have burned his jacket, the way he let it drop."

But did she ever know when *she* was wrong?

New Year's Eve, 1932. The middle of Helen's first year at Juilliard. Raymond throws a party. He's sure his sister will ruin everything by insisting she sit there like a log and play. But suddenly she acquiesced to her parents' good wishes and joined their group going to the Chanteclair.

Ray's was an open house really. Pool in the attic, poker and rummy in the living room. The girls went through the popular records and danced while the Victrola played.

Maxie had prepared a buffet. Assorted cold cuts and salads on the table, chocolate-covered almonds and raisins through the house, scores of charlotte russes in the refrigerator — promising '33. All to Raymond's taste, but tasteful.

Raymond never paid much attention to Maxie. Young people don't go cross-eyed focusing in on silver spoons. "Did I have all that?" he'd ask much later.

Ray and Maxie were generally polite and reserved with each other. Gentlemen rivals for the same hand. There were days Ray thought his father would get so angry, he'd kick Maxie out of the house. But Charley's explosions came up against something rock-like, the world run right.

"How are you this evening?" as each guest entered. Attached the proper name.

That's how New Year's Eve started, but after a while ashes spilled on the rug. Once Maxie came from the kitchen with no look at all on his face. Put a record on the Victrola and turned it up so he could hear it through the kitchen door.

Strange. At midnight the charlotte russes appeared on the dining room table in their bakery boxes; the supper was not cleared away. As Raymond licked whipped cream he noticed the mess. There was something wrong about crust half-circling mustard. Wrong about the yellowing top of mayonnaise. Wrong about the curling dried ends of cold cut skins. The remnants tugged at the corners of his heart.

In the living room the girls had gotten some of the fellows to dance. Ray's friend, crazy Dasher — in a bow tie that lit up — had gotten a circle to chug-a-lug.

These are the years we've all heard about, before Jews drank. Charley had had a bar built into his dining room closet. All through Prohibition he unlocked the door on his kind of surprise. Tonight the door stayed open. The Addises didn't mind Maxie mixing his special drinks for young guests.

Raymond couldn't stand the stuff. He was a Jewish drinker, one of the sources of the legend above. Two quick drinks and he threw up. Cigarettes were his vice. He lit an Old Gold to reassure himself and rejoined the poker game.

On the other side of the room couples were necking. On the mantel over the fireplace, cigarettes had been extinguished in the spongy ends of the charlotte russes. Dasher was fiddling at the piano, his glass on the exposed black top. No one had left a ring since Maxie's day.

Just like you! Ray could hear his mother saying tomorrow. Grim satisfaction — she could have predicted this — on her face.

Ray took a gulp of the next guy's Scotch on the card table. It scourged his throat.

CRASH! From the kitchen. The thunder of retribution?

In a college course a few years later, a law professor would simulate a crime right before his students' eyes. Then ask each one what happened. Raymond would never forget the disparity of accounts.

Things happen quick. A crack in what ought to be, and all hell breaks loose.

Ray saw Maxie run into the living room. If Helen had been at the piano, he'd have done a strange dance. He looked about wildly, then ran up the stairs.

Then, for a moment, Ray felt just as he did when he was hostage to his mother's taste and was forced in a darkened theater to watch the curtain rise. Some jerk's conception of a forest, town, or room — a sham of wood and paper and paste — would appear. And everyone would ah and clap because everyone else was ahing and clapping, until some fat singer squeezed into a costume that passed belief would start blasting away. Then just for a moment, madness was real, and he was mad.

A huge Negro stumbled into Etta's living room, mumbling obscenities as dark as mud. Stage center on the oriental, he discovered the knife in his hand. He made a full circle, red-eyed drunk, cutting the air.

Time stopped for passion. A soundless gasp of incredulity as he stumbled up the stairs.

"Oh, Mary, Mother of God, save me!" Maxie prayed from behind Helen's locked door as the wild man shook the floor with his pounding.

"Hail, Mary, full of grace —"

CRASH!

"Blessed art Thou —"

"Motherfuckinwhore!"

Dasher, the quick-witted, was the first to stir. They followed him up the stairs.

On the second floor, Ray looked up and saw heads on the banister peering down from the attic. "Help us!" he called.

The black man was pounding the door off its hinges. The sweat rolled down his face. His white silk shirt was limp, clinging to the muscles of his back and arms.

The stink of hard work cut through his perfumed body.

Raymond felt a stab of fear in his chest and saw Dasher, feeling no pain, grab the man's arm. Then there were too many boys on him for Raymond to join.

"Maceo, Maceo," the big man implored as the boys wrestled for the sharp carving knife. Once they had it, they spontaneously let the hand go. Mistake.

It took five of them to down him.

"Maceo," he moaned.

"It's okay, Maxie," Raymond called.

Maxie unlocked the unhinged door. He looked down. "Fool!"

The big man wept.

"All right, fellows, off him! He's *all right*. Can you stand, honey, can you? Let's try. Come on, fellows, let's get him on his feet."

Carefully, Maxie picked up the knife. It seemed to disappear as he took it to the kitchen.

Raymond in his mother's kitchen with his own friends. A black man on a chair, his head thrown back. Maxie's bravado: "It's hardly appropriate to say Happy New Year. But I do think, Raymond, it's time for you to say good night to your guests. Fellows, not a word to *anyone*. I'll take care of this."

Everyone left. Raymond sat alone in the messy living room, smoking, listening to the hushed sounds in the kitchen, smelling the coffee perk. Finally he heard the back door open and close and the stranger pass out of the driveway onto the street.

Maxie came in, picked up a cigarette, lit it — he needed a reason to exhale — and sat down.

Silence hung between them. They could see it in the forms that whizzed at the corners of their eyes so early in the morning. They could hear it in a buzz.

"Get some sleep, you look tired," Maxie said finally. His voice had no luster at all. He made himself stand up. Crushed his cigarette out. He never smoked! "Get yourself to bed, Raymond," he repeated slowly and looked all around the room. "I'll clean up."

Ray had always known Maxie was a fairy. But what did the term mean?

For Ray, a fairy was a man who had his mother's taste.

"What do you think of your dear Maxie now?" he asked his mother, confronting her alone in the kitchen the next day.

"He could have been killed."

"So could I!" When Raymond got angry the blood rushed to his face. His black eyes narrowed and his full lips drew tight. He was too scrawny to support his fury; his thin frame shook. "This colored stud, crazy drunk, came roaring through the living room slashing around with Pop's knife. In our house. Here!"

She poured coffee for both of them. She was wearing a pink silk peignoir that moved softly around her plump body as she served them and then sat down. "My father," she said, rubbing her forehead, "your grandfather," she recalled, "I don't remember him. He went to work one day — he worked for Singer. It was a bad neighborhood. He was shot to death."

"What does that have to do with the price of tea in China?"

"Things happen."

"*This* didn't have to happen. *You're* the one who had to have Maxie, no matter what Pop said. It's *your* fault!"

"Oh? So now I have two Charleys! What do you want me to

do?" she asked as if she had already addressed someone else. "Throw him out on the street so he can starve?"

Raymond stared at her in astonishment. She didn't even know she'd been wrong.

She didn't seem to give a damn that fairies did more than polish silver, that he himself, though he hadn't told her, had lain gasping for breath, heart pounding, till dawn.

"She only cares for herself" is the way Raymond's wife would one day phrase it.

"What if Helen had been home?" Ray hissed in pain.

Then her face went dead. "I have to think" is all she said.

Lilly helped her think. "What happened?" Lilly asked in a low voice, mouthing the words big. Her head slanted forward. News travels. She had walked over from Central Avenue as soon as it was decent on a New Year's Day. She sat on the edge of the couch that backed the front windows. Courtly motifs in needlepoint set off her simple wool dress.

Etta sat on the chair next to the side window, from which one could see the alleyway meet the street. She was still in her pink peignoir. "Looks like you could tell me!"

Lilly shrugged.

"So you want me to go over a tsimmes?" Etta said. She leaned forward too. Her small feet, buried in pink feathers, touched the floor. Once grounded, her legs, a crease of silk between them, held firm. She glanced around the empty room. "It's not a pretty story."

The sisters looked at each other. Did either of them go for light comedy?

"So?" Lilly's whisper sounded like something good to eat.

"So I was up till dawn with Maxie. And once he gets up, I've got Charley on my hands again."

"Such a hard life."

"The one that caused the trouble is someone Maxie was once sweet on," Etta whispered. "But no fine type at all. Maxie knew that. But he couldn't help himself. He had an urge."

"Urge?" Lilly mocked. "Passion. But it don't last." Well Lilly knew. The minute after she found out she'd have to marry her Alex, she realized she had wasted her life.

"Bad as he was, Maxie said sometimes he could be magnificent."

"Ha! I bet."

"But he was just no good. When he got out of jail right before Christmas —"

"Jail?"

"Don't you dare breathe a word of it!"

"Oh," Lilly answered knowingly, "have I ever opened my mouth?"

"When he *came back,* he wanted to take up with Maxie again. But by then Maxie was in his right senses and said he'd have none of him. This man got the idea Maxie was sweet on someone else. It just wasn't so. Maxie says since he came into this house his life has changed."

"Sure."

"Oh, *you!* You know *everything* — as soon as it's too late!" Etta brought her voice down. "Well, anyway, last night he came over to see Maxie, as nice as he could be. Maxie let him in. He shouldn't have done that. *There* he was wrong. And the two of them had too much to drink. What does Raymond know from going into the kitchen to make sure everything's getting done right? One thing led to another. This fellow began accusing Maxie of caring for somebody else. Maxie couldn't get him off the subject. He threw a chair at Maxie. You should see my wall! Then . . . he took a knife and chased him through the house . . ." Etta finished the story with a pause as if she were trying to gauge how it sounded to other people's ears.

"My, my," said Lilly, sitting back at intermission. "What are you going to do?"

"I don't know."

"What if the jailbird comes back?"

Etta shrugged.

"What does Charley say?"

"Guess."

Lilly patted out the wrinkles in her dress that had to do. "I wonder what your fancy friends are going to say about this."

"I'm sure."

Judge and Mrs. Higgins were overjoyed to get Maxie. They in-
stalled him year round in the clapboard on Cape Cod.

He took a Portuguese lover, who never stayed overnight. And
when he got drunk or too stupid, Maxie sent him home early to
his wife.

Life was quiet out of season, and Maxie took to it. He became
an islander.

And a legend. In season he gave parties that Etta clipped out of
the *Times*. "Maxie's this" or "That Maxie" appeared in cookbooks, though he never got a dime.

He didn't care, he confided to Etta. (Mrs. Higgins used to say,
in the right tone, that no matter *who* the guests were, Maxie saved
his best for the Addises' visits.) He could have named his price in
New York in the forties, but he stayed put.

The Higginses set up an annuity for Maxie that included his
tenantship in the house for life. It was there in 1951 that Maxie
nursed the Judge, then a widower, through his last tough year.

"What a swell couple they were," Etta would tell her grandchildren. Rose and Janet would look in the album at the two
couples, dressed in white, smiling, seated on a lawn. "They
couldn't do enough for us. 'Etta, how can we ever thank you suf-
ficiently for Maxie?' That Maxie. What a wonder he was. Remember, Ray? There was nothing that man couldn't do."

"I can think of one," Ray would answer in his tone that
changed things.

"Oh, *you!* Go get *you* to appreciate the fine things. Why
Maxie —"

"Sure, Mom, sure."

She remained proud that she had helped Maxie move up in the
world and get his name in the papers. And that through her the
Higginses gave him an annuity. But as her grandchildren grew,
she spoke of him less and less. Time passing and the tone of Raymond's voice.

When she said "Maxie" and when he said "Maxie," they were

saying very different things to each other through the years.

Raymond, of course, was saying, You're wrong. He only knew his mother to be *really* wrong twice. The second time — but here one could not dig deep — was about Helen. But *so* wrong. When he was angry at her, no matter how right she was being at that moment, she was wrong. To point this out, he made many perverse mistakes.

"How's your sister doing, Ray?" Angie the plumber asking, Clifton Avenue, 1943. Ray and his wife have moved in next door. Angie is crouched on the kitchen floor over the radiator register. A fat man whose stomach squeezes in between the heavy tools hanging from his waist.

"She's the same, Angie. The same."

Angie shakes his head sadly.

"Daddy has a sister?" little Rose asks after he leaves. Angie has fished her from the hole in the floor.

"Yes," Ellen answers. "But she's very sick and far away."

Rose sees her aunt: A grand lady sitting in a chair. Her legs are curved. There are crutches by her side. She sits in Europe.

❧ ❧ ❧

Helen didn't do well at Juilliard. All her life she had refused invitations to parties she didn't want to go to. College was an invitation she hadn't received.

Suddenly in New York the world was full of musicians and their mothers. Talent drowned the air. People sat at lunch and talked. Everyone else seemed to know everything ... No one cared.

She had trouble with the basic courses. At Dickinson, all she had needed were clean nails to pass. It hadn't been easy for Raymond to get himself left back. "It took me four and a half years to get out of high school and three to finish NYU," he'd brag.

Too bad high school had been such a breeze for Helen. If she hadn't been able to be promoted on manners, Etta would have realized she needed a tutor, as many musicians do.

If.

"You don't try," complained Etta.

True.

"You're giving up without a fight," Etta moaned.

It scared her, the world. She stayed home.

Pretorius believed it was artistic temperament. He roused himself and went to conferences with her teachers in New York.

Even in piano, she was not performing as she did for him.

Helen is the novice. In the world she lived to pray. She finds the convent imposes other obligations. During the allotted chapel time, there's rancor in her heart. She smells her stale breath rising with her prayers.

The school is officially concerned.

They respect Pretorius, and Helen is on scholarship.

They change her piano professor and tell Pretorius what she should take in summer school.

How very many Helens have they seen?

"Hello, Helen."

"Yes?"

"I guess you don't remember me?"

"I do."

His name was Michael Cohen and he was a waiter at the Chanteclair.

"What are you doing *here?*" he asked.

They were standing in the garden behind the Normal School in Jersey City on a hot July day. She was wearing a white organdy dress that had white, textured polka dots. Her light brown eyes and the lavender scarf around her neck looked cool. She carried new books that smelled hopeful. His were secondhand.

He meant just what his question implied. What in the world was *Helen Addis* doing *there?* She looked up at him. He had big blue eyes that didn't seem Jewish, and thick black hair like Pretorius. He had a long thin face and a cleft in his chin. When he waited on tables, he looked serious. She grew mischievous, thinking of how shocked he was going to be. "I'm here to make up courses. I'm on probation at Juilliard."

"That the place you got the scholarship to? I saw your picture in the paper."

"I looked awful."

"You did not. Though I don't see wasting money on girls. Especially when there's no work for men. And you, heck, your father could buy you the school!"

She froze in anguish. Then she rushed away.

"Hey, Helen, wait!" He followed her. Stopped her by grabbing the back of her scarf with one hand. "Turn around. Please! I didn't mean to offend you."

"Take your hands off me!" she screamed. People looked. The lavender floated out of his grasp. She turned. Her pale skin was splotched red.

"Honest, Helen. I didn't mean a thing. I apologize."

His voice sounded as miserable as she felt, and she heard it. New Year's Eve he *had* winked at her. It hadn't been something in his eye.

"Tell me the courses you're taking. Come on. Talk to me!"

"European History and Introduction to Literature," she mumbled, head down. What were they? she wondered, the names alien to her tongue. Who was he? his body looming in the sun.

"I can help you. History comes easy to me."

"Then what did you flunk?"

His laugh made her start. *"You're* here to make up courses. *I'm* here to get a degree. Might as well do something constructive with my days. This lousy Depression. Well, *you* wouldn't know. I help support my parents and a kid sister waiting on tables. That's why I couldn't ask you to dance New Year's Eve."

Should she sympathize with his waiting on tables? Should she apologize for eating at the Chanteclair? Should she thank him for wanting to dance?

She paused. "You're lucky you didn't dance with me. I'm no good."

"Heck, I can show you how to dance."

"I guess I can dance at least."

"You didn't dance New Year's Eve."

"I didn't want to."

"Don't you ever do what you don't want to do?"

She looked up at him and smiled. "No."

*

"I don't need college to play," she told her mother. Pretorius arranged a leave of absence for her second year. Then she wiped the grim look off his face.

In every artist's life there is an *annus mirabilis*. Helen had hers in her living room.

Etta hummed through the house again. She stopped to mark time with her fingers. On Sunday mornings she offered Mike Cohen a piece of fruit as he sat at the dining room table doing homework. Who was he to get upset about?

At first she was.

— "It'll do her good," Lilly said. "It's only right a girl her age should have a fellow."

"Boy, you sure can talk out of both sides of your mouth," Etta reminded her. For who had paid the bills for her sister's two pregnancies? *Lilly* had to be sent to a private clinic and be put to sleep. "Don't you think she's got time enough for all *that?*"

"Time don't wait for us to be ready."

"Then *we've* got to make time wait."

"How? You gonna grease its palm?" —

On Sundays Charley sleeps through anything till one. He, who has lost every single battle, at long last has won the war of Maxie. When he finally gets up, he walks through his own house in his slippers.

His son in the attic with the boys.

His daughter in the living room playing to a beau.

His wife in the kitchen training a Czech woman how to roast the way Charles likes to eat. Soon his Sunday table will be set for everyone . . .

Let the poor man have his pleasure.

Listen to that, Etta whispers to him. Have you *ever* heard music like *that?*

So what? he thinks. "No dear," he says. Cheerful, tactful victor.

Even Raymond, at the attic door, his cue resting under his chin, hears something incredible: the sound of his sister showing the whole world how magnificent a loser can be.

Some resemblance around her eyes, in her sly smile, has made him understand his mother is being fooled.

Helen is weighing down her first violin and heaving it as far as she can out into the lake.

Raymond assumes she'll be given another.

At sixty, Raymond, on the phone with his daughter Rose, will suddenly sound whole again.

At nineteen, the pitch of Helen's intensity moves those who love her and those who need her.

No facts remain outside of memory. No recording, cassette, video tape. No ruin.

She was good enough for Etta and Pretorius to believe she was right to leave school. She was good enough to be entered in the important competitions.

The suitcases of Rose Addis's prophecy come to Etta's mind. She looks at Mike Cohen to make sure he stays on the blotter as he writes. Soon he'll have to be cleared away. She listens to the crescendos of her daughter's call. Goodness knows how far she'll take them all.

And how she played! At his studio Pretorius listened. The music drove him past the hard lessons of sense back to vainglory. He was young again. But not as selfish. This time he gave himself away.

"Darling," her mother called her.

"Excellent, Helen," Pretorius found it in him to say.

In a rapture of self-containment Helen told Etta, "Don't pay the fee!"

Etta looked up from her accounts. "But darling, it's due."

"Don't waste your money, Mother. I don't want to be in any competition. I will never play in public again."

Why did she say it? She didn't mean it really. Yet every word she heard she knew was true.

Pretorius told her to sit down, but not at the piano. "What is this I hear?"

She looked perplexed. "From whom?"

"Your mother."

"She had no right to tell!"

Pretorius smiled, which in itself was awful. "How are we to make a secret of your shifts of mood? Shall we just keep quiet until each one passes? For instance, what shall I do about Queen Elisabeth of Belgium? Go ahead or wait for you?"

She curled up in her chair. Circled her clenched legs with her arms. "What do my moods matter? Whatever happens, every Saturday I'll be here."

He looked perplexed. "Then shall I go ahead with the arrangements?"

"Don't waste your time," she said, straightening up. "Since Mother told you, she told you. I'll never play in public again."

Pretorius rose and went to the window. He looked out — and in — on the dismal, sunless court.

He turned around. "Helen, you're trying my patience." Then he stopped himself and recalled what Mrs. Addis had asked him to do. *"Why* don't you want to play anymore?"

"Oh, I want to play. My life will be music. But not in public."
"Why?"

"I'm no good."

"If it's compliments you want, I'll give them freely. I have never heard anyone your age play like you."

She shook her head. "I'm no good."

"Is it this boyfriend of yours who is turning your head? Doesn't he want you to play?"

She looked at him suspiciously. "What are you and my mother up to?"

"She's worried about you."

"But you don't have to be."

"I've invested seven years in you." He looked at her as if he were watching them recede.

"And there will be seven more!"

"Then you'll play?"

"For you."

"For *me?*"

"And for *me* too."

"Are you out of your mind?" he asked her. "Do you think I've given you what I've given so that you can play for *us?*"

"Who else is there to play for?" she asked.

"Helen!" He controlled himself. I'm always controlling myself, he thought. He gestured toward the window and said in a high voice, "There's the world!"

"I'm no good, Mr. Pretorius, don't you see?"

"I'm beginning to," he said bitterly and sat down. He put his face in his hands, then shrugged and sat straight. "That's all for today," he said coldly.

"All? I haven't played."

"Class dismissed."

They sat silently, waiting for her reaction. "You're angry with me?" she asked quietly.

"No. I'm angry with myself. I'm terribly disappointed in you."

"Do you really think I'd be fit for Brussels?"

"I thought you were, until today." Then he changed his tone. "Where's your confidence, Helen?"

"You realize, of course," she said knowingly, "my father won't be there. In Brussels there would just be you, my mother, and me."

"I should hope we're enough . . ."

"Are we?"

"Let's make a bargain," he said, intent on putting his house in order. "You enter the New York competition, and after that one, you tell me. Let's just take them one at a time. Let's not think too far ahead."

"Okay," she lied. Anything to get to the piano and play.

The day of the New York competition, they couldn't get her out of bed.

She put her covers over her head.

That was that.

"Darling, wake up now." Etta sits on the bed, plumping up the discarded pillows.

Helen slowly opens her eyes.

"That's my girl. Sit up." Etta banks the pillows behind Helen's head. She fixes the neck of her nightgown, puts an angora shawl around her shoulders, carefully straightens her hair. The scar shouldn't show.

"You can come in now, Mr. Pretorius."

He walks in like a doctor without a bag.

Helen opens her mouth wide and gasps.

"Don't make such a face!" Etta cries. She grabs her daughter's hand. "Talk to us!"

"Ahhh," says Helen.

"Laryngitis?" Pretorius shrilly asks.

Helen brushes her mother's hand aside. Her face is beautiful in its rapture. Gently her fist marks time against her covered neck.

"So *that's* it," Etta says. "What a day to lose your voice, my darling. Are you well enough to stand?"

Helen wraps the shawl tight around her and sinks under the covers.

In the living room, Etta says, "Well, Mr. Pretorius, I guess it's one competition Helen will have to miss."

"More precisely, the first one, Mrs. Addis. I had better call New York."

Etta lets the sounds of his stiff explanation fill her mind. Next week she'll have the drapes taken down and the spring curtains put up.

"I wonder, Mr. Pretorius," Etta says at the door, "if Helen hasn't been practicing too hard . . ."

That may be it, for the next day Helen gets up as cheerful as can be.

The music she plays dances.

There's a load off her mind.

Etta forgets about her meeting at the temple. She gives *herself* the luxury of hooky. She sits and listens.

Dreams shift. The glorious structure stands. The beautiful daughter warms the mother's heart. Helen can have a different brand of everything. What is money for?

"I'm so glad you're feeling better, darling," she says at lunch.

Helen laughs. She's feeling wonderful.

"I've been thinking . . . Maybe that Mr. Pretorius has got you going too fast. There's no rush for you to enter competitions."

"Now or never, Mother,

Now or never, Mother,"

Helen chants.

"Then *never* if that's what you want. If that's what you want, it don't mean a thing to me."

"No more judges to buy, Mother," Helen trills.

Etta looks at her happy daughter and returns her nonsense. "Oh, I'd buy you the world, if I could."

"And I, Mother,
And I, Mother,
And Eyeeeeeeeeeeeeeeeeeeeeeee
Would have to pay."
Tra la la.

"There was nothing wrong with Helen." Lilly at eighty-two again. "She had a fellah and she wanted to get married. They wanted her to see the world. Go on trips. Meet other fellahs. They thought he wasn't good enough. He was a perfectly decent boy. 'What shall I do?' she came to me and asked. I can still feel her in my arms the night your poor father was born. 'Do you love him?' I asked. At first she could take him or leave him, I remember. Her head was filled with the piano and that strange little man — the Greek — who made her work too hard. 'Oh, Aunt Lilly, sometimes I think if I don't get married soon, I'm going to die.' 'So there's your answer,' I said.

"Three years. They made her wait three years.

"Do you remember what *that* feels like? For a young girl who don't know a thing? Three long years with everything inside her aflame. You girls must remember what that feels like — I still do."

She walked into Pretorius's studio after a month's absence. It seemed drab after the full spring days.

He seemed unreal. Tiny. The piano loomed.

"So you have decided to be an amateur." Spoiled brat is what his voice said. Yet he was still willing to take Etta's money.

Why not? was what he came up with in the end.

He'd simply control himself. But control can turn to ice. Helen had to duck to avoid the long thin icicles like those that formed off her bedroom window ledge in winter and after a day smelled like dust. They darted from his mouth. He had a lizard's tongue.

"What's wrong?" he asked.

Whoops! Another one. She ducked. Then laughed. "I'm cold."

"They've turned the heat off for the season and naturally *I* get no sun. No matter. Shall we commence?"

Commence.

The keys were cold. Like crusted snow. She was careful not to crush them. She felt so polite.

Then she gave up. She had to get warm.

She pounded out her octave exercises.

Over and over.

Over and over.

Harsh, grating, imbecile sound.

"Helen!" he shrilled.

"Bleep," she heard.

Toad.

A flame leaped through her. She thought of her brother, Ray — of all people — and laughed till the tears rolled and she had to stop.

Would *he* get the joke? She tore a page from her score, rolled it into a ball, turned around, and threw it at Pretorius. "It's too cold here. Put it on. Like this!" She tore out another sheet and balanced it on her head.

Pretorius donned his butcher's hat without moving his sleeves.

He looked so funny, she howled.

Outdoors it was warm again, like Mike. On Saturdays now he caddied at her father's club. She took a cab.

He was pleased and annoyed to see her. He was handsome in his knickers. His arms were daffodils.

"What are *you* doing here, Miss Addis. Isn't this your first day back with the great God Pretorius?"

"He's cold and he has no sense of humor."

Mike smiled broadly. "So you're finally growing up, little girl — Hey! I gotta get back." He pointed in the direction of the men who would know he'd been talking to Charley Addis's daughter. "You want to hang around? I'll drop you off before I go to work tonight."

On the way home, he stopped at the flatlands, where the weeds grow man-high and the refineries can be seen.

"What do you know!" he said as his arm went around her and she did not squirm. She let him hold her tight in his flowers. He kissed her, a long soft kiss until something wet slid in her mouth and circled her tongue. His tongue.

When he let her go there was a space between them. You could do *that* and afterward there was still a space. The space fascinated her. She stared at it. He stroked her bent head and said, "What do you know about that. You're growing up, little one. You are growing up."

When she got home she noticed a look on her mother's face. Not the one Etta reserved for Mike. In fact, her mother spoke to Mike directly. "Is she okay?"

"Never been better, as far as I can tell, Mrs. Addis."

"Mr. Pretorius called, Helen. He said you weren't acting right."

"Oh *him,* he has no sense of humor!"

Etta's look vanished. Her eyes narrowed. A short finger poked toward Newark. "I don't know about that man anymore. His voice over the phone gave me the willies. I think he pushes you too hard. I just don't know."

The next Saturday things settled themselves. Helen stayed in bed. Etta was just as glad.

Michael Cohen.

Just your ordinary guy. Medium height. Dark hair, blue eyes. Presentable. A serious demeanor, which substituted for what Etta called manners. The Depression whetted him.

Where is he now? Retired, on a golf course again, but this time playing? Is he still tight with a penny? Is he dead?

His first wife rocks back and forth, tick-tock, tick-tock, in Greystone. If a stick could be taken to the piñata of her catatonia, what brightly colored objects would tumble out?

Would there be a glimmer of him?

Does he / did he ever sight her on the green?

Who knows? Who could have known then?

All Etta knew was, Mike Cohen couldn't offer her daughter any life at all.

Etta wanted a bloody real M.D. for her Helen.

Although an extraordinary musician would do.

"A fine type" was as close as she could get to expressing her idea.

Etta watched like a hawk. "I don't want the two of you sitting out in that car!"

"You have nothing to worry about, Mrs. Addis. I respect your daughter."

"Well then, respect her right here."

"Oh, Mother!"

They waited. Do *you* remember what that was like? (Anyone out there wait anymore?)

Waiting transforms an ordinary boy in the eyes of a fairy princess.

Everything about Mike enhanced the texture of the wait.

The stiff cuffs against his wristbones. The fine markings of hair.

Each eyelash on her cheek.

The aftershave he used, the toothpaste smell.

The soft sandpaper of his tongue.

The bulge, sometimes, in his trousers.

The strong lean arms that connected her to him.

The facts about him:

His lips chapped easily in the wintertime.

He could only marry a virgin.

Even if he were the first, he'd figure if it hadn't been him, it would have been someone else.

His wife would live on his salary, keep his house clean, raise his children.

When he got a job in the school system (better days were dawning, and Charley, against Etta's warnings, did something for the boy), Helen thrilled at the smile on his face.

His dreams were what could be.

With his arms around her in the car, she felt real.

She wasn't real at home. Home became what Juilliard had been. When not at the piano she stayed in her room. Dreamed of Mike. Masturbated. Came.

Her mother didn't understand. What was all her money and all her parties compared to Mike? As a pledge of love she refused the clothes her mother wanted to buy her. She wouldn't go shopping or to the beauty parlor with her anymore. When Kat, the manicurist, arrived at the house on Mondays, she would *not* have her nails done.

Unkempt, she looked toward the future — away from her mother's admonition, "Boy, you're sure acting strange."

When her father glanced up from carving the roast and smiled at her — "I got a fine slice here just for you" — and licked his lips and made a slurping sound, she lost her appetite.

"Heck, your father could buy you the school." He had tried. It came to her one night, by way of a winged thought as she was drifting into a disturbed sleep, that her father had bought her the scholarship. He had rigged the Etway competition. She was sure. It came to her as quick as the Devil's wink, and was as clear and clever. How else could she have won? There was nothing special about her outside of Mike's arms.

She slept better. But she didn't talk to Charley anymore. "Speak up!" he shouted one night at table. His olive complexion turned red as beef.

She looked at him.

"Who the hell do you think you are, treating me this way? Have you forgotten I'm your father?"

"Charles!" Etta said.

"Say something!" He grabbed her out of her seat and shook her by the shoulders. Her head bobbed.

"Hey, come on, Pop," Raymond said.

"I'll shake your tongue loose!"

"Charles!" Etta wailed.

He let her go and turned to Etta. "You're so damn hot on manners, teach your daughter some!"

When they looked at Helen again — had time passed at all? — blood was on the tablecloth.

"Oh, my God," Etta screamed at Charley. "Look what you've done!"

Helen was grasping the carving knife by its steel.

Etta and the Czech woman cleaned the wound and dressed it.

Charles and Raymond stared at each other over the table.

There's a story told about them because they were both butchers. Charles fainted at Raymond's bris. Raymond passed out his
first time (and last) at ringside. Neither could take the sight of
human blood.

Charles was so sick with himself that Etta had to say "It's all
right now. It was hardly as bad as it looked. Let's forget."

"How could I have!" he asked her.

He went to his daughter's room. She looked pale as she slept.
Snow White. Blood Red.

A longing came over him for his mother, as profound as in the
first months of her death. Tears filled his eyes, big drops rolled off
his face. Mother, mother, spread your cards!

"Are you okay, darling?" he asked softly when Helen opened
her eyes. "Can I get you something? What do you want?"

She looked into his suffering face, for once not distorted by a
smile.

"Poppa." They both heard the lost little girl in her tone.
"Poppa, I do so want to get married."

The ghost of Rose — the trace of her hem — swept through
the room: Charley, your daughter is right.

Etta didn't give him any argument at all. What was left to say?

There were things to acknowledge, all right. Things as insubstantial as puffballs in the backyard in spring. Blow them away!

A puffball landed on Raymond's shoulder. Responsibility — as
light as it could be — for the dreams of his mother that weren't
going to be.

It's not a motive he acknowledged. He never separated his
piousness from his spite.

"College, who needs it?" is the way he told it to his young
daughters. "I wanted to open a store. But Mom had me for a talk.
We sat next door on the couch.

" 'Now that you're almost out of Dickinson, Raymond (it took
me four and a half years), what do you plan to do?'

" 'Be a butcher, like Pop.' "

Raymond didn't describe the look on her face — a daughter
about to be married, a son who wanted a lifetime of sawdust stuck
to his shoes — or her hold on his heart.

" 'Oh, Raymond! At least get yourself a college education! When you want to use it, you got a brain. If you still want to be a butcher after you've graduated, that's another thing. My God, being a butcher can wait!'

"If that's what Mom wanted, that's what I did. It cost her fifty cents. Twenty-five cents for me to take the Tube to the Village and enroll at NYU, twenty-five cents to come back.

"Don't forget, it was still the Depression. Anyone with half a buck could get in. Getting through was another thing. But I got that nonsense out of the way quick — three years. Then Pop bought me the store. I obeyed Mom to the letter of the law."

"She sure gave them a lot of heartache, right before your father started NYU." Lilly again. "She got it in her head that Charles had fixed the competition she won. Didn't want to take a thing from them. Until she was engaged. Then she let them give her plenty."

Mike convinced her.

A trousseau
A wedding
An apartment
Furniture,

these were theirs to give — until he carried her over the threshold and closed the door.

She looked at him. He was simply remarkable, sitting in the dark behind the wheel of the parked car. Wielding the heavy sword of logic, he came down hard. A blunt stroke cut a fine distinction.

She saw the severed thread.

He saw what mattered.

His arms, his lips, his Adam's apple knew how things should be.

"Come here, dopy." He drew her close.

This was life. His arm around her shoulder. The sweet smell under his arm. The warm wait out of which the future hatched.

"Come closer," he said. He bent his head to hers. His tongue entered her mouth, a fish out of a bowl. She heard the future in his shortened breath. The way of the world, the way he held her tight. The way, rather than ever hurt her, he pushed her off abruptly and moaned. This expectation was all.

She let the wedding preparations encircle her. Etta picked out the invitations, the patterns, the caterer. She masked and altered her disappointment with the exquisite, the expensive, the best.

Helen stared at the engagement ring that burned back at her. A better cut than Mike could have afforded alone.

In the midst of the activity at home she was as dreamy as a bride. She addressed the invitations, bumping her pen nib over the textured envelope, then lingering, watching the blue-black ink sink in. She began her cache of monogrammed thank-you notes once the first piece of silver arrived. She dwelled on the magical future: **H A C**.

At the fitting for the precious acres of her veil, she smiled through mist. For on or off, it didn't matter anymore. She saw through lacy, shadowy gauze down an awfully long aisle.

On her wedding day, dressed as Lilly described her, like an angel draped in a cloud, she stood waiting for her chord, unconscious of her father's arm. Everything was familiar: the soft weight of white, the long tunnel, the small figures hovering under an arbor.

She moved in perfect rhythm. Yet surely she wasn't the first bride to feel someone else reach the end.

A man was there. The rabbi called him Michael. He was doing a manly thing. Concentrating so hard on some small practicality that his intense preoccupation negated her. She wasn't there at all.

Etta took off her daughter's glove. Raymond gave Mike the ring.

A clammy hand reached what must have been her hand — she looked at it, rigid and white, filling the space. She watched through her haze as cold shaky fingers made shaky attempts — until with one harsh and clumsy shove against her flesh the ring was jammed in place.

A glass crashed. "Damn it! You could have *tried* to help me," Mike whispered as he lifted the veil to kiss the bride.

ᴽ ᴽ ᴽ

Something is wrong. In Indian summer Charley feels it stronger than he's ever felt a run of luck. A beautiful woman doesn't turn into an ill-kempt frump overnight. A young married woman doesn't sit in her parents' house hour after hour and play.

Something is wrong. Charley can't name it, though it's something he has almost touched before.

The weather is hot, damp, ominous. At odd moments electricity scratches the sky.

He takes off his butcher's apron one intolerably muggy day and goes to see his sister Adele. She's the pretty one whose son is at the bank doing well. When she smiles at Charley, Rose Addis jumps from her bright eyes.

She resembles her brother: olive skin, expansive features on a good long head. A kind smile.

She reheats the morning's coffee.

They remember his mother together. To please him she spreads the old cards.

The cards don't say anything at all.

On the spur of the moment she asks, "You want to see it? I still got it. I didn't sell the ball!"

She brings it to him. Unwraps it on the coffee table Etta gave away. All around it lies the yellowed news of yesterday.

Adele has some powers. She chooses her quiz programs with care. When she's feeling lucky, nine times out of ten she gets on the air.

For his Bar Mitzvah Raymond got a giant *Webster's,* inscribed "To A. A." She won it the day they asked if there was a butcher in the audience. She thought quick, raised her hand, and used her maiden name.

All around the dim apartment are her trophies, and there are the free meals, free tickets, cold cash you can't see. Yet all she can do with a ball is stare.

Charles stares too. Deep in the glass he sees troubled waters unchanneled by his mother's fine hands.

Memory teases him. A vague shape twirls.

The rare occasions . . . the distraught parents . . . They didn't want their palms read. Their faces were more telling than a crystal ball. Rose Addis saw the depths of trouble and spoke low. Charles sees those people now.

He hated them then. They turned his mother into something cold and strange. A French witch. Yet suddenly his heart cries out, remembering their pleas, their frantic begging. You'd go to hell to free your possessed child, you'd consort with witches. To have the Devil exorcised you'd do anything, anything at all.

Rose Addis would set up an appointment reluctantly. It took her back to Alsace and old ways. This was the only money she almost didn't want to make.

The date she scratched on her pad, Charley sat in the sweet shop with his sisters; they ate everything they ever wanted to. Then they returned to gloom. To the Cross of the alien religion hung on the inside of the door. To incantations in a scary French. To the mother's dipping water on each child's face.

At times life is too much for a widow with three children to raise. Charley would feel the sudden weight on his shoulders as, in a shadow of a moment, his mother turned frail. It was one of the occasions on which she *had* to lie down.

He was called to her side. *He* bathed her forehead with the holy water. *He* watched the tremors pass over her closed eyes.

Behind Addis's Meat Market, Charley keeps a yard. He grows white roses. Pink seeps into them when they bloom. Each spring he waits for the first one. The touch of the petal on a sunny day. The miracle of her closed eyes.

"Something is disturbing you deeply," Adele says, entering into his reverie in a soft, slow voice. "You can't put it into words. Let it stay unspoken, Charley. Let it pass away . . ."

The porch of Clifton Avenue the same stifling morning.

"Why don't you pull your hair back?" Etta says.

Helen runs her fingers through her hair.

Every morning she crosses the street from her apartment on Palisades Avenue to Clifton Avenue to play.

She comes to play her piano, and forgets to go home.

"You'll stay for dinner, Mike?" Etta asks when he comes after work to fetch her. They stay.

It's not right, and Etta and Lilly know it. You gotta please a man or he'll stray.

After his filling her daughter's head, Etta thought Mike would stand up for himself. But he don't.

Sometimes at dinner she thinks he looks surprised. Sometimes when he and Charley and Raymond talk, he talks like he's making up a lie.

He's a man; Etta thinks of all the things he should say.

"Don't pick that pimple, it'll spread!"

Helen with her left hand removes her right hand from her face. She pulls her head back and rocks in the rocking chair.

Oh, something is wrong, that is certain. What's going on is not right. But what is marriage if not a secret from the world? You get into it blind and it renders you mute.

Etta looks at her daughter. Is this the beauty that walked down the aisle? Her skin is splotched. Her clothes don't match. The sour smell of her body lingers in the close air.

Just one hair appointment in New York with Mr. Martin.

Just a little care with her clothes . . .

Etta doesn't see the extent of the deterioration. She's busy turning Helen into Helen again.

Twice a week, the minute Mike goes to work, the Czech woman is sent to Palisades Avenue to clean. Her daughter. Her son. Two slobs. Oblivious of how to care for precious things.

But a young married woman shouldn't act like a sloppy boy. Ah, is it too late to teach her the things Etta hoped she'd never have to learn?

Those hands, lean, muscular, competent (ignore the nails bitten into pink flesh). Hands for a concert grand. Hands for a washing board?

Etta sighs softly. She feels heavy with Helen again.

"Darling, let me run you a bath. With loads of bubbles, like you like. You'll feel like a new person, all cooled off."

Helen smiles lazily and nods. This will be the third bath she's taken at home. Etta is too busy running the water to count. Too busy taking the keys, going to the apartment, and picking out fresh clothes to match.

Back on the porch, the two of them. Etta has twirled Helen's damp hair into a chignon. A brand-new periwinkle scarf covers her neck and plays with the drops of blue in the silk frock she's never even worn before. Helen sure looks like a person again.

"Wait till Mike sees you. *Now* you do him proud," says Etta, who always knew it was not good, who fought against it till she couldn't fight no more. Here she is on this oppressive muggy day, saying what a man should say:

"You know, Helen, you got a husband neat as a pin. Meticulous as your father, you know. It's not right — a man don't like it — to let yourself go."

Helen looks through the dust in the screens and wonders once more where the other side of the street has gone. Is it up her ass? She smiles. If it's in her stomach, she'll need an operation. She frowns.

"Helen! Are you listening to me?"

"Yes, Mama." The wood slats in the screens are dark green. Verdi. Viva Helen Re of Dirt. Helen laughs.

"Helen! Have you heard a word I've said?"

"Yes, Mama." She straightens and sees her mother close up. What a wonderful bubble bath it has been. She is here for a reason. There are things she has been sent to say.

H A C

H elen A ddis C ohen

H ave A C ock

H elen's an A ss C an.

No! No! that's nonsense. Her mother is by her side. Hush, don't worry darling, it will be okay. I'll send it far away.

"Mama," Helen says tentatively. Then it comes out with force. "I don't like what a man and woman do together. I don't like it at all!"

"She came to me," Etta to her granddaughter Rose, Clifton Avenue, 1959. The two of them are on the porch. There's the still before a late summer squall. Etta looks past the screens at nothing. "Imagine, Rose, she said to me, 'Mama, I don't like what . . . what a husband and wife do together.' " Etta pauses. She's way back then. Something shuts down on her face. " 'But Helen,' I said, 'what did you expect? You're married now.' "

What did Helen expect? Hadn't Etta warned her? Hadn't that been the whole point? There's nothing that can be done *after*. After, it is too late.

It's a man's world. Didn't her daughter know it? Why did she think her mother hadn't let her sit out in Mike's car?

It's a man's world and Helen has missed her period, whether she kvetches or holds her tongue.

"Are you two for real?" His teen-age daughters had come to Raymond with the question.

"You think *we* wanted the abortion?" His wife wasn't there. He spoke out. "What kind of people do you think we are? We would have been grateful to have the child. Your grandparents would have taken it in like that! It was out of the question. Even now she can't stand to be touched. She never could. Where she is they've given up. They let her teeth rot out of her mouth.

"Old Doc Cooper came down the stairs and said to Mom, 'I'm sorry, Etta, but you've got a very sick girl.'" Raymond paused. It came back to him as it never could when his wife was shooing away the mention of it. "That's all he said to Mom. 'I'm sorry, Etta, but you've got a very sick girl.'

"We'd just seen that, all right." Raymond smiled shyly. "We really got an eyeful then. Ah, what's the use?" he asked, remembering, with a sheepish smile on his face.

Helen foamed at the mouth. They were sitting at the table. She stood up, put her hand against the wood, and with extraordinary power turned the table on its side.

It was a wonder Michael and Raymond weren't crushed or burned.

She proceeded to the living room, where she threw the Louis Quatorze at the front window. The chair wedged in, legs up, like an old lady with her ass — in clean underwear — exposed.

She took one of the crystal candelabras from the fireplace by its base. Crushed it. Made a glittering weapon of its remains.

She spoke in tongues and tried to slash her husband.

Etta grabbed her by the hair. Helen flung around and with her left shoulder knocked her mother out.

Raymond jumped at her. She gashed his arm before Charles and Michael distracted her.

She made ghastly sounds and twirled in a circle — the shattered glass in her hand kept them all at bay.

Etta moaned on the floor like a woman in labor.

Helen answered to the sound.

"Sacre Dieu" came to Charles's lips.

"Helen, oh my God, stop!" Michael cried. "See?! See?!" he continued, showing them all.

She whirled past dizziness — what were up and down to her?

"No! No!" Etta screamed when they lifted her up and tried to get her out of the room.

"Don't break into her circle!" Charley rasped. "Leave her! Let her be."

Alone in the living room she got to herself.

She had opened the scar on her neck before it was safe to return from the porch and subdue her.

"Etta, I'm so sorry," Dr. Cooper said, coming down the stairs. "We've got a very sick girl here."

Sedated, Helen was upstairs, asleep in her bed.

She was taken away the next morning, for the first time, and to the very best.

So Helen becomes a sound and a shadow. A voice from long ago. A stab of pain in the heart of the family. The irretrievable loss.

The doctors think like men. They attacked Etta with their book knowledge and their frustration. They hurt bad, but they don't destroy her. They only add small damage to great.

What were their lofty looks and sly suggestions compared to her Helen aborted, to the false hopes of insulin shock, to girls of Helen's age chattering in the clear air?

They couldn't make her ashamed of being Etta Addis. Who else was she to be? She was a very strong mother indeed.

She never became bitter. She never exposed her wounds for others to see. In her heart of hearts she never wished her luck on others. Life, after all, was what she always knew it could be.

Her punishment was to keep quiet — though on small issues she had a way of butting in.

If Raymond wanted to be a butcher, he got a butcher shop.

If he decided to marry a girl from a greenhorn family — so let it be.

A girl named Ellen. It could be worse. "Helen," Etta would always misspeak, calling her granddaughter. Little Rose heard her mother's name.

The doctors didn't deal much with Charley. He's a man. Hours: eight to six Tuesdays through Thursdays; Fridays and Saturdays, eight to ten. On Mondays he is off to buy meat.

He talks with them when he has to:

Fidgets.

Has little to say.

Appears at times not to understand questions.

Seems in control and unhesitant only when it's a question of what's to be paid.

A progression of doctors can't see him at St. Nicholas on Central Avenue. There's not a soul in sight when he draws holy water from the font. They don't see him wash his daughter's immobile face. They don't hear him murder his store of French.

Once he's almost caught. Helen opens a vein on her wrist with a small wooden cross he brought her.

He gives up. In his nightmares he lives his daughter's day.

"What do you want to bring that up for?" Ellen to her daughters. "It was a nervous breakdown. Something they could cure today with a pill. But in those days people were ignorant. They didn't talk about such things. They thought it was a disgrace. But believe me, your grandparents spent a fortune. A fortune. Those damn doctors took them for a ride. It broke your grandfather's heart. They say he's never been the same. But your grandmother, she endures."

It wasn't a nervous breakdown. It had a soon-to-be-altered name: Dementia praecox. Schizophrenia waiting its turn.

Actually, those were the days of great advances. New theories, new drugs, new hopes.

Years of hopes.

Really terrible years.

Helen responds to treatment.

They take her home too soon.

Too soon? She's strapped and carted back. A lifetime too soon. From sanitarium to sanitarium the Addises visit.

Etta sees her very sick girl.

Charley sees the Devil.

What does Raymond see?

He sees that life wears a smirk. He imitates it. Many things are not what they seem.

He develops his concept of the shmegegge. Any jerk who glides along blithely on the top of things. How he loves, with his tone, to crack thin ice.

He realizes that no matter what his mother thought, he's smarter than his sister. He begins to figure, to think. Ellen to Rose, to Janet: "Your father, what a brain." True.

If only he had started to think earlier, before there were things he was sure he knew.

There are some gravy years ahead. Good times surpass his philosophy. For a while he glides. Who says he of all people can't be a shmegegge? However, after he gets where he goes — he knows why.

Damn psychiatrists. Here he agrees with his wife.

Something in him is awestruck by his sister's ability not to budge.

Neither does he! Right from the beginning he knows better than to talk with them. He refuses to believe.

In the long run, even his mother admits that this time he's been right.

A still Sunday afternoon. Helen has been away for seven weeks. Raymond wakes up to a strange sight. One arm looks as if the wound Helen had inflicted has reappeared. The other looks as if it has spread.

He gets up groggily. Goes down the stairs. Not a sound. Charles and Etta are sitting in the living room, the big papers — Jersey and New York — uncracked. "Look at this strange stuff!" They start! He holds out his arms to them. As if ready to embrace, he shows the scales of his psoriasis to his silent parents. Their eyes are wary. Their hair is gray.

NEXT DOOR

ELLEN DIAMOND doesn't know she's beautiful. For her, a prominent nose, broken at the bridge, cancels — with a big X — that possibility. Her mark of Cain. She'll live with it.

Actually, it's the cracked nose, the wide shoulders, and the serious expression in her big blue eyes that turn this blonde from a doll into a beauty.

She has the type of looks men like. Raymond liked them. But some deep unease in her holds them off. She makes friends with them. She plays tennis, goes horseback riding, is agile.

Her high school essay on Lincoln won second prize in a city-wide contest and was placed along with the winner's in the base of his statue in Lincoln Park. But she never went to college. Her father lost everything — quite a bit — in the Depression. He had come from Russia — a country whose language he never spoke. Russia so close to Poland that maybe it *was* Poland. Once off the land, he picked up real estate. For better or worse, he brought his mother and his sisters and brothers over. They settled in Jersey City. Through the years the Diamonds filtered to Long Island, Miami Beach, St. Petersburg (Florida), and the casinos of Las Vegas. There is also a Brooklyn branch.

Jack Diamond kept a horse and carriage until Ellen was sixteen. Gave a buck to whoever needed one. When he was wiped out, no one offered him a buck back.

He was a short, square man with Ellen's colors and a cleft in his chin. An extremely handsome man. The Diamonds were handsome people. The mishpocheh that grabbed some money later on, overdressed for catered affairs and still looked good. Generally, looks — pastel coloring over expressive features — were their strong point.

Jack had been the one with initiative and spirit, and from her view of him Ellen inherited ideals.

After the pogroms, threats of induction into the Russian army, and the boat, America — which made him rich, which made him poor — could never let Jack down.

In his later years he watched Perry Mason on TV. "Now *that's* a lawyer," he'd say.

He married a plain young woman with water-blue eyes, who was born in this country. The youngest of a large family, the baby girl. She overfed her three sons, who were devoted to her, ignored her daughter, and, even before Jack lost money, kvetched.

"One day my mother said to someone, I forget who, 'Oh, Ellen wouldn't do anything like that. She's a *good* girl.' I thought to myself — how does *she* know I'm good — though I was. How does she know anything about me?"

Her mother was ashamed of her father's accent. That's the way things were; that's how ignorant people could be then. But Ellen's daughters, Rose and Janet, never heard the disparity between Pop and Nana Diamond's tone. Pop Diamond spoke thickly through his Yiddish, and drank shnaps in the morning. Nana Diamond said, "You dasn't do this" (for example, drink water from the bathroom tap), "you dasn't do that." She drank from a big bottle of seltzer and showed them how to mix jam with that bitter gas.

Perhaps Ellen was ashamed of her father's accent. It didn't sit well in her in-laws' living room. But if it pained her, she never admitted it. For Ellen as well as Ray there were things that ought to be.

Jack Diamond found what ought to be in America. He gave his daughter the land. It was up to her to burrow in.

"You know, Ellen, *that's* a good boy, that Raymond Addis. A serious boy." Ellen looked again.

By his early twenties, Ray was serious. He had learned to scan the silence of his parents' pain.

He tended not to be a joiner; he never learned to dance. His social grace, when he used it, was his manners.

With Jack Diamond he was extremely affable. He liked the man, he liked his accent. He felt free in the flat in Greenville.

And he was in love. He was in love and had money in his pocket. He jingled with power and worth.

He had graduated with a degree in accounting. He was clever with figures. Could do impossible sums in his head. For almost four months he followed Etta's way. He got experience in an office and waited to qualify as a C.P.A. For a pittance he worked columns. The grinding monotony was like sitting at an endless matinee with his mother. It was like crossing the ocean in steerage with Jack — of course with less nausea and fewer smells. He could not understand why his mother felt this road could lead somewhere. Was she being wrong again?

His psoriasis flamed under his white shirt. Charley saw his son grow pale.

Pop Addis bought him a store. A mile down, closer to the reservoir on Central Avenue. Then, within a month, Ray's eyes gleamed, a new vitality emerged. He was damn good at what he was doing. The money came pouring in. He didn't know what to do with it all.

If only I *had!* he'd think much later when his early years danced before his eyes. And his passion for Ellen came back to him, another lesson learned.

Passion is a strong word for this mother's son. As inadmissible as crying in public, to show you love out loud.

A weekday evening of the courtship. At seven o'clock, Ray, well dressed, arrives at the Diamonds' with a box of assorted chocolates under his arm.

He sits in the living room with Jack and his daughter while Minnie keeps the youngest boy and the dishes out of the way.

They eat their chocolate.

Jack drinks his shnaps.

They talk.

Ray often glances at Ellen, sitting on her father's footstool, radiant as day.

She looks at him.

He's dark-haired, dark-eyed; a strong nose looks good on a man. But his long face is too lean for it. Just as his lean body barely holds up his narrow shoulders, which slightly stoop under the good serge.

She looks again. Actually, he's more than just presentable. In his own way, he's handsome. It's "intelligence" *she* sees burning in his eyes.

The more he talks with Jack, the more she falls in love.

Real love. Far removed from a dark man with broad shoulders and thick muscular thighs across the court from her. Who raises a hairy arm, exhibits sweat, and, with a sweet deliberateness in his stroke and a mocking sensuality in his eyes, slams the ball back — within her range.

Ellen is a good girl. She tingles with virtue. Suddenly and irrevocably she chooses to do everything exactly right.

Raymond is a complex boy. He's getting smarter than anyone, except Ellen, thinks. Or Jack: this boy is bright. He is using his brains to ward off the world. Now he moves past it — one look at Ellen — to life.

She is a gift sweeter than any his father could conjure up. And it's so easy, so effortless — for example, to glide out of the house with Ellen. To put his arm around her in the car and to feel the soft angora of her shoulder, his fingers, his soul alive to the deep rich breast he should not touch.

A weekday. They go for ice cream. A mountain of vanilla with just enough — not too much — chocolate sauce. Sometimes they do, sometimes they don't have the whipped cream. They sit at a small round table, coats over the empty chair. The lights are low; the jukebox plays. They dig in, let the chocolate trickle, then slowly suck from the confectioner's cold spoons.

They are comfortable together, if sometimes quiet. Nothing intrudes on their belief in the other's good faith. Ellen knows Ray will be everything he should be, and Ray, about Ellen, knows the same.

It's so easy to look in her wide blue eyes.

It's so easy to think of using his name.

They park in front of her house. Ray pulls her toward him for a long good-night kiss. His hands sink into her sweater; he feels the angora swell. He thrills at the touch of her hands stopping his.

He walks her to the door, a final kiss there. Then a short, almost awkward, good night.

So easy, Ray whistling his way to the car. So easy, ten o'clock on a regular, sooty, burned-smelling Jersey night. So easy — his hand freezes at the ignition. It takes a genius like his sister to make life hard.

Raymond brings Ellen home to meet his parents. Clifton Avenue was in the Heights. Not an area Ellen would know. Most of the Jews in Jersey City lived in the Bergen section (centering on Lincoln Park) or farther still in Greenville, bordering on Bayonne.

Ironically, the modest Orthodox shul was in the Heights on Palisades Avenue. Jack Diamond and his brothers infrequently went there. While the Addises were driven to the temple they helped build — the glory of the Bergen section, Temple Israel.

Temple Israel in the late thirties was new and progressive. Ray had met Ellen there on a Young Adults' Night. He himself was an atheist. He had studied the Scopes trial at NYU. It hadn't surprised him that men come from monkeys.

He and Ellen met in the temple basement and agreed all the *forms* of religion were cant. True religion was in the heart.

"All of this," Ray said disparagingly, opening his hands out to the room. He looked at beautiful Ellen and was happy she knew the place was partly his to disown. The music began; he led her tamely through a dance. Afterward, how to keep her?

"Let me show you something," he said, continuing the main thread. He took her hand and led her from the recreation hall up the stairs to the temple. Ellen had never been inside before. It cost plenty to belong.

He turned on a light. "Do you think *this* will make my grandmother live again?" he asked. He pointed up to the elegant side window of stained glass. Lit from the inside, it was spooky. It glowered down on them somberly in splotched reds and blues and lead. "Ah, you should see it on a sunny day!" Raymond lamented, crasser motives obscuring philosophy. He walked over to the brass plaque on the wall. He rubbed his finger lingeringly along the indentations of Rose Addis's name.

Ellen sees the house on Clifton Avenue for the first time. An enormous white stucco with a slanted red-tile roof. A front lawn on each side of the entranceway. The entrance itself impressive. Some stairs to a long stoop and then a flight of stairs leading to a front porch flanked by white columns.

Ellen was not a person to notice *things*. But the aspect of the house etched itself on her mind even before Raymond reached her side of the car and opened the door. The house singled her out.

She was so convinced of the rightness of her decision, she had no fear.

A kind-looking gentleman appeared on the porch; he was dressed in a dark suit. Could he be a butler?

"That's Pop," Ray said.

"Welcome! Welcome! — Mother," Charley called behind him, "our guest is here!"

She was led into a room that seemed burdened by riches. Her first impression — "dark." Oriental rugs, tapestries, meant nothing to her. She would never know from décor. It, like organized religion, was simply the surface of things. Ellen had no patience with surfaces. If *she* had to dust, nothing got clean.

She was led immediately to a short, fat woman sitting in a chair. It seemed strange to Ellen to see someone's mother impeccably dressed up in her own home. Raymond's mother wore deep, dark purple wool. On her chest shone a cluster of jewels. Bracelets dangled on her plump arm. Has she gone to all this bother, Ellen thought, to impress me?

"Mom, I'd like to present Ellen Diamond. Ellen, this is my mother."

"I'm very pleased to meet you, Mrs. Addis."

"My, you're pretty."

Now Mrs. Addis should have said, "Likewise, I'm sure," not the first thing to come to her mind.

This was mild. Wait. "You're a tall one!" Etta will one day say to a gangling date of Rose's; or to Ellen's goyisheh sister-in-law, "Marcy, don't tell me you're pregnant again!"

Etta Addis said what she saw. The worst type of rudeness!

But in this case, she was admitting defeat.

"Now dear," Charles said, "don't embarrass Ellen."

"With the truth?" Etta smiled warmly. Leave it to her son to get stuck on a pretty one with no money whose family can't speak English. "Raymond, why don't you show Ellen around?"

In the attic, back to the pool table, he buried his head and kissed her covered breasts. "They love you," he said. He did.

Lilly came to dinner with her two daughters. Her Alex couldn't leave the store.

"So you're Ellen," said Lilly. "My, we've heard a lot about you! What a pleasure to meet you *at last!*" That's Lilly, she always starts off good. Ellen liked her right away. She was striking, and there was something real and wise in her eyes. That *at last* made them allies. Etta had taken her time.

Mr. Addis was immediately affable. "It's nice to meet you, honey." Not honey-of-the-streets, but honey-of-the-family, in his tone.

Mr. Addis, cutting succulent slices for her, "Here, take this one Hel——. Here's a fine piece, dear."

Raymond was quieter than in the Diamonds' living room. He looked both sheepish and proud.

All and all she was sure she felt at home. How could she be uncomfortable? Jack Diamond was as good as anyone there.

Though there was a moment she had to admit. They assembled at the table.

Etta at the foot said, "I bet you guys could eat!" Then without the slightest hesitation, erect and confident and with a vacant stare, she picked up the little blue and brass bell on the table. The tongue of the bell clicked.

The wedding had been simple. The two families, a few friends, in Rabbi Freemantle's parlor. Ellen already dressed in her traveling suit.

They had to wait a day in New York for the boat to California.

She woke up early the first morning. Her new husband was sleeping by her side. His hair was tousled, his mouth was open, he snored.

She had read the *Marriage Manual* intelligently. She knew not to expect bliss overnight. A warm feeling ran through her as he slept.

She washed and dressed and went to the lobby to wait for her father. Jack Diamond was to pick them up later for "a treat."

But he was there already, sitting, with a newspaper spread in front of him.

"Poppa!"

He looked up at her carefully. "How is my Ellen today?"

"Just fine, Poppa."

"That's good." He smiled. She turned away.

The paper was the scratch sheet. When either Raymond or Ellen made mention of their honeymoon in the future (not everyone then could take a six-week cruise to California — there's a picture of the two of them on board, her sitting, him standing behind and holding on to the cords of the swing), it was always that day.

Belmont Park in June. The sun shivering bright across the grass, the horses in their blaze of colors passing onto the track, their haunches high. For city people a country scene. The track itself, an oval sweep of rich brown earth. The dull clap of the hooves, the burned smell and sawdust texture of shit.

They held hands. "I could come here just to watch them," she told him.

He looked at the tiny men for the first time. Their colors to him were "costumes." Court jesters plummeting off the stage, landing on strong backs. They held stage whips in miniature hands.

He missed betting his first double. They stood at the rail and watched the race run.

Jack had reserved a table in the clubhouse, close to the finish line. His "surprises" had a poignancy that paralleled Charles's inventiveness. They didn't come out of a full pocket.

That he had managed to give them this day welled large in Ellen's heart — and in Ray's. It diminished the Addises' year's lease on an apartment and the furnishings too.

"Take, take," he said and gave them each fifty dollars. "Lucky money."

They sat at the table. Jack laid out the scratch sheet in front of Raymond and explained the odds. *Here* were figures that meant something!

An unspeakably tender pride suffused Ellen as her father in his unique English taught, and her bright husband caught on with alacrity. Father and husband huddled close over the *Daily Telegram.* In unison. Concentrating hard, the way men do.

Ellen could read a scratch sheet. Long since Jack taught her. She was good in a man's world. An efficient secretary. Her boss took her marriage (resignation) hard.

She was a good handicapper, though she hadn't the patience to figure too much. She went for long odds and hunch names. Then used facts to back them up.

"So? What do you see for the third?" Jack asked.

Raymond studied some more. "Maybe Chester's Pride," he said, looking at Jack earnestly. Handing in his exam.

Jack nodded solemnly. In a very slow English he drawled, "Certain-ly a poss-i-bil-i-ty." He paused. He looked out to the green. "But always remember vat is a horse race. In it each son-ov-a-vitch has a chance."

More than a year since that day. Ellen smiles as she heads to her father's office, remembering it. She is going to bring him good news — him first. He can tell her mother. Minnie has had children by squatting hairy-legged in the cave of darkness. Here's

Ellen taking a brisk walk in the clear light of day. Minnie would tremble, show concern. Ellen knows there's nothing to fear except fear itself — as Roosevelt soon will say.

But she is about to make what she will refer to in the future as her mistake. "The mistake." Eventually everything that goes wrong in her life is connected to it. Picture her as a kid at any one of those regulated little kids' parties she'll be committed to take her own kids to. See her blind-folded, twirled about, dizzy, staggering after her own outstretched hand. Wherever she pins her tail, it will always belong on *that* donkey.

Jack Diamond shares a desk at Garland Real Estate on Bergen Avenue. The Depression is over. Things are picking up. Jack never *really* picks himself up. He'll have twenty more years of getting an exclusive on a parcel here, moving something there. If he likes a young man just starting out, he'll give him a lead.

He's no loser. He's a winner taking a well-deserved rest. The past he looks back on is heroic. He has had one great pulse — one passion of energy. He has flourished and brought a family from across the seas. (He knew his daughter's California honeymoon was a blessing, but were they crazy to *want* to take a boat?) He had had his adventure, and in his view of himself it always shows.

Jack paces Jersey City day by day. What does he have?

His smile, his shnaps, his philosophy.

His house painting when things get rough.

His card games. The Elks. The track.

His oldest son, who in better days he had spoiled rotten.

His Ellen, who married good.

The younger boys, who'll never finish high school.

His Minnie. Every day when he turns his back on her and shuts the door of their flat, he commits murder in the good old-fashioned mid-European way.

He walks, he drives, he takes a swig, he lives.

Let's imagine he's an Italian who has saved his money. Why, he's back in Sicily. He's sitting in the town square. He's taking a walk. He's dropping in on a relative, whose doorway for *him* is as wide as opened arms.

The immigrant's native village, the immigrant's Jersey. The same thing. The place has been gained, the struggle is over. Both are in the world.

Stuck in it, a later generation might say. One that itself got stuck with learning English in the first grade, got stuck with accents, dictums, superstitions, old ways.

Not Ellen. She walked into Garland's office as if it were a spring day.

She tells her father she is pregnant with his first grandchild. Happy news. In the warmth of it she says, "My in-laws have made a very nice gesture. They've asked us to move next door."

"Have they?" he answers.

There is something more he wants to say. Later Ellen becomes sure of it. He was wise. He knew. "When I told my father, a look came in his eyes."

She heard more and more of the unspoken through the years. It sounded a warning resonant and clear. She'd be past his age before she'd fully realize the wisdom of his intentions.

Now in Ray's family there were subjects that bade you bite your tongue. No sense to blow against the wind.

In Ellen's family there were things you did not say. A word might knock a house down. It's true. If Jack Diamond had said a thing, Ellen would never have moved in.

"And that's why he kept quiet." Ellen recalling her mistake. "He was so wise," she would remember with pride. "He knew better than butt in."

❧ ❧ ❧

Ray and Ellen had two daughters. Rose was first. "Boy or girl as long as it's healthy." Ellen's refrain.

"Ah, come off it," Ray would rejoin. "That's why you always talk about having daughters."

"*Sisters.* I talk about sisters!" Did she have to spell it out? Sisters. Not like his mother and Lilly, always at each other's throat:

— You said that!

I did not!

I remember! —

They didn't know from sisters. Sisters to confide in each other. What wouldn't Ellen have been able to say to the sister she never had.

Still, boy or girl as long as it's healthy.

Not like Ray, who with all his education seemed to nurture a preference.

Ray was no athlete. Where the mind could direct his arms he was good: Ping-Pong, pool, sometimes golf in the spring. But he had seen himself in the yard on cold Sunday mornings, playing.

The phone rang early in the morning.

A girl.

Ellen had the will. More likely than not she'd make sisters out of her body with the same frenetic intensity with which, one needle under her arm, she knit.

Well, he had picked the name. His gratitude for this compensation welled out of him, making no sense at all, like the fancy gold cross on the delivery man's chest, like the bundles of herbs the women who came to his store put around their babies' necks.

"Oh, grand," Etta had said one night at dinner when they discussed the name Rose just to make some conversation. "She was a wonderful woman. I can hear her now." Etta hummed. "When she spoke French! Oh, Ellen, you should have heard her. Not *Yiddish.* She didn't know a word. Pure French. Remember how beautiful, Charley, when your mother spoke French?"

Charles seemed to step to one side as Etta did a fearless high dive into the past.

Ellen clenched her fork. "Would you be happy about that name, Pop?" Charley was Pop; Etta, Mothe*rrrr.*

"Would I be happy?" Charley answered. "Why, as happy as can be." He slid his carving knife under the hard, glistening rind of fat around the pork roast. "Here, Ray. Have some more of the rind. You got a taste for it."

How could Charley any more than Ray pass the piano, with its top covered with damask, without hoping for a boy's name? From Etta's side, from his. At dinner they rummaged through the dead with an eye to life. The men's names were too "old-fashioned" once you left the French side. Etta worked with initials. Raymond was bad enough, but its bearer realized it could have been worse. His mother turned Israels into Ians, Herschels into Harrises, without batting an eye. And she was very concerned about middle names, now that she knew from monograms.

"What about 'Ian Rutherford Addis'? That would look good on a shirt," Ellen whispered to Ray, even though they were on their own side. They laughed. Raymond had the uneasy feeling that for Ellen, Bob or Tom or Joe or Bill would be equally absurd.

Well, if there was a benevolent God, Ellen's dream of sisters aside, Raymond's first child would have been a boy. But there was only the world and X and Y chromosomes tossed like craps. At the moments in his life when Ray paid attention to this fact, he wished he could bring his father to it. But Charley could never accept the scientific truths of his son, who had gone through NYU in three years, absorbed the issues of the Scopes trial, and played Ping-Pong in Greenwich Village between classes. No part of the older man's soul responded to the harshness of the cold spheres. When Charley shot craps, he rubbed the dice warm between his palms, then breathed on them hard before he let go.

During the three-day labor, Raymond wished he could get in to see his wife. "Believe me, there's nothing to see," his mother told him. "It's better the way they do things now. Send them off alone. No one to hear them kvetch."

Perhaps it was. When he walked in, it was like nothing had happened. Ellen was propped up in bed, smiling and wearing blue. His constant flowers brightened the room.

What a difference twenty-five years later, when Raymond walked into the room of his younger daughter, Janet, and saw his one bouquet alone on the tray. And Buddy, his son-in-law, big shot, the son he never had, the sins of the father, smiling. Oblivious. "Hi, Pop! How does it feel to be a grandfather?" Ray would shrug. Raise his hand feebly toward Janet, take a seat without a word. Silently, he'd wait for Ellen, who parked the car on windy days. What did he have to say to a man who didn't send flowers? . . .

Jack Diamond stands up. "Congratulations, son. Lovely assortment."

"Yours are beautiful too, Poppa."

Jack Diamond raises a hand that says, Sssh. All is as it should be. Time for him to go.

Raymond takes his father-in-law's warm chair. He holds Ellen's hand. They smile at each other. What is there to say?

"Did you see your daughter?"

"Are you kidding? First things first. I want to see you."

"Just you wait!"

"You had a rough time?"

"Why bring that up?" Raymond's questions had a way of butting in. "It's over."

"Was it bad?"

"Well, I'll tell you one thing. Now I know why the women have the babies, not the men. If men had to have them, the human race would never endure." She laughs.

"I'm sorry."

"Silly. That's the way things are. It was worth every minute." She smiles, but looks very pale.

"You tired?"

She nods.

"Get some rest."

"They're beautiful." She turns toward the flowers. They were really, to her taste, too much of a display.

He gets up, leans over the bed, and kisses her on the forehead. His movement contains a presentiment that every time something important almost happens to him, he'll find her with her eyes closing . . .

He was not the type who could sit night after night with the other expectant fathers in the waiting room. Each tried to outdo the next in some movie version of how to act. You know, nursie with big tits, wiggle, vacant smile, sashays in:

"Mr. Robinson."

"MMMMMMMeeeeee?"

"You have a son."

"Oh boy, oh boy, oh boy, oh boy . . ."

"And a daughter."

And another son. In the movies, it works out to at least triplets.

Though Ray hadn't been able to sit among that nonsense too long, he knew his way around the ward.

Shmegegges. A new baby's a new baby. What was there to see? A red face? The wrinkled body of a plucked chicken? He saw himself at dinner with his parents. "Nah, I got a store to run. Had to get back. Figured I'd take a look with you tonight."

"Boy, you're something!"

Ray smiled to himself at his mother's admonition. He sure was something. If the umbilical cord hadn't lassoed him, hadn't dragged him to where he should be, he might have taken his own sweet time.

Nothing to do with the fact that the bands on the cigars that Charley had ordered would be pink. Honest.

What did it matter? Was he like the jerk who went running to the window with a catcher's mitt on, waving his southpaw and yelling whoopee? Boy or girl as long as it's healthy.

He stood at the glass, holding up his card. A masked woman brought his to him like he had all day. Slowly she rearranged the white blanket. Slowly she held the bundle toward the glass.

Great black eyes opened and stared into his. The infant started to yawn. No! Rose smiles. A smile of rapturous recognition: "Oh, it's you!"

This infant sees what she cannot see!

Raymond is smiling. Raymond in his heart is waving hello. Something has happened to him. Something as strong as the pull of gravity. But like gravity when everything is in place, it shows no sign.

At his store he goes into the back room and looks at himself in the small mirror over the toilet. He examines the long thin face, the prominent cheekbones and nose, the full lips. He looks into the big eyes that bulge slightly with surprise.

Rose will find the prototype for that face years later, walking through Petticoat Lane, watching London's Jews. No doubt Dickens found Fagin there. But for Rose, lack of rapaciousness, dogged intelligence, ill health illuminate her father's features.

Raymond won't have to go to London or read Dickens. Looking in the mirror is enough. He sees Fagin.

Yet, he had made a thing of beauty. With no effort at all. So much for fuss, for standing in line for tickets. So much for Etta's swatches of material. So much for hours and hours of practice until you've lost your wits.

Beauty, that ridiculous phony, that farce.

That surprise.

His daughter, with the pastel complexion of the Diamonds and his eyes. His child, who loved him right away.

Walking his parents through the halls of the Margaret Hague maternity hospital, he feels he has come of age.

November 1940. Helen has not yet been given over to the state. The closest to a hospital Etta and Charles have been was the public rooms of fancy country clinics. And earlier, each has stretched out beside a mother when she dies.

This is science. Etta's heels click along the scrubbed floors. She seems disconcerted by the sound.

"What are you doing?" Etta asks her son as he takes his card.

"Sssh, dear. Raymond knows."

He brings his parents to the edge of the crowd around the glass enclosure.

"Where's Rose?" Etta asks abruptly. This is like looking through Charley's window. Except all the white-clad butchers are women wearing masks.

"Take it easy, dear!" Charles says. He feels dizzy, the way he does in mezzanine seats. Detached.

"It's not our turn," Ray says.

There were people all around them. A tumult. Sounds of gooing. Love with its arms empty, gesturing.

"That's her," Raymond says, "little Rose."

"Oh, my God!" Etta cries. Her palms and breath fog the glass.

"My, my, my," Charley says, taking a step back.

"Come on now, Mom. There are other people. You've had a look. Let's go."

Etta stays moored.

An old woman in black comes up to her. As if giving vent to

years of experience no one cares a damn for anymore, she says, "Missus, dat's da most beautiful baby I ever seen."

— "It was something when you were born. Strangers wanted to see you ahead of their own. The Addis baby was all they talked about. 'Excuse me, Mrs. Addis,' they'd come right up to me and ask, 'is that your granddaughter? Oh, my,' they'd say. 'She is the most beautiful baby we've ever seen.'

"Your mother, you know, had the same room Nancy Sinatra had the week before." —

Janet was the second. It is chilly in the backyard. Ellen realizes her jacket will no longer button. She looks down at Rose and puts the child's hand on her stomach. "See how big my stomach is getting? There's a little baby sister or brother growing inside."

The right moment, after all the consideration, has simply popped out of the blue — out of the unusually clear sky and high, weak sun.

The child looks at her mother. She is four. She never takes a fact straight in the face. She squints her big brown eyes and tilts her head to the side as she thinks it over.

She hadn't noticed her mother's stomach grow.

"And we'll love the baby a lot, won't we, Rose? We'll love it together and help it grow."

Rose understands she's being told something very grown-up. Her mother's tone is portentous. The new responsibility impresses her. She smiles.

Ellen waits for:

How did the baby get into your stomach?

How does the baby get out of your stomach?

When?

After all, these weren't the old days when parents didn't know what to say to children, when infants suddenly appeared. The stork. What's a stork? "A bird" had been Minnie's mindless answer to her. Who was there to draw Ellen a picture? Did Minnie even *know* what a stork was?

Ellen looks down on her firstborn. Nothing normal and natural, and after all it *is* normal and natural, could be as terrifying as the big black bird of her childhood imaginings. The stork that suffocated and masticated children in its horrible mouth and then spit them out, little boys screaming and vomiting and having yellow diarrhea in her mother's arms. She could still see the black feathers ruffling, the huge empty beak opening into a colicky scream.

Ellen is ready for a tantrum. It's only perfectly natural for the older child, at first, to be upset.

Silence.

"Do you have any questions, dear?"

"No. Your stomach is growing because we are going to have a new baby." Rose would always be quick to grasp new ideas, if a little foggy on details.

Oh, how *easy* this can be if you just use your head, thinks Ellen, suddenly her mother's mother. "Rose, you're such a good girl! You're such a help to me. And you'll be such a good sister to the baby." The little girl smiles and hugs her mother.

Ellen rubs Rose's head as it rests on her stomach, and looks past the fence and hedges that border the Addises' yard on the south. She doesn't focus on the backs of the three- and four-story tenements that face her from Prospect Street. They form an irregular cityscape. They are there. Like the rationing and blackouts and bleak windy days.

But from their back windows, the people Ellen doesn't see, some her husband's customers, take a good look.

Right then, someone whose face doesn't count is noticing that she is pregnant.

It's news to women who hang out of windows to clip their wash to high lines. These women *wait* for Mondays. It breaks through their monotony like a blade to see two uniformed black maids come out of the Addises' two back doors with the laundry.

Ellen will never see them. At their back windows or in Raymond's store or at the track. Theirs is a world of superstition and poverty, and the Church. They are all Roman Catholics to her — including the Greek furrier across the way and the whites who will soon be drifting up from the South. Ignore. Ignore.

They don't ignore her, these onlookers who don't live lives of reason and roast beef. For them, a day is a day except payday and Sunday. And looking down on how Jews live is a treat.

They're all Catholics to her, and plenty are Germans. Ellen doesn't ignore the Brownshirts on horseback at the downtown German Club before Pearl Harbor.

Chermans. The horror is all around her. The dark smoky singe of history is not lost on her.

If Jack Diamond hadn't had the courage and determination and intelligence to cross oceans . . .

Thank God he had!

And because he had, she had this child. This child she must mold, she must teach. She stands there in the backyard, circling her daughter, who circles her, while she looks through the tenements, pointing toward order and light. "You'll love your little sister or brother very much. You're holding the baby now. She's right here in Mommy's stomach where she'll grow."

Up to now Rose's life has resembled the joke about the child who doesn't talk until she's six. One morning at breakfast she says, "This cereal has no taste, pass the sugar!" Her mother cries out, "But sweetheart, why haven't you talked before?" The kid shrugs. "Up to now everything's been okay."

Rose slips from her mother's embrace and goes to the edge of the yard, looking at the earth, the hedges, and the squares of green fencing behind them.

Chunks of dusty, pebbly Jersey City dirt. Last spring her grandfather broke up the lawn with a spade, and her father helped him plant a Victory garden. Only the onions and potatoes and carrots took. The makings of a stew. Rose tripped over the rake and fell on the oil spigot in the dirt. Two stitches high on her forehead.

Her baby blood in this yard. Her bronzed baby shoes in the breakfront.

This is the dirt Rose and Janet's canaries and parakeets, goldfish and chicks, will get buried in. Not completely satisfactory. The knowledge (via Ellen) that they have done all they have to do to right things in the universe isn't quite enough. After the ceremony, something besides the canary, parakeet, goldfish, or chick still seems to be missing.

Not yet.

The dirt, the bottom of the hedge, and the bottom of the fence mingle with Rose's state of well-being. But she doesn't focus on them any more than Ellen focuses on the tenements above.

She picks up her arms and spins herself around. She likes to watch the world whirl by.

"Watch out, sweetheart! You'll get dizzy." Ellen moves toward her.

Rose is breathless. "I'll . . . teach . . . the baby this . . . after she comes out of your stomach." She stops against her mother's leg.

"I'm sure you'll teach the baby better things than that. You know, sweetheart, you're a big girl now. I always tell you the truth. Some mothers don't tell their children that babies come from their stomachs."

"Really?" Rose is amazed.

"They say that babies come from heaven and are carried to earth by big beautiful white birds called storks."

Rose tilts her head. Her eyes slant into incredulity. The kids on Prospect Street don't know Santa Claus is really their own daddies. Even if they are far away, in Europe.

Nana Addis took her to Macy's and they waited on a long, long line. Rose sat on Santa's lap and touched his make-believe white beard and whispered in his ear what she wanted.

She knew the gifts would really come from the locked closet next door.

But her mother was angry anyway. "Now your mother's filling her head with *Santa Claus*!" Her father had a funny little smile on his face, like when he crossed the street to Rose and just missed, by *that much,* being hit by a car. You always have to look *both ways* when you cross a street.

Rose said to her mother, "How can they believe in the stork? There is no stork!"

What isn't isn't.

Can't be.

Like the holiday Pop Addis took her way up the Avenue close to his store to give her a treat. They stopped by a man with a mustache and funny clothes. He was cranking music out of a box.

He had a little monkey, but it was dressed in a suit, like a midget. The monkey took off its hat and held it out.

"Here, Rose, put this in."

She clenched her fists.

"Come on, dear. Don't be such a scaredy cat. Put this in his hat and he'll bow."

"I'm *not* scared." She was surprised to find she was in tears.

"Sssh, sssh. Here, look at this, Rose." Pop put the money in the monkey's hat, the creature bowed and put his hat back on without dropping a coin. The organ grinder and her grandfather laughed.

Then, was it the same day, it was as unreal, he took her to a black roof top filled with pigeons. So many pigeons that they had their own wooden house because they always came home. "Look, Rose!" She was supposed to have fun while Pop and a tall lady with long earrings talked.

"Both your grandfathers. What wonderful men. How they love you."

One day she was alone with Pop in his living room. Something got into her. She started to giggle wildly and to dance.

"Don't!" Pop Addis yelled, and before she could slow down, dizzy from the circle of her spin, he slapped her face.

She was too stunned to cry. She never told a soul.

They knew. No matter how many games of gin they played through the years, they were never close.

"Does Nana know about the baby?"

"Yes, dear. And when I go away for a week to have the baby — I'll be away for one week and then I'll come *right* home — you can sleep next door."

Rose paused, then smiled and trotted in her grandmother's back door to share all of this interesting news.

Ellen allowed herself to sit on the bench with her back to the hedges, facing the back of the house. She let out a sigh of relief.

There was a lot to shield a child from in these grim days. Her mother had two stars on the banner she hung from her window. Her youngest on a trawler, her next-to-youngest in North Africa.

Lilly's son-in-law had been at Pearl Harbor. Leave it to Lilly. He was missing from the first day of the war. Lilly wore her older daughter's grief. She was not part of the intense hope and strained exhilaration around her. Take a good look at *me,* she seemed to say. Ellen wanted to turn away.

It shouldn't happen to her brothers.

"Why does Daddy wear this?" Rose had asked.

"He's an air-raid warden. He makes sure all the lights are out on the street so we can sleep."

Rose's baby's head bent under the heavy white helmet. At nap time she points out God to Ellen on her ceiling: an impassive yellow face in that helmet. She points herself out too before she falls asleep. Little Rose in her WAC uniform, she stands straight in her jeep leading her troops to victory. In the purse of her regulation shoulder-strap bag there's box after box of the Jujubes she is now allowed to eat.

Let it be a girl who doesn't have to go to war, thinks Ellen. You'd have to be crazy to want a son these days.

And it was a girl. "Dear Rose, you have a lovely new little sister named Janet. She is very cute. You will love her very much and help Mommy take care of her. I miss you very much. Be a good girl. We will both be home soon. Love and xxxxxxxxxxx, Mommy."

Raymond delivers this evening missive, then goes to bed on his side. He stretches out luxuriously — smoking in the dark, ashtray balanced on the blankets over his stomach, watching the glowing butt. No one to say, Sit up.

The big empty house emits night sounds; it snaps and hums around him.

Crrrk!

All alone.

He's reminded of the nights before Rose, when the back bedroom was empty.

When he couldn't catch his breath, he'd get out of bed as quiet as could be and go there. He'd sit in the dark on a straight-backed chair, gasping in long, low whispers.

In between gasps, his perspiration cooling, he'd look out of the

naked windows — one facing Prospect Street, one New York —
he'd look out into the black night. It was like having a secret. It
was like being very wise . . .

Etta has a game. The perfumed gray-haired women — "the
ladies" — in brilliant clothes sit around the card table set up in
the living room. All the doors have banged open for Rose since
her mother went to the hospital to have the baby taken out of her
stomach (and then she'll come right home). She can stay on her
side while Loretta reads her magazines in the kitchen; she can go
next door.

She can catch a draft, standing in the vestibule watching for the
lady with the chauffeur who comes from New York.

She can walk into Nana's in the middle of a game and cause a
big rumble.

"Hello, sweetheart!" the lady from New York says in a voice
like a man with a cold.

"Bub-e-leh!" another shrills.

"How do you feel, bubbe, with a new sister to steal your grandmother's heart?" Silly old lady, putting an idea like that in a
child's head, she'll hear her mother say.

"Here, give me a little kiss right here," the dummy (that means
the fourth hand) says.

"Rose, darling, say hello to the ladies!"

The confusing and vigorous celebration of her arrival lasts less
than a minute. Then the faces shut down. Back to the game.

She's free.

She climbs the stairs to "her" room, on Nana's side, next to the
one that used to be her father's. Her father's is Pop's office now. It
has a desk and under a bunch of ruffles a safe and in the safe a gun.

"Her" room is special. Nothing is the same there. She walks in.
She goes to the window. She opens the window seat. By the time
she can share these mysteries with Janet, the contents of the window seat will be in the cedar chest in the attic. It will give the
sisters no end of afternoons, that chest. Always it will be the top
layers, the treasure trove of scarves, that awe them.

Rose undresses down to her white underpants and undershirt.

Then she chooses her scarves. She picks out a rainbow one she can see through, one appliquéd with bright blue and black sequins she can feel, and one that she senses is past understanding way before she sees a peacock's tail spread.

She drapes herself. She struts. She hums. She poses in front of the mirror. She lets the sequined one spark from her arms as she spins round and round and then plops, stomach up, on the big bed.

When the ceiling settles in place she rubs herself down where it feels good and talks to her ceiling people. She sniffs the soft tickling hairs of her free arm while she masturbates.

Spent, she rises from her sweaty bed and readjusts her scarves around her body and her head. She closes the window seat and then climbs onto it, her back to the room.

The two side windows of the bay are trimmed in stained glass. She squints at the white wall of the Loys' house turned blue, red, and yellow, turned all bubbly and out of shape.

No one is looking for her. No one is calling her name. Alone, she enjoys the hours. Her father's daughter. But it is a complexly colored, magical universe she hears in the steady rhythm of her own transformed breath.

Raymond opens the drapes in his living room. It's a beautiful, crisp Sunday morning in March. You couldn't ask for better weather to bring your wife home.

He picks up his keys and goes next door.

The smell of his mother's coffee tempts him. It blunts the fear of bombs, while he is away; of his parents not getting Rose to the cellar in time.

"Hey, Mom, you gonna set a place for me?"

"Look who's here, Rose," Etta answers.

Rose is drinking her "coffee." ("I'm away one week and she teaches a four-year-old coffee!") But it was Charley's trick. A glass of milk with a spoonful, drop by drop, of coffee. Raymond remembered his grandmother's steaming bowls of café au lait. Turned into a kid's game in America.

His mother had Rose in an impractical dress she'd outgrow.
"Have an egg, Ray? You got time."

The two of them watch Etta take more butter than she should
and put it in the pan. When it melts she cracks two eggs in it
(she never breaks a yolk), puts the heat very low, and covers the
pan with the pretty plate that will be Ray's.

"Why do you cover the eggs with a plate rather than a cover?"
Rose would one day be asked.

Because.

And on certain evenings of her life, alone and vague, she'll
make a pot of tea and cook her grandmother's breakfast for her
supper.

As the eggs slide onto his plate, Ray says, "Today's the day,
Rose."

"I know."

"Your mother's coming home," Etta says.

"And Janet," Rose reminds her, Rose who gets a note each
day.

Raymond puts a lot of sugar and cream into his mother's coffee. No matter how good it smells, it is always too strong.

Rose watches him sop up the yellows and then eat around their
dried remains.

"How would you like to come with me to pick up your mother
and the baby?"

It wasn't really a surprise. She knew. Nana had told her. That's
why she had to wear a dress.

But her mother and father *never made false promises.* So they
never told her anything at all until the very end.

"I took the same ride to pick you up," Ray told his daughter.
He glanced over at her.

Her head was leaning on her elbow and she was looking out the
window into her own world.

"Sit up straight, Rose. If the door opens, you could fall out!"
She adjusts herself. "Where's the hospital?"

"Close."

"When will we get there?"

"Soon . . . You'll be glad to see Mommy and the baby, won't you? It's been a long week for you."

What did he expect his daughter to answer? What he felt?

She felt it too. *They* — she and her father — had been away. *They* had had an adventure.

Hell, Ray would have had her sleep on his side if it were done. It would have been wonderful — in peacetime — to come home, tiptoe up the stairs, and find his daughter sleeping in the next room.

That's *you,* he could hear his mother or his wife saying. And who'd put her to bed? (Loretta's a day girl.) And who'd stay with her?

So he'd go next door after the hospital or his air-raid warden's duties. "Rose, you still up?" he'd whisper into the dark room. No reason for his sister's old room to give him the creeps.

"Yes, Daddy."

"Here's a kiss Mommy sent for you. Now get some sleep."

In retrospect, it's too bad it can't be done. Having her on his side wouldn't have been much different from being alone.

Rose sees them come toward her from the car window. Her mother, transformed because she walks so slow, her father, and the nurse, with Janet wrapped up in her arms.

The car swarms and squeezes with warmth. "Rose, my big girl!" her mother cries. "This is for you!" Not her sister, but dark brown branches with cotton tips.

"I want to see the baby!"

The nurse, in the back seat with her and the pussy willows, opens the blankets and shows the little sleeping face.

"Oh, how cute," Rose cries. "Hi, Janet, hi!"

"She's sleeping now," the nurse says and tucks her away.

"Can she breathe like that?"

"Of course."

But for the next two years Rose will push aside any blanket.

Rose touches the cotton buds shaped like Jujubes. "These are nice!"

"Yes, and they are for *you!*" her mother says, turning. "Let me see my big girl."

"Your mother bought them for *you,*" Raymond repeats.

The pussy willows glimmer. The cold sun flickers on and off them through the window of the moving car. Rose is overwhelmed, as she always will be when someone offers her a gift, at the same time half-suspecting it wasn't really meant for her.

But since Janet is tucked away from all of their germs, sleeping (not suffocating), her mother calmly explains, in the strict woman's arms, Rose slumps in her seat and gives herself over to the brown-black branches and gray-white buds she'll always wait for in their season.

❦ ❦ ❦

So Ellen had her sisters. Rose stood by like a sentinel. "Ma! Ma!" she'd cry, rushing into the bank or post office or store if the infant turned over and lay face down in her carriage.

Was the terror she felt at Janet's smallest movement or complaint the horror of her own black heart?

Rose had to ask herself this question when she was older. When her generation began to raise their children permissively. Biblical names came in, and with them Cain and Abel.

It appalled her to hear "I have to keep Jeremiah and Adam (or Salome and Rachel) apart or they'll *murder* each other." It astounded her to see the little demons try. It seemed to her (not having children, she was entitled to pristine convictions) that everything these parents read in a book they wanted their kids to act out. "Oh, Jael and Habakkuk hate each other's guts. It's *sibling rivalry.* It's normal. They should."

Should they?

Should *she* have?

Had she?

"Oh, no," she'd tell a mother she'd had Psych 201 with some years before, during an afternoon cut through with war cries and blasphemies. "My sister and I were always very close. I mean, sure we fought. And sometimes we'd disguise our voices and phone each other from next door and then run like crazy back home to hosie a chair. But *murder* each other? Honestly, I don't know how you can even use such a word within their range."

The looks she got. You might be smart in some areas, but your Freudian slip is showing, Rose.

Okay. Maybe it's repressed. So she had to go back and ask herself the question: Had she stood by Janet's carriage like a hawk, actually waiting for her sister to die?

She had to go back long after the forties receded to scratched black and white in her mind.

To the mushroom cloud at the movies.

To the movie Loretta told her about: A family around a piano like the one next door. Singing. Smiling. The Germans come and shoot them down. The blood flows so high, their bodies and the piano float out the door. The story crawls along her skin as cold as pee in bed.

To WACs and WAVEs and crushed tin cans and Rose leading the troops.

To Tokyo Rose.

To V-Day, which was more than a Catholic holiday. For the Addises came off their stoop and cheered. Pop Addis had a little flag for her to wave.

To Ellen's sobs as Eleanor Roosevelt's voice shakes and splinters over the radio.

To Harry Truman campaigning on TV in '48. To her knowing as well as Pop Diamond, who had a hundred riding on it, that no matter who said what about Dewey, when the President stood up to speak, the music played. He'd win.

To him winning. To Jack Diamond collecting. To her mother's pride.

To squared shoulders and monogrammed blouses and little tea hats that are coming back.

To the song hits of the forties revived, as every decade is, by the camp and hype of nostalgia, that soft-core porn which teases sleepy memory.

When these naïve days — it made people naïve to fight a just war — were as removed as the newsreels — George Bernard Shaw rolled off the plane in a wheelchair — she'd feel she had to go back.

The least she could do.

The nurse sterilizing her mother's tit with white gauze. Her grandparents, her father, her, upstairs in masks watching the baby suck.

The loud noise at dawn. Her mother falling down the stairs with Janet. The whole flight!

And after that the sterilizing machine for bottles, her mother's bandaged ankle, Janet's crossed eyes.

Did she hate her sister when she was carried, vulnerable and cute and half-smothered, from the hospital?

Did she blame her mother for telling her they were going to raise the child together?

But how could Ellen realize that her bright girl would fall for it, that she would assume the burden of maternity, would be such a dope?

Did Janet hate her?

"What about when I brought you across the street to see old man O'Grady laid out?" Rose asked. "Remember how we knelt on the bench in front of the coffin while you cringed in the back and then couldn't sleep for weeks?"

"Yes!" Janet smiled. "And remember when you bought me that wonderful stuffed Pluto and told me you hoped it wouldn't remind me of the poor chicks we just buried? That did it!" She laughed.

"What about when you had a slight nose bleed, and to get your mind off it, I took the roll of toilet paper I'd used to stop it and draped it around your body and you laughed so hard you hemorrhaged and had to be taken to Christ Hospital to be cauterized!"

"You were just trying to cheer me up."

"But, Janet, I could have killed you!"

"For goodness sake, you always read to me and bought me gifts and let me hang around when you were with your friends. The only thing stinky about you was, when we fought, you bit!"

"And pinched."

"And called Mommy if you were losing."

"I was a scaredy cat."

"You were a dirty fighter."

Through the years the two of them often went back. It took a
lot of conversation to bring a family memory up to the luster
you'd want to rub your fingers against a million times more. You
couldn't repeat yourself *enough*. At worst you'd turn bronze
golden.

"Do we have to go through *that* again?" Ellen, here, a notable
exception.

Rose would remember her mother's diffidence when she came
to be shown other people's antecedents hung along drafty halls
and staircases. "Do we have to go through *that* again?" kept her
polite smile fresh.

Just as when she met a certain type of winner she couldn't help
being tickled. The type of person whose every word articulated
self-worth. Usually an older man careful of his clothes, his teeth,
his phrasing. "Hey, Rose!" Raymond's voice from the grave.
"This one's a real Popcorn."

How Etta Addis would have loved the family portraits, right
down to the sheen of satin and glimpses of the chair. Her short
legs would have stomped the staircase. How delighted she'd have
been to meet a Popcorn.

Rose would share these thoughts with her sister, who couldn't
care less about bad paintings or pompous asses, and showed it.
Raymond's look of half-sleep would appear on Janet's face. Without one iota of his bitterness, she'd shrug and turn away.
Mommy's baby simply didn't care.

So they got together, these sisters. At a table or at a bar. Where
planes met. In New York, Vegas, London, Rome, Union City,
they'd dig up Clifton Avenue. Follow the cord.

How did their mother manage it? they wondered. Any time
they had a tiff — Mommy, Rose bit me; Mommy, Janet won't
leave me alone — "There's nothing as wonderful as having a sister. Wait till you're grown up. Listen to your mother. Believe me!
You'll see."

On Rose's birthday and on Janet's they both got gifts. Still, Rose was clearly Etta's favorite, and Charley and Janet were thick as thieves. "I'd follow him down to the cellar while he laid his traps."

Favorites? Nonsense! It was all in their heads. Children get the strangest ideas.

They were both loved equally. The one who was too smart and the one who was cute, the one who read books up in her room and the one who played ball with the boys on the block. In the eyes of the family — or any mother, father, nana, or pop who deserved the name — they were equal, equal, equal — the same.

Actually, the harsh inequalities Ellen saw to one side, in heart they did not vary.

"Do you know, I was over twenty before I stopped thinking, Sssh, you'll wake the baby, if someone made noise after dark?" Rose, thirty-five, still striking, if slightly matronly against the leaner line of her sister.

"Is that why you never had a child?"

"Partially. Having you was enough."

Her head drew to the side, her eyes slanted. She was thinking. "Only one lifetime. God, I knew early what I didn't want. Do you think I could have raised a child the way you're raising Laura? Let her pick some frozen shit from the freezer and warm it in the toaster oven if she's hungry enough to eat? It would have been bacon crumbs on top of the fresh spinach, like Mommy used to do, if she were mine.

"Or, I've thought about this" — you could see she had — "say I could still concentrate on my work. Do you realize how cold concentration is? Mine, at least. It excludes everyone. When Laura needs you, you're there. I'd either turn into a Helen or make one."

"That's what really got you, isn't it?" Janet asked.

Rose looked at her sister the way her Alsatian great-grandmother once looked at the cards. "As early as I knew anything, I've believed that what happened to Helen when she was pregnant could happen to me if I got knocked up. I can't say I've made a choice. My blood told me what to do."

"Well, then," Janet drawled, as she often did after one of Rose's huger pronouncements, "your blood sure has smarts, sister."

"It sure has!" Rose said, stretching. This time they were in Janet's kitchen on Central Park West. "And I have my memories. You can't imagine how cute you were, just out of the hospital with this immense mammal in white trying to smother you in the car. Believe me, you were worth everything I went through, and more!"

"It should have turned out differently," Janet said, shaking her mop of curly hair. Her glasses drooping down on Ellen Diamond's nose. Three years before, she had talked about her sister in therapy. She had written Rose a long letter that ended:

> *. . . Thank God you in some way got through some of our parents' control. If you had been under it as much as I, you would never have been able to reach out to me the way I feel you always have. We could not — would not — be capable of loving each other.*
>
> My thoughts suddenly run out. But it is what I underline that I most wanted to say. Whatever the whole story is — it ends up that I love you very much.

"How did Mommy pull it off?" Janet asked.

The sisters howled.

"What's so funny?" Ellen's voice came out of the wall plug by the kitchen table where they sat.

But they couldn't stop.

It was late at night. They hadn't smoked. It simply was that funny.

Here they were, two grown-up sisters, talking, sharing everything.

"So, what's so funny? Tell me! That's the big laugh? That for once you realize I was right?"

❧   ❧   ❧

What had being right ever gotten Ellen Diamond?

Turn on a light, answer a phone, open a door. Always the chance it would be Ray with something new.

The first time she was still weak after Janet. He let himself in the back door too early one night.

"What are you doing home?"

"I quit."

You do not *quit* a defense job that you've just been lucky enough to get, and that's keeping you out of the war. By now, they were calling up people with two kids and asthma. Maybe it was a joke?

A fever?

A national disaster?

The end of the war?

Of the world?

"That idiot!" she realized.

"Nah, it wasn't her. She can go to hell."

The woman who worked next to him at the tracing-paper section of the shipyard blamed the war on the Jews: "Oh, go on! Honest, Ray, I never woulda guessed. But I don't mean *you*. You're nothing like the others."

It wasn't her. On her he just perfected, night after night, his famous look.

And it wasn't the way the rest of them grabbed everything they could. Oh, he brought home a few sheets of tracing paper to show Rose what he did. But the others were vultures. It made him sick.

Still, it wasn't their rapacious and petty avarice. Or his being tired after a day in the store.

It was the monotony.

"I was standing there like a shmuck and all of a sudden I thought to myself, they can take this and shove it. I stopped what I was doing, I took off my mask, and told the foreman I was going home. You should have —"

"You're crazy!" Ellen cried.

Nothing could make him go back and apologize. She asked her mother-in-law to try.

"Get *him* to do something, once he's made up his mind?" That's where his dear mother left it.

She was too ashamed to tell her father. Jack Diamond dropped by in the mornings, after Ray left for work and before the girl came. She poured. "Drink hearty!" he said and downed his morning shnaps.

"Ahhhhhh! So how's my Ellen, the baby, my Vrose?"

She'd sit there while he discussed his Lenny. It rankled him that his oldest went somewhere in America night after night to pack black-market eggs. What could she say? My husband walked off a defense job? "Don't worry, Poppa. Lenny's a big boy now. Whatever happens to him, he's responsible. There's nothing we can do."

Of course, Ray was honest. He'd never take a cent. He'd sit in a restaurant adding up the long column in his head. "Hey, you, you've made a mistake," he'd call out in that tone of his, but then he'd prove he had more to pay. He never touched one of Lenny's eggs.

Still, he could act, he could *be,* peculiar. She'd watch her father down the shnaps as she saved him from this revelation. This son-in-law that he respected, that she knew in her heart was as good as they come, could at times be very odd.

Then one dark morning she fell down the stairs with Janet. With her ankle bandaged and her milk dried and little Janet out of danger, she made him promise.

When he returned, he shrugged. "Nothing doing."

"They wouldn't take you back?"

"You heard what I said."

He robbed her peace.

But nothing happened. The war ended without a trace of retribution. Somewhere, in the flux of history, Raymond's unfulfilled transgression got lost.

"See, I told you," he said.

"Brother, you don't know how lucky you were."

"Just listen to me for a change."

Then there was Belmar. There's a picture of the four of them there. Ray and Ellen are seated on white wood-slatted chairs in front of the Braymore Hotel. (On the porch you can see happy guests and around it flowering bushes.) Ellen holds Janet, an infant; Rose in her disheveled pinafore stands in between her father's tanned legs. Ray is slim and looks confused or thoughtful, and young. Caught by the camera held by who knows whom (Rose's expressive face questions a stranger), Ellen smiles. Surrounded and set off by the riches of life, she is at the center of gravity. Serene, caring, content in her sunsuit.

Let the moment last! It doesn't.

Ellen loves the ocean, the smell of salt, the weight of the air. She lies on the beach with a paper shield on her nose, and suns. In the water she rides waves.

Ray at the beach: the water stings; sand gets in his suit. At the hotel, the food is kosher. At night you have to walk down the hall — for God's sake, Ray, use the sink! — to pee.

"What do you like about this place?" he asks.

She loves it. Hers is mermaid love. From full breast to sedate fin she loves the sea and sun.

"Do you begrudge me?"

"Wh*aaa*t begrudge?"

"My pleasure."

Did he?

From the moment it was warm enough in Jersey to put the deck chair in the backyard, she'd steal an hour. There she'd be, in her bathing suit and nose guard, stretched out, oiled down, sunning. The old men of Prospect Avenue and the 4-F's she didn't see sure got an eyeful.

They thought her immodest. That, she could never be.

But there was something she surrendered to the sun. Ray would catch her off guard in these moments, enjoying the hot pressure.

It irked him. Though he never knew why.

And the irritation grew in summer. He entered her life on Saturday night and went away on Monday. "See you soon," she'd say, with a smile and a peck. To her it was only four days; to him a week. "Have fun," he'd answer. Who's to stop her?

One weekend of the very summer of the photo, sitting on the beach, he said, "Maybe we'll try again."

Was he crazy? Two children was the right number. And tough enough. One was unfair. *Three?* An accident. Four: immigrants, ignorance, Catholics.

"Let's be thankful for what we have," she said.

He looked into her blue eyes. "Not right now. I meant later."

She closed her eyes against him and sighed. Stretched out.

He looked beyond her glistening, high-breasted body to the sea.

He had spoken carelessly. It had been the *trying* that had interested him. Like maybe after lunch. He felt foolish. Then he felt worse. Before he'd known anything, she knew she'd have two.

"Yes dear, yes dear," he mimicked, "whatever you say." He scooped up hot sand and buried her feet.

Very lazily, Ellen murmured, "Come on, don't be silly, Ray."

Belmar wasn't his fault.

The heavy moist salt air was too much for his lungs. He began the season of the photo by sneaking out of bed. He'd sit on the empty porch, alone with the smell of wet wood, and gasp out into the damp dawn.

But then one night he tore off his sheet like a bandage. Put clothes over his pajamas, picked up his car keys, and left. Drove, drove, drove. Finally pulled over to the side of the road and slept where he could breathe.

The two drinks were his fault. Two drinks were one too many. Something new.

They had a set. People Ellen had known all her life. People who came from nothing, married each other, and after the war made good.

Ellen didn't have to read *Pilgrim's Progress* to know that life resembled a huge bazaar. She herself passed the merchandise by quicker than Christian. The important things were always in front of her eyes. Still, she knew when to keep quiet. She didn't make a federal case of the frivolousness around her on a night out. "You don't know how bad you can sound to people." He always thought he was just being funny. Ha! And as the years passed he got worse. "Honestly, Ray, you dignify their nonsense. If every time we go out you have to go around contradicting everybody and spoiling things, and come home throwing up what you shouldn't have been drinking to begin with, I'd just as soon stay home."

"Ah, you're a stiff like the rest of them. You just can't take a joke!"

It was a joke. All these characters who knew from nothing running after baubles the way his mother had years before. Getting, grabbing, following, without a speck of Etta Addis's finesse. There was no decorator they could use, shop they could discover, New York restaurant they'd try that he hadn't known all his life.

He had broken away from the people who had known them in the old days. His mother complained that he never saw old friends. Except for crazy Dasher, who Etta called the big baby. Him he saw.

He and Dasher had driven cross-country when they were sixteen, in the heart of the Depression. They had stood at the Mississippi and not taken pictures because it was dry. Ray experienced all kinds of weather — much of it supposedly better for his lungs.

You can have Arizona.

Dasher agreed. After med school in Switzerland he came right back to Dirty City. Left the fresh air to the goats.

But the others from those days had moved far out into lush suburbs. Tract housing had not yet encroached on their lots. Ray could never dissociate the long drive to God's country and the embarrassing boredom once he was there from the similar drive to the sanitarium to see his sister. Helen and the others sat in an excess of lawn. She, mute as stone; they, with their additions and frosted Tom Collins glasses. Their small talk, their white toothy smiles jingling like loose change. He'd opt for the small glint he sometimes caught deep in his sister's uncommitted eyes.

He'd opt for the couples he and Ellen ran around with, though every once in a while he tried to tell something to those shmegegges who were blinded by what they could so suddenly buy.

Take a look at me, was what he was saying. I'm an object lesson. Learn.

Look at him.

What had Raymond Addis seen but money? He had lived through one of the great economic reverses in history, but it had passed him by. They were the others at NYU who for a dollar ran

errands for the Commies. Soon, recuperating from his heart attack, he'd feel a wash of sympathy for the others when he saw
them — badgered and ruined by McCarthy — on TV.

He lived through the Holocaust, a nonpracticing Jew in Jersey
City, while the others like the Addises in Alsace lost their inns
and their lives.

And he was spared World War II. The others went into the
war to die. Or to return, hundreds upon thousands, like Ellen's
brother Moe, who married a shiksa, to live in a cheap house in a
project built out in God's country — so new a development on
upturned land that the mud seemed never to dry.

Only now was history catching up with Ray. It was whispering
its pedantic complexities in his ear. Still, he wasn't cooped up
with the others. He was becoming part of statistics while holing
up alone in his store. He was keeping things going while the customers he had been fair to during the rationing ran off to the new
supermarkets, and while the pigs who had been in the black market made it big.

New Year's Eve, 1955.

Other people's houses, smells of perfume, static from new car-
pets, smiles of friends. He'd smile back. Horse around. Stuff his
face.

Only at the card table with the men in a rich haze of smoke did
an evening right itself. Poker faces. Hands.

Gussie and Phil, apartment all dolled up by Bea Mann, who his
mother had used before she had a name. Ray and Ellen wouldn't
touch Bea Mann, though she was offered to them with ribbons.
"You guys," Etta despaired, "there's more to a home than making
sure the colors don't clash."

But you see, his mother knew that; Ray and Ellen personally
didn't care. But these other jerks, they needed Bea Mann to tell
them. They paid for things for which they had no idea.

He felt like holding up a mirror and saying, Take a look.

Around midnight Gussie insisted the men's poker and the girls'
kalooki stop for Father Time. She turned up the sound of her set.
There were more drinks, her shvartzeh put out a spread.

She was common-looking. Under the bleached hair and thick

make-up she had a pitted face. And a Venetian vase. Two vases. "Aren't they gorgeous?" she exclaimed. Bea had been lucky to find — Gussie had been lucky to pay for — a pair. They were wired into lamps as garish as a kid's motley marbles in a pile.

"They're ugly as sin," Ray observed.

"So are you."

Ha. Ha.

She turned the lights out at New Year's — the way kids do. There was swaying and kissing and singing. He had had enough Scotch to sway and sing too.

And kiss? Someone stuck a tongue in his mouth. At their age! He wished he remembered who.

They got louder and louder. He could have sworn he saw Ellen dance with big Al Francis.

He sat it out. He had funny pains, shortness of breath. He remembered another New Year's Eve. He remembered Maxie. What was all this when he had had all that?

He had only meant to turn on the damn lamp. He couldn't find his cigarettes in the dark. The switch was slippery; he tried to hold it when it slipped. CRASH! Then the lights went on.

He bent down among the marbles to pick up the lampshade. He put it on his head. "Happy New Year."

"Beast!" Gussie cried to Raymond. Tears were blazing paths, connecting ruts down her face.

Ellen said, "For God's sake, Gussie, don't fuss so. It was an accident. We'll replace it."

"Replace?! Do you have wool in your ears? Replace?! It's priceless. It's a pair!"

"Raymond," Ellen rasped. "Take that shade off your head! It doesn't help matters."

He died with his lampshade on.

It was at that moment, when he reached up, that he really felt sick.

At first he thought it was the usual attack, but he had had too much to drink to be quiet about it.

"Whatsamatternow?" Ellen mumbled from her side.

"Gas."

He was breathing like he was sucking.

"Can't you breathe?" She forced herself awake, though she would rather have slept and he would rather have been alone.

She turned on the light. Her hair — which she kept blond — was caught up in a net. She wore dark, checkered cotton pajamas. Late night, aggravation, and cold cream turned her pale. He took a very sharp look.

Whereas it took her longer to focus. She *felt* before she *saw* something haywire.

His gray pajamas shimmered and stuck like silk.

"It just pours off." Her mother-in-law describing the steam baths at the milk farm. If it cost enough, sweating became something wonderful to do.

Ellen now saw sweat pouring off. "My God!" she cried in a voice that could wake sleeping girls.

What now? He had already made a fool of himself. He had already (she listened) retched and gagged over the toilet.

He looked at her in her hairnet with her face white as ice. This was no ministering angel. He saw cold fear in her eyes. This was not his mother in the middle of the night, her upper arms and big breasts and stomach swathed in flowing gowns. Nor his grandmother, who caught the scent of trouble before it came, and warded it off with a caress, a look, sweet chocolate. This was his wife.

"Do you want anything?" He was obviously too sick for her to stay angry.

He did not turn his gaze from her. His head wobbled no.

"What are you staring at?"

She was *there*. Standing on the other side of the double bed with the receiver in her hand. If one strained in dead silence, one could hear from next door his parents' muffled snores. They were there. The children . . . whoever they took after, would be . . . right now they were in their places.

This is what flashed in front of his eyes: the white stucco house with green shutters and slanted red tile roof. He didn't have a favorite color or a flower, he never noticed a finishing touch, yet he could see this house he'd never taken a good look at, encircling him.

He already had an invalid's instinct for the signs within him. So he knew:

The shortness of breath was not asthma.

Nor the sweat.

Nor the pain that kept his arms pinned down, that crushed his chest.

Any minute he might leave the room forever.

He was in the grips of death. Father Time with his white beard and scythe. The skeleton costume all smiles at Cheap Sam's that Rose used to stare at on Halloween.

The Swedish art film. He had showed up for Brigitte Bardot after the picture changed. Well, he was already in New York ...

It was Death who entered the carriage, hooded Death who played chess by the sea. He got the point — it's all a game. Though it took a lot of saying from the Swede.

He kept his eyes open as Ellen tried to reach a doctor. The short form, the ample breasts blunted by the sensible pajamas, the concern against the sides of the tense blue eyes. Ellen Diamond Addis on the phone. The closet door was open; its full-length mirror was behind her. He did not see himself.

He fought a tidal wave of nausea and dizziness within him. It wanted to pick him up and toss him from this room. He fought it like a madman, he gasped like a swimmer, and just when he believed he was riding the black wave peacefully, he realized he'd been duped. His eyes were closed.

No scythe. No smile. No hood.

Open those eyes!

He did.

The electric light had turned the room orange and yellow while detached pieces of night whizzed through his head. Ellen's scared blue eyes were like static electricity. He struggled against the blind spots snapping between them.

"I can't get anyone! Dr. Loy doesn't answer. Dasher's out. I'll ... I'll call the hospital."

He could lift his hand. His straight palm meant no.

"But you're sick!" she cried. My God, she didn't want a false alarm any more than she wanted him sick. The roar of sirens, her in-laws up, the neighbors sliding out of bed to darkened windows.

"It'll pass," he whispered hoarsely. It was passing. His breath was coming back. He was in the room with the bedroom set and Ellen. Shivering.

She crept into the hallway silently and brought back towels. Very slowly she was able to strip the soaking pajamas. He mopped the places that she missed. He helped her help him on with fresh pajamas. Checkered, like hers.

"You look better," she said. "Try to get some sleep."

"No," he said and pointed his thumb down.

Over her insistence that it was sleep he needed, rest for both of them, he kept his thumb jabbing to the floor.

With dread, she let him lean on her and helped him down the long staircase. She remembered Janet in her arms when she stumbled and they fell. Now he was supported by the banister and by her side. The possible plunges in life . . . What you don't expect can happen in a blink. What you *do* expect has some power to save you. Slowly, slowly, testing the carpeting on each stair. Sisters lay asleep overhead. One false move . . .

She got him to the chair, sat him down, brought a hassock over, before she felt the raw strain rip through her side. Without realizing it or wanting to, she carried his weight.

He was gasping. He held on to his left arm. He had never done that before. The gesture was eerie. It was crazy what they had just done. But if she had refused, God knows what new trick he'd be up to.

She sat by him, watching, the way Rose used to watch Janet's nose and her blanket.

She had always kept a reasonable distance from horror. What's over is over. Nothing left to do. A closed coffin. Think of the living. Pay respects. She'd never viewed a corpse.

Nothing protected her at the moment. Her rationality, her sense of values, her wifely feeling were as impotent as the big insurance policies locked behind the breakfront's bottom door. She was on the razor edge of panic.

Disappointments, who doesn't have them? You got married and you matured. It was enough that the children knew from nothing and your parents crossed your threshhold with pride.

The pangs of childbirth, the quarrels, Etta bursting in at any time with her keys jangling, Ray's store making less of a go, the tepid sex, the realization at thirty-five that with a little luck you have thirty-five more of the same to go. This was life. You put a pleasant face on it. No one should know.

But now she was beyond it all. She was scared out of her wits. Every fiber of her body, every stretch of her will, breathed with Raymond.

He saw her panic. It was a mirror of the pain he was going through. See! See! For years I've kept this from you.

They sat there in the living room, one listening, one staring. The greenhorn's daughter. The Addises' son.

He held watch on the curve of his wooden banister, the mate of the one next door, while she saw the side of his nostril expand and contract, his mouth open quick — as if for a sharp word — then slacken.

Time ticked out on the Swiss clock on the landing's wall. Next door the grandfather's clock tolled out each quarter-hour, like Big Ben. Then a whole song and the chime of five.

"Ellen, a blanket, hah?"

"You okay?"

"I'm okay."

"Do you want to stretch out on the couch?" she asked as she fetched him a cover.

"No, I wanta stay up."

"Sleep's the best thing," she said, as she tucked it around him.

"Not now."

Then he said, "What a pair we make, hah?"

"We don't do so bad."

"Good old sis and me."

"Why bring that up?"

"What a pair we make."

"If you want to talk like that, I'm going back to bed."

"I wish you would."

"That's the thanks I get."

"It's late, El. It's late. Go. Go to bed."

"You okay?"

"Yeah."

"You sure?"

"I'm just weak."

She'd be up there. He'd be here. The night would pass. He'd see the morning.

He felt like a child again, being so weak and warm under the blanket after a quick, violent illness.

She knew everything was in the breakfront, didn't she?

"Leave the light on!" he demanded before she crept up the stairs.

A few years later Rose would come home after her first term in college, her face burnished with excitement, her eyes too bright. At dinner she'd place her grandmother's crystal and silver salt and pepper shakers in front of her. "The question is, if we were not here to see them, touch them, know them — would they exist? Would *they* be here?"

"You have to take care of good things!" Etta interjected. Charley was gone. She looked around at a table full of careless heirs.

"Look, Miss Smartie, calm down!" Ray's face was getting red in an attempt to steady her, his tone nasty in an attempt to teach her modulation. "I don't know what your fancy professors are teaching you. But your father can answer that straight out, here and now."

"But Dad, what I mean —"

"Listen to your father!" Ellen admonished. "He's telling you something."

"Calm down!" Raymond insisted. "I know what you mean better than you think. Let me tell you something for your information. These things don't give a damn for us."

"Oh, *you.*" Etta sighed.

"Mothe*rrrr*! Please don't interrupt Raymond when he's explaining something to Rose."

"These things don't give a damn for us. You go tell your professors. Your father says, when we're all six feet under, they'll still be here!" . . .

The sturdy couch by the front windows, the heavy durable winter drapes, the round coffee table with its painted pink wood bottom and its foggy-glass top, the sensible armchairs, the blond breakfront, the wall-to-wall with the old stains.

In the dead quiet Raymond felt sudden exultation. He'd get some more wear out of these things.

Things. Boo-hoo. Cry if they break. Fuss over them, cry your heart out. Are you crazy? Would they whimper for you? You should be celebrating, Gussie. You outlived a lamp!

I should be celebrating, Raymond thought. I've outlived one too.

A small sour smile crossed his face. The type Ellen would try to erase. But she was upstairs asleep now, so would never know it was there.

He lit a cigarette. Many an asthma attack he'd ended with a smoke to clear his head. But something was wrong. He couldn't get the smoke down without something wanting to come up. He crushed the cigarette out.

I think I've had a heart attack, he said. He thought he said it. He thought he could see his slippered feet and hear his words. But his head was thrust back, his eyes were closed, his mouth open. He was fast asleep.

He was sitting abnormally straight in his chair when his daughters came down the stairs the next morning. Ellen had prepared them.

It was immediately obvious that he had no power over the chair, over being downstairs in his pajamas and robe. His hair was sticking up. They could see a white patch of psoriasis near the scalp.

They stood on the landing with embarrassed looks on their faces, their eyes averted when he saw them. He was embarrassed too.

"How you feeling?" Rose asked.

"Yeah," Janet concurred.

"I've never felt better."

They took two steps off the landing and went quickly into the kitchen. Janet first, Rose making an attempt to stroll.

They went about their breakfast. Rose was chubby. Many of her friends had already "developed" and "had figures," whereas she was the type about whom grownups rave, "What a face!" Kat, too, the black manicurist who still did the Addises' nails on Mondays and carried all sorts of news along with her heavy case, had said in her declamatory voice, which she underscored by emphatic nail-filing, "I was by Mrs. Saltzman and do you know what she said? That Rose Addis has the face of the Madonna, God bless her. I most certainly did agree."

Her grandmother hadn't yet let go of the story. Evidently it was a special compliment to look like the Madonna, even though the Madonna was Catholic. It was a splendid exception to a fairly established rule.

Janet, on the other hand, needed to be built up. She earnestly overpoured chocolate into her milk. Behind her thick glasses one eye refused to center. That slightly out-of-focus look, curly blond hair, and frail body were cute.

"It doesn't look very good," Rose whispered with a throb.

"What?"

"I just don't know," she continued prophetically.

"He said he felt okay."

Anyone who'd lived more than ten years on Clifton Avenue certainly didn't go by what people say. But a child could have her mind on her chocolate milk.

"I don't want you to worry," Rose said.

Janet looked up from stirring. "I'm not."

"You sure?"

"Positive."

"I'll call Russell." Russell had a driver's license and was taking a group to a fantastic ice-cream parlor in Englewood this New Year's Day. A car had to have someplace to go. Also, Russell's father was dead. "He'll understand. There'll be room for you."

"For *me*? You're going to take me?!"

"You have a mustache, Janet. Wipe it off."

Russell's voice cracked, as Rose felt it would. The back seat would move over.

"Thank you so much, Russell." She said good-bye softly and hung up. Everything was quiet. Her grandparents had not yet been informed. She made herself a bowl of Cheerios and banana.

She was struck by the drama of her friends' concern. She was struck by drama. "Sarah Bernhardt," her father called her. She saw the world spin round her and reorder poignantly. "What does your father do?" A handsome senior from Bayonne at a Y dance. The revolving ball of mirrors twirls light into the darkened room. "I . . . I lost my father." His arm tightens around her waist. "Poor kid."

"Hey, don't start crying," Janet said. "He'll be all right, Rose. Wait and see."

All the king's horses and all the king's men. Will they put Humpty together again?

They were upstairs dressing when the ambulance came.

Rose debated with herself. She knew she shouldn't — her mother wouldn't like it at all. Even her grandparents were not to excite him. They stayed next door. Etta, in fact, was by her living room window, unconsciously rubbing her chewing gum into a smooth ball between her thumb and forefinger, just the way she did when she listened to the Texaco opera on the air. Charley was in the cold vestibule.

Also, Rose was scared. Scared to look at him again. Scared because by the rules of this house she ought not to and because she was afraid of what she would see.

So she crept down on the staircase to the point where they couldn't see her and she could listen.

But she didn't move away when they carried him out. She saw him at the doorway, strapped down to the litter.

He caught her eyes. He wasn't a bit angry! *This is what it's all about,* his look told her. *Don't let any of them fool you. Take a good long look at me.*

Daddy!

Until they edged him out of the door, he didn't take his eyes off her.

❦   ❦   ❦

Brothers in the dead of winter, three strong, look big. Important, even. They enter Ellen's living room in heavy coats, heavy looks of concern in their eyes. All bundled up — "Button up your necks," Jack Diamond's winter cry. The cold clings to them.

"What's up, El?"

"What can we do?"

Lenny the oldest, Moe the handsomest, Barney the baby doing the best as he tries to keep up with his big brothers.

"Oh, hello, Mrs. Addis," almost in unison.

Etta is sitting in Raymond's chair.

Lenny's "Mrs. Addis" is slurred and careless.

Moe's is distant and respectful.

Barney's eager.

What can they do? Etta thinks. They could move something around.

"I'm awfully sorry, Mrs. Addis," Moe says.

She nods. He's the best of the lot. If you hand him and Marcy a perfectly good piece you've no use for anymore, they appreciate.

"Awfully sorry, Mrs. Addis," Barney agrees.

"How's Zelda?" she asks him. He married good.

Lenny, he's past redemption. The only time he opens his mouth is to eat. And drink. Shnorrer.

She gets up. "I'll see you boys later." She goes next door.

Ellen shows them a sigh of relief.

Lenny says, "Any time you need us, sis, we'll scare *her* away."

Ellen puts her finger up to her lips for a violent "Sssh!" Her mother-in-law shouldn't hear. No one should hear. Anything. Ever.

"How's Ray doing?" Barney asks. He had gotten into the revolving racks of hair-care accessories in chain drug stores and supermarkets — and on the ground floor. Ray had loaned him some money; he wouldn't take interest or, for some reason, a share.

"He's doing okay. But it was a pretty bad attack. If he . . . gets through today."

"He'll get through today," Moe says. Marrying Marcy had rubbed off on him. A person could arrive up to a half an hour late at his house — even on a snowy day — without being assumed dead.

Ellen nods. She agrees with Moe. Maybe you have to be in the middle of catastrophe to measure how long it can last.

"Don't worry," Raymond had told her under medication. "I'm going to live." He said it drowsily, but stubbornly enough, if you knew him.

Dasher had dashed in. He wore red, blue, and green checkered pants and a bright green sweater. He drove his sports car where his patients could see. A nudnick. His style of living was ten years ahead of his profession.

"A heart attack?" he demanded in a surprisingly high voice for a tall man. "No kidding, Ray! Jesus H. Christ. Figure it. It just don't add up. Anyone can see you're a textbook perfect cancer type!"

Ray struggled to whisper with — incredible! — delight, "Fooled you . . ."

What were these people made of? Ellen wondered. People like Ray and his mother. "Oh, dear." Etta's face just shut down when she was told. She didn't shed a tear. Just sat there looking past her. Probably saw a new scratch on the piano, the way she stared.

But oh, to have three strong men when you need them. She looked up to her brothers — not too far; for all their bulk, they weren't tall.

Men in the living room with their boots on and their coats closed. Handsome men.

"Take off your coats," she said. "You'll catch cold."

"Nah," Lenny answered. "I'm going to drive over and tell Ma and Pop. These two will take you back to the hospital and make sure everything's okay. Barney's friends with some big heart man in Teaneck."

Where had the little boys gone, with their loud insistent farts and obscene gestures, filthy games, naked parts? Now she forgot even the bits and pieces she admitted to of those days.

Here were three men to appreciate. Her brothers.

Raymond lived through that day and the next and the next . . .
They kept you very quiet after a heart attack. Ray learned to do
less and less. He was washed by a terrible weakness, his frail body
blended into the hospital sheets. His thick hair and black eyes
greeted Ellen and Etta, Charley and the kids. Then the family
could make out the smallest smile at the lips.

Exertion, the Devil. "Don't *run!*" screams mama after bubeleh,
"you'll *sweat!*"

Ray shouldn't exert himself. The worst thing. Any accelerated
life sign is like sticking your thumb to your nose. A dare!

Sssh. Relax.

He is fast asleep. Ellen covers him for the night. A wave of
tenderness overwhelms her as she looks at his defenseless features.
For all his small perversities, he's better than his fate. A new sympathy has developed over the last three weeks on the Christ Hospital's cardiac floor. The New Deal Democrat and the rich man's
son root for the underdog. Him.

They have each other. For how long? Oh, the blessed monotony of life on Clifton Avenue. The precious portion. She looks
back over it as she lights a cigarette in the hall. She never smoked
before she was married, just as, according to Etta, her son had
never been sick.

That's a mother, Ellen thinks, inhaling, at the same time extin-
guishing the match with nervous flicks of her wrist. Exhale. The
world rights itself, falls into a pattern around her cigarette. The
things we never appreciate until it's too late. Take away the thin
rectangular box of Parliaments that she's putting in her purse.
They don't make it anymore. Remember forever the box sliding
open, the tingle of silver foil against a well-manicured nail, the
clear white filtertips exposed in two layers. The first puff snatched
just in time.

That's a mother who makes her own good times to see her son.
Who comes to the hospital after a game or before a meeting.
Who stays too long when she has nothing better to do. For a real

mother the whole world would drop away. A real mother would drop away.

The resentment on Clifton Avenue that erupts when Ellen hears the jingle of her mother-in-law's keys in her living room. "Helen!" she'll call into the emptiness year after year, meaning not even Ellen, meaning Rose.

"Oh! Here's where you guys are!" You couldn't make a pound cake in peace.

The same resentment when Ellen comes into Raymond's room and feels suddenly that she has interrupted something. What? Etta on the chair. No emergency puts a wrinkle in her clothes or face, or takes the blue rinse out of her thick white hair. Raymond in bed, absent-minded, his hand on his elbow. With his mother there he stops short of scratching the scab. What is Ellen interrupting? A silence? A knowledge? A look?

She comes into any room quick. Now she always has a lot on her mind and errands on her list. She can feel the static of her energy rising in the air and jolting them.

"Oh, hello, Mother*rrr*. No game today?"

"It's *Wednesday*, Ellen."

Oblivious. And all Ellen has to muster is understatement.

A real mother with a son so sick? Like her own mother? Eat! Eat! Like herself? Can the born Platonist define a Real Mother? Ellen, can you define your terms?

Don't talk nonsense! I mean what I mean!

She finds herself walking too fast. "Take your time!" Raymond will yell through the remaining years. "Where's the fire?"

She gets into her car. She always brings her skirts above her knees when she puts her foot on the pedal. In the car she works her shapely legs shamelessly, like a man. She means business. She has places to go.

At the same time she's looking back on it all: when she creeps in the back door praying Etta is on her own side; when she gets Rose and Janet to sleep; when she goes into Janet's room the next morning. Her baby who always wants to oversleep. Warming Janet's feet she thinks. Squeezing orange juice. Getting the girls off. Leaving block-letter instructions for the maid. Going up Central Avenue. Shopping for her. The bank for Ray. Walking through the corridors. Back in Ray's room. Fixing his blankets. Finding the nurse. Adjusting the bed, the shade.

"Why don't you sit down?"

She's looking back all the time. When she's busy, she can think.

The world as new as her marriage. The big white stucco house. Etta "beginning to entertain again." The expectation, the pride in Jack Diamond's eyes.

The ordered days march on. Ray off in the morning, then the girls. Jack Diamond's shnaps. First Loretta, then May, now Claudine arrives. The phone calls. Setting up the games. The errands. Stopping by Ray. The afternoon of mahjong, kalooki, lately canasta with the girls. Home for dinner on the Addises' side. Out at night, to an even faster game. The Golden Age. The progression staggers her. Till it's over, you don't know what you'll miss.

What's over?

The belief in endless prosperity and abundant good health. Youth. She's thirty-five. She's getting stuck with what she has. And like most people, she finds it not what she expected.

When Jack Diamond appears at Ray's room each midday with his heart in his eyes, she feels like crying out to him, "It's not your fault!"

Her nerves!

In another week Ray's coming home, God willing. Coming home with that time bomb of a heart in his chest. They are going to be very, very careful. Coming home to haunt the upstairs.

"Why don't you get yourself a game for the afternoon?" he asks, watching her from the bed. As if she'd play!

"Huh?" She looks up from his get-well cards. Today she's sorting out all the ones she'll have to answer. She's ripping the addresses off the envelopes and clipping them to cards that send a big cheerful THANKS!

"Get out of here, is what I mean. Relax."

With him like this? She looks at him. He'll never understand.

"I'll relax when you're well."

He smiles. The hospital bed is in sitting position. "Don't hold your breath."

A silly thing to say. She ignores him.

"You don't have to sit here all day!"

"Don't I?"

"Get the hell out of here! Go! Why don't you just go!"

She understands. She has to. He's bored, he's restless, he's ungrateful, and he's sick.

Relax, hah? Alone at night she relaxes. Alone, she can't afford her daytime looking back. Without a sweater to knit, the kids to rush downtown for a haircut, a malted to sneak into Ray, she can't endure the vision of the big house as she saw it for the first time; the just expectations of an earlier day.

It would drive her crazy to lie there in bed, feeling the weight of dissatisfaction and the endless craving, the need.

For what?

What does she need?

She's angry with herself. She needs her husband well; that's what she needs. She has a home, Ray, two fine children. She didn't lose a brother in the war.

When has she ever had to scrub a floor or bend over an ironing board?

What would the starving people in Europe, in China think of her needs?

What if she had married Al Francis? He asked her. What if she had married one of the big ones with no brains?

Where did brains get Raymond? Where did they get her except in this cold bed?

Brains. Her mother-in-law didn't have the sense she was born with and look at how well she endures.

And Al Francis made a fortune in scrap metal just because he hadn't had the brains to say no.

"I'd sure like to be back playing tennis with you again, Ellie."

He was getting paunchy. He was getting bald. The virile ones go bald.

"You never change a bit," he said to her.

He was still flirting.

She was still saying no.

Some women are flattered by that nonsense. But any woman can have a man if she'll do what they want. She knew what Al Francis wanted. And he wasn't going to get it from her!

Al's poor wife said to her: "You know I'd give this all up" (and "this" was amounting to a pile) "if I had someone with whom I could talk."

Well, Raymond had the brains to talk. That was sure. Sometimes with Rose he'd control himself and make a lot of sense.

There were endearments she would have liked to hear from his mouth. Reassurances firm and manly and without rancor that would have warmed her heart. Compliments he could have paid. So many words he wouldn't say.

"Why don't *you* ever talk?" he'd retort.

Now what in God's name would she have to say?

She couldn't get enthusiastic over a recipe like Etta, or repeat endearments succulently like Charles, or talk about a book she'd read like Rose. She was quiet like Janet.

What did he expect from her? Whereas he . . .

Did Charles and Etta talk? "Oh, yes, dear" is what Charley said. Always a smile, a kind word. What went on in his head? When she heard rumblings she'd put her ear to the dividing wall. With no one listening, boy could they fight!

Did her parents ever talk? Ah, if her mother hadn't had her nose buried in the boys, if she hadn't turned around to Jack with a complaint, he would have given her everything. Each of them now talks to her. Minnie with her infernal whine against him. Her father with his "you-can-tell-her-vrom-me-she-knows-vhere-she-can-go."

Ellen tracking him down through relatives, phoning him, phoning her. Whispering, her hand covering the receiver's mouth and her own. Two sides of a conversation, modified and shaped through her lips, till they're back under the same roof.

Enough at night! She turns on her radio, low, her talk show next to her ear. She continues her way of sneaking sound even though Ray can't hear. "Turn that jerk off!"

"You should listen, you could learn from him."

"Sure, sure. *They* should listen. I could tell them all a thing or two."

The politicians.

The show people.

The authors with their books . . .

That's Ray.

Oh, it's going to be Victor Reisel tonight. This should be good. In the dark, huddled close to the sound, Ellen relaxes. All thoughts of her own drift out into the night. As Reisel introduces the man with whom he'll talk.

Raymond's coming home. Ellen looks around the bedroom. Her brothers have moved his favorite chair up and Lenny has gotten a deal on a secondhand TV for the bedroom. She looks at herself in the mirror. She has on a gray tweed skirt and a light blue cashmere sweater set that her daughters had bought for her thirty-fifth birthday. They had included a note with a funny poem from Rose; now she was ready for Nature's spelled backward, Serutan. Blue sets off her eyes and hair and minimizes her nose.

She affixes scatter pins, small doves with glinty red eyes, to the inside sweater. Do they look all right? She is about to go next door. She, Ellen Diamond Addis, has made up her mind for her husband's sake.

She goes downstairs and presses her ear to the wall. "Ma!" Janet would protest if she saw. "Sssh," Ellen would respond, moving her finger nervously against her lips. In anyone else, Ellen would consider listening deplorable. But she never saw herself as eavesdropping, privy as she was to her reasons, confident as she was of her own discretion. On the Day of Atonement, she'd stand and move her lips with the rest, though she had nothing to say.

In this instance, she is just checking to make sure that Kat has gone. She wouldn't have been able to abide the manicurist's high-voiced chatterings. Any more than she could abide, after what she's been through, dinner next door. For weeks she has taken her meals at the hospital — eating off Ray's hospital plate the food he couldn't stand. Tepid sweetbreads and a roll loomed in front of her as an exhilarating promise of freedom.

They give her the strength — on hearing silence — to pick up her keys and go next door.

Her in-laws are both sitting in the living room this Monday. Charley in his chair, with its back to the doors of the dining room; Etta on hers, near the window, her plump feet dangling. She is checking her newly polished nails the way she'd look over your shoulder. They seem as interesting to her as new drapes or the timing of a roast.

Charles has been running both stores and looks tired.

Ellen sits on the steps to the staircase landing. She can't stay. She only has a minute to tell them that when Ray comes home tomorrow they'll take their meals on their own side. None of the reasons comes out of her mouth at first. She simply tells them.

Charles and Etta look at each other across a long, long room.

The past month, every night, Charley had entertained Janet with her favorite trick. He'd set the stem of one spoon under the cup of another. With a deft punch on the first, he'd spring the second into a glass of water. Its silver clink mingled with ice and crystal. "You never miss, Pop!" Janet would shout with joy.

"He's the champ there," Etta would say, tending to Rose's seconds.

Charles felt he could hide wax whistles under his grandchildren's linen napkins once more or sneak in baby chicks, telling them the chirps they heard were the teapot's whistle. Surprise!

After dinner Charles would set the cards together deftly. Wait expectantly for Janet to pick up her hand and find, after a bit of shuffling, that she was already gin.

Rose would go next door to do her homework. "I'll keep you company," Etta would say.

"No thanks, Nana," Rose would answer patiently. Like Greta Garbo, I vant to be alone.

When Rose was very young, Etta would wait for Ellen and Ray to go out. Then she'd go next door and charm the sitter to silence. She'd go up the stairs and enter the nursery. She'd pick Rose out of the crib and hug her. Without a mask across her face, in utter defiance, she'd love that child to death.

Ray didn't want to "spoil" them. He, who had never heard a no. Spoil, phooey! This month Rose poured as much catsup over her meat as she wanted, talked over the phone without Raymond shouting *good-bye,* and sprawled on the couch as she read. What harm did it do her? How they picked on that child. You could make a record when report cards came out. "What's wrong with gym?" Ray would growl (her only B). Then he had something for all the A's. "Big deal! Why the hell don't you relax. Go out and play."

Janet went out and played like a little ragamuffin. And she managed a few B's.

"A or B or C," Ellen would say. "The important thing is to do the best you can."

"The important thing is to have fun while you can. It took me four and a half years to get out of Dickinson and I had a ball."

"Oh, Ray," Etta would say, "a fine example *you* are for the girls."

"Mothe*rrrr*."

Silence.

Shut up, glared from Ellen's eyes. These are *ours.* You have no business.

So Etta should have known it would end up like this. She wasn't superstitious like Charley, but she had a feel for when things could break.

"I don't use salt either!" Etta who has high pressure (not the type like Ray's that can kill you) snaps.

Ellen, caught in the older people's silence, has started to enumerate the small issues. She is up to restricted diet.

"Dear," Charley says, "the children have to do what they have to do."

"What the doctors say," Ellen adds. He has a heart, this man. Hearts break.

Part of Ellen wants to cry out, We'll stay, Pop! We'll eat with you every night, dusk after dusk after dusk. If only —

"The doctors say he should not be excited in any way," Ellen concludes.

"Some excitement, dinner!" Etta answers. She looks around. "What's there to get excited about here?"

You!! is what Ellen would have liked to scream in her face. You selfish old woman! Every time you forget your son never touches chicken liver, lima beans, mushrooms, rare meat — every time you butt in — I can see my husband slowly burn!

"He'll be lucky if he'll be able to come downstairs for dinner at first," Ellen says. "Let's think of him. One step at a time."

Etta turns with a tight smile to her husband. "Let's think about Ray a little, Charley."

"Mothe*rrrr*! How can you?" Ellen shakes. Tears well in her eyes. She sits there, the living example of the month she's been through.

"One step at a time," Charley picks up. "One step at a time."

"Yes," Ellen says, regaining control. "Let's just try this till Ray is well. It won't be that long," she continues, getting a feel for how this new wool unravels. Not too long, you selfish old woman. Just forever.

❦   ❦   ❦

"Maybe she's trying to kill him," Etta said to Charley at dinner. He was at the head, Etta to his left, where Ray used to sit at that long table. They were having calf liver — medium rare — since Ray wasn't there.

"What, dear?" She brought Charley out of the gray haze, where he wondered silently about the blood in his spit, where he wandered vaguely along Central Avenue after a healing correlative. He found himself looking up at the spangled light enmeshed in the Venetian chandelier, looking at the mirrors behind Etta's back, looking at the handblown glass panes in the door. Looking for a crystal, looking for a clear and less ominous light.

But he didn't find one. His eyes glazed with disappointment. The moments when he tried to peek past shadows made him appear absent-minded; when he looked up, he seemed to be slowing down.

His wife pointed a finger next door as a reminder. "I know what they're having. Eating bland, hah! Spaghetti and meatballs.

I'm telling you he was never sick a day in his life before her. And now she's over there feeding him slop!"

Sure enough, next door, the slop has already been swilled from four red-stained plates. "Don't gobble!" Raymond's admonition on seconds, his own bathrobe stained. A mass of overcooked number eights (not even Etta has yet heard of al dente), tough meatballs (that's right, tough), and spare ribs — really white and brown bones, their meat floating around in the tomato sauce, have been consumed.

It's one of Claudine's best. One of those the sisters will remember. Here's the list of favorites:

Chicken fricassee (just off the bone) with smaller tough meatballs — spicy.

Pot roast, overcooked Jewish, with potato pancakes. Claudine's a depressive. Often she sits in the kitchen and broods. When she comes out of a spell, she grates potatoes and lets them gray in ice water all day. She fries and offers them at night. The sisters will never make or find others as good. "The secret may have been in the graying," Janet much later would opine.

Fresh chopped kale with bacon rinds. Soul food before they knew it. And for Rose unduplicable, in Georgia, from Bird's Eye, or in Rome.

Spaghetti and meatballs.

What can you do? Even after all the years of Etta's fastidious supervision, these meals tasted good.

Here, when you eat, you eat. Don't talk about it. There was an absence of Charley's shivery slurps and mock drooling, Etta's analyses or raves. Food was food. Sometimes it was so-so; sometimes it hit the spot. Always it was overcooked. When you get down to the bottom line, you hungry? Eat and shut up.

Still, no one was trying to kill anyone. In fact, it is extra silent at dinner because that day "You'll kill yourself!" happens to be exactly what Ellen did say.

"Will I?" Ray answered bitterly from his bed. You had to live with a recuperating heart patient to appreciate fully how he plays. At that moment Ray was quite willing to see his life hang on the balance of one overcooked spaghetto. It pleased him enormously.

Meatballs weren't enough. "Throw in some sausage and spare ribs or I won't come down." *So there.*

So kill yourself! See if I care.

Raymond punctuates the postprandial silence with a loud, triumphant belch. He's feeling better. "Ah, that tasted good!"

The girls giggle, but he's playing for his wife. A shorter belch breaks through the barrier of the silent treatment.

"You're just like your mother," Ellen can't resist. "You both should own stock in Tums."

The girls howl.

"It's true. They both belch like the world's deaf. Come on, enough's enough. Claudine has got to get home. Let her clear."

Standing's not exactly easy. Ellen supports Ray. Slowly they walk to the landing. One step at a time they ascend the stairs.

Ah, Ellen, this forever will be altered. Not so easily will you chip away at your mistake. Next door a man is slowly dying. And widows have to eat. And live, Ellen, and live and live and live . . .

After six months of recuperation, Ray goes back to work. "How you doing, Ray?" ask customers who never sent a card.

"Never felt better in my life."

He no longer smokes; he does not drink.

He and Ellen sit at home.

There's a lot they do not do.

There are two schools of thought.

Crazy Dasher's: "Move your ass! Take a walk. Screw! For Chrissake, come hunting with me."

Hunting?

"Your father in a cap, up at dawn, can you imagine it?"

After a year of Dasher's prodding, Ray goes along.

It doesn't kill him.

Dasher's friends are regular guys: A saxophonist from the Copa, a big bookie from Bayonne, an orthodontist (when orthodontists were few), the horse-shit king. "I kid you not," Dasher explains. "They *pay* him to haul it from the track. He hauls it straight to south Jersey. How the hell do you think mushrooms grow? In actual fact he's the mushroom king."

"I wouldn't touch one!"

"Ah, you, you're too finicky. I'm a doctor. I'm telling you, shit's good for you."

Where does he get off, traipsing in a field before the sun has hit the air? He does not carry a gun. "Fellas, this one's here on doctor's orders. To move his ass, to get some color, for Chrissake to live."

To live?

Is that what it is to share a bunkhouse with a group of men? At home their heavy watches, loaded wallets, and loose change plunk down on pretty dressers before they strip to sleep. And they wear pajamas between their wives' percale sheets.

Here they tell raucous stories. They outdo Mickey Spillane. To hear them talk, they've lived.

And prospered.

And drunk their share of beer. Ray takes a can and listens. Let them talk.

When the lights go off, against all private reservations, he sleeps — exceedingly well.

He wakes up to the sound of someone almost not making any noise at all.

It's dark and cold. Through half-opened eyes he watches the bulk of Dasher, scurrying around. Dressed to his teeth. Light on his feet. Happy as a bird.

Last night he laid claim to stompfing nurses end to end. Incredible now to watch him prance as fresh and innocent as a baby or a bride. This guy's the new day dawning.

And what's bringing the boyish glee to his step, to his shadow? He has built a fire. He tiptoes out the door with a big pan. A woodsman's breakfast for all. There's not a thought in the doctor's head. He's just gonna warm some stomachs.

And when he wants a table at the Copa he'll get one. On a bad losing streak he won't have to look behind him on the street. Should he have a dozen children, all their teeth will be wired. At the track he'll sit at the finish line by the king.

Warmed stomachs don't growl.

Ray sits up in the gloom and wraps his blanket around him, slips on his shoes, and goes out. The air is warmer than inside, like years ago at summer camp. He pees against a tree.

"Ah, you're up already. You're no guy for a surprise. Come sit by the fire."

Raymond squats on a log. "A little caffeine's good for yah," Dasher says. But he's already fixing Ray his Sanka. "Like old times," he says.

Ray doesn't get it. It's his first time here. But then he realizes Dasher's way back when. They used to have fun. "Old times?" Ray contradicts. "Then we were young."

"We still are."

"*You* are."

"You are too. Don't think, don't worry, don't aggravate your rashes. Be like a surgeon. Chrissake, you know what it's like to cut meat. Calm, collected. Finger out of the way of the knife, mind on the scale. You didn't drop dead, don't you forget it. Don't let those fancy heart guys make you act like you had."

"Nah. I'll go out and do a jig."

"Why not, if you could dance?"

Ray shakes his head slowly. "It's not so easy," he says into the gray.

"I know, pal."

"Just think of it, Dash. Helen rotting away out there. Me rotting away in here." He puts his hand on his chest and then leaves it there to scratch. "I wonder why."

"You've got the wrong attitude, Ray. Old pal, if you don't watch out, your attitude will kill you."

"I know. I shouldn't talk. What's over is over. Past. Kaput."

"Exactly the opposite. You should talk. About how you feel. About Helen. Jeez, remember? She was quite a lady, your sister. To me, I mean I was younger then, she was perfect. Sometimes I still see her by that piano. Remember the New Year's old Maxie's sweetie pie went nutty?"

"Remember? What a scene! Leave it to Mom's helper, hah?"

The two men laugh.

"What a night that was, Ray. The times we had. Boy, oh, boy. The two of us together."

"Mom still doesn't forgive you for pawning your five-dollar argyles at poker games."

"Etta's never gonna forgive me that. 'You, a doctor?' That's what she says when we meet on the street."

"She's no dope."

"I admire her. I think — no kidding — I think way back then I had a crush on Helen. But I was too young. She never looked at me."

"She never looked at anyone — except that Greek jerk and her ivory keys."

"Did she look at you?"

"Me?"

"Did you two ever talk? Share things? Could you figure out earlier that something was going wrong?"

"To tell you the truth, Dasher, all I knew of Helen is what you saw, her sitting by the piano."

"That New Year's Eve, I was real disappointed she wasn't there."

"No bull? Really? You *liked* that eternal playing? Jeez, was I relieved!"

Dasher nodded and started to mix a mess of pancake batter.

"You know," Ray continued, watching him, "I'm starved."

"Sure you're starved. The air's good for you. The talk's good for you. I want you to become a regular. We do this once a month. I want you *here*."

"What's in it for you, Dash? I don't discount my meat."

"You're a hard guy. You're not easy to love."

"What's that? A proposition? Is that why you're not married? You queer?"

"Look at you. One word about emotion and you run scared."

Ray smiled sheepishly. "Maybe so." He paused, then he said, "I wonder what it's all about."

"What's it about?" Dasher smiled. "It's about staying alive and it's about nothing at all."

"Then don't worry about me," Ray said. "I'm going to live to the year two thousand. I'm not gonna die. Even though it stacks up to horse shit."

"If you got the right attitude, there's a good market for horse shit," Dasher said.

Ray watched him pour the batter into the pan. "You know," Dasher said as the heavy rounds began to sputter, "you should see this S.O.B. heart attack as an opportunity."

"An opportunity?" Ray questioned, relaxing into the good smell.

"Yeah, an opportunity to get to know yourself. You're an anxious guy, Ray. If you came to grips with that, you'd feel better. You want to do more than breathe to the year two thousand. You wanta live."

"Back to me doing a jig, hah?"

"Nah, nah. But it would be a good idea if you could hash things out with someone. If you could get to the roots of your anxiety."

For a moment Ray didn't believe his ears. Then his eyes squinted into the fire. He could feel a helpless tug of rage in his chest, as if he'd been cheated again.

Dasher made a pile of pancakes. "Here, help yourself to syrup, and test these before I wake the others."

Raymond looked at the offering on the plate Dasher put in his hands. The pancakes steamed into his face.

"Listen," Dasher said, "don't get mad. I've thought about this, Ray, baby. There's too much eating you. You're no heart-attack type. Psoriasis, asthma, heart. All psychosomatic illnesses. Forgive me if I talk like a doctor, but you're a fuckin' neurotic like the rest of us. For Chrissake, do something about it, *talk* to somebody about it, express yourself, before it's too late."

"Crazy Dasher," Ray said. Just looking at the pancakes made them stick in his throat. He thought of expressing himself. Then put the plate down.

The flames slapped Dasher's face red and shadowy in the gloom before dawn. Made him look like he was sweating.

"You worry about yourself," Ray said. "There's nothing wrong with me."

The second school of thought is what Ray follows. "Use common sense" is the way Ellen phrases it.

For example, Eisenhower's heart attack. At first Ellen is astounded by the daily bulletins. The interruption of a program when the President moves his bowels. She has no idea of the protocol of courts or the physicality of kings. It's common sense that emperors must wear clothes.

They put the President on anticoagulants. Here's something new. She goes to Ray's checkup with him. She confronts the venerable specialist, Dr. Young, face to face. Like any doctor worth his salt, the more he talks, the more he bucks. But he doesn't throw her. She keeps hold of the clean reins of her intent. What's good enough for Ike is good enough for Ray.

"Tell me, doctor," she says, cutting through all she's not listening to. "I just want to know one thing. If it was your brother, would you put him on anticoagulants?"

The doctor's mouth shuts down.

"I'm not holding you responsible, doctor. I just want to know, if it was your brother, yes or no."

"Well . . . if it were my brother . . . yes."

The pill joins its fellows.

The magic pill. Ellen's. Ike's.

"You should throw those phenos and the rest of them away."

There's supervision, extra blood tests involved. No matter. This is the pill one dreams about. The scientific discovery made just in time for you.

The thinned blood courses through Raymond's veins. He's proud. Ellen, despite the doctors, has saved his life.

A merger of the spirit. A thrust against the odds. A soar of strength. Like a winning day at the track.

"Win or lose, it's not important," says Ellen. "We go to enjoy a day, to relax."

They live a quiet life. "I wrapped up my silver and put it away."

They stay away from dizzy friends on a dizzying spiral. No more matchcovers with smiling faces.

They strip down to essentials. They have a sixth sense that what the gods don't hear about, they don't take away.

But every Monday they break even. They take their pleasure quietly, leaving by the back door. If Etta catches them: "Where you guys off to?" Raymond answers, "Out."

Etta on a spring day before the screens go up, standing by a column of the porch looking down at the scarlet buds of her azaleas.

The kids' car swings out of the driveway. Etta looks up.

Ellen stares ahead of her. Through closed teeth, frozen lips, she manages, "I knew it! Keep your eyes on the road!"

The big car drives down the block.

Etta watches, her face set, her corseted back to the granite.

Sssh. The walls have ears. Not just at Clifton Avenue. All over America. McCarthy's showing just what happens if you speak above a whisper. And how many names scream out in the headlines, JEW!

It's best the neighbors don't know where they go.

To do what? To place their two dollars. To have a meal in peace. To relax.

Raymond has done his ordering for the week. Ellen has left lamb chops for Claudine to char for the girls. If Aqueduct proves therapeutic, they'll dine at Roosevelt.

It's their relaxation. On a beautiful day like this, away from every care, it's a shame to be cooped up in the clubhouse. They take reserved seats near the finish line in the clear air.

Ellen looks down to the grandstand. The whole world is milling around. It's an endless Prospect Avenue out of doors, in the sun. Why aren't they at work? On the Mondays of her life she'll always be amazed to find these others here.

Now the crowd roars. Ray and Ellen come to their feet. She can hear the horses' hooves thud in her heart as they hit the dirt. The crowd roars louder; on each side of them they hear, "Come on, Gold Rush!" "Five, Five, Five!" "That's a baby!" Raymond sings out noncommittally, "Come on! Come on! Come on!" He must have a hot one. In tandem, two horses, their backs as sloped as those of the jockeys on their backs, go over the finish line. An orgiastic moan wells up among the cheering. The board lights up PHOTO. "Four is how I see it," Raymond says confidentially.

"I just don't know how you can call one that close," Ellen says admiringly.

"Four."

"You have it?"

"Sssh."

She has it. It's the first race of the double. She had placed her traditional two-dollar bet on her wedding day, one-six, and then two looked good in the second, so she bet one-two. Four was such a long shot in the first, she put two dollars on four.

"They're putting it up," Ray says. A howl from the crowd. It's official. Four! A spray of yellow hits the air. She can never understand why they tear them up so fast. For a few minutes after there *must* still be a chance!

"Wwwhoooo!" Ray whistles. "Look at that price."

"You got it?" she asks.

"I got it riding on the double — four-six."

"I got it straight."

"No kidding! Good girl!" His face lights up in the sun. "Look at that price! It'll bring us even." He takes out his tickets. "Look at this." He holds up number three, which came in second. He had it to win.

"Oh," she sympathizes.

"I was standing by the window, thinking four. Then I said, nah, it's too much of a crazy long shot and I have it in the double already. So I go up and say three, thinking I'm smart. When all along something's telling me four."

"Well, anyway, we have it."

He shrugs. Flicks a few tickets away. "But I coulda —"

"Coulda, woulda, shoulda, Ray."

He takes his sheet and figures, figures. He looks young, with a pencil behind his ear.

She reads what the handicappers are touting. Finally, she says, "I'm going to collect. You see anything?"

There's a long pause while he continues to study. "Ah," he says finally, "go on."

"You sure?" She doesn't like him doing too much walking, taking too many steps.

"Positive."

On the way to the win window she discards her losing tickets, adding them to the sea of yellow at her feet. She takes her time. Goes to the ladies' room. There's no line at the win window. "So, you had it, blondie," the cashier says. She looks into the admiring face of a gambler and smiles. "Win some, lose some. It's a lot of fun for two dollars." She collects $89.20.

She walks slowly through the unconscionable crowd. Only Monday. Think what it looks like here the rest of the week! The odds are on the board for the second race. The horse she likes at five-to-one still looks good. The odds aren't *great,* but she'd kill herself if she didn't back the second digit of her wedding day and it won. While she's at it, she backs the second digit of her girls' birthdays. These doubles, she thinks. They're made for suckers. For the rest of the day she'll bet one hunch name a race, and that will be that.

She joins Ray, who's sitting in his seat eating a hot dog. The mustard gleams in the sauerkraut. "I bumped into the shit king," he said. "He tried to tout me."

"Can I have a bite?"

"Sure. Here." He gives it to her and sips his root beer. "He spoke to the trainer and the horse is ready. Glory Bird in the third."

"Maybe he knows something?"

"He knows nothing."

"Not a bad name. You sure this isn't too salty for you?"

Ah, once a week, Ellen, let him live.

And they'rrrrrre OFF!

They pick out six in the far field. It has the lead. It's way out! But the race is not often won by the starting lead.

Will he hold it? There's eight sneaking up. And three.

Come on six!! Come on six!! Come on six!!

They're neck to neck and then —

"Is that — ?"

Raymond doesn't let her say the number. "Yeah, yeah."

It's over suddenly amid a great noise.

"Wait'll they post those prices," Ray says, sitting down.

"Are you sure?"

"Chrissake, El, it wasn't even close. Six."

"Then you — you have the double!"

"Look at the board!"

It's official!

The double, four-six. And just look what it pays.

She has the first race. He has the double. She has two dollars on six. He has a five-dollar combo.

Some days you feel it in your blood. Everything clicks. You're hot. When the results are posted, God, you feel smart.

"I'll walk with you," he says.

They've got a lot of collecting at different windows.

Together they make their way through the milling throng.

Ray can't help thinking of the look on the shit king's face. He's the type who always asks, "Did yah have it? Did yah?" Ray will nod.

Ellen's thinking, What the hell. She'll drop a few on Glory Bird. If it wins, they'll have it.

Tonight they'll come home late.

The kids will ask, "How'd you do?"

"We broke even," Ray will say.

Ellen: "We had a very relaxing day."

And so with common sense and anticoagulants, phenobarbs and pressure pills, with eating on their own side and Mondays at the track, Ray heals.

He no longer has asthma. Why? (1) He doesn't smoke. "I quit. It was easy. All I needed was to be scared to death." (2) A bigger fear (heart) replaced a smaller (breath). Dr. Dasher. (3) "I might never really have had asthma. The shortness of breath, the pain. It could have been heart all along." Raymond toward the end.

He sees a lot of Ellen's family. After all, Moe has begun to work with him. He's gone from one job to another since the war.

Lenny rents one of the apartments on top of the store. Jack and
Minnie often drop by on Sundays. So does Barney. So do Moe and
Lenny.

Pandemonium on Sundays. Barney has the youngest boys, Ron
and Tim. They bang the piano, they crash into walls. "All right!
All right, fellows!" Barney jumps up. "Just once more, *once more,*
and we GO." They stay.

Lenny and his wife fight. Their two daughters hate each other's
guts. They whine about each other to their mother.

Moe and Marcy stop by with their four kids as if it were normal. That damn church! It runs your life. Their usually well-be-
haved brood comes into contact with Barney's blond monsters
and go mad.

Calm them down. "Time for a treat!" Ray calls into the fracas.
That works. What's commonplace to Rose and Janet since they
were as young as their youngest cousins is magic to them.

The pantry shelves. A third of them, from where you bend
down to where it's too high to reach, are stacked with Raymond's
candy. More Cracker Jack than you've ever seen, grocer's boxes of
chocolate twists, Milky Ways, Mars bars.

"Say please to your uncle," aunts croon.

"Uncle Ray, can we —"

"Sure, sure."

He reaches up to bring their orders down. He helps himself.

At six, whoever is there eats Chinks in the kitchen, scooping
chow mein and foo yong from the boxes to their plates. Minnie
jumps up before the meal is through to do the dishes. Ellen won't
have it!

"I'll do them, Ma."

"No, no. Let me."

Usually it ends up, Ellen washes, Minnie dries.

"They'll drain, Ma! The girl will put them away tomorrow."

"I want to help."

Sometimes they tug at each end of a dish towel as if it were
each other's neck.

Mr. and Mrs. Addis *know* they're welcome. But at most they
come in and say hello.

"Oh," Etta will say, as her sturdy walls begin to clatter, "they got the Bolsheviks over there again."

And Charley, goodhearted as he is, silently agrees. That brood screams past the grace of childhood.

Rose HATES these Sundays. She doesn't see herself as related to her mother's side. "Don't be so smart," Raymond reprimands. "Get down off your high horse and have some fun."

Fun? A house full of younger cousins. Sunday going on and on and on.

Ellen herself only bears Sunday thinking of what Monday brings. By nature she's no one for a racket.

But for Ray, little Ron and Tim, and their cousins Jamie and Shaun can't make enough noise.

Barney can't jump up and scream, "*Okay now fellows.* This is it. *Final!* The last time. Let's GO!" loud enough.

Unemployed Lenny can't crow, "Shut up already, it's Sunday, get off my back. Give a man a day of rest," mockingly enough to his working wife.

Ray smiles, he helps himself to a little beer. He gives up the prize in his Cracker Jack to whatever kid can catch it.

"You're encouraging them," Ellen reprimands.

"So what? They're young, for Chr——" (Marcy's there) "creeps sake. Let them have fun."

"Daddy," Rose whispers, just before he goes out to buy Chinks, "it's not that I wouldn't love to stay." (She's been forced in the whole afternoon. "Stay home for once. Forget your stuck-up friends. Find something to say to your cousins.") "But your parents have invited me to go out to dinner. I feel it a duty to go."

"Don't be such a wiseacre!" But a featherweight of responsibility lifts. She'll keep them company. Of course she can go . . .

Sitting in the back of their car, coming home in the dark over the Pulaski Skyway, Rose joins her grandparents' deepening quiet. She'll hear it more and more.

She'll butt into it the night before Charley climbs his stairs for the last time. Startled awake in the living room, he will stare at her mutely. She'll sit down for a minute before she asks to use their phone.

"Cee, Dee, Eee, Eff, Gee, Aay, Bee," Etta will suddenly hum from her chair. Her legs dangle just above the rug. Her hands stretch across keys no one sees. "The C scale," she'll explain proudly, as if she were counting to ten in Deutsch. "Remember, Charley? Gee whiz, remember?" She'll close her eyes and hum and play, "Cee, Dee, Eee, Eff, Gee, Aay, Bee, Cee."

In the car Etta makes a restless little shift of position to ease gas. She ate too much. Everything was so good. She remembers how the waiter cut the rosy rare London broil at their table. And put it juicy over the thin wedges of garlic bread, right in front of their eyes. Now she suffers for it. Her flesh bloats, her stomach churns against her garment. She belches. Her mind fogs with food. She is on the verge of a curt nap that will only punctuate her discomfort.

In the back seat Rose slits her eyes so that the lights of the flatlands below her sparkle. The rancid smell of industry and rendering plants is blunted by the cool, damp night air. Still and heavy, it waits for morning as the moving car creates its own breeze.

She's above the tall weeds, swampy waters, and round tanks. She's speeding.

Before the Skyway tumbles down into Jersey, the whole gaudy face of Manhattan will sparkle straight in front of her half-closed eyes.

At the wheel, Charley can no longer see well in the dark. Looking past his windshield he must avoid the tricks of looming things. It takes all his concentration.

Born in Hoboken, raised in Jersey City, nowhere else in the world he ever wanted to go.

Now, night-blind, he can feel Jersey City approach him. The soil rises through concrete for him to smell.

Witch's son. His Buick is magical. "I'm going to win it," he told his wife, his grandchildren, his daughter-in-law, his son. On the day of the drawing he sat by the phone. It rang. He won.

He'll make it home.

❧ ❧ ❧

"The children don't understand." Adele at seventy. She's talking about death. Her older sister is gone and now the baby brother.

Two hours ago, when she had stood at Charley's open coffin, she could have sworn she saw the chest move. There were impenetrable swayings, like muffled sobs, along her brother's stiffly tailored suit.

Adele sits in Etta's living room, her big eyes wet. Her face has wrinkled deeply at all the points a smile touches. The wrinkles afford her an etched-in kindness. Her dark skin — once so much like her brother's — has turned leathery. She has a plump mole on her chin with hairs on it as white as those coming out of her head.

Every year she remembers her grandnieces' birthdays. Looking at her aunt's creased and shiny fingers, Rose can picture the worn and crumpled five-dollar bill in her hand. She can imagine her slipping it into a birthday card, then tonguing the envelope.

The sisters rarely see their great-aunt.

"How come we never visited *your* grandmother?" Janet will ask Ellen when she is under analysis.

"Buba?" Ellen will recall. "What makes you bring her up?"

"Why not? She was my great-grandmother. We lived in the same town. You loved your father. How come we never visited her?"

"A lot of good that would have done. All those years she never learned one word of English. Now *you* tell me. What the hell would there have been to say?"

The absence of Charley's sisters was different. Rose and Janet shared an image of them passively chained in their addressless flats on Central Avenue.

"That *Cherman*," Etta would spit. (She always meant Adele's Cherman. She preferred the pretty sister.) "He keeps her locked up swell."

Every late spring, called, who knows, by the memory of those early dance years, Adele would manage to slip away for a few reckless hours of freedom. She'd be rocking with Etta on the porch when the sisters returned from school. "Rose! Janet!" she'd call. She had the wet-lipped voice of her brother. "How you've grown! What a treat!"

Every Thanksgiving she sent a fruitcake home with Charley. A fruitcake that had been kept in a dark place since the year before. One whole year! When the tin was opened, the cake looked and smelled like hoarded jewels. So rich, it was hard to eat.

Now on leave for a funeral she says, "The children don't understand."

Rose didn't understand. She was lost, observing the people who walked in the opened door. Each hesitant at first. Unsure. It's an adult act to walk into a room.

But the morning following Charley's death, Lilly had rushed in. She had cut through the quiet gloom with a shriek. She and Etta staggered across the room to each other, met in each other's arms.

"She's stirring Mother up," Ellen complained as the two women embraced.

It was as if they didn't see each other every week. It was as if Lilly came in after years of silence, bearing special knowledge that Etta recognized at a glance. They howled. They moaned, in the middle of the room.

They were Mary and Elizabeth, not pregnant in the flesh, but filled with significance when they met.

"So tell me, how did it happen?" Lilly asked finally, sitting down, taking a tissue, wiping her eyes.

Rose didn't understand why the sudden death was such a surprise. Grandfathers are old men. Grandfathers die.

> *The woods decay, the woods decay and fall,*
> *The vapors weep their burthen to the ground,*
> *Man comes and tills the fields and lies beneath,*
> *And after many a summer dies the swan.*

Rose sees gray heads being lopped off. Trees falling. Saplings growing. She wells with just nostalgia, carried along by the grand sway of Tennyson's verse. She sees the poignancy of men coming, men going, while in passion and expectation she is always almost sixteen.

"They just don't understand," Adele, the oldest, repeating like Charley, repeats. What does Adele understand? Miss her turn or not, sooner or later, she's next.

Rose had been at the center of action. She was doing her home-work on the dining room table. Her parents were out playing cards. Janet was already in bed. The phone rang.

"Helen!?"

"It's *Rose*, Nana," she said with mock patience for the ten bil-lionth time. "Mommy's out."

"Come quick! Hurry!"

She ran next door and then up the stairs. She stood at the bed-room door, ashamed to look at her grandfather. He was propped up in bed, his head back. That dark-skinned man was ash-white, like a statue. Next to him was a basin of blood.

She ran downstairs, still in her bobby sox, no time for shoes. She went out in the dark. Halloween. Boo! She rang and rang till she stirred the slight, deaf doctor who lived next door. He had to be ten years older than her grandfather. He had lived all these years quietly and childlessly with his slight and deaf cousin-wife.

How many times had she been at the entrance of the Loys' liv-ing room. Once? Twice? Always the pleasant smiles. Even when they had to ask (often in the earlier years) for the girls not to bounce the ball off their outer walls. It was unprecedented to meet like this. "My grandfather! Come quick!"

The old man, spry as a cricket, picked up his bag, came across the way, and in a hop examined the patient. Then he got on the phone. "An ambulance!" he screamed in the high-pitched voice, like the two back legs rubbing. "You heard me! And you'd better be damn quick!"

"Dr. Loy said damn?" Raymond later said. "Then it had to be bad."

Rose went next door before the ambulance came and called the game.

"No, not my father!" she yelled at the hostess. "Get my mother to the phone."

"Yes?"

"Ma. Pop Addis is very sick. You'd better break it to Daddy as easy as you can and come home."

"What do you mean?"

"The ambulance is coming!! I can't explain now. Just come home."

The sheets of the bed were bloody. Rose stripped them off to be thrown away. She took the basin to the bathroom while Etta was downstairs, and emptied her grandfather's blood down the drain.

She went downstairs and said, "They'll be here soon, Nana. Don't worry."

Etta sighed. "Maybe I should have gone." Dr. Loy had told her to wait for the family. She really didn't need much convincing not to ride in an ambulance . . .

The three of them, Ray, Ellen, Etta, came back from the hospital. Rose was sitting on her grandmother's side with Janet. "What's she doing up?" Ray snapped.

"She should be here too," Rose said.

Janet, huddled in her oversized robe, wanted to ask "How's Pop?" But a lot of good it would have done her, so she said nothing. She sat on the couch and waited.

"Now don't get excited," Ellen called.

Etta had taken off her coat. Uncharacteristically, she swung it over the banister and sat down.

Janet stood up. "Where you going?" Ray demanded. She shrugged and went past them toward the kitchen.

"Let her go, Ray," she heard Etta call.

"She should be in bed. Tomorrow would have been time enough, Rose."

"She should know too," Rose argued.

"Quiet!" Raymond called. "Enough!" . . .

Why hadn't Janet come over tonight? Been with him when he unlatched the door. The door in Pop's kitchen that they didn't have on their side. It went down into the cellar. He'd snap on the weak overhead light and, flashlight in hand, lead the way.

"Watch these stairs, honey. They're steep, Janet. They're steep." He'd lead her down, a puddle of light left for her on each step. She'd sit on the rickety chair near his big work table while he set cheese from his store into the immense traps — "Careful, very, very careful," he'd rasp in his juicy voice — or mixed white powders, or swept up. It was an ugly, scary cellar. Etta must never have been down there for it to look that way.

He'd let her light the match for his Camel. He'd work with it between his lips. His ash would bend and then fall to the floor, even when he was giving the place a sweep.

She reached up and unlatched the door. She snapped on the light. She took hold of the wobbly wood banister. "Careful, honey, they're steep, they're steep . . ." She took three steps and then sat, looking down at the work table, somber in the weak light. Had he been here tonight? "Pop?" she whispered. Where was he, she wondered.

Her skin crawled with the thought of roaches. He could crush enormous water bugs while she stayed by his side. "Easy does it. Careful, careful, careful . . . WHAM!"

"Oh, don't cry," she heard him cheer her. "Don't cry, don't cry, don't cry. Or we'll all get so wet we'll never dry."

We'll drown, she thought, smiling through her tears at him. She tasted salt.

Then fear crept over grief. She couldn't stay down here alone. She dried her eyes first so that no one could see: "What are you crying for?"

She stumbled on a stair, tripped by her robe. "Whoops! whoops! honey, too fast." She turned out the cellar light and bolted the door. She stood in the kitchen, and, making the space for where he would be, she looked up.

Then she returned to the living room. "We're all sensible people," she heard her grandmother say. "We must make arrangements."

Rose looked up. "Come sit with us, Janet."

Janet shook her head.

"Where you going?" Raymond asked.

"To bed."

"Janet," Rose said, "Pop —"

"I know."

Janet understood.

*

Ray and Rose were alone in Charley's store. She sat at the desk in the office, piling photos that till now had been under its glass top. She looked long at her aunt.

There were also fronts of greeting cards — Charley had a preference for the colors of Easter — and a few prayers to saints. In the top drawer she discovered light ruby rosary beads — and a rabbit's foot she knew Janet would treasure.

The pile of the accumulated years, with its brown-edged photos, the one of his mother hand-painted so her beauty was rigid and glared, its daffodil-yellow bunnies against purple dyes, its paper chains of paper dolls, and its out-of-place prayers, jarred Rose. This was the work of someone who'd press gardenias between pages, who'd live in rooms that had white crocheted doilies over the chairs. Feminine, goyisheh, and alien, it was as mysterious a part of her grandfather's nature as the gun he kept. Or the whisper at the funeral that in business he was tough. Or the postcard from the woman librarian on Central Avenue that said simply, "A man is dead."

Ten years later in Alsace-Lorraine, she'd find the one née Addis left over by Hitler and time. A shrunken old lady, white hair, dark skin, demented in a country clinic outside Gerstheim. A marble plaque to her family on the front of her door. All over the walls inside her sanctuary were tacked photos, greeting cards, prayers, and paper dolls.

Ray finished the tape he was computing and slid down from the high cashier's chair. He was dressed up in a suit in the store closed for mourning. He looked proprietorial and sure.

"These last years he's been running this store as a hobby," he said. "I'll keep George, but the new guy, Pat, he's gotta go. What do you have there?"

"A rabbit's foot for Janet. The pictures and stuff for Nana. What should I do with this?" She unfolded the rosary beads. "You want them?"

Ray toyed with his father's diamond ring, loose on his finger. "Leave them. I'll give them to Pat."

"Go with my blessings, son," she mimicked.

Ray shrugged. "I wish I didn't have to. But I can't afford him. For Pop — well, this was his pleasure. Right here you can see it. This tells the story." He pointed to the long white paper tape. "He was playing it like a game."

"Are you going to run this one?"

"Yeah."

"Well then, can't you switch Pat down to the other store to help Moe?"

"If he wants to work on weekends — only for a while . . . Rose." He pointed out past the glass. "Eight butchers, ten sometimes. What a business."

"I have a picture of them here."

"Yeah? Let me see."

Then they walked out of the office. He stopped and put his hand toward the inside pocket of his jacket. "Have I taken my pills?" he asked. A day didn't pass when he didn't wonder, but he always had.

Rose looked at the enormous old-fashioned scale next to the office, with its weight like a round clock at the top.

"It's an antique, all right," Ray said.

They could both remember swinging on it and being weighed.

"It goes like that," Ray said, snapping his fingers. "You turn around and it's all gone. 'I'll go to Hoboken.' " Ray smiled at his father's standard answer every time his mother wanted to take a trip. " 'It's nice there in the spring.' Well, he died with his boots on. Too soon. But you can't knock the way he went. Look around you, Rose. Here you have it. He played it like a hobby at the end." (Suddenly, Ray, like Charley, was repeating.) "But here you have it. A man's life."

He said it with pride. He was not asking what does it all add up to, what does it mean? He remembered the days his heart had pounded as he lifted the sharp knife to the big bologna.

Like his heart pounded today.

Rose became the cashier for him in Pop's old store on the busy Saturdays around the holidays. Ray looked better than he had since his attack. He greeted fat Italian ladies he had known since childhood, and worn-down thin old men. His banter with them was easy and funny. When he laughed he didn't snicker; he laughed.

That spring, awkwardly, he went into the overgrown backyard, and tended, as best he could, Pop's roses.

"Mother, you just can't eat alone here every night."

"Why?" Etta asks, looking carefully at her daughter-in-law. She is trying to locate Ellen's special knowledge, her stubborn list of cans and can'ts. Is it somewhere behind her blond tight face?

"*Why?*" Ellen repeats in astonishment. She looks past the open doors of Etta's dining room. Sees the long table where night after night for more than a year her mother-in-law has been served. Just visualizing it gives her the creeps. But as usual her words stay away from her sentiments. "Don't you think we should cut down?"

"Send Claudine home before dinner and come eat with me."

"We've been through that!"

"But mine can *cook*!"

Ellen keeps quiet. Gives Ray a look. Hadn't she told him? It's her stomach she's concerned about. Herself. This is some mother, who would choose to sit by herself for a dish.

Now what would a Real Mother do?

A real mother would hear her footsteps echoing in each large and empty room. This place would be too much to keep up. She'd move into a small apartment. She'd stand in an efficiency kitchen and fix a little something for herself that she'd eat plain.

She'd think, I've got a sick son. Let him run this house. Let him make some rent from my side. What do I need with this headache?

And Ellen would drop by often to visit. For with a real mother you can talk.

"Cook?" Ray rejoins. "What are you talking about, cook? You put a pan over a fire and you cook." He laughs.

Son-of-a-bitch! thinks Ellen. Now that's the way to rile her up. Won't he ever learn!

"You, what's the use?" Etta snaps. "Everything's a joke."

"Raymond wants you to eat with us, Mother. We've talked about it. He just doesn't know what to say."

Etta, from her deep seat, looks at her son in Charley's chair. "Does he?" she asks. Her eyes glint. "What's a matter, Ray, cat got your tongue?"

"Yeah," says Ray in a voice that has turned to disgust. "Do what you want. Just do what you want!"

"What I want, hah? That's what's important to you?"

What she had wanted was Adele's son Paul to handle the estate. He had offered his services for free. "Sure, sure, he'll do it for nothing and take a good look at what you have." So, what was she, ashamed? No, she had to let Sig Lewis do it, Ray's friend. "He's done me lots of favors, let's give him a little business in return." Three thousand dollars! The bill just came. That's what Sig Lewis's services cost. Even though Paul had said, "Aunt Etta, let me handle the estate for you through the bank." Almost for free.

"She'll bring it up," Ellen had warned him. "Learn better than to give her advice. Everyone's advice is more important than her son's!"

"Sure I want you to do what you want," Ray allows, more mellowly. "What's wrong with you?"

"I got all the headaches."

"How many times have I told you, let me help more with the house."

"Sure," Etta says disparagingly. "I'm a landlord. I'll raise your rent."

A real mother wouldn't take a cent.

"This house is too big!" Etta says.

Finally, Ellen thinks.

Then Ray has to ruin it: "Maybe we should all move out."

But Etta doesn't hear the spite. She has her idea. "We could find a big enough apartment and sell this."

We, Ellen thinks. All of us? Oh, crap! "Mothe*rrrr,*" she says, "this is our home." And her whole life would have been different if she had never moved in.

"I'm not kicking you out on the streets," Etta continues, actually able to entertain the concept! "I'm just thinking of what we should do. I could use some good advice!"

"Go have lunch with Paul!"

"And what's wrong with Paul, wise guy? That he wanted to do me a favor cheap?"

"*Cheap!* That's his middle name. Paul Cheap Cherman! When'd he ever do anything for you?"

"Ray, don't get excited."

"He'd sit around this house at every party. 'Aunt Etta,' he'd say so nice. What did he ever bring? Maybe a bottle of liquor the bank repossessed? That guy still has his first penny."

"Oh, *you,* it's too much for you to remember that once he brought me a case."

"A case of liquor for all those years he sat there" (Ray points to the needlepoint couch) "and drank!"

"Mothe*rrrr*! His face is red!"

"Well, Ellen, for crying out loud, what am I to do!?"

Don't aggravate him!! she felt like SCREAMING!!!

But she holds her tongue.

Ray looks at his mother. She always fell for a smile. Treat her like a lady and she'll give you the shirt off her back. Invite her to the Square for lunch, she'll run to pay.

"So," Ray asks, "are you gonna eat with us or not?"

Etta looks at him. "Is that all you got on your mind?"

Ray shakes his head and smiles a bitter smile. Looks at Ellen, points to his mother. "It's like talking to a wall."

A circling embankment.

They had run around. It had even been suggested that they move into one side together. This one never even got to which side. It landed where it should, without a touch of sweet reasonableness to guide it — nowhere at all.

But dinner? The more Ellen dreaded having her there five nights a week — ah, if only it were Pop! — the more guilt she felt, the more she felt she must.

"It's terrible to think of you eating all alone here, Mother," she says quietly. "Wouldn't you rather eat with us?"

"No" pops into Etta's head just like that, but she doesn't say it. She doesn't even know if she means it. It's no fun being a woman alone. It gets you into other obligations. She looks at her daughter-in-law's tense face. She looks at her son's clamped lips. His cheeks sucked in.

Claudine puts too much sugar in her salad and sets it out too soon. By the time you get to table, the iceberg is soggy and the ice in the water has turned to sweat on the glass. Ellen and Ray pick on the children. Janet has the remorseful look of her father; Rose often looks far away and sad. *They* never hear a word she or the children have to say.

"I don't like to impose."

"What impose?" Raymond drawls, his left cheek almost reaching his eye.

A swell invitation. "Give me time. Let me think."

A real mother would have . . .

"Ah," Ray says with a shrug of his shoulder, "what's there to think about?"

"I'm used to it here."

"So you'll get used to it there." As he stands up, and he stands up slowly like an older man, he turns to look into the empty dining room.

In the cold hallway, without even lowering his voice, "Why *not* eat next door?" he asks his wife. "Here or there, what does it matter?"

He got the silent treatment for a week.

Etta finally acquiesced. An (approximately) seventy-year-old widow, no matter how straight she keeps her checkbook and how well she manages her affairs, must ultimately listen to the children.

"Yes, the children," she'll say to Lilly, "insist I eat with them."

"How come they don't move in?"

At first when she hears Ray's car in the driveway, and later, anticipating him, she'll pick up her keys and go next door.

"Whatcha doing?" she'll ask Rose, sprawled on the couch, reading. "What you watching?" she'll ask Janet at the set.

"Where's your mother?"

Lately, if Ellen's home from a game, she's upstairs.

Etta goes back and asks Claudine, "What have we got to eat?" She takes the lid off the pot.

She comes back to the living room, keys dangling, and sighs, the cushions depressing, into a seat.

The days grow longer. She grows hungrier. She can't wait till Ray gets home and they all sit down to Claudine's slop.

"A girl doesn't need college," Ray says at table one night. Especially one that gets all A's and never stops reading.

"Get your nose out of that book and sit up!"

"Sit up!" Rose will probably hear in her coffin, and pay as much attention.

It is clear to her that her father doesn't mean what he says. How she came to this half-truth is hard to fathom. She didn't doubt his love or her intelligence, though neither helped her make her way in the world. In fact, her conception of both stymied her.

She was his blood, his love, but the love of a sick man who had no luck. You understand, his eyes said, whenever a shmegegge wants to sweet-talk you, just take one long look at me. I'm smarter than all those bastards. Look at them with their rosy baby cheeks and fat stomachs. Just take one long look at me.

She was smarter than they were too. And obviously, like her father, the very force of her intellect would stymie her. It ran deep in the blood. It was fated. She had no luck.

Under her sense of humor with her friends and her courteous submissiveness to her teachers she harbored bitterness.

One of her teachers, Miss Rush, who knew her better than the rest, suggested she apply to the Seven Sister colleges. A dose of the Ivy League might change her.

Radcliffe? Cousin Paul's son, young Paul, went to Harvard. Hahvahd Yahd. All those shmegegges walking around in beanies and blazers.

Her a Radcliffe girl?

You could have it.

She had her father's sawdust in her soul.

She came by it the hard way. She had spent an excruciating time in grammar school.

"Do you know what you are?" Bill Novack asked her. He had just found out. They were both six in Mrs. Shea's class. He was her boyfriend. He had a square build and a square face with a cleft in his strong square chin.

"What do you mean?"

"Do you know what you are?"

She squinted.

"Come on. Are you Polish, Irish, or Jewish?"

"No."

"Come on! Everyone has to be something. And you're one of those. I know."

"I'm Irish." She liked the way that one sounded. Iherish.

"No you're not! You're a dirty Jew. Jew! You killed Christ!"

"I did not!"

It was an amazing turn of events.

Just that September, Pop Addis had surprised them. She and the baby woke up one morning to two sets of swings and a sliding pond. After school kids came to play.

Suddenly she was alone in the backyard.

Ellen read a book, *One God,* to her. Basically we are all the same. Her former friends chased after her: "Jew! Dirty Jew!"

They were ignorant. Christ was Jewish too.

She hid in the phone booth in the drug store and called the maid to take her home. Hardly a tactical coup. But she was afraid of being beaten up. So she used cunning. Rich Jew.

Why hadn't her parents told her earlier? The war was just over; perhaps during it they didn't want to make her scared. It was enough she didn't believe in Santa Claus or have a Christmas tree, wasn't a Catholic.

Ellen took her to Hebrew classes at the temple. The kids on Prospect Avenue went to Sunday School. She went to Tuesday and Thursday School. They had trouble reading the catechism forward. She was supposed to read mumbo-jumbo backward. They were named after saints. Her parents and grandparents had to phone a lot of people to find out the Hebrew name for Rose.

And she was still followed home.

"Fight back," Ray advised.

Two times a week, in the Bergen section at the temple, she was to make Jewish friends. But these little girls were sissies compared to the kids on Prospect Avenue. And just as ignorant. The rabbi would come by and read them fairy tales and make believe he believed them himself. And they fell for it.

For Rose, the fairy tales were the last straw; she wouldn't go back. "It's the *Bible*," her parents told her, visibly amused. She wouldn't budge.

"Not everyone is against you," Ray would say.

It would be during a burst of sadness when she would cry herself senseless on the couch. Her parents would circle round her, wondering what to do, till all hours. Her father never went away.

And he'd call from the store the next day. "Did Rose fight back? Is she okay?"

During those sessions reason cut through the night air.

Ray was right. It was mainly Bill Novack and the two other Poles, and Louise, a rough girl from the South. They hated Jews.

And they forgot about her lots of times. She wasn't chased every day.

Her best friend, Gail Sheehan, lived across the street. But she went to parochial school. And the two Jewish boys in the neighborhood went to Stephen's Prep.

She wanted to go to private school too.

Then Ray would flare. In the late night he would be as concentrated and beautifully insubstantial as an angel. There would be just his wide brow, dark eyes, and finger motioning up threateningly. NO!

You have to face this. If you run away from this you'll run away from the next thing and the next thing and the next. And before you know it you'll be running all your life!

He was certain. It was one thing he *knew*.

It was Boston University, B.U., that was under consideration at the dinner table.

"You don't need a degree to roll a baby carriage," Ray continued. As if she'd ever.

"It's something she can fall back on," Ellen said.

"Then let her go to the Normal School!"

"The Normal School," Rose sneered.

"Don't use that tone, young lady, or I'll wipe it off your face!"

"Ray!" Etta butted in.

"Mother*rrr*!"

"Why do you always have to pick on her?" Janet mumbled in rage.

"The Normal School," Ray continued, "is good enough for a lot of people in Jersey City. It's good enough for you. Too good!"

"It's for IDIOTS!" Rose screamed. "It's not good enough for me!"

"Don't excite your father!"

"Miss Fancy Pants."

"She's right," Etta said.

"I don't know why you're making a federal case out of it, Daddy," said Rose, calming. "I just want to go away to college. Everyone else is."

"You're not everyone else!" Ellen reminded her.

"If everyone else jumped off the Brooklyn Bridge," Ray philosophized, "would you jump too?"

"Probably. Anything! I'd do anything. Anything! To get away from you!"

"That's a nice way to talk," Etta whispered.

"So go jump," said Ray.

"Is it the money?" Etta asked. Ray was driving her to the sanitarium. Once a month now he had a sister he had to take his mother to see.

"Nah, don't worry."

"Why are you so against her going away? So you'll miss her awhile. She's gotta grow up."

Ray blushed. "That has nothing to do with it. She's too big for her britches. Her head's always in the clouds. The Normal School's okay. It'll knock her down a peg or two."

"She'll never go there."

"She has a choice. She can commute to NYU like her old man. Or go to Fairleigh Dickinson. This isn't the boondocks. All she has to do is open her eyes. We have plenty here."

"Oh? What'd she say to that?"

"What does she say? She's a baby. She wants every bit of it all her own way."

"You always got your way."

"So did Helen."

"My God, Ray. Let the poor girl live. Don't worry so. She's got a good head."

He took a sideward glance at his mother. Ready to start it all over again. She could go through what she had to go through and not be afraid. *Herrrr? She doesn't have the brains she was born with.*

"This is what's no good for your health," his mother said. "All this worry for nothing. I wish you and Ellen could just relax and have some fun. Do something better than go to the track. You never saw a track before you met her. All that gambling and worrying. Some fun. Why, when we were your age — the house was always full. Remember, Ray?"

"You always gave a great party, Mom."

"Yes," she said. The car turned into Greystone. She could see ahead of her the endless walk over the endless lawn. "I think Boston would be good for her. After all, she'll meet fine people there. Find herself an educated fellow. What's waiting for her at the Normal School? Some fellow like Helen found? It's the best thing for her. She can call up young Paul; he'll show her around."

"Sure, sure."

Ray parked the car. He sat for a minute, as he always did. "Remind me, when we get to the first water fountain, not to forget to take my pills."

"Room and board as well as tuition. It's not cheap for you," Etta counted.

"Wasted money for a girl."

"So she'll have a little fun, gain a little experience before she's married. What's wrong with that?"

"For fun I'd pay! But all that money for her to sit in a strange town with her nose in a book. She might as well be *here,*" Ray said, not without meaning.

"She has plenty of friends. You're always yelling for her to get off the phone."

"Bad as her. She picks the real lulus."

"So in Boston she'll find better types."

Ray was quiet.

"Let me blow you," Etta said. "Let me pick up her room and board. For me it would be a real pleasure. Let me treat."

❧ ❧ ❧

Ellen and Ray sat at a round table on plush seats at the hotel. The lantern in the middle of the table was already lit, though the spring dusk equalized its light. There was a hushed, dignified silence. The occupants of the other linen-draped tables spoke under it, lending their muffled tones to the quiet end of the day.

The well-being she felt reminded Ellen of the summers at the Braymore in Belmar, before Ray's old asthma and the changing times chased them away. Today had been such a beach day. The air made her feel she could go for a swim in it. She and Ray had followed Rose and her friend Hildy to the Charles. Young people sunning on the grass. Topless young men rowing flat boats in the river.

Used to Jersey City all her life, she tended to think of New England — once you got on the Merritt Parkway heading north — as country. The Back Bay of Boston, with its brownstones and blazing magnolia trees, with its youths carrying books, wasn't exactly real to her. Any man with a pipe she thought must be a professor.

Ray was pleased because Hildy, even though she was a scholarship student, could name the cars they passed going toward the river. Ray couldn't. But later, in their hotel room, he said with relief, "That Hildy has her eyes open."

Hildy and Rose had gone off to the university to see if their marks were posted. After Rose had said if-you-keep-walking-you're-sure-to-find-it, Hildy had given them directions to Isabella Stewart Gardner's house as if she had a road map etched into her brain. They decided to take a slow walk back to the hotel instead.

They had a nice lunch, just as if they were at the track. And even though he had pills to take (Ellen figured pills and liquor didn't mix long before the first reports), they each had a whiskey sour.

"See, it's not so bad," she said.

The hotel room was sparer than its price would have suggested. But it had a good-sized bath. Just the two of them in a room in which they had nothing to do with the furnishings. Whatever sounds came in from Mass Avenue, there was no jangling of keys.

The room was real. It was enough.

He touched her shoulder. "What do you say?"

They were both a little tipsy. After you eat, it's particularly no good for your heart.

But suddenly he didn't seem concerned at all. Nor she.

They felt like the teen-agers they had never been, taking off their clothes. She put on her hairnet and went for a towel. He found the Trojans he had carried just in case.

They stretched out on a bed together, naked in the middle of the afternoon. They had done this before they had a household; they had done this at the Braymore after the hearty Sunday meal.

But what they wanted from each other they had never had.

"Let yourself go," he used to say at the beginning. How could she, if he didn't sweep her off her feet?

They had other things.

Today they had each other. They kissed; he fondled her. He got on top of her and entered. She closed her eyes. It would all be ruined if she saw his face was red. He thrust into her with energy. There was no one they knew to hear. It was almost four years since his attack, but still, as her pleasure increased, she thought, Let him get it over with, please God, and be well. Like on Valentine's Day: it's not the chocolates, who needs them? It's the thought that counts.

Ray's needs were less Platonic. At that moment she was the blond broad, he was Mickey Spillane. Riding high in the middle of the afternoon in Boston, he was feeling like a man.

When it was over they wiped themselves off right in the bed, without one care for the sheets, and fell asleep in each other's arms. Ray first. This was the best part. She heard his regular, emphatic breath before she rolled over.

When they woke, they showered. As she splashed Tweed over her clean body, she tingled the way she did in Belmar after a day in the sun. He shaved, covered by a hotel towel.

They watched television in their robes to kill some time. Laughed together at the announcer's twang. They sure talk funny in Baaahstin.

The whole day was like a warm handshake. Friends well matched, arms stretching across the years.

So she could say in the restaurant in the glowing dusk, without a shred of conscious irony, "Wouldn't your mother have enjoyed it here." She was back in picturesque Boston. The maître d' could have had a Harvard degree. Etta would have enjoyed that. And of course with all of Rose and her gear to get home, there was no way that they could have been expected to ask Etta to come along.

"Yeah, this is the type of place," Ray said suspiciously, "they'd cut up mushrooms in the sauce."

"Well, we'll just ask," Ellen said, "to make sure."

If ever there was a day meant to end in harmony, it was today. But they didn't need Etta, it turned out; they had Rose.

Right now she sees them and rushes by the maître d'.

She's wearing a trench coat; from under it a yellow skirt hangs. Sneakers on bare feet. Her hair, which had been caught up in a bandana earlier, falls past her shoulders.

"Hi! Guess what?" She takes off her coat. Her yellow piqué top is split under the arm. She hasn't shaved.

Raymond rose to take the coat. "Don't get so excited, sit down."

"I'm sorry I'm a little late," she said. "I had to go back to the dorm to sign out and change."

"Why bother?" Ray asked. She had looked neater at the river in her jeans.

"Oh, Daddy! Did you have a good day?"

"Up to now."

"Ray!"

Rose, with the habit of years, ignored his harsh tone.

"What's the use?" he asked.

"Let's order," said Ellen.

"Hey, I have good news!" said Rose.

"First," said Ray, raising a hand, "what do you want to eat?"

He was wearing a good light-weight wool suit his mother had picked out for him. "Let me blow you to a suit that fits." He wore a white shirt and a tie of blue and maroon. Any tie he picked out had maroon in it. Just as all his suits were blue.

Ellen wore a crisp white piqué blouse in a square cut with pearl-colored buttons and a strand of Majorca around her neck. Etta had discovered Majorcas two years ago; she had friends who brought them back. She pounced on them like a new dish. Whoever went over, she commissioned to bring back pearls. Under the table, Ellen had on a tailored herringbone-patterned skirt, hemmed to her knees. In this outfit, with a gray cardigan over her shoulders, she could go anywhere.

"Pull your hair back," Ellen mouthed silently to Rose as Ray studied the menu. Then she pointed her head anxiously toward Ray, giving what Rose knew was a Significant Look.

Rose screwed up her face into a pout. One minute back alone with them and she was ten.

"Get that damn hair out of your eyes!" was Ellen's equivalent to Raymond's "Sit up and put that book down." Though Ellen in cooler moments used psychology. "I'm surprised at you," she'd say in a just-between-us voice. "A girl with a face like yours. Why, you should be proud to show it."

Right now, one mute hand, fingers in comblike position, darted toward Rose's forehead. Rose's hair immediately grew a quarter of an inch in each direction in retaliation as she jerked away. All of this under Ray's downcast eyes.

Ellen sighed, her lips curled over her teeth in exasperation. She went back to the menu. An atavistic urge had once more been thwarted. Her own hair sat on her head like a crown. Not too long, not too blond, not too teased, it was back-combed, laquered, and off her face. Like a wig.

"Some nice broiled calf liver with bacon." Ellen changed the subject. She liked to pick something — not too expensive — that she didn't eat at home.

"Me too," said Rose, who also liked liver and was also sensitive to her father's paying the bill.

"Well," Ellen said, after a pause, "it's silly for *both* of us to order it. I had my eye on the broiled flounder as well. How about I order that, and we'll share, Rose? That makes more sense."

"Order what you want," Ray mumbled.

"Ray," Ellen coaxed, "there are some nice chicken dishes."

He held up a hand.

"Let's see," Ellen said, filling in the gap, "both the flounder and the liver come with two vegetables and a salad. That should be plenty."

"Have a first," Ray growled.

"New England clam chowder," Rose said, her spirits rising once more in her position of cicerone. "This is the place for it! Even better than Paddy's!"

The waiter arrived and Ray ordered for them. "And I'll have the crab meat cocktail, back fin, right?"

"Yes, sir."

"Otherwise I don't want it. And the pork chops with red cabbage and applesauce."

"Oh, no, Ray! That's too heavy."

"It's what I want," he said stubbornly.

She *knew*. He was eating his heart out over Rose.

"There's no sauce on the pork chops, is there?"

"As you wish, sir."

"No mushrooms?"

"Would you care for a side order of mushrooms, sir?"

"No, no." Ray smiled. The waiter *couldn't* be serious. "Mushrooms you can have."

This is ridiculous, Ellen thought. There they were, away, out having a good time, and they were acting as though they still had Etta on their back.

"You've really enjoyed your year," Ellen said, making some conversation.

"It's been incredible. Just incredible. You know," Rose said, and leaned forward. Her head tilted to one side and she squinted. She took a Parker House roll as an object of contemplation and put it not on her bread dish but on her plate. "When I first started, the first semester, I thought everything was separate. I mean there was English Comp and Introduction to Art and Introduction to Philosophy and Trig.

"Don't forget gym," Ray imposed.

"And gym — and German. And they were all different, number one-o-one this, and one-o-one that. But this semester — it came to me in a flash. I was in Art. Imagine, you sit in a room, the lights go out, and there's someone up there whose job it is to tell you all about all these works of art that flash on the screen. It's absolutely fantastic. There was a Cézanne on the screen. He was a nineteenth-century French artist. In a sense he owed a lot to an earlier French artist called Poussin."

"Sure, good old Poussin. Poussin, hah? Poussin who?"

"*Nicolas* Poussin, Daddy, but that's not the point."

"The waiter!" Ray warned.

"Enough!" Ellen mouthed as Ray inspected his crab meat for cartilage. "Enough." Out loud she said, "That Hildy seems like a nice girl."

But try to keep Rose from her point.

"It came to me," Rose said, and her face was flushed with enlightenment, "that Art one-o-two and English one-o-two and Philosophy one-o-two are only separate in the catalogue. To spoon-feed those who can't understand."

"*You* understand, hah," Raymond said with significance.

"It came to me," and at that moment she resembled her great-grandmother, the world was a crystal ball, "that all of these subjects related to one another. Break down the barriers and they're all intertwined parts of one enormous whole. There's not English this and Art that and German. There's culture. There's Western Civilization. There's the whole!"

"My God, Ray. Don't let her upset you!" Ellen cried out in the sharp falsetto of a wounded animal. "She'll grow out of it!"

Jolted, Rose saw her father bend the prongs of his cocktail fork.

"Be careful, Daddy!" On his anticoagulants, if he scratched himself, he bled.

"*Now* you worry," Ellen said.

"What have *I* done?"

"She's right," Raymond said to his wife with a small white smile on his lips. "What has she done? This is normal dinner table conversation in Baaaaaaaahstin! Let me take care of this."

"Eat, so the waiter can clear."

"We're not at home, Mother! The waiter doesn't have to catch a bus."

"See! Listen to your daughter. This is *education*. I only wish Mom was here!"

The entrée was served to silence.

"We're lucky we came early," Ellen finally said. The restaurant had filled up. "Some very interesting types. Rose, by the way, what was that good news you had for us? Let's have some good news!"

"Oh, nothing," Rose said, not without a throb of self-pity. "My marks were good. That's all. I made the Dean's List. Forgive me. I'm sorry."

For Rose it had been incredible news. She had watched the older girls in Jersey City prepare for college. She had even been invited to watch her Jewish "Big Sister" in high school, Gloria Stern, pack. Nubile, small-waisted, experienced, Gloria bent over a veritable steamer trunk, preparing for the voyage of life, a cigarette with a lipstick stain resting on a tray. Gloria was more sensible than a lot of the girls who hung outside the Y on Tuesday nights eyeing the fellows. Yet she was armed with cashmere, tweeds, and the right intentions. Ellen had picked up an appropriate farewell gift for Rose to take her. A plastic tube of brightly colored panties, inscribed "Monday," "Tuesday," "Wednesday," right on through the week.

"It's not like high school," Gloria leveled during spring recess, when Rose was a senior at Dickinson and Gloria a Wisefool at Syracuse. "In college, work as hard as you want, you're lucky to get a C. Yes," she continued with a dreamy look as she exhaled. She was pinned. The pin — it looked like a small cuff link —

hung over her tit. The boy *puts* it there! "A C is equivalent to a high school A. I guess *some* get A's, but I bet they don't have *any* Social Life."

Here she was a year later, Rose Addis, accomplishing the impossible. And had she and Hildy missed one Ford Forum or an interdenominational rush? She had worked hard, and the only C's she'd seen were last semester in Trig and gym.

"We're very proud that you've made the Dean's List, Rose. Aren't we, Ray?"

"Dean's List," Ray repeated. "Well, I've got a question for someone who has made the Dean's List." Then he chewed some pork.

He looked at Rose with all the old cutting edge of his personalized logic. "It's a theoretical question. If Albert Einstein were invited to a formal dinner party, should he wear a suit?"

At Einstein's death, the Young Philosophers' Club of Dickinson High School had sent a condolence card to his wife. Rose Addis was signing it once more as she thought. "Should?" she answered finally. "I don't think he'd *have* to, if that's what you mean. After all, he was *Albert Einstein*. If he wanted to he could go to a ball in his sweater."

"Why?" Ray asked reasonably. His Socratic method was smoothly exposing his daughter's lunacy.

"Why?" Rose beamed. The truth cheered her. "Why, he was Albert Einstein. The greatest genius the world has seen in centuries. He could go anywhere he wanted, any way he wanted."

"He was a genius," Ellen lamented. "He could forget his socks. He didn't have to comb his hair."

"Mommy, really," Rose said condescendingly. Her mother, unlike her father, had no way of approaching an issue.

"Don't talk to your mother like that!"

"I haven't said anything."

"It's the attitude. Don't think you're so smart. Let me tell you something, young lady. Albert Einstein or no Albert Einstein, if he is invited to a formal dinner, he *has to wear* a suit."

"Why?"

"It's the right thing to do. Genius or no genius, if he doesn't do the right thing, he's no man."

"Anyone would be honored to have Einstein at his dinner."

"I wouldn't. If he came in like a slob with no respect for his hostess, with his hair all over, I'd throw the bum out!"

"Oh, *you!*" she said.

"And what would *you* do?"

"I'd throw all the rest of them out! All your respectable people doing the right thing without a brain between them. One wearing a suit because the next one is. I'd say, '*You,* Albert Einstein, great genius of the Western World, *you* stay!' "

"Genius, spenius! If he doesn't know how to dress for dinner, the hell with him, he's no man."

"He was a great man. If he wanted to, he could have given his lectures in his undershirt. No one would care."

"Is that what they're teaching you here? Be careful, or I'll yank you out of this place so quick you won't know what happened!"

"Conformists! All the rest of them are just conformists, and you'd have Albert Einstein live by their rules!"

"Do you know what happens if you don't live by the rules in this world?" Raymond's face was as red as the lobster he had almost ordered. "You know what happens to 'geniuses' who come to dinner looking like slobs? You know what happens to people who don't comb their hair?"

"They make great discoveries. They lead humanity on!"

"That's where you're mistaken, sister," Raymond hissed. "They end up carted away to the booby hatch."

"Albert Einstein died in Princeton! That's where real geniuses die!"

"Dean's List, hah? Where the hell's your common sense!?"

"Sssh, Ray, people are turning," Ellen warned.

"Let the bums look!"

"Look," said Rose, close to tears of indignation, "I made a special effort to run back to the dorm to dress for this night. So I just hope to God you're not talking about me."

"Oh, no. Oh, noooo. I'm talking about ALBERT EINSTEIN!"

"Is everything all right, sir?" the waiter inquired.

"Ducky."

Ellen said, "Why don't we share a dessert? I saw a parfait coming out. They're big."

"I'm not hungry," Rose said.

"Bring the ladies parfaits! . . . She made a special effort to come looking like this." Ray pointed.

"Oh, Rose," Ellen said. "Can't you see it's killing your father. Just a little care of your appearance. Is that too much to ask?"

"Because if you're talking about me and not Albert Einstein, let me tell you one fucking thing. I'm not ending up in any booby hatch. I've seen this in your eyes for years. I'm not like your sister. Once I got away from that damn city and came here, I didn't worry about it a moment more."

"Worry?" Ellen said. "What nonsense have you been keeping in your head? Why none of us ever, ever thought —"

"Oh, no? Well, here I'm not so unusual. Here there are lots and lots of people with the same ideas as me."

"And they let you all walk the streets and use four-letter words. You know why?" Ray glared. " 'Cause you're all spoiled brats with rich parents who can afford to send you away to school to learn this nonsense. But this isn't the world — it's a dream. You're in for a rude surprise when you get out in the world."

"I'm not the crazy one," Rose said. "You are."

He was close enough to grab her by the throat.

"This is what they should have done to Albert Einstein!"

Then he saw all the faces. It wasn't their looks, but the fact that he could focus once more that allowed him to let go. Rose touched her neck.

"They should have done that before it was too late."

"This is what we've come to," Ellen said after a while. She was watching the mint sauce stain the whipped cream and thinking of her mother-in-law. "Even with her off our backs it doesn't matter. She taught us how to ruin a day."

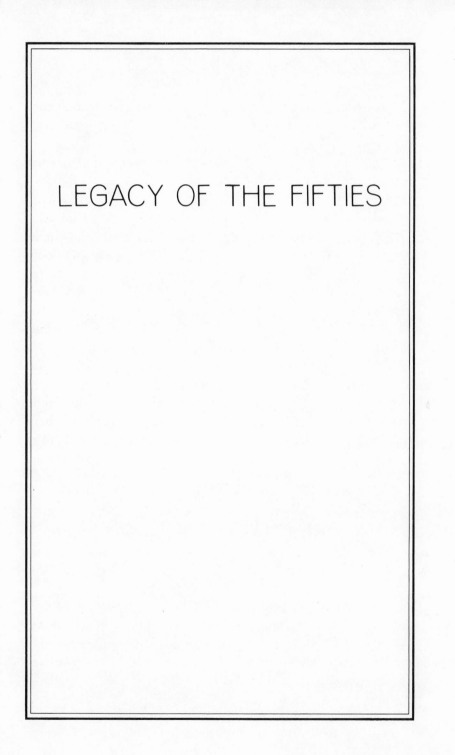

LEGACY OF THE FIFTIES

"WE NEVER SHOULD have sent her to that place!" Ray said to Janet when her turn came. "You want an education, here's thirty-five cents. Take the Tube and see if you can get into NYU."

"We never should have sent her. Didn't I tell you?" to his wife and mother. Ray over dinner would-could-shoulding another loser.

Ray had no more idea than Rose then that Boston University's aim, the same as Ray's, had been to calm her down.

Take Professor Zeno Beni. He hadn't wanted Rose to live the Predicament of Man in the Modern Novel any more than he wanted her to be rowed to hell with Dante. But she didn't understand why, when she presented Carl Sanchez to him, Beni glared like her father.

Beni wanted the Great Books of the Western World to do for his crowded and popular classes what they had done for him — they had taken him out of the moral morass of Boston's Little Italy and made a Christian of him. He had left audacity behind him at Harvard, where it belonged, among those who'd get a chance to use it in the world. He had remembered his undergraduate roots and had come back to the B.U. that had made Harvard possible. Now he wanted to raise others up. He wanted to make

good citizens (in the Platonic sense) of these students. He wanted
the sons of Boston Irishmen and daughters of north Jersey Jews to
be better businessmen and technicians, husbands, fathers, wives
and mothers, by learning how to think.

But he was too inspired a teacher. Peasant-short, dark, and
ugly — the face of St. Charles Borromeo, Rose would realize later.
Not even the best of Italian art could tame the expansive features,
and there was no paint to erase the five-day shadow. Beni too had
his revelation. Without realizing — egotist that he was — the *extent* of his powers, he brought literature live into his classroom.
Whole. Fraught with all its dangers. The dangers that Zeno Beni,
Abstainer, Family Man, Methodist, escaped by teaching the Great
Books.

In the throes of explication he could often make a student *experience* as well as *think*.

A student like Rose.

An A student.

But not dangerous, this excellence, thought Zeno Beni. Time
and again it was the young girls — the future wives and mothers — who took the best notes.

These young girls would have the leisure and learning to begin
the educations of their sons that his own mother, sacrificed on the
slow turning wheel of every day's same needs, had never had.

"I'd like just five minutes alone with that Popcorn!" Ray said.

So would Rose, years later, when Beni saw her on TV and sent
her a letter, the old avenging voice amplified through a long tunnel, a hollow of time. Ah, the hell with Zeno Beni! What Rose
would have given then for five minutes with Raymond alive. Or,
that failing, for him to have seen her on TV, the image like a telex
to the spheres: ALL O.K. WORKING OUT. WAS NOT NECESSARY TRY
KEEP ME DOWN.

Rose had met Carl during her senior year in Boston, when she
had lived on Marlborough Street.

> *On Marlborough Street,*
> *blossoms on our magnolia ignite*
> *the morning with their murderous five days' white.*

She, Rose Addis, lived on the same block as Robert Lowell. She had written a poem about the shock of clenched magnolia buds blooming the same spring Lowell contemplated his. That summer she had stood on a trolley with his *Life Studies* in her hand and read of them. She missed her stop.

She thought she might have actually seen Lowell roll his daughter young enough to be his granddaughter down Boston's hardly passionate Marlborough Street. Was the child in flame flamingo infant's wear? She imagined so. She never looked again. Down the street of art the poet rolls his daughter once.

Instead, on that street, she met Carl.

"Why don't you go out and meet some normal people?" Naïve Ellen.

Rose didn't *want* to meet them. So it took her longer than it might have to realize there weren't any.

And to distrust all those who pretended to be.

Carl was talking to Hildy. "Rose," she said, "this man wants to meet you."

She had been warned off him already. He was Carl Sanchez, who had once had a play produced in Boston.

There was the smell of the notorious about him. Some said he lived off women.

For art, is the way he would phrase it.

"Rembrandt sketched his wife as she lay dying," he said to Rose by way of greeting. There was a flicker in his eye. He stood shifting weight from one foot to the other. Like a small dancer. A Laurentian type of man.

"Laurentian," i.e., D. H. Lawrence, the genius. Cunts stuck with flower petals. Sex, the ambiguous life force he mixed his metaphors for. Sex beyond words and conflicting images and confusing body parts. Sex star-cold, inhuman, and forever.

"I hope she didn't bleed on his pad."

"I'm serious, you know. Don't mock me, Rose Addis."

"I see you know my name."

"I know *you.*"

Interesting.

"I was thinking," Etta Addis said to Rose some months later.

"Lilly is always after me. I'll go to Europe with her this summer if you'll come along."

Europe?

The Old World seemed to Rose a middle-class ploy against sex — and Gentiles.

"Carl wants you" was the factual message Hildy the journalism major left on Rose's bed.

"Tell him I'm busy," she scribbled back.

Then a manuscript on her bed and a note: "Please do come to visit me at the above address. There is even more than *this* that I have to say — to you. Yours forever, Carl."

Yours forever.

He opened the door. He saw she was flushed, and he smiled. He led her in with the sure, economical grace of a delicate man who has learned to use every inch. He couldn't afford a slouch, an ungainly gait, or a high voice.

He was not handsome. But he had wild tawny eyes and curly, unkempt, sawdust hair that together cast a golden glow.

You needed eyes for this man.

"Excuse the mess," he said familiarly. A desk predominated in the small dark room, and papers flooded it.

He led her to a wooden chair — there were two. In the alcove she saw a mattress on the floor.

In Rose's Republic all mattresses would land on the floor.

"Oh, it's lovely here," said Rose, meaning it.

"I wish you could have seen it when I had my books."

"Where are they?"

"Women," he answered.

Aha! Just as in his manuscript, his wife must have sold his books.

"I'm sorry," Rose commiserated.

"I *like* you," he said significantly. It was understood somehow that he already loved her and lusted after her.

Rose felt sublimely comfortable. A deceptive feeling she'd later have at interviews for jobs she didn't get.

"What do you think of that?" he asked, pointing to the manuscript she held reverently.

"Did you really work at McLean?" she asked after a hesitation. In the glorious twilight of the New Criticism, she was timid about smearing the artist with his life.

He nodded.

"That's where Lowell was committed."

"I saw him there. I knew the attendant who was reading *The Meaning of Meaning.*"

> *The night attendant, a B.U. sophomore,*
> *rouses from the mare's-nest of his drowsy head*
> *propped on* The Meaning of Meaning.

"Really!?" Rose, like her grandmother and her Aunt Lilly, was a star-watcher. *Disgusting! Ogling people who are just flesh and blood like you and me.* "How did he feel about being in the poem?"

Carl looked at her searchingly. When he was on the make, the artist in him swelled. "What does it matter what *he* felt? What matters is the poem."

"But *Lowell,* what was he like?"

"Withdrawn, remote, much as he pictures himself in *Life Studies.*"

"It's a wonderful book," Rose said.

"I like that."

"What?"

"The way your eyes shine, the way you go beyond yourself when you speak of what you like." He stood up. He swayed.

"Oh, I'm a great appreciater. In kindergarten, you know" (she had already picked up one of Carl's Britishisms), "the teacher organized a band. I remember at first I was put with the singers, then I was given the triangle to play, and finally the teacher came over to me and said, 'Rose, *you* are going to be the listener!' So the band played and the singers sang and I sat in the first row all by myself. Listening."

Carl had swayed to her by then and reached his hands to her.

"I ran home from school so *excited.* 'Mommy, Mommy, I'm the listener!' "

He took hold of the hands she must have offered and raised her.

"I've been the listener ever since."

"Then listen to me, Rose Addis." He kissed her.

It was as strange a kiss as he was a strange man. She could feel the pressure of his arms and legs. There was something spiderlike in his embrace, as if his feet had left the floor and were encircling her ankles, as if his arms had intertwined with hers.

Since early childhood she had had moments that chilled her. Moments like this one. When she wasn't there.

Her stubborn intelligence told her she was in this room with this man. She could feel the force behind his delicate frame wrapping her in this spider embrace.

"NO!"

"What's wrong?"

"I don't know you."

She looked at him.

Alive. Excited. Cunning as an animal. Halted. Yet ready to spring.

"I don't know anything about you!"

A room. A desk. A mattress. A man.

"What about this?" He pointed to the manuscript. "You seem to want to avoid it. Didn't it tell you anything?"

"Oh," she said, "I loved it."

She walked away from him and sat down. What he had written was dense and rich and confusing. She followed the gold vein through it.

"Do you believe in it?"

"Yes."

"Oh God, Rose, then help me with it. I haven't had a minute's peace since I first saw you." There were tears in his eyes.

"Ohhh," she groaned. *Don't let them tell you it'll make them sick if you don't. It won't.*

"Do you think I'm mad?"

"No. No one who writes like you do is mad. *They're* mad. They don't want you to be what you are." She thought of the nemeses of his novel: poverty, bad luck, the wrong women. "They're afraid of you. They're fools."

"Yes." He rose to it, seeing the fright lessen in her eyes. "It's

what's out there — it's the world that makes us doubt ourselves.
They send the Black Maria after us and we believe its screech-
ings."

The shmegegges, Rose thought. Suddenly the weight of a
daughter's devotion shifted to him. She saw starved greatness in
his eyes. This wouldn't be like going to bed with anyone, like losing self-respect. She saw Ellen Diamond in a toga, pointing upward, upward. This would be entering the Platonic heaven.
Where the idea of things, the pure Ideal, is Real.

"You're better than they are. You *must* believe that. It's the bad
marriage that hurt you. I can see it as clear as day between the
lines of your book."

"Yes. But I'm no saint, you know."

"Do I ever!" responded Rose, the careful reader.

And they laughed. They laughed like anybody.

"Look at us!" he said with a real smile. "You bring me luck!"

"I'm not lucky," she said. "I come from people who have run
out of luck."

"Don't be silly! Look at me. I'm a lion again!" he declared,
tawny and skillful and posturing, like the King of the Jungle.

"You're ruining your life," said Ellen.

"What did I tell you?" said Ray.

"There's something wrong with him," said Etta. *"I wonder if he's a
little — what we used to call — fruity."*

He stood in front of her and unbuttoned his fly. He took his
penis out. The closest she'd ever gotten to a penis was Raymond
at the top of the stairs in his underwear when a date came to pick
her up, saying hello, meaning screw you, and scratching his balls.

"Come to me," he said.

Transfixed, she obeyed him.

He put her hands on his penis.

"I'm a lion again," he rejoiced. "I'm hard."

Significance poured into things.

Rose was far from the day when a room would be a room, a
desk a desk, a mattress a mattress, a man a man. Or pleasure pleasure.

Denotations were like the starter apartments she'd hear about

through Dr. Lizbeth Courtney's walls as she waited for the stern
old dike to fit her for her illegal diaphragm. Denotations were ir-
relevant. Rose could hear the new brides, the normal people, feet
in stirrups, legs spread, Dr. Courtney's cold instrument stuffed up
their vaginas, chatting about refrigerators that self-defrost, sinks
that eat garbage, wall-to-walls, waiting *all day* for the custom-
made man.

They seemed as detached as Dr. Courtney's anatomical draw-
ings from the connotations of their cunts.

"Cunt, cunt, cunt." Carl mouthing her.

With Carl in her arms, the tumble-dust of meaning fell all
around them.

She was Venus; he was Zeus disguised in a rain of gold. Carl
talked like this. After he had two beers, she found him hard to
follow.

Still, the loss of her virginity happened in that small room, once
she forced herself back into it. It was a spectacular event, too
grand to be commemorated or even connected to an invitation
list, a registered pattern, a ceremony, a catered affair, and a big
cake.

She was initiated in a rite of their own imagining. Together
they took a bath.

He told her she wouldn't get pregnant. He'd withdraw. Then
he entered her on the mattress on the floor.

"You can do what you want," Ray said calmly to Rose. It was a
hot August day. He was in his air-conditioned bedroom, where he
could breathe. Ellen stood nervously by her bed. He sat in the
chair turned toward the TV.

Rose had a moment when she believed it was going to be easy.

"It's a free country," he continued. "But when I look at a man
like that, I think, he's no man, he's a bum!" He put his hand out
to stop her. "Wait one minute, Rose!" he snapped, but then he
calmed himself again. "Don't get me wrong. I'm just giving you
my opinion. Just the way you give yours to us. I have the right.
How old is he? Thirty? No job. Just sits home and writes. Thirty,
Rose. Why by the time I was thirty —"

"Your life was just about over!"

"Rose!"

"That's okay, Ellen," Ray said as sweetly as a D.A. who had just made a point. "She's twenty-one. You heard her. She can vote, drink . . . Whatever! She has a tuition scholarship to NYU. She's a big shot. She's all set.

"But let me tell you one thing, sister! If that bum is what you really want, you'd better forget about graduate school and get a job. You won't get a cent from your grandmother or a cent from me. You want an apartment in New York? Go out and work nine to five. That's a real education!"

Her father looked at her with murder in his eyes. "We never should have sent you to that place."

"You're ruining your life," said Ellen.

❧   ❧   ❧

"You have a choice. You can either stay in school or get married," Raymond told Janet at the end of her freshman year at NYU.

"Oh," Janet said. She was eighteen. They were in the parlor on a vacant Sunday. Ray had cheated pancakes, sausages, and syrup for breakfast. The sugar was coursing to his heart. Ellen was in the kitchen, doing dishes quick — before Etta could jingle in and see what she had missed.

Janet could feel the odd hollow echo of the place since Rose was gone. It made her spirits sink. It was like every Sunday at one o'clock without Charley's footsteps reverberating down the stairs next door.

Her grandfather always woke for first breakfast at eight-thirty and then went back to bed till one. Sunday in, Sunday out. A never-varying habit. A monument. A niche in time.

Broad noodles on Friday night.

Here, sweetheart, here's a nice slice, oh what a slice for you. The creak of the stairs.

Next door there were other footsteps gone as well. Music she would never hear. A special void, a distance she felt when she disturbed her grandmother.

She stood now and walked over to the stairway landing.

Her father was in his favorite chair, the one marked by the flakes of his psoriasis no matter how often (not too often) Claudine vacuumed. He had a stubborn proprietary attitude toward his chair. He did not plan to leave it.

His younger daughter had a good build, straight and tall with something of the careless grace of an athlete or of someone who hardly thinks of body at all. She had a sallow complexion, though outside the house there was often color in her cheeks. She had his long bony face, Ellen's strong nose as well as her teased and laquered hair, sitting too high on her forehead.

Janet saw her father's point, of course. Free will ran rampant on Clifton Avenue. Here there was always a choice.

Rose was given a choice too.

"I don't like school," Janet said, sitting down on the stairway landing.

"Why? You do well."

It came as a surprise to him that she had finished her first semester at NYU getting all A's.

"Well?" she mocked. "You call it doing *well?* I memorize."

"Nothing wrong with memorizing!" Raymond said, relieved now that he knew the short cut she was taking. "I used to see guys crib notes on their cuffs." He pointed to his head. "I cribbed in here."

"It doesn't mean anything."

"Don't be a jerk. Take a look around you. The people that get the good jobs, the people that are going somewhere, they don't give a damn what it means. They memorized. Don't be a sucker. You memorize too."

"Rose didn't memorize."

"She took everything too seriously. You're different. You're like me."

She looked at her father. Once when she was a baby, toddling and transfixed by the snow on the block, she reached up to his gloved hand dangling by the pocket of his camel hair coat. Her hand was taken so warmly, she was surprised. They walked together briskly. At the corner there was a man, also in gloves and a

camel hair coat, facing them, steam rushing out of his mouth as
he laughed. It was her father. Laughing at her. Laughing at the
kind stranger who had accepted her proferred hand.

Apathetically now, she acknowledged to herself that she probably was like her father. He was a stranger to her. And she was a
stranger to herself.

"Buddy's a nice boy," he allowed. Doing less and less these
days, Ray had time to savor life's ironies. His brilliant, beautiful
daughter was in New York wasting her life with a bum. While
Janet was being courted by one of the richest young men in the
city. She had a chance to have all the things he pooh-poohed.

"Of course, college comes first. And I strongly recommend that
you continue." He launched into the advantages of an education.
Propelled perhaps by the secret confidence that she would not get
one.

She shrugged, got up, and turned to climb the stairs.

"Where you goin'?" he called. But it was more of an ultima-
tum than a question.

Hers was the middle room, juxtaposed to the one next door to
the aunt she had never known. "Promise you won't tell." Rose
years ago telling her. Her big sister had expected her to respond to
the drama of Helen. But nothing her father excluded from her life
surprised Janet even then.

Janet too had bay windows but with no stained glass. In front
of the bay there was a dressing table. It had an oblong, heart-
shaped glass top, legs disguised in a frilly white skirt.

She had had that table there since she was thirteen. Neither she
nor anyone else thought to change it. She sat down at her old
Snow White table now and looked in its mirror.

Mirror, mirror, on the wall . . .

She was cute.

"I believed I was cute the way my mother told me. Then one
day, I must have been fourteen, I took a good long look at myself.
Cute? I thought. Is she crazy? I'm not cute at all."

She was, in an irregular way. She had a no-nonsense approach to her looks. She, unlike Ellen and Ray, was not upset by her sister's greater beauty.

What did she need beauty for?

She wasn't going to make a great scene, take the choice handed her, and then go to live with a writer in the Village.

Beauty would have been a waste in her life.

She lay down on her bed.

Unlike Rose, it had always been difficult for Janet to rise in the morning. Sometimes, when she got up, there was a wave of dizziness that rushed her down. An inertia dragging her to her fate. Mommy, rub my feet.

When Buddy held her in his arms in the dark, finished basements of Jersey City where her crowd necked, she'd catch herself sliding to sleep.

The beer, the music, the long kisses blurred.

She didn't like basements. Beyond the upholstery and the built-in bars, the paneling and the parquet floors, she'd hear ever so faintly and mournfully the snap of her grandfather's traps. She did not like messages from the underground, brought up by roaches that gave her the creeps.

It was indistinguishable to her in her dazed, dozing stage, bugs or Buddy's hands crawling on her skin.

School or Buddy.

She had an eight-by-ten colored photo of Buddy by the bed. He did everything extravagantly. His family's middle name was money. In a restaurant he always ordered steak.

She reached for the picture, propped it on her tight stomach, where it held on its standing frame.

Buddy smiled out past her to that realm of self-worth where people have their pictures taken.

He had a nice face.

"Gorgeous," said Ellen. "How I love to look at that face."

It was the round face of a twenty-two-year-old. Minute acne scars gave it a tone of roughness that was more attractive than the wet and shining cheeks that peered out from the frame. She liked the feel of his face in the car. When she closed her eyes she could feel him strong and manly on her wedding night.

He had big eyes, bigger than hers, but much lighter brown. The pretty lifeless quality the photographer captured was real. He had a small nose and thin lips and a thick neck.

Everyone liked him. When he told a joke, everyone laughed. Buddy. Everybody's buddy. The big tipper, the happy handicapper.

As Ellen put it, the good boy.

As Etta put it, Boy, that Buddy can dress.

"Hi, Nana," he'd boom at her. "How's my girl?" He'd take her to a movie.

He saw every movie in northern Jersey, New York. Every ball game. Every play. Doing, doing. With him you always did.

He was finishing up NYU the way Ray approved of. Without giving it a thought. But he didn't have Raymond's brains. "That's okay, believe me," said Ray. "Five years, six. He's young. He's regular. He's got time."

Janet took the picture off her stomach. She held it up and looked at it till it became the icon in that teen-age room.

A surge of rightness left her weak. And more dramatically than was her wont, she brought the glass-covered cherry lips to her lips for a kiss.

"Buddy?" Rose said, greeting her sister at the door of her apartment. Rose and Buddy had graduated from high school together. And she had seen him with Janet around NYU.

"Come, sit down." Rose walked about her bare apartment in her bare feet. Leaving Clifton Avenue meant leaving umbrellas, buttoned sweaters, socks behind. She liberated herself from the weatherman. When her mother called and asked, "Is it as muggy/windy/cold/snowy there as it is here?" Rose often didn't know. But none of this meant she was free.

What's free?

She had no idea.

Hildy, adding the mechanical wonders of photography to her checklist of accomplishments, had taken a picture of Rose in her senior year at B.U. Rose sat on the railed wrought-iron balcony of her single room in Marlborough House, holding a sprig of pussy willows, wistfully wondering.

Rose wore a black skirt and sweater; her thick hair agitated to her shoulders. Her dark eyes burned out against her pale face. Her head was slightly tilted, and she looked at and past the pussy willows, which the sun lit, turning them into a spring day.

Rose had no idea how hard it was to photograph black, or that in Hildy's fine picture she was dreaming in a cage.

She looked wild and wonderful now, her long thick black hair electric with thought. Her big black eyes and full lips took over her pale face, which was held aloft on a tall, slender body. Love would always make her lose weight; in the case of Carl, she also had to work very hard.

She had her mother's iron will and her father's brains. A streak of melancholy ran through her like a pulsing blue vein. But she didn't see it. If forced to analyze herself, a process she avoided, she'd probably say she had a good sense of humor, was funny.

Which, when she wasn't tearing through to the heart of the matter, she was.

She looked at her sister intently.

Cards, crystal, the creases of the palm. She did not need them. Buddy Hensh hung in the air between them, and Rose saw.

"Do you like Buddy?" she asked.

Janet nodded.

"Do you love him?"

"I don't know."

"Well, if you don't *love* him, it's not fair to him to keep him on the hook. It would be fairer to let him drop."

"You think so?"

"Absolutely. The choice is yours. Make a commitment, or, if there's the slightest doubt, believe me it will be better for him in the long run, *let him drop.*"

Janet, this man is not worthy of you. I have seen in his eyes his lack of core. His goodness to everyone is not goodness. It's ease, it's what he can afford. Everything in life he'll try to mold to his comfort. There's not a spot to wade in at, even at his depths.

The unspoken prophecy. Rose was claimed by the Diamonds. A word will knock a house down.

"Tell your sister a nose job would make her as pretty as can be, Rose. To you she'll listen."

"A nose job? A little button for her nose? Her nose has *character!* What's wrong with her nose?"

"*Character?* That's all we got around here. You're all characters!" . . .

"Rose, she listens to you." Her mother's worried whisper on the phone. "Not one of your smart-aleck remarks against Buddy Hensh. This is your sister's *life*. Don't ruin it. Don't do to it what you're doing to your own."

It wouldn't have mattered. Alsatian Rose could have told her. *That* was a witch. People won't see what you see if it's not what they want to hear.

For example, Rose has just given Janet a Raymond-dose of logic. A clear choice. "Not fair to him" is what her sister thinks. "Drop him" is what Rose lets ring through the air.

Not fair to him.

Marriage or college.

Janet leaves, a bit more convinced.

Part of Rose tries to leave with her. But that part comes back after Janet shuts the door. Rose does not know what to do with it. She walks aimlessly about the stark rooms.

Who is she to give advice? There Ellen is right. She wouldn't want her little sister to live her kind of life.

The life of the heart.

Ah, Rose, intuitions are not like hand mirrors. Alsatian Rose could have taught you: the twists and turnings of fortune you meet will vary, will often surprise. But the one thing you'll never see in the crystal is your own eyes.

Rose, you are too young to know your own heart. Too searching, too ambitious, too bright. That feeling you're feeling so deep inside is in your brain.

"My brain?!"

Yes, your brain. It's crying out for someone else's talent, someone else's rise . . .

Petal-eyed Rose Addis, long since gone. What the gangrene left isn't even worms' meat anymore. But in your time you knew your business. You saw it every day. When the force of intellect strikes, it strikes early. And with its own passion and drive it can carry the heart away.

"I used all my power to try to send Carl out into the world," Rose will say one day. "It took me a long time to realize the extent of my own motivations and ambitions. And after that even longer to begin to know myself. I think the more intelligent you are when you're young, the longer it takes you to learn how to feel. My father used to say youth was wasted on children. Maybe they don't have the emotions for it."

"Don't be too hard on yourself," Jennifer Potash will respond. Dr. Jennifer Potash. One hell of a witch. "How you ever accomplished what you have accomplished out of that background of yours is a miracle to me."

"I don't know," said Rose.

"What don't you know?" Raymond asked. They were walking from the movie they had just seen, *General della Rovere*. One day Raymond had taken the Tube over to Rose's fait accompli. Sheepishly he began his weekly visits. He'd drop her off an order of meat and canned goods and then wait for her idea of something they could do.

Walking in New York, Raymond was what he was. A forty-six-year-old man in uncertain health, being squeezed by the supermarkets.

What would happen to Addis Meats if Dasher withdrew the hospital account? And what had happened to Raymond's life, that his business hung by Dasher's hospital? Dasher would never in a million years withdraw the account. This added to Raymond's aggravation.

Since his heart attack and loss of weight, he was always cold. His good overcoat grew big on him. He'd taken to wearing a black hat too small for his skull.

"So-what-*could*-be-new" was now the permanent look in his

eyes. And he responded to morsels of absurdly bad news with a smile of sheer delight.

Yet he greeted the buildings and the sleazy shops along Times Square with interest. Almost as he greeted Rose. In spite of himself he couldn't get rid of the presentiment that maybe he'd missed something they had to say.

He and Rose stopped at a Chock Full o' Nuts. He liked the hot dogs and she liked the plain wheat doughnuts.

"I don't know how serious Janet is about Buddy," Rose continued.

"Butt out."

"Do you know?"

"It's none of my business. It's her life. Let her lead it."

"Sure. That's why you didn't let her go away to college."

"She didn't want to, wise guy. She was smart enough not to want to end up like you."

"That's pretty smart, I imagine. But what do you think about Buddy?"

"He's a regular guy."

"You like him!"

"What's not to like? He has a smile on his face, he's a gentleman to my mother, he combs his hair, he has money."

"Yes, but I wonder, I wonder if there's any . . . any depth."

"He's no Einstein. But he cares for your sister. She's no Einstein either."

"She's smarter than either you or Mother allow."

"Yeah, she's smart all right, but like a normal person."

"I don't think Buddy will satisfy her."

"*Satisfy?* What book you find that in? Who's satisfied in this world? Come back to earth. He's a damn worthy fellow."

"I don't think he takes things seriously."

"Neither did I at his age. But he'll learn, he'll have to, just like me."

"I can't believe this!"

"What?"

"You *identify* with Buddy Hensh. He reminds you of *you.*"

Ray looked at her with that slightly embarrassed smile on his face. Screwed up as she was, she was the only person who knew anything about him at all.

In later years she'd wish her father could have had a mistress. That the times he was most himself were not when he was alone laughing his head off at Laurel and Hardy or in New York with her.

"He's like I was when I was young," Ray admitted. "He's got parents who can't stop giving him everything he wants. I mean the son *and* the older one, what do you expect? And he likes a good time. Even before he dated your sister, I'd bump into him at the track. He shows a girl a good time and respects her.

"Sure, he's wet behind the ears. Wasn't I? I let Pop give me the store on a platter. I should have gone off on my own.

"That's what I tell him. 'Buddy, we all come from monkeys, but don't end up a jackass like me.'"

"You and your monkeys."

"I take things for what they are. I know where we came from and I know where we're going — nowhere fast. But a young man like Buddy, with every advantage, why not take a stab at the in-between?"

"Why don't *you* take a stab?"

"Me?" He raised his hand and pressed his fingers to his palm, dismissing the days of his life.

— "What do monkeys do?" Jennifer would question Rose one day.

"Hell, they eat bananas and masturbate."

"They do what feels good." —

"Why *not* you?" Rose asked her father, along Times Square.

"Don't talk nonsense. I tell him, 'Buddy, don't be like me. I'm an example. When I started out, I didn't know what to do with all the money coming in. Now if I didn't wholesale to the Doctors' Hospital, I couldn't even keep the store. What looks like easy money in the beginning can turn to crap. Don't be like me! Don't take. Start something yourself. Go out on your own!' 'You got a point there, Pop,' he says."

"Good God!" Rose said. "Does he really call you Pop?"

"Something wrong with that?"

Rose shook her head. "You see him developing a sensibility he hasn't the slightest awareness of. Be careful —"

"Advice yet! Save it. You need all the advice you can get for yourself."

"I just don't know," she repeated abstractly.

"So who asked you?"

That night she said to Carl, "Look at this." She had written a description of a man — a middle-aged man — who believes we all come from monkeys. This man buys a small black hat. Slowly the hat turns him Jewish.

"Damn good," said Carl.

"A lot of Gogol there, don't you think?"

"Don't be so cerebral. A lot of you."

"Maybe you should go to work and I should stay home and write," she said jokingly. One of those bad jokes.

❦ ❦ ❦

The women were in the small room. Etta, Ellen, Rose, Janet.

"Put a smile on your face!" Ellen snapped at Janet. Etta at such close proximity rubbed her nerves raw. "You're getting married. A bride should smile."

Janet, dressed in her short white dress and starched veil that did nothing for her, indeed did look pale.

"That lipstick's too light," Etta offered. "Doesn't anyone have a darker shade of pink with them?"

"All a bride needs is a smile to make her beautiful," Ellen answered. "This one doesn't seem to know she should be smiling."

"Ma, leave her alone!" Rose pleaded.

"Oh, I've left her alone, all right."

Ellen, dressed in crisp blue, was still burning. When Ellen Diamond knew she was right, nothing could change the current of her conviction.

"This Is My Beloved" was her choice for the wedding march. It summarized love. Kismet. This was good luck, this song. This was a smile on the face.

Janet insisted on classical. During the weeks of preparation, it was the one point Janet was adamant about. Chopin.

"Chopin," Raymond moaned, as if she were starting up. He was so viscerally offended by the choice that it led her to great obstinacy.

They shared a secret now, which made her father tread a little lighter.

During the engagement Buddy had taken to sleeping over in Rose's empty room.

One night Janet was filled with fiery intent. Ah, if we were only brave enough to accept what the night tells us.

Strategy, however, would never be her forte. On the way to Buddy she met her father coming from the bathroom.

"Where you going?" he whispered fiercely.

Why didn't she say to the bathroom?

"I want to speak to Buddy. I want to break it off." Her voice was trembling.

"Why?" Ray's tone altered perceptibly.

"I don't think I'm in love."

"Let it wait till the morning. Don't disturb his sleep."

"It's important."

"That's why," Raymond explained. "It's important enough to sleep on. If you feel the same way in the morning, you tell him exactly how you feel. Believe me, wait till the morning. Sometimes moods like this pass. And if this one does — or either way — nothing's lost. Let the poor guy sleep."

So it was Chopin.

Rose felt slightly dizzy in the closed little room. And the slightest dizziness turned her nauseated with fear. She sat down, vivid in her cheap pink dress, which looked good on her. But when she sat down, it pulled up a bit too tight.

"God, can we turn up the air conditioning?"

"It's cool enough for me!" Ellen replied defensively.

Janet was getting married at the Ritz-on-Bergen, close to Journal Square. It was a dowdy, respectable place. Two of Etta's cronies were permanent residents there. Rose and Janet would always believe Janet was the only Jewish girl ever married there.

In fact, no Jewish girl from Jersey City ever got married in Jersey City as far as they knew. *So, you'll start a trend.*

People had big affairs. They sent engraved road maps. You went around eating and drinking somewhere on a Route and trying to figure how much a couple. There were hors d'oeuvres, rooms with tray-bearing servants loading you with Chinks and caviar and pastrami. Then there was the sit-down dinner, offering not only innumerable courses but a choice and lots of wine. And lately, after dessert, there was the Viennese bar, pastry, coffee, liqueurs, and, if it was Saturday night, the Sunday *Times.*

In Buddy Hensh's family, if an aunt and uncle dropped less than half a grand to the newlyweds, it was a disgrace.

Buddy hadn't even been thinking Jersey; he was thinking, as usual, big, New York.

"What's wrong with the Ritz-on-Bergen?" Ray threw out.

"Why not at Father Divine's?" Buddy kidded back.

They were at dinner on Clifton Avenue. Even Janet had to admit that the meal had picked up since Buddy.

"I'm serious, pal. What's important about a wedding — getting married or letting the world see how much money you can spend?"

"Hey, Pop, I mean we're talking about my wedding. To me, after all, what I always imagined was an event. I mean, it's a big day. A step for life."

"Well, that's just what Ray's saying, Buddy. It's a big day, but not for anything that money can buy," Ellen elucidated.

"Hey, listen, you know my folks. They wanta pay."

"We're not talking about money," Ray tried. "What we're discussing are *priorities.* What makes a marriage, that it takes place at the Waldorf or on Journal Square or in front of a justice of the peace?"

"What do you say, Nana?" Buddy asked Etta.

"It's none of my business, this wedding."

"I don't think the place is important, Buddy," Janet said. "We don't need a big deal."

Buddy looked around the table uncomprehendingly, but with a smile. This was a young man who lived in harmony with the universe getting involved with a family who liked to make things tough.

When Mrs. Hensh served up a platter of caviar to Buddy's specifications, run through with chopped onion, Ray would mumble, "Fish eggs." And in the summer, Janet, whose mother scooped out balls of cantaloupe and watermelon onto a big plate, would be offended by his eating pounds and pounds of fresh cherries.

He had been doted on so long by parents who could afford it that he saw no line between his comfort and the meaning of life. Everything good flowed to Buddy Hensh in its season.

Ritz-on-Bergen was so off the wall that it amused Buddy. He liked his future father-in-law, whom he considered, not without due cause, the wackiest man he ever met. *Wacky, Buddy? It's time you learn from some real common sense.*

"Ritz-on-Bergen is a good, solid, decent place," Ray continued.

"Mr. and Mrs. Hensh may have their own ideas, Ray," Etta interposed. "That's why they want to pay."

"What's wrong with you, Mom? I'm the father of the bride. Do you think I'd let *them* pay?"

"Well, I'm not paying!" she answered.

Ellen turned pale in humiliation.

"Who asked you?!" Raymond snapped.

"Raymond, be sensible!" Etta continued. "This is your daughter's marriage you're talking about. Like Buddy says, an event. If the Henshes want to have it some place swell, let them be happy. Let them spend! Is it a sin that people should be happy, have a good time?"

"I can pay for the Waldorf-Astoria," Raymond said. "I could hire a steamship and have them married on a boat if it were the right thing to do."

"Look at him!"

"But I'm telling Buddy something. It's not the cost that makes the event."

"But it sure makes your friends happy, Pop." Buddy smiled benignly. "Everybody remembers a good time. Like my Bar Mitzvah —"

"Not again!" Janet cried out. "How many times do we have to hear of your Bar Mitzvah?"

"Calm down," Ray said.

"But can't you see the point?!" Janet asked Buddy in exasperation.

"I can't see the Ritz-on-Bergen," Buddy answered pleasantly enough.

"I can!" Janet said. "I can see getting married with the smallest fuss and the least expense. Ritz-on-Bergen is fine with me."

"Don't be so quick," Ray admonished. "Let's just discuss."

One day in June, half of Jersey City did things Ray's way for a change. Plain, simple, styleless. With moral intent.

Rose felt regret in the little dressing room. She wished Janet were seated in one of those plush prenuptial parlors reserved for the bride, with a photographer snapping as her sister looked into the mirror and pretended to adjust a longer, more stylish veil. One of those preceremony movies should have been made to kill time, with the bride walking serenely down the aisle toward the rabbi played by the caterer's son. Why shouldn't Janet have memories other than the electric nervousness of the moment? Why not the trimmings? Rose felt the disdain of the lapsed Catholic who regrets the changes of display in the church she no longer attends.

Janet was a lamb being led to the altar of the Jersey rich. So why couldn't she have a few riches? Why in the midst of plenty must she stand out so pale and plain an Addis?

"Maybe there's still time, sweetheart," Ellen said, dazzling in her blue.

Janet looked up at her hopefully.

"I could ask. All you have to do is give the word . . . and they can switch to 'This Is My Beloved.'"

Janet closed her eyes against her tears. In a tremulous voice, fighting for control, she hummed "To Love Again."

"What's that?" Etta asked, coming out of the doldrums of the close quarters.

"Chopin! It comes from Chopin!" Janet bellowed.

"Oh my God," Etta moaned. It was a magnificent moan. It incorporated her entire despair at the situation, including the badly placed tables reserved for her friends. "Don't tell me *that's* the Chopin you've chosen? What kind of people are you? That's the Funeral March!" . . .

"Ceremonies you can have," Janet would say to Rose in the future, her parents' verve against forms gone wild in her. "I got married to the Funeral March at the Ritz-on-Bergen. Do you find any significance in that?"

"You certainly had a good time at the wedding," Rose said to Carl back in New York. He had been introduced as a friend from Boston. Marcy took him up. They discussed the Pope. He soul-kissed her — Rose's aunt! — good-bye. Now he was dancing around the room, shedding his jacket and loosening his tie.

He was the son of a factory worker in Quincy. To him, the Ritz-on-Bergen had been a real spread.

And liquor — he was Portuguese, Irish, and an eighth Cherokee. Liquor ran through him on the warpath. It turned his eyes to fire. It released his wayward soul.

In ten years' time he'd find out he wasn't a star-crossed genius, but an alcoholic. At forty, scared out of his wits by the D.T.'s, he'd do something about it. He really didn't know what he was doing now.

It had often been a woman, sometimes a man, who supported him. They'd lift him out of the confused impulses of his strange nature.

But never had he been with anyone like Rose. Right now she undressed, unmindful, untidy. She sat cross-legged on the mattress, back to the wall, hands on her stomach.

She had taken her love seriously. She had carved a life for the two of them. No dishwashing anymore for Carl Sanchez. He was pinned to a desk. Write!

"You frighten me," he'd say to Rose. "You can be so cold, so abstract."

"What?" she'd answer, coming down from the clouds. She,

who had thrown her life out in front of him like a rug and said, My prince, take a walk.

She had simply settled in with him, a married man whom she temporarily couldn't marry. Under the cover of their bohemian life style she was able to express all her Platonic intentions: devotion, fidelity, struggle, hard work.

She didn't doubt for a second that they were forever. She didn't know how unfaithful he was.

"Ah, it doesn't matter that much," she said sadly, the first time she caught him. "We're all human. Just as long as you write."

"Wouldn't you like to take a lover?" he'd ask some nights.

She, incredulously, "Me?"

At forty-five, five years dry, if he had met Rose Addis on the street, "I say," he'd say, "I wasn't very good for you back then, was I? But back then, I wasn't very good for myself either." (He'd pronounce it "eyether.")

"How have you been?" she'd ask, always polite in a tight situation.

"I'm off the booze. Booze was my bad man, you know."

"I heard. It struck me that when I was with you, Carl, I had no idea you were an alcoholic. Even after that night when you were so loaded you pushed your hand through the windowpane."

"You were beautiful in the cab, rushing me to the hospital."

"You prayed."

They'd smile at their shared memories.

"You're doing well now," he'd say. "I see your books reviewed."

"I can't complain."

"I always knew you were the one who could write. It used to scare me."

"I think I *used* you way back then, Carl. I've thought of it often since. What I expected you to do was what I really should have expected from *me*."

He'd think, Should he try to make her — I used to live with Rose Addis — one last time.

She'd think, Should I say something real, right to his face? My only regret about you, Carl, is that with all the women you had known, with all the moaning and groaning and heaving and jabbing, with all the positions and words and gestures, cock and mouth, you never had the inclination to teach me the first thing about pleasure.

"Pleasure!" Alsatian Rose interjects abruptly. "Pleasure comes from the heart." . . .

"Why are you staring at your stomach?"

"I'm five days late."

"Five days is nothing, Rose."

"I'm never late!"

"And if you are — so what?"

Carl had taken his wife from Radcliffe and left her with two kids on relief in Somerville.

"So what? So I can't finish school, I can't work, you can't finish your book."

"Catastrophe! Catastrophe! Why, my dear Rose, do you always see so darkly?"

Carl dances out of his clothes.

"You don't give a damn!"

"If you're five days late, you don't have to fiddle with your diaphragm."

He grabs her hard, pushes her down on the mattress. "I can take you now." He thrusts into her, endlessly repeating movements and his peculiar animal sounds. The drink in him impedes conclusion.

"Oh dear," she says later, after a long scalding bath, "you didn't bring it down."

"And the male's sperm fertilizes the female's egg," Ellen had read to Rose from *Growing Up and Liking It.* (You'll like it! You'll like it!) Rose at twelve had finally asked. They are sitting at the kitchen table, mother and daughter, studying. "Just think of it, Rose. The fertilized egg is so small, you can't see it with the naked eye." Ellen points to the tip of her long polished nail. "And from that small egg, a child grows. Isn't science itself a miracle?"

"Remember, Rose." Four years later. "Remember, no matter

how careful you think you are, accidents happen. All it takes is the smallest, most minuscule drop of sperm."

The smallest, littlest, tiniest, teensy weensiest bit and WHAM!

The minuscule dynamo swam through Rose's head, year in, year out, so fast, so small, you couldn't see its tail.

"You're leaving this house," Ellen had said. "You're breaking your father's heart. You think you know what you're doing. If you get yourself in trouble, just don't come home to me."

Awake before dawn, she watches Carl's easy sleep. She puts a finger up her vagina and it comes out clear.

"You're ruining your life!"

She'd seen lives ruined.

Maureen De Lupa comes to her, washed in the cool air. She sees her in home room in Dickinson High School, 1956. She has a clean, lean beauty. The network of muscles and veins are tight in her upper arms. She smiles in her self-contained, modest way. Her hair is dark and clipped into an Italian boy. Maureen could do all the things Rose had never had to do. A multiplicity of daily chores: wash dishes, iron her own clothes, make her bed.

When she displeased her father, he took a strap to her.

How was that done? Rose wonders. She remembers the girls who came to school with welts and red eyes. There was a sense of secret shame. Did their fathers strip them bare and whip them? Rose too polite, too scared to ask.

"I'm in trouble," Maureen whispered over the phone. Rose's moral universe snowed. Getting in trouble was something Maureen De Lupa and Gil Hutchinson were too good to do.

"Only once. Only once, honest."

They were married in the church. Maureen had to leave school because she was pregnant; Gil because he had to go to work.

> *They tried to tell us we're too young,*
> *Too young to really be in love . . .*

"But they seem so happy!" Rose said at dinner. She was thinking of their tidy little apartment, their shared lives, Maureen in Gil's ex-football-playing arms.

"Wait," said Raymond.

The baby looked just like Gil. A sort of gentle blond on a strong pudgy frame.

"Gentle?" Maureen picked up. "Gil? You should know him like I do!" she said with an irony lost on a virgin. "Well, from now on I'm going to be careful. There'll be days we can and days we can't. He's not going to have me to blame if he doesn't go to night school next term. Anyway," she summarized mysteriously, as she grilled cheese sandwiches in her electric frying pan, "one's enough."

"What was it like?" Rose asks over lunch.

Maureen, sweet sixteen and a half, blue running under dark eyes: "When you're brought in, you say to yourself you'll never scream like the rest of them. I mean, at first it's not that bad. Or you think, if you gotta scream, you won't be like them and curse who did it to you.

"But when it gets bad you spill your guts out, just like the rest of them. You can't help yourself. It's like being in hell.

"No one tells you how bad it's going to be. But how can they? You can't explain the pain. No matter what a person's done, that pain is worse. I was forgiven that day. I know it deep down. No priest can tell me different. Whatever bad I've done in my life, I've paid."

Maureen on Journal Square a year later. She bumps into Rose. She's rolling Gil Jr. She has a swollen stomach, a sheepish smile, and a black eye.

By graduation, a lot of girls had to drop out. One gave herself over to the Carmelites. Rose sees her again. A notoriously promiscuous girl with a trapped light in her mild eyes. Seeing her all dressed and walking in the halls, you wouldn't know she went down. Her rebellion and her desire led to the convent door closing.

But they were the Catholic girls, Ellen's *others*.

"What happened?" Ellen repeats Rose's question. "Well, okay, you're old enough to see what can happen. The Kleins did what had to be done, then spent a fortune getting Kim to Europe. As far away from *him* as they could. Imagine, he still called! I don't know why your father doesn't fire him. I know he's just as upset as me! But all it takes is everyone saying something's right to do for him to say it's wrong."

"What *had* to be done?"

"Well . . . an abortion, that's what. What else was there to do?"

"They could have let them get married! Why didn't they? They wanted to!"

"And ruin her life? Kenny Douglas, your father's goyisher delivery boy, and a baby. Talk sense, Rose, please!"

Don't come home to me.

There was a Negro girl in high school they say brought it down with a knitting needle.

In college a friend of hers had it done without anaesthesia and almost died.

God almighty. Clamped down on a table with some grad student in math cutting her insides out.

Another, who could go home, had a therapeutic abortion.

Would two psychiatrists declare Rose Addis insane?

The phone rings, punctuating Rose's terror. Ellen's anxious voice. "I knew you'd want to know the minute we did. They made it safe to the Islands. Everything is fine. Janet just called."

"Great. Everything's just fine."

"You don't sound well."

"Mother, it's seven-thirty."

"Oh, I woke you, sorry." Intonation: *A sister's a sister from morning to night. A mother's a mother all of her life.*

In Ellen Diamond's universe a plane doesn't rise without intent to fall. That's why it is important to exercise control over every bit of life you have any power over at all.

The eensiest, weensiest, tiniest bit.

Rose is overwhelmed with a depression so violent, she doesn't even realize it's a good sign. Hanging the phone up, she bursts into tears. She sees her pale sister once more. Allowed to land safely, to tan in the tropics. She sees the knife at her sister's throat. Her own parents and the Henshes watching over the two cradles, listening to weather reports, monitoring flight patterns, making sure the neighborhood is safe, the carpeting wall-to-wall, the nest padded. Stifling her sister's life. And now, stifled hers. Pregnant by a man who would sketch while she delivered. Trapped by her body.

Aunt Adele comes up the stoop to the porch. She speaks to Etta of her daughter. "She used to say, 'Mama, why do you do so much for Papa?' (The Cherman.) 'Why don't you say no? *I'd* never do what you do for any man.' 'Ha,' I said. 'Wait. You'll see.' I remind her of it now." Adele's voice rises in triumph. "When I see her down on her *own* hands and knees, 'I told you,' I say. 'You see?!' "

"What's wrong?" Carl wakes to Rose, hysterical beside him.

"The world! We have no luck, my sister and me. We're doomed. Oh! Oh! Oh!" she screams, racked by her vision.

"Calm down, Rose," Carl pleads, shocked by her extremity.

"I'm scared. I'm in trouble. I'm doomed."

"Rose, Rose, remember the day you read to my children? How beautiful you were! You could be a wonderful mother to our child. You'll see."

"Are you crazy? When have you last seen your two children? If I have a baby, you'll leave me just like you left them. And my life will be over. Do you want me on relief like your wife?"

"It's you who frighten me," he said, caressing her. "There's something cold at your core. Something you will not share with me."

Was there?

What Alsatian Rose saw in her crystal.

What Etta clung to in the high sheen of things.

What Helen broke.

What Ellen didn't have to see to know.

"You'll leave *me*," he said. "There will be many who'll come after. They will suffer too. They no more than I will get through to you."

"Leave? You're impossible! I'm pregnant. I'm chained to you!"

"You bitch of a bourgeoise! You'll leave me. You'll run home to Daddy. He'll fix things for you. You'll run home and marry a dentist." He grabbed her in rage. Forced her onto her hands and knees and mounted her from behind.

"I'll never marry a dentist," she moaned.

He exploded within her. She was wet with his sperm and her blood.

The summer is a tropical nightmare. One night in August she sits in their apartment at the kitchen table with his three note-books in front of her.

How did she get them? He guarded them, and she was not one to pry.

She could not really distinguish the days of these last months with him. Overworked, overtired, she submitted to his odd ab-sences, his crazy scenes, and finally to the women he brought home.

"I say, why won't you join us?"

If he came in with a woman past the hour she felt safe in the streets, she'd study at the kitchen table, heat-blind to the roaches, smelling gas.

Simple solutions never occurred to her in those days — like kicking him out. She was standing sentinel over her sister's crib again, this time keeping a man alive. She was signing the marriage contract she hadn't signed, in blood.

The book, the blessed book.

She opens the first notebook. No wonder he didn't want her to see it. He hadn't written anything new in it since he had last read to her, months and months ago.

She opens the second. "Rose . . ." he pants plaintively from the mattress, where he is screwing someone else. "Why, why, won't you join us? I'm waiting, we're waiting, for *you.*" She closes the book guiltily.

She hears Zeno Beni playing the children's role in St. Augus-tine's conversion. "Take up and read! Take up and read!" Beni calls in a falsetto.

She does.

At first she doesn't understand.

It is the moment before revelation. They were making quite a bit of it in her graduate Art History class uptown. That moment

before sight, quite important to Caravaggio's painting of the conversion of St. Paul.

What she sees without seeing is the title, *The Little Black Hat,*
and then her story, painstakingly copied out, dated fragment by
fragment in Carl's deliberate schoolboy hand.

She leaves it open in front of her and goes on to the third notebook. READING NOTES is scrawled with grand intention on
the otherwise blank first page.

She leafs through the pages. A nightmare!

Where's your sense of humor, Rose?

For the first time one of those realities with a small "r" comes
to her: a man and woman can live together day by day and de-
ceive. A heavenful of weightless Platonic Ideals falls from the
skies.

An example from notebook three:

Heading underlined: *George Eliot (Mary Ann Evans, 1819–1880)*
Work Printed: DANIEL DERONDA
Written by hand: Very pertinent comments.

A whole fucking notebook of Rose's opinions on everything she's
read.

Back to notebook two.

She looks at the careful hand until she sees Washington Square.
Carl is on the grass. Reading to the next grad student he's going
to seduce, perhaps the cow now in the next room. He looks up
after dramatizing one of Rose's fragments. Roguishly, he says:
"I'm Portuguese, Irish, a bit Cherokee, you know, and, of course,
a little Jew."

"Oh my God," Rose cries.

She sees his head rising from in between the woman's fat thighs
in wet-mouthed and delighted anticipation. She feels the weight
of each notebook leaving her hand for his head.

As she heaves, she screams: "You fucking bastard! Do you
think I'm going to *screw* her for you too?"

                    ❦   ❦   ❦

Rose slept in Helen's room. The tiny maid's room behind the
bath she used as her study. From her desk she could look out over
the garage and backyard.

Late at night she'd lie in bed and hear her grandmother's breathing. It reminded her of the month after Charley's death, when she was sent next door to this room so that her grandmother would not be alone. Then as now loud moans rose and turned to brutish snores. Deep sleep seemed to liberate the hell in her grandmother's heart. Etta always woke refreshed.

On the nights when Etta's moans woke Rose, she would go to her study, set aside her school work, and write. She did short descriptions of the people she saw on the Tube and bus, snatches of dialogue overheard. Nothing complete. Fragments.

She was twenty-three. But something seemed arrested, stopped in her. She tried not to dwell on it.

She dwelled on her master's thesis. She found consolation at the New York Public, the Morgan . . . at the grand, silent places where one could think.

She was not much meant for life, she thought. Yours forever, Carl.

"I love you," he wrote her finally from Boston. "But I don't think, in your heart of hearts, you ever really did love me."

Though she didn't marry the dentist from Bayonne that he predicted.

I'll never marry, she thought, back on Clifton Avenue on her grandmother's side. Men are very bad for me.

"Just leave her alone," Raymond cautioned Ellen. "Let her come and go as she pleases."

"But why did she go next door?"

"Not one word."

"At least your mother could have told us. Just like her. I walk in one day and Rose is there."

"I've been through this before! You listen to me this time! Just don't you say a word!"

"When did I ever have a word to say around here?" she asked. She did what she did more and more often. She walked up the stairs.

Etta Addis drew a hot bath every morning. She moved along the deep-carpeted hallway, unconscious of her nudity after years of massages, milk farms, and the steam. A small puddle of flesh carrying a peach-colored towel under the softest part of her arm. She powdered herself after her bath and went downstairs in a clean peignoir. Her underclothes, nightgowns, dressing gowns, all were meticulously tasteful and clean. There was not one bit of old lady's negligence about her in 1964, when she must have been somewhere in her late seventies. The fat that gave her high blood pressure seemed to suffuse her with the glow of health. It softened the harsher aspects of her earlier, heavier-corseted days; it pampered her skin, her face. It kept all of the wrinkles where you couldn't see them.

In the kitchen she put on the coffee. Rose would wake to the comforting smell of its perking too strong.

Rose would wake and look around the room, "her" room. The stained-glass trim of the side windows, the white lace bedspread, the Chinese rugs, the fine-lined furniture. There was a picture of Helen now in the frame on the bureau. Another thing a person was allowed to exhibit once she was old. This room, in the fullness of her education, appeared to Rose like one of those pre-Raphaelite paintings done after a poem by Keats. "The Eve of St. Agnes," but with no man sneaking up the stairs.

Downstairs, her grandmother was preparing a tall white meat chicken and tomato sandwich for her to take for lunch — on Arnold bread. Next door they still used Wonder Bread, from the store.

She thought of her father and Helen being made sandwiches like this that teemed with abundance, hope, optimism, life. What went wrong?

You don't see that woman. She has all the sweet smiles for you. Boy, can she be sweet to her friends she can't do enough for. And to you. But she has another face, let me tell you.

"We all have more than one face, Mother."

"Some of us do."

"Her sweet smile," the rabbi would remember at the service so many years later. "In the midst of the deepest adversity, I still remember Etta Addis's sweet smile."

"You're up, sweetheart. Oh, you're wearing the dress. You look grand."

It was a lavender wool that Lilly had picked from her department in Bloomingdale's and mailed out on Etta's orders. The discount Etta didn't need, but if Rose hadn't time to go shopping with her, she had to rely on Lilly's taste.

"It fits like a glove. You got a good figure."

"It's comfortable," Rose allowed. With Carl out of her life, she seemed to have retired her jeans. She saw the approving light in her father's eyes.

She saw her father.

Some Mondays they went to the track together.

Ellen had made a major step in her life. She had registered as a temporary typist with an employment agency. "I was so nervous. After all, I'm so *rusty*. But I couldn't believe it. It opens your eyes, to see some of the idiots who walk in looking for a job."

Rose remembered the old days of the Normal School debate. "Teaching is something you can always fall back on," Ellen had said.

Rose pictured herself, young Jewish-doctor husband dead, two half-orphaned tots frantically reaching up to her apron-clad waist to embrace her. They topple her over. She falls backward into a classroom.

"Talk sense," Ellen said. "You'll see. Even when you have a good husband and fine children, even when you don't need to, it gives you a sense of self-confidence to know you have something to fall back on. It's a security. A satisfaction. Why, when the children don't need you anymore, you can always substitute."

Substitute? Had her mother no remembrance of *substitutes?* What did she think: Good morning, class. Jane Eyre is ill today. I'm Mrs. Goldblob from Livingston, who always listened to my mother. I'm sure we'll get along. I'm the substitute!

Substitutes were the wretched of the earth, reluctantly walking into minefields. Usually men, whose suits showed threads.

"I'd rather play canasta!"

"Don't be so smart! What I wouldn't give for your opportunities. But what do you know. The *hours*, Rose. The summers. Go learn the hard way."

Her mother had learned the hard way. Days of canasta with the girls, dinner with her mother-in-law, the jangling of the keys, the jangling of her own nerves. Rose watched her mother struggle out of the entanglements of the day. "It gives you a sense of satisfaction. The employers offer you full-time jobs on the sly."

Seated on the 99S bus, Rose watched the familiar scene of Palisades Avenue, the humble frame houses, the stores, the park that rose as a surprise and then tumbled down so that you could see New York.

The New York Public Library never ceased to amaze her. The mixture of scholars at the long tables with bums keeping warm, the sweeping aristocratic expanses and the small economies, the place for everyone, and, presenting her pass at the locked glass doors of the Berg Collection, the inner sanctum of the elite. Ten years from now the library would have all portable grandeur stripped, every small amenity vanished. She would look at the sign in the ladies' room, which warned against combing hair on the premises, and feel that this great place had become a locked razor. Or the palace after the revolution. Stripped of everything except — thank God — the books.

In 1964 she took her place in the plush seat at the center table of the Berg Collection (which would be unscathed by the purge). The letters she was working with were brought to her.

She put on the table the notebook and the sharpened pencils she was allowed. Got to work. The listener. Reading other people's mail.

Nineteenth-century mail. Postmarked, water-marked, black-edged if within a year of death. Spidery handwriting, first horizontal, then vertically crisscrossed along the sides. Early in the century, the person who got the letter paid. People receiving hatched letters; for the few pennies genteelly saved for them, they could ruin their eyes.

Rose didn't ruin hers. She had a feel for the nineteenth century the way Etta Addis's mother had a feel, from fist to shoulder, for measuring silk. If you can read the heart, you can read the hand. Particularly the Victorians. Oh, those great, brooding figures despairing over the death of God.

Now there was a concern you could sink your teeth into.

"The God Within: A Study of the Effect of German Biblical Criticism on the Work of George Eliot and Robert Browning." By Rose Addis.

She picked two optimists. She stayed away from Clough, who ran to Rome, sobbing there is no God, boo-hoo, boo-hoo; Tennyson, who fought despair with vowels and resonance; Arnold, too modern in his small self-doubts, too cautious and unproven in his sexuality. She stuck to George Eliot, the Brain, who translated volumes of complex German while still Mary Ann Evans, home nursing her father. Only after she laid him to rest did she go to London and plunge into affairs with men who used her mind. Oh, those secret days before George Henry Lewes involved her in the most respectable illicit relationship of the nineteenth century and isolated her in the country, where he got the prose flowing. Eliot, the great agnostic apostle of the Jesus within. Yet Eliot's early days came back. Near sixty, she married for the first time — a man half her age. And she outraged England. She had become by then the Queen Victoria of the Concubines. Hubby tried to kill himself on their honeymoon in Venice, but lived to write her Life. Strange Victorians. So vocal about death, closed as a coffin about sex.

Robert Browning, the man who had to be an optimist to live. How well she, Rose Addis of the great sense of humor, could fathom his fear of despair. Browning, her thesis stated, in certain key poems used the exact tenets the Germans used to prove the Bible was not written by God, to prove that man can never disprove the experience of God.

"I think you have something here," Robert Heret, her thesis adviser, said. "At least it's convoluted enough. It *sounds* like Browning."

The sons and daughters of the affluent society, Galbraith was writing in these years, no longer connected to their immigrant past, no longer needed by industry, will have the privilege of time to study. They will find homes for themselves in the universities, where they will educate others in the contemplative life, the life of the mind.

In the late seventies, when Rose would be invited to universities to lecture, she'd lunch with the Galbraithian sons and daughters of the affluent society. Talk about their crabgrass, their love affairs, their tenure disputes, their disillusionment with academia, their surburban, embittered, underpaid, paltry life of the mind. "Zeno Beni was the last humanist," she'd often say.

But even in 1964, Raymond Addis's daughter had considered Galbraith's economic Utopia soft. He was speaking like a man riding high. He thought he was seeing the future, but he was actually extending his own time. He'd have to revise *The Affluent Society*.

Had she been born in Eastern Europe, Rose believed she still would have had to use her brain to survive. Therefore, as a woman in a shtetl, she wouldn't have.

She'd have done okay in Alsace. She would have run the inn frugally, impeccably. (Sloppy herself, she was excellent in administering cleanliness.) She would have had her visions. Listened carefully. Married a New Yorker on a visit and become a fortune-teller and abortionist on Central Avenue.

But she was better off at the New York Public in that short-lived heyday of affluence. She had, at twenty-three, what the theoreticians were talking about, a life of the mind. She came into the world with it. She squinted her eyes to one side so that she could see. It was her one confidence, the realm of her salvation, her destiny. She had her father's peculiar ability to look past the horse shit, but she didn't share his perversity. What she saw, she wanted everyone to see. At the bases of her brilliance was a blessed proletarian blind spot. She didn't doubt the value of understanding. An Ellen Diamond–like assumption. An I-know-what-I-know-so-don't-tell-me.

"Get your nose out of that book!" Raymond Addis trying to save his daughter by eradicating the means of her salvation. Fulfilling his own destiny by trying to ward off catastrophe with the exact advice to bring it on.

She sat at the Berg Collection, light years away from Carl and confusion and financial responsibility, in her ivory tower, her head in the clouds, absorbed by the great questions of others, writing a thesis that in a hundred years perhaps a hundred scholars would read, fifty ignore, thirty call useful but wrong-headed, the rest misquote, and one or two see.

She sat at the Berg Collection, absorbed, soaring, alive.

Rose married a Victorian scholar.

"A professor," Ellen said. "What could be better? They'll always have something they can discuss."

"Let's hope they understand each other," Ray said. "No one else can."

They did, in fact, have everything to discuss. David Willner entered Rose's life in a clean sweep.

" 'I love your verses with all my heart, dear Miss Barrett . . .' That comes to me as the appropriate beginning of a letter to you. Your article on Browning's Higher Criticism in the fall issue of *Victorian Studies* has knocked me off my feet."

David Willner wrote that to her on Columbia University letterhead. *David Willner!*

He invited her to the Russian Tea Room for blinis. He had seen her before at the Modern Language Association meeting with Bob Heret. He had found her attractive then, but later he couldn't believe her mind.

He himself was attractive. A tall lean man, with a shock of black hair. He had a prominent nose, high cheekbones, and small slanted eyes. When David Levine caricatured him for the *New York Review of Books,* he dropped his lips and chin and accentuated his temples.

"You have *ideas,*" he told her, as if in the circles in which he traveled this was unusual. "More!" He put his fourth finger to his thumb to make the exact differentiation, leaving behind the spoon and the sour cream. "You have the *intuitions* that get *to* the ideas."

"I'm quite flattered," she answered. "But you see, I come by it dishonestly. My great-grandmother was a witch. I'm descended from innkeepers and witches with horse sense," she said, keeping her genealogy to one side.

He had a very nice laugh. Slow, quiet, full of appreciation.

He was charmed.

She was charmed.

This man was what they used to call, in front of the Y on Tuesday nights, a catch.

She felt the change come over her. She became the lady Rose Addis in her lavender dress. No more on all fours being screwed in the Village. Now the pride of the Addis family, the beautiful, the true, and the good.

"We read your *Victorian Hell Fire* in Professor Heret's seminar," she said. "I did the report. Do you know what the rumor is about you among the grad students at NYU?"

"No," he said, a bit disconcerted.

"It's rumored downtown that you delivered your Bar Mitzvah speech in Greek. One of the girls in the class is the cousin of someone who was there."

"It probably did sound like Greek," he said, with a shy smile.

"You're very modest," she said.

"I have a lot to be modest about."

"Do you?"

"Well, if you'll give me a chance, you will, unfortunately, find that out for yourself."

It was a courtship. Honest to goodness.

She went with Etta to buy clothes.

She waited for the phone to ring.

He picked her up, took her to New York, then brought her home.

They stopped at his big apartment on the West Side. He did not rush her. "I want it to be right this time," she said.

"It will always be right if it's you and I."

Always.

She looked incredulously at the love in his deep eyes.

When he won a Guggenheim, she thought she'd burst for joy.

They would spend their wedding year in England and Italy. He was going to do research on the expatriate Victorians.

"And you?" he asked at a French restaurant in the fifties. "He knows all the places," said Etta.

She looked down shyly. "I have an idea," she said. "I don't know how good it is. I don't want to do anything academic next year. I mean, except any help I can give you.

"You know the letters Elizabeth Barrett Browning sent her father after she eloped, the ones she sent on black-edged paper in mourning for his love —"

"I don't remember that *that* was the reason they were on mourning stationery."

"Well, for my purposes, it won't matter. She sent them from Italy, and even though they were black-bordered he didn't open them. He mailed them back sealed."

"I must introduce you to Jimmy Craig. He's been looking for those letters for years. He's convinced they're extant. If anyone will find them, he will — or you."

"I'm not looking for them."

"So you'll find them quicker."

She smiled. "I want to write them."

David Willner absorbed new ideas. He was shamelessly open to them, indiscriminate, unflappable. It was the whore in him.

She had broached this subject with Robert Heret and with a few other academics and had seen the light go out of their eyes.

"Write them?" Willner asked. He was excited.

"Yes, date them, put them in sequence, and then write them. *Letters to Father.* Sort of an existential historical novel."

He shook his head in delight and sealed her destiny.

"Of course I believe in women's liberation!" she'd shout one day on a talk show. "All I'm saying is that in my life, from my own personal experience, as they used to write in English composition class, in my *career,* there has always been a man. I don't recall ever having done anything completely alone, even if it might look that way today.

"Sure, sure, it could have been a woman who encouraged me," she was cornered into saying a few minutes later. But then, her father's daughter, she couldn't resist it: "— if I were gay!"

She'd one day shout. And one day she'd do things alone.

Not then. Not in 1965. If David Willner had said, "Won't that

be a bit . . . a bit *popular?"* If he had had any of the intellectual
fifties in his soul, she would have become Dr. Rose Addis. Emi-
nent Victorian (Scholar). Politic. Soothing her colleagues about
their crabgrass. Ignoring the hushed yelps of climax coming
through the thin walls of the English department offices. She'd be
called a workaholic behind her back. Tenured and still writing.
She'd have had regular pay and regular hours. Her way would
have been paved much earlier and at less expense.

"Waiter," Willner called. "Champagne."

"Letters to Her Father," he toasted, altering the title slightly.
You can't waste champagne.

After the bottle was empty he took her hands in his. "Let's go."

She always carried her diaphragm with her. "Be prepared," as
Tom Lehrer sang during her college days. She stopped at a drug
store for Koromex and then stumbled about David's big bathroom inserting it. The feel of the jelly on her fingers and the
cornstarch on the rubber lingered.

She came out in a bath towel. He was in his pajamas.

There was a lot of Jersey City in her, and even in her drunken
exhilaration she felt she was a bit too klutzy among his fine
things.

But he didn't seem to mind at all.

He took her hand and led her to his bed. She remembered being
extremely excited.

She remembered the two of them making love in the dark.

Ellen said, "Why start?"

"She asked. It's time for her to see," Ray answered.

"See what? Why drag it all up again?"

He brought a finger to his lips and exaggerated his *sssssh.*

So on a beautiful spring day, Rose and Etta and Raymond
walked slowly across a wide expanse of lawn. Etta, always on
shipboard over her short stout legs, was a bit ahead.

"Calm down, Mom. She rushes," Raymond said to Rose.
"Nothing has changed in all these years, but still she's got to rush
to see."

"You wait here," Raymond told her finally. Rose would later realize that she never saw the inside of Greystone. *What is there to see?*

> *On what wards — I walked there later, oft —*
> *old catatonic ladies, grey as cloud or ash or walls — sit*
> *crooning over floorspace — Chairs — and the wrinkled hags*
> *acreep, accusing . . .*

Ginsberg didn't see anyone propped on *The Meaning of Meaning.*

"You wait here," Raymond repeated. "If we're lucky, *maybe* she'll come out. And remember what I told you. No matter what you expect, there's nothing much to see."

Rose sat on the bench in the kingdom of the mad and watched her winded father follow her winded grandmother into the big building. She waited for the ghost of the past. Helen. The person she, in bravado, had said in Boston she would not turn out to be. She had been right. But only now, dressed in trousseau clothes, life with David stretching out in front of her as endless and ordered as the continent she was going to see, did she believe it.

In her light orange dress on the bench amid the lime-green grass, under the shining blue sky, she felt buoyed by the springtime of her own rationality and by her aesthetic sense, which more and more put things into perspective.

She saw them from a distance. They walked out the door, Ray on one side, Etta on the other. In between a woman who seemed as old as Etta, just as fat, a little taller. Slowly, they approached her. Rose stood up. Helen and Etta sat on the bench; she and her father on chairs.

"This is Rose, Helen," Raymond said in the loud, emphatic voice of a tourist speaking English to a native, of a man speaking to the deaf. "Rose wanted to meet you. She's my older daughter. She's smart. She writes. She writes the way you used to play the piano. Remember?"

The old woman had stark white hair like Charley, small eyes

like Etta, a bloated face, and white hairs on her chin. The eyes were not empty. Way back in them there seemed to be something that could say, the way Lilly could, and Etta, Ray, and Rose could too, "Well?"

Helen was wearing a gray housecoat and had slippers on. Over her white socks her swollen legs were bruised. You could see a woman like this sitting on a stoop on Prospect Street, staring ahead. Rocking, rocking, like Helen.

"This is my daughter Rose," Raymond repeated.

Helen said, "Oh."

"She's just got her master's degree. She's getting — soon she's going to Europe."

"Hello," Rose said.

"What's that bruise on your foot, Helen? It's new?" Ray asked, irritated by it.

Helen turned from Rose and looked secretively down at the bench. Very slowly she lifted a hand and began to rub her mother's pocketbook as she rocked.

"You like it?" Etta asked.

Helen rubbed it for a long time. They all watched, intently.

"What?" Ray asked, seeing his sister's lips move.

Helen said, "Very pretty."

"It's a good one," Etta answered.

They went for a little walk. Raymond got to the water fountain. He had his pills in his hand when Helen, all by herself, walked over.

"What?" he asked. "You want a drink? Sure. Sure. Go ahead. I'll hold it for you." She bent down over the spout, exposing the backs of her sore and varicosed legs.

Then Ray and Etta took her back in. When they came out, Ray was smiling.

"Boy, it must have been Rose being here, hah, Mom? See how interested she was."

"Why, Daddy, she wasn't at all interested."

"She certainly was," said Etta. "She liked you. She stayed out a long time. Ray, did you see the way she looked at Rose?"

"I sure did." Then he laughed. It was a very nice laugh. It was the laugh of a boy. "Hey, Mom, she walked right up to me by the fountain and you know what she said? 'Oh, Ray.' Real annoyed like. 'Oh, Ray,' she said, 'you still always have to be first!' I couldn't believe my ears. That's more than she's said in years. 'Oh, Ray,'" he imitated, "'you still always have to be first!'" He laughed again. "Where'd she ever come up with that?"

❧ ❧ ❧

Rose's wedding was Etta's last affair. The house was open. The liquor was out, as in Charley's day, and all the silver gleamed.

Walking downstairs early that morning in September, Rose felt she was walking into the past as well as the future. The present was not on her mind.

"Ah, your grandmother's just a peasant with money," more than one friend would say through the years. She was one of nature's aristocrats to Rose. Oh, the palaces, the country homes, the exquisite art Rose was soon to see. Never would she look at a Gobelin tapestry, an inlaid table, or an eccentrically spectacular room without thinking: Here is something Nana could really appreciate so much more than I. She sent postcards.

The house, with the fresh autumn flowers run through it, as brisk and sparkling as the day, and with Etta already ordering big men around, seemed to grow young again and to fit into Raymond's tales of plenty. The living room and dining room had nothing of the immensity of royalty. But they were the unerring display of one undaunted imagination.

The concert grand had long since been moved next door. Her mother had tried to get Rose to take Popular on it, really believing it would make her popular! Janet played. Today someone professional would come to make music — to get the crush from the reception to circulate next door.

Rose sat for a moment on the landing, facing the fireplace. She wore the dark peach satin nightgown and peignoir that Aunt Lilly had sent her from Bloomingdale's. With her black hair pulled into a chignon and her face fuller now and expectant, she fitted among the orientals and the chimney pieces.

Backward in time, almost like sliding down the mahogany banister the way Janet used to, she came to earlier autumns. She and Etta bumping into all the Jewish girls on the Square at all the better shops. The season of the High Holy Days. Shopping for outfits. To be prepared for the crush outside of the temple during the Days of Awe.

Everyone so smart. Not like shiksas in their Sunday hats. Smart. The perfumes, the furs, the suits. How can you distinguish money from money? And yet when it was time for that noisy and raucous crowd to pay lip service to the occasion that bound them, there was a special stir when the Addis family walked into the temple where they owned a window. Charles and Etta leading the way, six tickets always, to their eighth-row-center seats. The rabbi's wife, a lady and a star of the legitimate stage, turning around respectfully to greet them. That feeling of special power rose up pleasurably in Rose again.

The Day of Atonement. Then afterward breaking fast at the Addises'. All the old friends driving in from their suburban temples as well as the finer types from Temple Israel. The house on Rose's wedding day hadn't looked like this since the forties, the early fifties, when Charles was alive and Raymond wasn't sick. All the gentlemen in their good dark suits served their whiskey by the portable bar. Scotch and water and a little ice. These men didn't drink gin and vodka and bourbon and rye. "What will you have, doctor?" Scotch and water, a little ice.

She could remember her father among the people of his youth. Something kindled in his eyes. He wasn't nasty when he talked. He was very polite. Her mother? Where would she be? Somewhere inconspicuous. Not another Diamond there.

The Day of Atonement. The congregation rises to recite their sins. Ellen Diamond turns to Rose and Janet and whispers conspiratorially, "I move my lips like the others. But going down this list" (she points to the prayer book) "there's not a thing here that I do. I have nothing to be forgiven for."

On her wedding day, Rose smiles, as she fits into the family tradition. Later she will remember: O Mother, Mother; then atone for that. Atone for disappearing in your mother-in-law's living room, for keeping up a smile, for not speaking your mind. Atone for all the goodness in your heart that you transplanted into the hearts of sisters. Atone for expecting them to do as you, take those hearts and hide. Atone, Mother, for not knowing sin. Atone for being faithful to Daddy. Atone for not knowing that you did not know. Atone for not taking any one of the china serving pieces now in my possession and throwing it straight at Etta Addis's antique fireplace mirror or at her head. Mother, atone on the next Day of Atonement!

Etta Addis came into the living room. "Darling, you're up!"

"Everything looks so beautiful, Nana."

Etta smiled. She was not flustered. At seventy-something she could still give orders, expecting to be obeyed. She could take a few minutes to look at her granddaughter without kibbitzing her to rush. A party came naturally to her. Who was she, with her plump body and nothing much to say, to get flustered? The center of attraction? Phooey! Parties emanated from her. Spread from her kitchen, from her enthusiasm, from her eye. She knew how to make a good time.

And today she was inspired by beauty, by Helen! Helen! Ellen! Oh, I mean, Rose! Rose!

"You're beautiful," Etta answered. "What a day!"

What day for Etta Addis? September 1965? V-Day! This was the wedding she had longed all her life to give.

She looked at her granddaughter as if Bea Mann were with her, displaying a cloisonné piece that without Bea's skill you couldn't buy for love or money.

Her beautiful talented granddaughter, who she used to bribe the nurse to hold and hug and kiss, was marrying a fine type.

All the aspirations of Etta Addis's life were redeemed. All of them! You want to live to eighty- or ninety-something? Then you have to know this trick — *Be oblivious, care for nothing and no one but yourself.*

No, no! Be fair, Ellen.

Have moments! Have moments beyond death. Times when your daughter doesn't rock, tick-tock, tick-tock. When your son's not picking his scabs. When your blood flows and energy courses through you. When you see everything you've always believed in in front of your eyes.

Grab these moments! Run with them! Quick! Don't think. Take what you can have.

Etta looked at her granddaughter. Everything is in front of her once more.

So Rose was married in her grandmother's living room at a service for the immediate family and then watched the house fill up with other relatives and many friends.

The conversations ranged from the chicken liver to Beckett and Mondrian. Buddy sought out art historians to find out how much his horse prints were worth — now and after the guy died. He was no more outlandish than an ordinary collecter, but Janet rolled her eyes.

Lilly conversed with David.

Raymond offered a toast to the bride and groom. He pulled out this amenity as if time hadn't touched it. Look, this was another thing that, if he wanted to, he knew how to do. "To Rose and David," he started brashly, and, then, glass high, quiet descending, he changed his tone. "A happy, healthy future together," he said. He looked around carefully and then at them. "You got a good start from your grandmother's house here. Couldn't ask for better. May all good things come from today."

"What were Aunt Lilly and you so close about?" Rose asked David.

"She was telling me all about you. Things I didn't know. How beautiful you are and how you've always been smart."

"And . . . ?"

"And . . . ?"

"Come on, honey. With Aunt Lilly there's always a zinger."

"It was more like a pass," David answered. With a serious look, he embraced her and whispered in her ear, "She said you reminded her of her when she was younger and that I was the type of fellow she could have had if only she'd used her head."

"That's my aunt. She can't come to a wedding without getting half-married herself."

"You got a Somebody there," Aunt Lilly told Rose.

Rose changed into her traveling suit. She checked in her shoulder bag — passport, traveler's checks, plane tickets. They'd spend the first night of their marriage in the air. Tomorrow this time would be a different time and they would be in London.

She picked up her trench coat and looked at herself in the mirror. There was a knock at the door. "Rose?"

"Janet? Come in."

"You look great."

"Think so?"

"I just wanted to say good-bye. I hope you have a wonderful year."

"Janet!"

They put their arms around each other and kissed. "Now you come and visit, Janet. You and Buddy. I'm going to miss you a lot."

"I'm going to miss you. You know, it was really a beautiful wedding."

"I don't know. I sort of missed the Chopin."

"Speaking of Chopin . . ." Janet went over to the picture of Helen. "You say she doesn't look like this anymore."

"You should go with them yourself some Sunday and see." Janet shrugged. *"Her* wedding must have been something."

"Aunt Lilly says she was an angel draped in a cloud."

"Are we angels draped in clouds?" Janet asked.

They looked at each other. Then Rose turned her eyes to the room. "Well, this is good-bye to 'my' room. It has kept me safe and sound and sane for a year and a half."

She looked at the bed that she had slept in, dreamed in, masturbated in. It looked unperturbed. It kept secrets well under its beautiful hand-crocheted white covering.

The sisters didn't stand on ceremony. They walked down the stairs together.

MONKEY MAN

THE HOUSE on Clifton Avenue was sold in 1966. "The stairs are no good for either of us, Ray," Etta Addis said one night at dinner.

Ray did not need to answer. He was having all his teeth out, two at a time. "Get 'em out and put in choppers!" That was his answer to more bridgework. He had had enough. Had suffered for his sweet tooth and his chemistry all of his life.

When he did speak, it was from behind a napkin. Why bother now? His mother often threw into the silence of the three of them sitting there her latest calculation about her "headache," this house that had grown so big for them. "She just drops her stupid remarks out of thin air," Ellen would say. Though any comment any of them volunteered at dinner appeared to be a non sequitur, coming as it did from the spaces in which they avoided each other, each hoarding a precious and well-guarded store.

Etta, however, was naturally the most loquacious. She would sit on her side of the house regaling poor Lilly, who still worked, with the rich widow's plight: someday, if things kept up as they were, Etta Addis might have to dip into capital.

At dinner, sporadically, she dropped bills, high blood pressure, upkeep.

But this night Raymond noticed that his mother's face was flushed and that her eyes had narrowed ruthlessly. Her breast heaved and her breath came short and hard. It was as if she had suddenly landed at the table, pulling him, as she did, from his own flight. She was about to excite herself. He was about to warn her. But she was too quick for him.

"I've listed with Ruby on Central Avenue. I'm gonna sell."

Raymond rubbed his tongue against the raw beef of his gums. He tasted blood.

He'd taste it again, in the dark of night. When a stab of angina made him sit up against his pillows. While his dentures were in the bathroom, smiling in a glass.

His mother was like the stranger he had once read about in grade school. Who arrives at the inn, tells a tale by the fire, and in the chill of the morning, before anyone else is up, departs.

"Wait for me!" screams Raymond's heart. "Wait!"

He glances at Ellen, who has come down to a sock in the mouth. Her "mistake" has long since become the condition of her life. Right now, she's stunned.

"Big deal," he'll have to answer in the future. "Big deal," when she reminds him his own mother kicked him out of his own house. Not that it wasn't a blessing in disguise.

"Big deal" comes over his face now as he picks up his napkin. "How much you asking?"

"I want to give you a share. It'll draw interest. You'll see."

"That's not what I asked!" he whistles nastily.

"Ruby says we can get twenty-five."

"Thirty-five!" Ray says, pointing his napkin at her. "You're always in a rush, aren't you? You tell that jerk Ruby your son says thirty-five and not one cent less!"

"Wh*aaaaaaa*t are you worrying for?" he'll tell his wife later. "Who'd ever come up with thirty-five for this old place?"

"Maybe we coulda got forty," he'd say when it was too late. Each year he'd add another ten.

Rose returned from Europe to the flurry of activity.

"So you've finished a book," her grandmother found time to say. "Then I'll see you on TV."

Etta glued to the set. Ellen rolling her eyes.

Liberace in tux at his sleek black Cadillac of a piano. A candelabrum on its top.

Liberace's Mom. His brother George.

Really, Motherrrr, how can you watch that man? Can't you see what he's taking you, what he's taking the whole country for?

Jeweled fingers. Ivory keys.

"Oh, Ellen, how he can play!"

Letters to Her Father did not get published. Trade publishers suggested university presses, and university presses suggested trade.

"But it's good," Rose moaned.

"Too good," raged David.

"We cannot get up sufficient enthusiasm," said the letters.

It would be a long time before Rose Addis would be asked if she wrote in pencil or pen, on yellow-lined paper or a machine. Whether she worked every day and how many hours and how did she think all that stuff up and were any of the characters people she had known.

She would have years of solitary: pencil in hand, eyes going over the intricate pattern of Etta Addis's former dining room rug.

The pattern in the rug. Sometimes she'd think of Henry James. He'd always be esteemed by the intelligentsia of northern New Jersey. He put all the passion of his regulated life into form. He never made an ass of himself at a dinner party. His family called him Angel. Fellow American! His perfect life deserved his perfect art.

He compressed everything onto a page.

Rose attempted to compress everything onto a page.

She believed if anything dripped over the sides, she was lost. She was wrong.

But art doesn't come from being right. It comes from having something to say.

In the sixties, Europe itself still had something to say. She went to it American, came back with a slant on American life, wearing a dress and a stylish babushka.

Janet was still in jeans. And though Laura could not yet talk, she was consulted on decisions.

"You're so damn *American*," Rose said.

"What're you, Chinese?"

They were sitting on Etta's couch, looking in at the disheveled riches laid out on the dining room table.

"Oh shit," said Janet, knowing what they were in for.

"I couldn't write this morning," said Rose, meaning, oh shit.

That's the way she judged a day. By what she wrote and what she got in the mail. Her intensity was like a pair of blinders, veering her straight. Only success would give her the time to look back to the side of the road and wonder. (So what else is new in the etymology of ambition?)

She was a third-generation immigrant. She had no way of separating who she was from what she wanted to become.

She wanted to redeem the past by becoming a Popcorn.

Her genes were right. In them were a mad woman tinkling the keys and a sane woman spreading the cards.

Only, for a long time, she had her father's luck.

Her father, her mother, what had their limited experiences taught them? Don't-run-you'll-sweat. Don't-talk-you'll-end-up-in-front-of-McCarthy. They fitted into their times. Don't expect what other people get.

Sometimes the others seemed to get it simply by a smile. But Raymond, on principle, would never smile.

Oh the *assumption* of success. For years Rose could not fully accept it. That marvelously uncomplicated assurance that with a smile and a handshake and enormous energy a project had a better-than-even chance of turning out good. That a person could discount the possibility of disaster and catastrophe that lurks in every act without giving himself a canary.

Oh the blessed simple-mindedness of a Popcorn, gracefully skating on thin ice.

Zeno Beni lecturing on the Bildungsroman, the novel of development. Portrait of the Artist as a Young Man.

What kind of novel of development could you write about a woman? — David supported me. I sat at my desk and wrote — Rose believed that as a form the Bildungsroman belonged to men and Germans.

It would not occur to her that through the years she sat and wrote with an audience of David, Janet, and a poet-friend, her determination and the lust of her ambition were her Bildungsroman. Zeno Beni lectured on James Joyce's Stephen Dedalus, the artist-hero.

Dublin 1904

Trieste 1914

Joyce dated his book. The century began in a flurry of artists' wings.

It would not occur to her then that silently and secretly she was fitting into her generation. Hers was not the generation of the garret, of La Bohème. And more and more, those who now expatriated themselves for the muse, like Joyce, had less and less to say. If God died in the nineteenth century, the glorification of the artist died by the middle of the twentieth.

Her father took the spiteful view of the predicament of his times. We all come from monkeys, so there! But he took no responsibility for what we are left with. No saints. No artist-heroes. Only people.

Zeno Beni would accept none of the crasser aspects of human development. He saw the further decline of Western civilization in Rose's later appearances on TV. Etta Addis, had she lived, would have seen that her granddaughter was a writer.

Rose saw, by the time she was promoted as a Jewish writer — "You?" Ellen howled — she was even less a Jew. She was an American. She had something to say and many things she wanted to do. Zeno Beni, Plato, Goethe and the nineteenth century aside, there was only one place and one time, here and now.

But this comes later. In Etta Addis's living room she is staring out at the dining room rug, which will soon be in her study. "At least it's not the family jewels again," Janet said.

The one gold piece Rose had really wanted was her great-grandmother's gold watch with their shared initials.

When she and David toured Italy, she had left the watch rolled up in a sock in London. It was still there when they returned to their looted apartment. She was so relieved that it took her a few days to realize she had lost most of the jewelry that Etta had given her. Or did David realize it first? So much for protecting yourself from the thieves of Naples.

All the beautiful things of this world. Sought after, worked for, paid for, desired, stolen, bought back at flea markets, auctions, on the black market, in stores. She really wanted to hold on to her great-grandmother's watch. It caused her anxiety to realize she probably wouldn't get through life with it. Someone would come and take it away.

Where are Etta Addis's gold-link bracelets, matching necklace and gold-ball earrings today?

Janet lost things. Left them around in the rubble she accumulated. Probably dusted them right off bureaus when she occasionally got up a blast of energy and cleaned.

One thing about these sisters. They'd never haggle over a will. "It doesn't seem right," Rose would say some years later. "It's almost irresponsible, the way you disregard things." Of course she wasn't talking about *things* but the principle. She'd been to Europe many times by then and seen objects weightier than their gleam.

And yet for Rose as well as Janet, the value of money was dreamlike. After all, the Addises had been rich during the Depression. Random history had kept her family, even in bad days, from being cheap. To Raymond money was a moral lesson. Now you have it, now you don't. Ellen said as long as you're healthy.

And no amount of money can make you wise.

Rose herself was always at the two-dollar window taking a stab.

Eventually she'd write about people who knew a lot about money.

The day on which Rose would philosophize on Janet's cavalier attitude toward things, Janet would be sitting in her big apartment overlooking Central Park. She'd be literally surrounded by neglected conveniences. The only similarity between Buddy and the later men in Janet's life would be that they all seemed to come to her with updated versions of kings' ransoms. They'd set up hi-fis and video recorders and dehumidifiers all around her and she'd ignore.

This was the kid who'd been cute. In jeans, as in her tomboy days, and no make-up, and the cut-the-shit Raymond look in her uncommitted eyes, she was irresistible to high-rollers, to men who had a lot of ambition, not a few hang-ups, and who found it hard to relax.

Janet was relaxed.

She wasn't after anything.

She'd find by the time she was thirty a new reference for her old preference, the bed.

She *looked* like somebody's mistress. Yet though she lived with a man who could afford to keep her, she kept herself. She'd be damned if she'd get married again. After she left Buddy, she went back to school and became a masseuse.

Neither Ellen nor Raymond could say the word.

Ellen said she went to business.

Raymond said nothing.

Their daughter put her hands on people's bodies.

Actually, she became a sort of Bea Mann of her field. Fashionable. She jammed her portable equipment into her car three long days a week. Zoomed around town from penthouse to brownstone. Never dropped a name. Relaxing famous flesh.

Janet hadn't asked for the things she neglected, so Rose's criticism surprised her. "Look who's talking about the value of things," Janet would say to her sister. "Why, you live so sparsely you don't even have a TV."

"But if I had one I'd take care of it."

"Why don't you take the Sony we're not using" (it was stashed with the bicycles in the third bath). "It'll give you something to dust."

"Smartass!"

"Come on, Rose. Have you forgotten your upbringing? 'Don't cry over anything that won't cry over you.' "

A pair of silver grape shears with clusters of silver grapes affixed to the handles could not enjoy Etta Addis. But that day on Clifton Avenue when she had the sisters in to divide, could she enjoy them!

Her twenty-fifth wedding anniversary had supplied her with more silver utensils than there were purposes. In the silver flat-

ware Rose finally took there are a dozen spoon-shaped implements
with pronged forklike edges. Grapefruit? Melon? Ice-cream cake?
What the hell was the Idea the craftsman was trying to imitate?

They were in for it that afternoon.

"David would like this," Etta said of the Dresden porcelain.
And indeed he would.

And the hand-stitched tablecloths and the lace tablecloths,
either one of the sets of extra dishes, and all the silver. The lamps,
the needlepoint, the furniture they didn't make anymore. The oriental rugs. What was there not to like?

The relish in her grandmother's eyes?

It's disgusting the way she drools over things.

"Aren't these shears beautiful?" Etta ogling the *Ding an sich.*
"Why won't you girls speak up. Take!"

"Now don't get excited, Nana," Rose said, trying *not* to sound
like Raymond.

Janet said, "These are your things. You can take the grape
shears with you. They can still be yours to enjoy."

"But I want you to enjoy *now.* I can't live forever," Etta Addis
said. She paused. *"Can I?"*

"You have many, many good and healthy years ahead of you,"
Rose said.

She had.

Only in the last months of Etta's life, and then, fully, after her
death, did Rose fathom what was hushed up by her grandmother's prodigious vitality. Of all the people Rose had ever
known, her grandmother, all through her life, had been the most
afraid to die.

Maybe if she could have gone like an Eygptian.

"Now, Rose, these boxes and rugs are for you — and Janet,
here are the cartons I've marked for you — and those things over
there, I got them all wrapped up good in Saran Wrap now, but
when the time comes, those are for *me.* You'll find instructions on
how everything should be placed in the tomb. Rose, *you* take care
of this. Please, please don't leave it to your father to mess up."

But to go like a Jew.

At least not like the old days, in a white shroud and pine box.

The Addises had bought a prime plot years ago. "Plenty of room for all of us," Raymond would say. A choice plot and a well-cushioned, hermetically sealed metal coffin. At least.

But these meager trappings could not blind Etta Addis. The day her granddaughters divided up, a few months before she left Clifton Avenue forever, she was aware of it as always. Even under the thrill of pulling out all her things, telling their stories one more time, and then passing them on to flesh and blood. Even while imagining their immortality in new surroundings, where she could inquire after them. She saw it as clear as the cartons she was packing. But you didn't pay specific attention to it any more than you did to a plain cardboard box.

Etta Addis would leave the earth the way she came to it — a pauper.

❧ ❧ ❧

Ellen and Raymond's first years at the Jersey Towers were idyllic. What price could you put on privacy, Ellen would often say. What price on a girl who comes once a week, and for dinner good hamburger from the store or a quiet barbeque chicken.

Raymond gained some weight. In the pictures of that period, his face seems fuller. He came dangerously close to a smile with his mouth full of undecayable white choppers. It was not until 1971 that he had his second heart attack.

Etta moved to a furnished one-and-a-half with a view of Lincoln Park. She tipped the janitor to get rid of most of the furniture and replaced it with her own. She was pleased by the wall-to-wall, indoor, outdoor carpeting that they'd shampoo for you on request, and by the three vents above her miniatures of Napoleon and Josephine, which blew in hot air in the winter and cold in the summer without a thought from her.

Her dressing room–toilet smelling of powders and good soaps, her stand-up kitchen with its miniature fridge, her view of Honest Abe sitting in Lincoln Park and the girls from the best Catholic families being structured by the nuns, spoke to her. Even the small toaster that Rose gave her, small enough to fit on the counter, popped up with "You're free! You're free!"

As were Ellen and Ray.

From the Jersey Towers you had to walk two windy blocks to a bus. From the Berkowitz Apartments you walked out the door. On a good day you sat on a bench. If it snowed you called Mahoney the robber to deliver. A pleasure for a few pennies. And if you didn't have taste and energy, like Etta, you didn't have to lift a finger to fix your place up. The Berkowitz was filled with old ladies.

"Kvetch, kvetch," Etta would say. " 'My son never calls.' 'I got a no-good daughter.' 'I got a pain here, I got a pain there.' 'Can you help me with my insulin shot?' 'Can you pluck a hair from my chin?' It's amazing what strangers will tell you on a bench. It's gotten so some days I stay in with the conditioner rather than go out."

The area was safe. The riots on Jackson Avenue never got as far as here. That boarded-up, bombed-out stretch became Martin Luther King Jr. Drive, to parallel Etta's Boulevard, which became Kennedy. During the many years of Etta's residence, only one woman, on the third floor — Irish, "but real lace curtain, you should have seen her things" — got murdered walking down the street. In broad daylight a man took a hatchet from a shopping bag and split her up. But that was an aberration, less ominous than it would appear. He was white.

Still, old Dirty City, corrupt and alive, was changing. It was turning into something you heard a lot about on TV, something that sounded as stark as one of those defoliated jungles they also talked about — an "inner city."

Even the Bergen section was going. In the big old apartment houses that had once had a lavish air, they'd take anything that wasn't chained down in the lobby.

So they chained things down.

No wonder people with businesses holed up at the Jersey Towers. No wonder old ladies ran to pay for other people's furniture in the well-maintained Berkowitz.

This was the type of place a successful son whose mother wouldn't fly would send his mother.

Etta sent herself.

She knew what each age demanded. Though she often led, she never parted from what Raymond called the sheep.

Naturally *her* son gave advice.

"For the same price you coulda had a real spread at the Duncan Arms and had a place for some of your furniture."

Him. When had he last been to the Duncan Arms? Had he seen its cavernous lobby picked bare but for one tattered couch shackled to the past?

Rose Addis thought all the efficiencies must be as bright and airy as Etta's. Until she stayed at the Berkowitz, in the apartment of one of Etta's friends who was in Miami.

Rose had come back from England in 1971 to visit her father, once he was out of the hospital. She had wanted to come on the news of his attack. But that would have scared him.

So she waited.

Her New York apartment had been sublet for the year of David's new grant. And she hadn't wanted to stay at Janet's with Buddy and little Laura around. "I vant to be alone."

Sadie's old lady's room pointed a finger at her. Better to land up like this?

Why did Rose vant to be alone?

She regretted by then that she hadn't spent the year and a half after she walked out on Carl by herself.

She hadn't been afraid of being *alone.*

She had been afraid of the next rap on the door.

Still, she must have done the right thing. For she had ended up with a wonderful man and a wonderful life.

Sadie's room had green walls and dormitory furniture and an odor of must. Till then she thought her grandmother's ivory walls, which she had paid extra for, had simply been included.

There were cigarette burns in Sadie's sheets and used matches interwoven in the pile of the uncared-for carpeting. There was a general uncleanliness about the place, beyond the surface that Etta had paid to have scrubbed. Secret dirt you had to live with to acknowledge. It spoke of a pained hip or shoulder, a cataract, a loss, a daily malaise. This is what we come to in the end, said the room. Have a drink, said the liquor in the closet.

This is what happens, thought Rose, if you let things spill over.

"I'm the one who almost killed him this time," Janet had said, driving Rose in from the airport.

"What did you do?" Rose asked.

"I'm seeing a shrink."

"What??"

"Now don't have a heart attack."

"Very funny," Rose said, looking at her sister behind the wheel. In profile the cast of Janet's face was hard. As if there were certain things in her life she would not listen to reason about and reconsider. "What's wrong, Janet?"

Janet shrugged.

"I'm surprised you'd tell Daddy."

"Me? Do I look like the type who'd confide in your father? 'Hi, Dad, I'm coo-coo too?' "

"Oh."

"That's right. *Buddy.* He's like a sieve. In fact, the only way you have of knowing anything has gone in his head at all is if it comes out. I warned him. But he couldn't keep his trap shut."

Janet's life was spilling over.

Still, Janet *had* married Buddy. They had a child. She had made her bed . . .

Now lie in it? thought Rose, stretching in Sadie's. She was up at dawn. Jet lag. Etta would be up too. Age.

The transience of American life is something she discussed with close expatriate friends when she visited them in Bath. Flitting around the world had made them steady. After all, there was a *way* to do things. There were *forms.*

"She don't feed him right," said Etta, setting up breakfast on her bridge table for Rose at six-thirty. Ellen now had a full-time job.

"Yesterday I saw that he ate, Nana."

"I sent him over some grand chopped liver I had left from my game. Along with some stuffed cabbage. Not a word."

"Nana, he does not eat chopped liver and he shouldn't eat stuffed cabbage. Too rich."

"Too rich? I don't put in a speck of salt."

Etta sat well-dressed and rosy in the pretty efficiency she had
spent money on. *As if she'd live forever* (*not that I'd put it past her*),
said Ellen.

Can I?

She smiled at Rose, who could see in the center of her lively
eyes the points of her pupils that were blind to her son.

She had raised Raymond. Catered to his whims. Knew his perversities.

What else was there to do? Tell him, That's right, Ray, black is
white?

There was nothing wrong with Etta Addis's chopped liver.

Etta sat like a short, ample, and big-breasted goddess in armor.
She reminded Rose of a fresco in a small room. Piled around her
in her niche were her brightly painted attributes. Each thing ac-
crued had special importance, though the exact allegory went un-
studied on a minor ceiling.

There was not a rent, not a cigarette burn on the surface. And
around Etta Addis's heart there was enough fat to wrap secrets —
enough to kill a man.

"She don't feed him right," repeated her grandmother, serving
Rose's sunnyside eggs at the bridge table where she also played.
"He needs to be built up. He's thin as a rail."

He was.

Yesterday Raymond had dozed so often in his chair, his legs on
his footstool, that Rose had a lot of time to study his hands over
the afghan. Long delicate bones delineated each finger. Shone
through luminously like his eyes, when he woke, piercing out of
his ashen, emaciated head. When he opened his mouth, indepen-
dent of meaning, an oversized set of choppers grinned.

Today when she opened the door with her own keys and entered the vestibule, she was surprised to see him far down in the
living room, awake. He sat in an unaccustomed chair, his back
braving the draft and the view of New York. As she came closer,
she saw the kindling of hope in his eyes. There he was, a burning
specter covered by a *Barretts of Wimpole Street* afghan Etta had
knitted years ago after seeing the play. How d'ya like *these* apples?
his eyes seemed to say, as if he and his daughter were sharing a

joke. You had to be familiar with chronic illness to get it. Raymond Addis only *looked* dead.

He put a long, thin, ivory hand up, held it there, as if he was an old Pope. The gesture was self-conscious. He presented himself, invalid that he was, as an animated memento mori. There was someone else in the room.

"This guy waited to see you, Rose," he mumbled.

A big man stood up. She saw the uniform first. "Yes, officer," her father would say when forced to the side of the road.

She would look down. In her whole life it had never seemed necessary to look at a cop. Till now.

"Hello, Rose. Remember me?"

"My God!" she said. She had just walked into one of her recurring dreams. She's at a fashionable restaurant, at a party, in a crowded plane, being greeted by the stranger who knew her all along. "Kenny Douglas!"

"Told yah she'd remember, Ray!" In his wide smile she noticed that the one thing that had been at all unsightly about him, a stupid space between his two front teeth, had been fixed. Her father's old delivery boy took care of himself.

She could have been sixteen again. That's how sorry she felt for Kim Klein.

"He visits me," Ray said, as if exposing a secret life.

"You're doin' much better. A definite improvement since I saw you last week, believe me."

"I'll live," said Ray.

"He'll live," said Rose.

Kenny smiled quickly. "How're things in London?" he asked.

"Oh, all right," she answered. "And with you?"

"Oh, all right," he repeated. "I guess we're in the same boat."

"Why did you say that?" she asked him early the next morning.

"A girl as smart and pretty as you gets out of this damn city as far as London and things are only just all right? Something's gotta be wrong."

"Why in the same boat?"

He took a deep breath, as he did when he lifted weights, and then let it out. He didn't talk for a while, just lay there with her in Sadie's dissipated room, tracing the crack in her ass with his finger. "We don't have what we want," he answered.

"Not even at this moment?" she asked, optimist as always.

He stopped tracing and began to pet her. The first night they were together they made love time and time again.

Later she would say that the most intense moments in life are not fit for hard covers. "Pure paperback original," she'd say.

"Don't we have what we want at this moment?" she whispered again.

He could have been Zeno Beni doing *Faust*. He said, "This moment won't last."

In her father's living room, Ray said as if he were bragging, "Kenny's gonna be made a detective soon."

"I'll be out of these," he said, pointing to himself and sitting down. "But I'll still keep an eye on your store."

"Don't do me any favors," Ray said, seeming to gain strength as he pointed a thin finger. "They see you trying my door in regular clothes and they'll shoot you dead."

"I guess a detective can take care of himself," Rose said.

"Wiseacre, don't give me lessons! Or if you are . . . it's time for my phenobarb. How's about my phenobarb first?"

After she gave him his pills, Kenny made his move. "I gotta get goin'. Pick up my partner. Rose, want to walk down with me? I'll show you my squad car."

They smiled, each remembering the Addis delivery truck as if it were yesterday. "How can I resist?"

"You better get back here quick," Ray growled.

They sat in the patrol car in the parking lot looking out to the skyline of New York.

"History repeats itself," Kenny said.

One night on Clifton Avenue they had sat together in the Addis delivery truck.

"Where the hell's your common sense?" Ray had sputtered at midnight. "Your mother wouldn't let me go out there and drag you in. But I shoulda!"

"We were *talking*."

"Where the hell does a girl like you get off having something to say to him?"

"He's been through hell."

"I'll fire him this time! You just see if I don't."

"I won't sit out with him, I won't talk to him. Honest!" sobbed Rose.

"It's funny," she said to Kenny in the patrol car. "I haven't thought about that night we talked for years. But at this moment, it's like yesterday."

"It would be nice to talk again to somebody who understands."

"Why not?"

That night they sat in a bar in Bayonne.

"If any of the guys drop by, they'll think I have a girlfriend." He was dressed up as if he had one.

He was myopic. The few men in her life that she had considered very beautiful were myopic. Did myopia develop from staring at a glittering reflection or trying not to?

When he faced her, there was still something open and boyish in his blunt eyes, in his smile, in the cleft of his chin. In profile, though, when he raised his drink and stared beyond her, she saw the toughness of his jaw and the quiver of his throat when he swallowed.

"Do you ever think of Kim?" Rose asked as naturally as if they were in the delivery truck. Then she surprised herself by adding, "The last time I really thought about her was eight years ago, when I mistakenly thought I was knocked up."

"Good a reason as any. I thought about her when Ray told me you were coming home. I don't know what it was about you Jewish girls. So quick and smart."

"We were supposed to be good lays," she said as if she had never left Jersey City. As if a bar in Bayonne wasn't a culture shock. An ocean away from the pub where David and her friends had conversations eighty-five percent of the world's population not only wouldn't understand, but couldn't care less about.

"You were that."

In the delivery truck Kenny had shown her picture cards of the effect of syphilis on newborn babies. That's as far as they ever got.

"What are you smiling about?" he asked.

"Your syphilis sportscards."

"God," he moaned, "what a memory!"

"Best thing to have at a reunion. This *is* like a reunion."

"And you're looking great."

"You do okay yourself, Kenny."

"I try to keep in shape."

"So tell me more about the Jewish girls."

"I've only been with one. Mature. That's the word. She wanted it, you know. It never would have occurred to me to try. Jeez — she was like, like you . . . But she really wanted it."

"Did that surprise you?"

"Then? Sure it did. I was brought up different."

"But then . . . even then you must have had a lot of experience."

"An eighteen-year-old hood who just about made it through Prevocational?"

"As I remember, you looked like you were fucking the whole world."

"I wasn't."

"It must have been the D.A. Too bad you had to cut off all that gorgeous hair for the force." Gorgeous. A word she'd never travel out of Jersey. She smiled at him. He was the most beautiful man she had ever seen. And no one could call her out of the truck.

He put his hand to his hair, absent-mindedly, as if to feel the weight of what she had to say. "Do you think if I had experience I'd have let Kim get in trouble?"

Rose shrugged.

"I'm the careful type. My wife must have had to work real hard to get herself knocked up."

His cold gray eyes turned to steel. She could see the crease of his contacts. His jaw tightened.

"I guess her parents didn't insist on an abortion?"

He laughed. Signaled for another round. "They insisted on a nice church wedding. When I gotta go to church these days my blood still boils."

"*Gotta* go?"

"Christenings, holidays. I got kids, Rosy."

"How many?"

"Two, and one in the oven. They're with the wife at her mother's in Florida. They are," he said distinctly and bitterly, "away."

"So you're on holiday."

"Are you?"

"I wish I were."

He looked down at his glass. "It makes me sick to see Ray sick. To see him never get a chance. He's a prince among men."

"You drink too much."

"I'm Irish."

"Oh, Kenny, that's a stereotype."

"Like most stereotypes, there's truth to it."

"Like Jews being grasping and greedy?"

"The Kleins, those bastards, were grasping and greedy."

"And my father's a prince."

"Don't confuse me with facts, Rosy. Don't forget I'm just a dumb cop. A pig. I betcha that's what your friends call us. Pigs."

"Pigs, shmigs. Don't you bother yourself about it. The Irish are charming."

"Jews are real smart."

"You know, Kenny, if my husband were here, we'd never get away with this."

"I'm sure," he said shakily.

"No, no. That's not what I mean. I'm a big girl now. I'm allowed to have my friends."

"Oh?"

"I mean I have a lot of men friends. That doesn't mean we go to bed."

"What are they? Fags?"

"Some are. But that's certainly not the point. That's what I mean, Kenny. Irish, Jews, Fags. We'd really be in for a lecture."

"Because we're talking carelessly?"

"Exactly. See, you're really not so dumb."

"Streetwise. I know your husband's type."

"That makes you a good cop. That's why you're getting promoted."

"And you're a good daughter, that's why you came home."

"Maybe I came home to see you. So you can tell me about my father, the prince."

"He's got principles in a stinking world. I can tell you stories of what I see every day, *on* and off the force, that would turn someone like you into a crusader."

"Not you?"

"Me, Rosy? I hope you didn't come home to see me. I'm part of the shit you see all around you."

"Not to me."

"Or to your dad."

"I kinda see what he sees in you."

"He saw me cry. In the freezer. The day I called Kim from the store. A personal call like I shouldn't. Must've been the tenth call. That bitch of a mother of hers answered, so I just breathed. I hear her voice like the voice of my dreams. 'I know who you are. One more call you hoodlum and you can bet your bottom dollar I'll call the police.' Just like that. She'll call the cops. She cut my kid from Kim's belly and then cut us apart and then *she's* gonna call the cops. And you know what, Rosy, she could do it. She had all the cards in those rich, ungreedy, ungrasping little hands of hers. Do you know what it's like to have nothing, to taste dust? I mean, I couldn't put two and two together in those days. Honest to God, I don't remember even *thinking* before I met Kim. I walked in the fog of youth. You could write a song to that. I got off the phone and I just headed into the freezer. There were two empty hooks. I put a hand in each and hung there like what I was, like a side of beef. Only the rest of the sides just hung, I was bawling. Or trying to. The tears stuck in the cold. Ray comes in as thin as white smoke. Sees me there."

"Jesus," Rose said, "that's just the type of scene that would drive him up a wall. What did he do?"

"Why . . . why he comforts me," Kenny said, as if she must have known.

"He comforts me. 'There, there,' he says. Pats me on the shoulder. Gets my hands out of the hooks. 'You finished now?' He gets me to the back room and pours coffee down my throat.

"Then he says, 'You can't fight City Hall. You can't fight the little women.'

" 'You can't fight the little women.' Shit, I'd do a lot for that guy. I wish he had an even chance."

"Oh, he's not going to die, Kenny, if that's what you mean." There were tears in her eyes. But her hands were in his. Her thumbs were rubbing his thumbs.

"'Hey, Rosy, I don't mean to upset you, but life's life. Ray looks bad."

"He'll look bad for a long, long time, Ken. Believe me. I'd know if he were going to die."

"What are you, some sort of witch?"

"Some sort. It's a talent I come by dishonestly," she found herself saying to another man at another table. "My great-grandmother was one."

Kenny looked uneasy. "I hope she was a good one."

"She . . ." Rose bit her tongue before she went into the abortionist aspect of Alsatian Rose's trade. "She saw things. And she was a professional. She knew how to get things done."

"And you . . . ?"

"I'm a professional too. I write."

She sat cross-legged and naked on Sadie's bed. Sadie had times like this, passed through Rose's head. The room had lost all identity, was only a backdrop for what she felt for Kenny. It was the first time place had no importance — had not become wed to what a moment had to give. Some of her best times with David were at the edge of a vista, admiring a view.

Kenny, bareassed, was bending over the small fridge, getting ice for Sadie's Jack Daniels.

So you really couldn't say Sadie wasn't there.

She was an unseen accomplice. A friend. They referred to her.

Sperm ran over Sadie's burned sheets. No one ran for one of Sadie's towels.

"What are you writing now?" Kenny asked, getting back in bed.

"I've just finished a novel about Americans living in London."

"What about Americans living here?"

Her rejection slips would read: "As impressed as we are by your handling of setting (London, Paris, Rome) and by the bleak interior landscape of your international cast of characters, we are more intellectually impressed than we are emotionally moved."

— "What's a bleak interior landscape?" Rose would fume.

"Emotionally moved," David would mock. "Not only can't they read; there's evidence they can't even write in English."

"I've been emotionally moved in my day," she would find herself answering impatiently. "Haven't you?" —

To Kenny she said, "What *about* Americans living here?"

"Whatever. I'd generally just be more interested in those living here than those living in London. I don't mean your book, though. Of course I want to read it."

"What do they read on the force?"

"Cop shit."

"Maybe I'll write about you."

"Be my guest."

"What would your wife say?"

"Don't worry. The last book she read was *Dick and Jane*. See Dick run. That's her level."

"See Kenny fuck."

"Now that, Rosy, that has promise."

"It's like your prick has hands," she whispered as he entered her.

"Not a bad line."

"I've got a way with words."

"God, Rose, you feel good."

"So Kenny's driving you to the airport," Ray said, looking at the two of them. "It looks like you're getting out of here none too soon."

"I'll get her there safe, Ray, don't you worry."

The three of them sat in Ray's living room. Ray was dressed. He wore pants too big for him, a wash-and-wear shirt that Ellen hung up to dry on the shower rod and which was wavy if not exactly wrinkled. "That's not what I was worrying about."

"What do you have on your mind, Daddy?"

He put his hand up. A resigned look appeared on his parted lips.

He wasn't going to die and he wasn't going to live. He was going to sell the store. He was going to go on social security early just as Rose suggested. He was going to take a walk around the Jersey Towers on days there was no wind. He was going to think.

In that apartment with his wife off to work and "The Dating Game" on, he was going to watch the world turn.

Two days a week he'd man the cash register at the Paramus outlet store to Buddy's family's factory, and make sure that two days a week the kid was not robbed blind. Through Ray's stern justice the store lost clerks and customers two days a week.

Ray lost faith in Buddy. Buddy the workman's friend. Taking the help out to lunch with a big cigar in his mouth and talking big figures to their face.

He'd run that part of the business down to the ground before his own father was under it.

And if they ever handed him the clothing factory itself— watch out.

Two days a week he did what he could until Janet and Buddy came to the apartment one night and after Ray took his phenobarb told Ellen and him that Janet wanted a divorce.

Who could blame her, Raymond thought, though he simply nodded his head. In a sense he had married Buddy; this was his divorce.

What would a guy like Kenny be able to do with a factory? A guy like Kenny who had his feet on the ground and knew men?

Ray was going to deal with complexity, see the joke all around him, do nothing, feel the pain in his heart, grow more and more bitter and more lost.

"Don't you worry about me," he said to Rose and Kenny in

his living room. "I'll let you in on a secret. It's not easy to die."

He meant it takes time.

"Me," he said, "I'm gonna live to the year two thousand."

He insisted on walking them down. First he put on the gray sweater Ellen had knitted for him. Sweaters. Afghans. Not to go crazy. Something to do with her hands.

Then he put on his overcoat. And his little black hat.

Outside on the bright windless day he pecked his daughter on the cheek. His lips were moist. "Thanks for coming," he said.

"I'll be back this summer," she said. "Take care."

Ray stood outside while they drove off. Rose stared back at him from behind the rolled-up window. Stared into the eyes of the small bent figure, mute.

"I know how it must feel, Rosy. To say good-bye to someone you love as much as him and not know if you'll ever see him again."

She turned to Kenny. Watched him. She didn't put her hand on his prick the way he liked her to while he drove. That was useless now.

When she came home he'd be a detective with a wife and three kids. Maybe there'd be three kids more.

Last night she had offered never to leave.

"You'll get over that," he said. "Once you get back to your own world, you'll see."

"What makes you so smart?"

"I'm a family man, Rosy, I gotta be."

"Life," Rose said to him, trying to hold back her tears. "Life, Kenny, turns out to be a hell of a lot like Kim's mother."

❧ ❧ ❧

"I'm beginning to feel like myself again," she told David on Christmas Eve.

They had gone to Rome for the holidays. The six weeks since she'd been back she'd been withdrawn, remote, depressed.

"Oh, I guess I'm just waiting for inspiration," she told him listlessly, waiting for the letter that didn't come.

"Rome works," David said with a smile.

They were eating at a small trattoria near the Pantheon. They always had the spaghetti all'Amatriciana and the baby goat.

It was a clear cold night. They had walked through Piazza Navona, which was crammed with the seasonal Christmas stalls and tawdry wares. The Romans celebrated Christmas like any other festa. Its individuality was obscured.

Rose fingered the twig of holly at her table. The harsh green leaves and the red berries were as close as the city came to the holiday as it was known in the north.

She poured some more wine. "A lot happened to me in Jersey," she said, feeling as if — if she could somehow give it shape . . .

Yes, that is what it all needed. Shape. Contour, like the Pantheon. She could hear the low "baaa" of the bladder music the shepherds blew. They came down from the hills on Christmas Eve and played the old horns. People tipped them. Whether or not there were still shepherds in the hills, on Christmas Eve the shepherds came down from the hills . . .

That was the way things should be. Nothing spilled over. Her head was clearing, just as weeks before the swelling in her vagina had gone down.

David was waiting for her to speak. He knew long before anyone else that she had something to say.

To the world he was the successful aggressive scholar.

The world didn't know he had waited thirty-three years to find someone who was related to magic on the paternal side. Someone who could do the most amazing thing with an idea, a special day, someone else's mood — make it live.

He felt his work was ultimately useless. What would it be in seventy-five years? What would Professor Willner say to a student who used a seventy-five-year-old reference?

David Willner had turned away from generation after generation of lawyers. An alien among his relations. Had followed his early successes in scholarship from reward to reward. Once you get one grant you get them all, he'd often say.

His mind was always working, but he hadn't seen where it was taking him. His excellence shielded him from his discomfort among men.

Close to forty, he wondered if he couldn't have done better for himself than writing about and teaching English literature.

Victorian Hell Fire had launched him, and on it his fame would rest. He went into the subject like a good surgeon. He didn't murder to dissect, but he did isolate the components of Victorian angst about the Death of God with a clarity and urbanity unprecedented in his field. His own attention to detail and his ability to lose himself in research enriched the work. And disguised his detachment from the subject. For he did not believe in God. And he certainly didn't believe in the Devil. If forced to it, he would not be able to understand why any intelligent human being would mourn or despair of forces that never were. He had begun his research with amused detachment, and the sheer weight of his intellectual intensity and his own years of labor turned the work passionate.

He would never equal it and he knew it. He did less research now, did it mainly in relationship to grants, and at his core he did not care.

He assumed he'd be exposed by a bright graduate student one day. But at the present any voice against his work was tinged with envy. For David Willner was a name in his field. Once you are invited to one conference, guest lectureship, festschrift, you're invited to them all.

Yet the Immortals pointed a finger to the next century, when his Library of Congress cards (and there was quite a file under Willner, David 1932–   ) would sit undog-eared, unperturbed. In his field the bottom line was immortality. You dealt with it every day; the lust for it rubbed off.

The Immortals pointed to the woman he loved.

He waited for Rose to speak.

"Janet," she said. Yes, it was Janet who had made things spill over. She felt the truth of it as she saw him relax. Here was something David Willner could fix, be reasonable about. His lack of a cosmology did nothing to liberate his senses; it fixed his stars. To

Rose, order was a learned response. A talisman. Under its auspices, provided by David, she could sit at her desk and write. She needed it no less than he. For she had inherited a much more unruly nature.

Society had always needed both the God and the Devil David didn't believe in, plus guilt and the family, to keep people like Rose down.

"Janet? Because she's seeing a shrink?"

"Because I didn't know she was so unhappy. She never let on. All the nights the four of us have spent together. All the times I've been with her alone. It makes me realize there were whole aspects of life I knew nothing about. That were hidden from me. Or that I refused to see."

"Don't be so hard on yourself."

"But why didn't I see?"

"People need their privacy. She let you in on as much as she wanted you to know."

"Do you think it's all so rational?"

"Well, I don't think she is a self-indulgent person. At least not yet, until the shrink gets through with her."

"You think it's self-indulgent to talk about your problems?"

"I think married people should try to work things out between them without letting the whole world see. I realize here I part company with most of my colleagues, not to mention most of my countrymen. Actually, I have a certain sympathy for the way they do things here in Italy."

"Can't you see that things are changing here?" They had come back to find everyone in Rome — everyone! — wearing jeans.

"On the outside, maybe. But the family is still strong. And there's something to say about working things out without recourse to divorce."

"Oh, my God, are you going to call that 'civilized,' the way the Christian Democrats do?"

"For the sake of argument."

"But this isn't just an intellectual argument."

"Still, no matter what goes on in your sister's head, in the Eternal City certain things will always be the same."

David Willner, who knew England better, said this in 1971, just as postwar Italy began unraveling.

The world was changing. Soon in Italy there would be divorce. The pious poor southern women the Church relied on voted for it. Many of them had understood inexplicable misery. Even they wanted the dream of being free. As much as David Willner wanted the dream of order.

Rose too. "I'm certainly not advocating divorce. As much as I always knew Buddy was the wrong person for her, she *did* marry him, they *do* have a child. I'm hoping they'll work it out. What I'm talking about is the misery beyond it all, the pain."

"You exaggerate," said David.

— "I made my bed," said Kenny. "Even though my wife made it for me."

"But there's still room around all that for us."

"Dream on, Rosy. There's *now* for us."

"There's got to be more. Now's almost over." —

"I don't exaggerate," she said to David. "There's more pain, regret, and loss in this world than I ever imagined."

"We all know that."

"But do you *feel* that?"

"Do I feel for the whole world? No, Rose. Not like you."

"It's not the whole world. It's me — it's my sister."

"I feel for *her*."

"It's my *father*. My father. He's never lived!"

"Well, maybe he hasn't lived the way you'd have him live, but he's lived."

"No he hasn't."

"How do you know?"

"He's just like me."

"What does that mean?" David asked.

"We're alike. I sit all day and write. He sits all day and suffers."

"I didn't realize we lived such a dull life," David said. The coolness of his voice went through her like a stab of regret.

"I'm not talking about us," she retracted. "My God, David, look at all we have." She put her hand in the air.

His admonition made her pull up tight, take stock, be grateful.

It would all turn out all right. She'd put the pain to use. Things would be perfect again. Ellen Diamond had never allowed a night to close on a fight with her daughters.

When she gave her husband the silent treatment, she'd wink at Rose and Janet as soon as he was out of the room. "It doesn't mean a thing," she'd whisper. "Everything's fine. It's just that he's got to see he's been wrong." Wink. Between us girls.

Everything will work out hunky-dory, fine, okay.

— "Why you crying?" Kenny asked. They were lying together. She put her head against his chest, she pressed against his body. —

"Why are you crying, Rose?" David asked from across the table, concern on his face.

Her father put on his sweater, overcoat, little black hat, to face an autumn day that shone like a giant yellow mum.

She poured more wine and sipped it.

"The ends of things make me sad."

"Is that all?"

"Believe me, it's enough."

"Well, you've just ended a book, we're ending a year, and there's the possibility that Janet and Buddy . . . that they *might* be ending." He made a list of it, put it into perspective.

"I don't know what I'd do without you," she said.

"You'll never have to do without me," he answered.

"Never is a long time."

"Not for me. But for you it probably will be. Someday you'll leave."

"Why do you say that!"

"I don't know. A feeling, I guess. Even now. You're not exactly here."

She smiled for him. Focused on him. "Come on, it's Christmas Eve. No time to be sad." She could not bear the responsibility for human sadness. She did not know everyone must bear his own alone. On David's sadness she practiced alchemy.

"Now you're remembering you have me."

"I always remember that," she said cheerfully. "If I seem abstracted, it's that I think I have an idea for a new book."

"Oh?" said David. "So *that's* it." Relief.

She felt relief too. Tipsy on the wine and suddenly good.

"I don't think I'll write about Europe anymore. This would be a new book from an old idea. A story . . . some people years ago . . . thought quite good. It's about a man — a very intelligent man — who has the wrong temperament. He never gets what he wants. It's really about America. And loss. I used to call it *The Little Black Hat*, but now I think I'm going to call it *Monkey Man*."

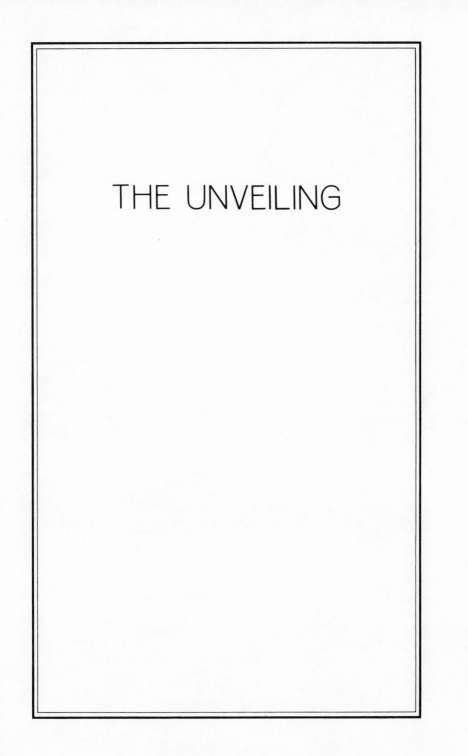

THE UNVEILING

It was a beautiful day in Jersey City, and the sisters were way down Palisades Avenue, almost in Union City. The April sun splashed the entrance to the Hebrew Home and Hospital Complex. The old people well enough to sit among the plants on the patio looked as if they were in a park. They watched Rose and Janet carefully. Suspicion and expectation in their eyes.

There was a parking lot in front of the complex, and some of the spaces were reserved for the big donors. Their names were printed in concrete.

"When they die," Janet said, "they bury Levy, Shapiro, and Fein in their parking spaces, right under their Cadillacs."

"I don't know," Rose said. "Maybe, after all, Levy, Shapiro, and Fein built what they could in this life. And at least here they took out Nana's catheter."

"That was something."

"And something has just *got* to be better than nothing. If we can't see that, if we can't *act* on that, we'll end up just like Daddy."

It was 1976. Rose had just finished *Monkey Man*. She felt a sudden affinity to God, who on the seventh day took a look and saw it was good. The Bildungsroman might belong to men and to the

Germans, but last month, the day of the crumb buns, she swore she'd be a success.

Before the glass doors opened, the sisters were reflected in them. In their jeans, their bodies erect, at thirty-one and thirty-five they looked like slim children with a gold and green paradise of the elderly at their back.

The clean halls brought them into the shades. Janet knew the way to Nana's room. They passed a one-legged man in a yarmulke, conspicuous among the old women in their wheelchairs, old women with greedy eyes and withered bodies.

Janet had told Rose that Nana was holding her own, improving.

"Sure, sure," Raymond had replied last night, "I'll-tell-him-when-he-comes-in."

"Raymond!" Ellen had admonished. *You're scaring your children away,* she had warned him before they came.

"He's *alive*," the sisters had told Ellen Diamond in privacy while Etta was still at Christ Hospital.

"But he's *sick*. He doesn't mean what he says."

These were the days Rose had led her grandmother down a path of half-truths, hopes, and illusions in order to get her to the Home for rehabilitation under the auspices of what was left of Etta's own will. Exhausted, Rose had gone back to Boston. David at forty had taken a chairmanship there.

"Of course he means what he says," said Janet, who had completed analysis. "He's telling us something."

"Of fear, of dread. He's a sick man. I know. Maybe I've kept too much from you girls through the years. "

"Maybe you have," said Rose.

"A lot of thanks I get!"

"For trying to keep us in a fool's paradise," Rose said.

"I'm the fool," said Ellen.

"But this ain't paradise," said Janet.

"The two of you, the two of you!" Ellen said as if it were a revelation. "Who'd ever believe you'd both be so hard, both be so alike!"

"Mother," said Rose, rising to her stature of older daughter, "let's try to be reasonable. Janet mainly, because she's in New York, and I as well, have the whole burden of this on our shoulders."

"What do you mean? Your father is taking care of this."

"My father," said Rose, "is taking care of losing nurses."

"Round-the-clock nurses! Do you know what they cost? How he worries?"

"It's *her* money," said Janet. "Nana is going to die the way she lived."

"He wants that too. That selfish old woman, just lying there. Be careful or you'll lose him first. *He's* the one to worry about, not her."

"Maybe so!" screamed Rose. "But we've got an old woman lying at Christ Hospital. And the way he carries on, she'll lie there forever. Every time he gets near the social worker for the Home he costs us time. He's a liability walking along a hall. He's paranoid, he's nasty, he's not in control!"

"He's a sick man!"

"He's *alive!*" Rose reiterated what had at first been Janet's line. "As long as he's breathing he has a responsibility."

"We won't treat him like a dead man until he's dead!" Janet insisted. "We're not *you!*"

"What ever happened to you girls? Where are your hearts?"

You should be proud of them, she said to Raymond later. *The way they care.*

"What time is it?" Rose heard walking along the hall.

"It's two-ten, Mrs. Maisel," Janet called back.

"What time is it?"

"What time is it?"

followed them.

"You should see Mrs. Maisel when the aide walks her along the railing," Janet said, crouching along the rail in imitation.

" 'I can't do it.

'I can't do it.'

While she does it."

Janet laughed. She was an initiate into the world of the institu-
tion. "Wait'll you meet Nana's roomie, she lived on the Grand
Concourse when it *was* the Grand Concourse!"

"Hi there!" Janet nodded to a woman parked in front of a door.

"Janet, you know everyone."

"I spend enough time here."

Rose let her sister go ahead. She was proud of her kindness
along the ward. She induced team spirit, the way she had when
she was one of what Rose called the Elizabeth Thirty-seven. She
had been arrested in an anti-Nixon march in 1971. Ellen, arriving
with Chanukah gelt for Laura at the apartment in Jersey that
Janet still shared with Buddy, had to use the fifty dollars to bail
her daughter out.

In front of one room a small old lady sat in a green sweater, her
ancient head sagging toward the belt that kept her from falling
from her chair. Janet bent over, took her hand and rubbed it. She
called Rose to her side. The woman slowly picked up her head.
Rose was confronted by the anonymous mask of age. There
wasn't even the glint of suspicion in the eyes that looked out
from the mass of fallen flesh.

"It's *Rose*," Janet said.

"Rose," the woman repeated toothlessly.

"Rose," the woman said before Rose realized this must be Etta
Addis.

I'll-tell-him-when-he-comes-in.

"Hey, I'm sorry," Janet said later. "I see her every other day. To
me she was looking better."

"I didn't know her. I thought you were being kind. I looked at
her and I didn't know her. I had to surmise."

The Hebrew Home for rehabilitation. The Final Rehabilitation.
The Hebrew Resolution-Complex.

Resolved: Contrary to family pressure, Etta Addis will not die
the way she lived.

"I'm a pisher now," she told Rose.

Peeing in her pants seemed to upset Etta Addis as much as the
catheter had in Christ Hospital.

She always felt she had to move her bowels.

"Reggie, Reggie," she cried.

"Around here," Mrs. Roth, Nana's roomie, informed them, "you wait."

A big black man came in.

"Do you have a buck for him?" Etta cried.

He put her on the pot.

She sat strapped on the pot, blowing air out of her mouth. Pwoowf! Pwoowf! Pwoowf! Red in the face, nightgown over her stomach. Pwoowf! Pwoowf! The sisters watched Nana try to go.

"Around here," Mrs. Roth informed the sisters, "if you want something you gotta scream like hell."

Mrs. Roth was a good-looking old woman. She could still stand, with assistance, because eighteen months ago she had refused to let them amputate her leg. It was easier for her to get her clothes on right. And she managed to wangle extra beauty parlor appointments, so her short white hair was perpetually set. A light wool shawl of rose and blue made expressly for Bloomingdale's covered her shoulders. Intelligence and sharp humor glinted in her half-blind eyes. She wore a strand of pearls the size and shape of the balls of dark flesh that dangled from under her chin. Nana's roomie.

"What time is it . . . ?" Mrs. Maisel continued.

"Hear that?" said Mrs. Roth, looking at Rose. "She was once a brilliant woman. A schoolteacher. She can't help it now. Only the ignorant taunt her. That lousy Mr. Greenberg, the skunk. 'You should have had *her* brains when it mattered,' I told him. I open my mouth.

"Like your grandmother." When Etta was returned from the pot, the two sat in their wheelchairs at each side of the entrance to their room. "She can't help herself. Even though she wears it everyday, she thinks I stole her green sweater. They steal like hell around here. I warned your father when she came."

Etta beckoned Rose with her good hand. The right side of her body still moved.

"Roll me," she whispered.

Rose and Janet took her down the hall. Sat on the couch in the lounge opposite her.

"No good talk in room," she struggled to say. "Wires! S.O.B.'s got it bugged."

"Oh, Nana," said Rose. "That's not so. Your room is safe."

"Have you checked TV?"

Rose turned to Janet.

"As far as I can make out she thinks her TV caught fire and burned her apartment up."

"Terrible," commented Etta Addis.

"Listen to me, Nana!" Rose said with great conviction. "You must have had a bad dream. Your apartment is just as you left it."

And Rose walked into the apartment once more, the way she had two months before. The gold and white cut-velvet couch glistened in the sun. The day bed was made up. The plants were being watered by a neighbor. The pictures, including the miniatures, hung straight on the walls. In the desk drawer, Etta Addis's affairs were in neat, accurate order. The rent check ready to be sent out. The checkbook balanced. "Cash it immediately," she'd say each time she gave a check to Raymond or one of the girls.

There was an unsealed envelope with a St. Louis address. Rose had looked inside. A contest from the newspaper had been clipped out. There were three questions and, under each question, blocks that Etta had filled in in pen with a deliberate hand. A Singer sewing machine was offered. Etta's answers were right. In the silence of the room and her heart she had aspired to win the prize.

Rose's head spun. She had to hold on to the vanity table. She stared at her grandmother's hand mirror and immaculate ivory-handled hairbrush. Suddenly she understood the room of Albert's that Queen Victoria preserved. And Garibaldi's bedroom on Caprera, the bed turned so that he could look out the windows, see Corsica as he died. The bed encased by glass, his medicine on view, his clock stopped in commemoration.

"No!" Rose had said to her father that evening. "Just pay the rent."

"She'll never go back there."

"We don't yet know for sure. She's strong! She's determined. They'll give her therapy at the Home."

"Let's close it up!" He sat in his chair in his living room, his face away from his daughters.

"And who's going to pack everything up?" Rose asked. "I will not do it."

"I will," said Raymond.

"Oh, you will?"

"Sure. I'll throw everything out the Goddamn window!" He laughed.

"Now you listen to me," Rose said. She tried to make sense. She couldn't tell her father she never wanted anything in her grandmother's apartment to be changed. "Don't make a liar out of me. I've just convinced Nana to go for rehabilitation before she returns home. We *cannot* strip her of her apartment the minute she's away."

"If the therapy is at all successful," Janet said, "she might be able to go home with a nurse."

Raymond looked at them with disgust. "What are you, babies? She must be ninety years old, she's had a stroke. She's going nowhere!"

"The master of realism," Rose mumbled.

"What?"

"You're the man who three months ago didn't want your mother to buy a cane!"

"She was okay then!"

"What's the use." Rose sighed.

"She saw her friends get canes and she got the bug. That's her all over. She could walk perfectly okay then if she took her time. If she started to get dependent on a cane, then where would she be?"

"I guess nowhere else than where she's now," said Rose in desperation.

It still bothered her that her father was the only man she could imagine who'd argue against an arthritic mother, maybe ninety, using a cane.

❖

Something else had bothered Rose about the affair of the cane. When she had called her father about it from Boston he had said, "This is none of your business, big shot. Just butt out. Sell your books if you're so damn smart."

Sell your books if you're so damn smart.

She had given him the manuscript of *Monkey Man*. He never read it.

"It's beautifully written," Ellen had said, "but to get published you have to throw in lots of sex."

Had *she* read it?

He hadn't come to the talk she gave on Elizabeth Barrett Browning at the Modern Language Association meeting in New York.

"In the morning, Rose?" her mother, who took the day off for it, said. "On a winter morning to go out in the wind?"

The day after the talk, David and she had visited Etta before returning to Boston.

"You're not going to stop by your father?" Ellen said over the phone from work.

"For what?" Rose asked. "To have him tell me I'm a jerk?"

"He doesn't mean what he says."

"Maybe I am a jerk. Maybe no one will publish my books because I'm no good. Maybe he means what he says."

"Rose, I'm surprised at you." Mommy's big girl.

But she had gone to see him after visiting Etta. It was something about her grandmother's tone.

"I tell him prune juice," Etta had said. She sat on the straight-backed bridge chair. Her short arthritic legs just missing, as always, the floor. She was home from the hospital after a violent illness — a new pressure pill had almost killed her. She was not fat anymore; her face was drawn. But she was lively enough and meticulously attired. "I thought I'd had it this time," she had said with shame. "But I didn't," she had added in triumph. "I'm a tough old bird."

Now she was on prune juice. " 'Ray,' I told him, 'Mahoney delivered it by mistake.' The unsweetened kind and Lena said what's a matter with you, Etta, keep it. In the morning, first thing, a glass with the juice of one quarter of a lemon and see if you don't have relief."

Lena was standing by the door as Etta spoke. She was on her way out. She was a wizened thing with unkempt gray hair, wearing a housecoat printed with faded green leaves against white. She wore white anklets and had thin little-girl legs marred by the blue veins of ancient marble.

"And honest to God, I'm regular."

Lena nodded.

"You remember Mrs. Tuttle, don't you, Rose?" Etta said.

Lena Tuttle. "Of course," Rose answered, recovering. "How could I forget?"

She used to wait in the vestibule at Clifton Avenue for Lena Tuttle to arrive at her grandmother's game. Chauffered in from New York. Thin as now. Long-gloved hands, holding her furs to her chest, as the chauffeur opened the door.

She wore hats with sparkling mesh veils. A kept woman for twenty-five years, before he died she married Tuttle.

"I never would have recognized her, Nana," Rose said after she left.

"Really?" Etta answererd. "Like everyone else, she's got her story.

"I'm worried about your father," Etta continued. "Hard as he tries, poor guy, he can't go."

"David," Rose said, "I think I'll call him."

"I told you we should drop by," he answered.

"Take a look for yourself," Etta said.

To her you'll listen. Rose could hear her mother in her head.

Over the phone he was slow but not belligerent.

"Nothing," he answered when Rose asked what they could bring him.

"You're sure? Come on!"

"Weeell . . . Crumb buns."

"Crumb buns?"

"Yeah. I'm just in the mood."

But when he opened the box his face lost interest. It was almost as if he were saying, "Again?"

She felt a surge of compassion, seeing him once more find something he didn't need.

"What's wrong?"

"Nothing."

"You said crumb buns."

"From the Italian bakery."

"The Italian bakery? *They* make crumb buns?"

"Terrific ones. They sell out."

"But why didn't you tell me? We always went to Five Corners."

"Didn't I?" Raymond asked, scratching at the white patches near his temple. A thin man snowing. Stoop-shouldered, pensive, he walked away from the table in the dining area and sat in his accustomed chair, where he could look past the big room to the windows. See the weather for himself.

"Come on, Ray," David said. "Eat. A crumb bun in the hand is worth two in the bush."

Ray looked up at his son-in-law. The chairman of an English department trying to cheer him up.

Kenny Douglas would not say a crumb bun in the hand is worth two in the bush. Kenny would stand up, go out, buy the right crumb buns.

When Ray's mind brought Kenny and his daughter in conjunction, he separated them, one appearing over each eye. They'd hang there sometimes like a magician's trick, showing him something he might be able to figure, but whose inner workings he didn't want to know.

The double image did more. It brought back the past, the years-ago past when his grandmother would gossip with his mother. In some way it recalled the texture of life on Central Avenue in Jersey City. It made for an eerie continuity, a sense that his daughter would never leave the city or the sawdust or him.

For as much as Rose admired Etta, right smack at Rose's core Raymond saw Charley.

"Seen Kenny lately?" Rose asked. Right in front of David she acknowledged what her father was thinking.

"He brought me over some crumb buns last week."

"What is it with these crumb buns?" Rose asked. She took one from the box and split it in two. "You have an affinity for them because they flake too?"

"Ha. Ha," Raymond said. He was on his best behavior.

You're scaring your children away! Ellen warned over the phone from work. *That big mouth of yours. They're beginning to believe what you say.*

"Ha, ha," he said and suddenly he wanted to tell his daughter something. He was back to the old days and Ellen wasn't there. He had something to say.

"You know, yesterday I had this craving. I got up, it wasn't too late, maybe eleven, and I thought maybe with a little luck, it's early yet, they won't be sold out.

"So I get all dressed, take my pills, and go out the back way. You know you can cut right through the parking lot, cross the street, and you're at the Italian bakery. I figured it's clear. What the hell. If I keep the scarf over my nose, what's a little wind?"

"Too bad you couldn't do that a little earlier. You could have come with mother to hear my talk."

"It would have been worth it," said David.

"A little wind, I think," Raymond said, bending forward in the chair. "I try to walk. The wind's pushing me back. I try to walk. It pushes. I can't breathe. All of a sudden — WHAM!" Rather than falling back in his chair, Raymond stands up to emphasize. "I'm sprawled on the ground. The damn wind knocked me right off my feet." A merry smile of embarrassment comes over Ray's face as he pats his rump.

"Lucky I'm off anticoagulants. I'd really be black and blue today!"

"*Off* anticoagulants?" Rose asked.

"Yeah, young Young has me off them. It's not like in his father's day. Cholesterol too is no big deal anymore. There's two schools of thought now. It's all fancy guessing.

" 'Are you all right, sir?' 'Sure, sure, never been better.' One of those snot-nosed kids wanted to help me up. A Spic. You can't tell with kids these days, white, black, indifferent. Long hair. Are they gonna help you off the ground or are they gonna mug you?

'Just keep your distance, buster,' I told him. I sat there a while. Finally caught my breath. Got myself up.

"It should have been a warning, but I was so damn close. So I pick myself up and I keep walking. I got cross that damn street and got into the damn store."

"Oh," Rose sympathized. "And now you're going to tell us you got there too late and all the crumb buns were sold out!"

"A lot you know, sister," Ray said, sitting back down. "They had trays."

"So you bought a half-dozen and ate them all?"

"*Sssssh.*" Ray put his hand up. "I walk in. They got a line. You need a *number.* I'm standing there like a shmegegge with a ticket in my hand. I'm waiting. Ah, the hell with it. Who needs it? I turn right around and walk out."

There was a long pause. Rose said to him softly, "You never read *Monkey Man,* did you?"

"I'll wait till it's published."

She walked to the picture window. Looked over at the skyline of New York. Turned to him. "It will be, you know. Something inside tells me. Your grandmother, maybe."

"She was a magical woman," Ray said plaintively. "Alsatian Rose."

"I feel things will soon be changing for me. I very much want you to know."

He smiled. "I hope you're right, sister."

"*Monkey Man* will be published. I feel it."

Raymond looked at his daughter with interest. He was not used to people saying positive things.

She was not used to feeling them.

"The talk at the Modern Language Association went over very well. I wouldn't even be surprised if *Letters to Her Father* makes it one day. Things are changing. I feel it in my blood."

"I never heard you talk like that before," David said later, back in Boston.

"I never felt that way before." She was in a long white nightgown that picked out both the dark brown and the silver in her

hair. She looked quite beautiful, though she didn't buy her lin-
gerie for him.

She made a fist, as if to fight the possibility of tears. As if to
fight. "In this world, if you really put your mind to it, it has just
got to be possible to buy yourself a crumb bun!"

Now, in the Hebrew Home and Hospital Complex, sun
streaming in, she watches the half of Etta's body that can, shiver.

She holds the good hand. Janet has her Intensive Care Lotion
and is rubbing it in the bad arm.

What could they do for their grandmother, except what was
never done on Clifton Avenue: touch.

It had driven Raymond crazy at Christ Hospital, watching
Janet massage the old lady, watching Rose hold her hand and talk
about the canned asparagus Etta hadn't liked at lunch.

It made Ellen mad. Rose she could understand, but Janet. She
was a lucky old woman that even Janet cared.

In Christ Hospital, the sisters fell into an allegory of devotion
on each side of the old woman's bed.

"That's enough!" Raymond would cry. Humiliating, shameful,
to see them acting out what should be kept quiet.

His devotion was to struggle to the Home every day Janet
wasn't there. To take a seat, the two of them in silence.

Raymond, she'd scream in a tone Ellen said she'd never show the
girls. She'd bully him to unlock her closet.

Frail as a rail, he'd go from closet to bed with the dresses. Two
at a time. Never convincing her what she knew was stolen was
there.

"You can be *too* good," Mrs. Roth said of Raymond Addis.

"He's so devoted," said one nurse.

"He's cute," said another.

"Cute?" asked Janet.

"Yeah. He reminds me of that TV show, 'Mr. Peepers.'"

Holding her grandmother's hand in the lounge, Rose asks the
magic words that got her to respond at Christ Hospital for the

first time. "Nana, tell us what you're feeling. Tell us what's on your mind."

"You know," Etta Addis says, looking up. "They told you."

"Nana, you're so wrong, believe me."

But nothing could dissuade her. She was sure she had had an operation in the intensive care unit at Christ Hospital. Through her haze she thought she had heard the doctors talk.

Rose sighs and looks at Janet on the incredibly sun-filled day.

"You know," Etta repeats.

Nothing could convince her otherwise. What she had silently dreaded for a lifetime surfaced with her shock.

Tied into her wheelchair, paralyzed, and confused — arteriosclerosis, stroke were nothing to her. She confronted the only demon strong enough to kill her.

In an ancient parody of her once-young daughter, she had her visions, heard her voices, and if she had been able to move she'd have gotten Mrs. Roth, the bum.

The tapes were in her room, her television was burning, and the doctor's voices came over the tubes. This was Armageddon. Stripped bare, all that was left of Etta Addis was the instinct to survive.

Yet her life was being stolen by the enemy.

In the dining room she threw her food and rattled her silverware with one hand.

At night she screamed. "She can't help herself," said Mrs. Roth, who couldn't sleep.

Her granddaughters were not sent to hurt her, that she knew. But they kept the truth from her.

"You do *not* have cancer, Nana," Rose says into the clear light of day.

"Rectum," Etta answers.

The only death bad enough to claim her.

They wheeled Nana back to her spacious double room. Her bed was next to a wall of glass doors. Outside you could see the hedges of someone's backyard.

They waited in the hall for Reggie.

They watched him lifting old ladies in wheelchairs onto the huge scale while the nurse recorded weights.

He strode over to them when he was through. A big man, he took the physical exertion with a smile that showed his power. "I didn't have a chance before. You're the one from out of town?" Reggie said to Rose.

"Right."

"You married?"

"Yes."

"Children?" He eyed her up and down.

"She's the sister with the husband and no children. I'm the one with the kid and no husband," Janet said.

"What's that?" Mrs. Roth, sitting by the door, asked.

"N*ooo*sy," said Reggie.

"So who asked you?"

"Forgive me, Mrs. Roth. I keep forgetting you is from the Grand Concourse when it was *The Grand Concourse*. Before us'n came along." He whistled at the girls and cast his eyes to the ceiling.

"Not an easy job," Rose said.

"They're nice ladies, all in all. Like your gramma. What's Mrs. Addis after now?"

"The pot."

"Could have guessed. Let's see if I can talk her out of it."

He sauntered past them.

"Hey, you made a conquest," Janet said.

"If a man's got bulging pectorals and a prick that could be divided in half and then some, he comes after me."

"You complaining?"

"I'm just stating a strange biological fact. I must secrete a Tarzan-Jane fluid or something. The older I get, the less I understand about sex."

"Ha," said Mrs. Roth, rolling herself over. "You're just too young to know a thing or two. To be honest with you girls, I do. Rose, you could write a book. If I knew *then* what I know *now*, boy would I have done things different. But I came from a very Orthodox household, girls. Right was right and wrong was wrong, and boy you better know it."

"That's awfully nice of you, Reggie," Rose said from the doorway, seeing he was going to comply with Etta's wishes.

"Got a buck?" Etta called.

"My father's father was a rabbi in the old country. What did I know? My husband did me dirt. In bed with whoever while my brother-in-law is putting him through school. Right in my brother-in-law's office, he's shtupping the secretary. 'Don't leave me now,' he tells me. 'After all, there's no one left for me to fool with, you won't have to worry anymore.' "

"Boy oh boy," said Janet. This was a new Mrs. Roth. She'd seen it happen before. People talked when Rose was there.

"I had two young boys, one sick as hell, but right was right. I said, if I stay with you, you're going to step over me till there's nothing left. So I'll do it to you first. I walked right out the door."

"That's more than right is right. That's survival."

Mrs. Roth lifted an ancient hand to confute Janet with.

"Let *me* tell *you* about survival. If I knew then what I know now, I would have done what they all do." She leaned toward the sisters. "I would have kept my mouth shut and turned the tables on *him!* You know what I mean, girls?" Mrs. Roth asked with a wicked gleam. "Had my own fun on the side like you see all around you. Even here! You should see what goes on on the third floor, where they can walk! But not me. I leave. Good-bye. I'm telling you, Rose, there's a book in me."

"Did you marry again?"

"I'm being perfectly honest with you girls. I had a wonderful sister. Like you two have. She did plenty for me after I lost my little boy. My own place on the Grand Concourse — not the way it is today, you wouldn't know it, but when it was grand. A little job, a son to raise, and a wonderful friend. I'm being perfectly honest, my friend would have married me any time I said. Like I'm sure yours would marry you, Janet."

"You didn't want to get married again?!" Janet exclaimed.

"Why should I? What was I to Roth? Three meals put on the table, the skunk!"

The sisters sat at a bar in Union City on the same hot April day. Janet had left her car off for repair while they had visited Etta. At the last minute she'd try to group errands together. You never knew beforehand, because Janet never planned.

They were drinking beer and smoking from a pack of cigarettes they'd decided they needed and had bought from the machine.

The air conditioning wasn't on to meet the unprecedented early heat. They were both flushed.

"How do you like that Mrs. Roth?" Janet asked. "God, for a month I was figuring her straighter than Nana."

"Sometimes I think no one in the world has ever been as straight as our family. While most people attempt to appear respectable, *they* etched respectability into their flesh." Rose shuddered. "And I'm just like them."

"You do okay, sister."

"Do I? I guess I do what Mrs. Roth says everyone does. I take a little fun on the side."

"It bothers you?"

"It's nothing I ever thought would happen. I try not to think about it. Make it go away."

"How do you do that?"

"I work."

"So do I."

"I guess it's harder not to think about when you're rubbing flesh."

"I like rubbing flesh."

"Damn it, so do I."

"Why the regret?"

"David."

"Well, you have to balance these things. Like I really have a good relationship with Roger, but I don't tell him everything."

"Jesus Christ," said Rose, on her second beer. "Mother made a big mistake. She should have ordered brothers."

"Or twins."

Rose took a deep breath. "I'm going to make a phone call."

"Good for you!"

"It's the one thing I'll never understand about this modern world."

"What?"

"How everyone cheers when you go against your better self and do something wrong."

"I was hopin' you'd call," said Kenny. They were in a motel off Tonnelle Avenue.

She never went to McDonald's, ate plastic food, watched TV, or knew anything about sports. She took all of her America in Holiday Inns, Great Westerns, and Ramadas.

She didn't answer, Why didn't you call me? She had set the precedent in '72, had been the one to call when she returned from Europe. She had discussed it with Janet first. Janet said she did the same thing herself occasionally. Took a stab. Made a phone call to the past. An old lover, even if he betrayed you, gained something as time passed. Years later you could meet for a drink and still see something of yourself. Something important that, if you didn't want to, you didn't have to face every day. But something that was there.

"I'm always here" is what Kenny had said the night, when, back from Europe, she sat with him in their bar in Bayonne.

"Why didn't you write?"

"Hopeless to write."

"Are you so *sure* it's hopeless?"

"Except when you're sitting right here."

"You were a fool to let me go."

"I don't have you to let go. You're the fool to start up with me again."

"Who's starting up? I just asked you to come for a drink."

He grabbed her wrist. "You're too close to talk shit, Rosy. Do you think if it were in the cards for us to be this close, I'd ever let you go?"

"I figured David would be with you for Passover," he said in the motel on Tonnelle Avenue.

The Addises had never celebrated Passover until Janet began living with a record executive.

"Why ruin a beautiful friendship?" Ellen Diamond answered valiantly, when some buttinski had the nerve to ask why Janet and Roger didn't marry.

Of course, Ellen Diamond's parents had not lived to see what they could never understand. With the rate the world was going these days, Ellen often thought of her beloved father peacefully sleeping with his dream of his old America still intact in his handsome head.

Twenty years before, they draped the mirror when you married out of the religion. Now there was no such thing even as living in sin. You were having a relationship.

There was no more getting into trouble. An unwed mother had a one-parent child. If she was stupid enough to want to bring a child into a world like this. Who would *want* to bring a child into a world like this, she often asked Rose.

Janet's lover treated Laura better than Buddy did. Not only that, Roger was a good Jew. Ellen, the man who thought we came from monkeys, and, till this year, Etta, went to the first night of Passover. Laura asked the questions.

Raymond responded when he had to. He was polite to Roger. Never interfered. He was not the first father in history to see his daughter given presents. To find, despite himself, his estimation of her rise with their value.

"He did come for Passover, but he had to get back to school."

"Ray didn't say."

"Probably on purpose."

"Why? He doesn't know what's up."

"In a way he does."

"Jeez!"

"And he approves."

He sat up in bed and looked down at her. "Approves?"

"Sure. He's always looking for the son he never had."

"To commit incest with his daughter?"

She giggled. "Honest to God, you're quick for a cop."

"And double-quick for an order boy. If he *knows*, and if he *approves,* how come he led me to believe you'd be here all week with David?"

"How come you *wait,* but never call me?"

"Now you're getting out of my depth."

"Sure, sure. Play possum, play dumb, play dead!"

"Don't get pissed, Rosy."

He got out of bed. "Pour me one neat!" she called.

"Oh," she sighed, gulping it. "Today I didn't recognize my own grandmother."

"Ray says she's pretty bad."

"So's he."

Kenny nodded. "I don't like what I see."

"Or hear?"

"He's gotten pretty sharp. Sometimes he forgets who he's talking to."

"Even to the person who brings him the right crumb buns."

"I told him I think he must be pregnant."

"It's the beginning of the end, Kenny. He's beginning to die."

"That liquor turns you soft. He'll be okay like always."

"He'll live as long as she does. I hope my mother's right. I hope Nana's heart keeps pumping till she's past a hundred. 'Cause he won't go first. He'll stay with her; she'll keep him with her. But I don't give him more than three months from the day she dies."

"Shades of the French bitch. Here, give me that glass! You got me here. Now have your way with me. How about let's fuck some more?"

She stretched, looking up at him. "Fucking you is a great pleasure."

"That's 'cause you don't have to do my shirts."

"I'd send them out."

"You would too, wouldn't you? You'd find a way."

"I have found a way, I guess."

"Have you?"

"Sure. At least that's what the old-timers would say."

☙ ☙ ☙

She wanted to tell David. David, I have a lover.

And there has not just been Kenny. Maybe to convince herself that there has not just been Kenny.

He took her to Locke-Ober's to welcome her home. They always had the chicken livers there. He ordered a very good red wine. Rich as a special night abroad.

He was a handsome man too, she thought. His face was intense and rugged. A marriage of the minds, Ellen Diamond said. He probably could have any student he wanted. The great professor. But he didn't want.

"Neither would I," said Kenny, "if I had you."

"The Venetians had the right idea," said Rose.

"Really?" answered David, amused. She often broke into thought through non sequitur.

"I mean the Lords and Ladies of Byzantium. With their high marriages and their lovers and their trains."

"I'm sure it looks in retrospect more orderly than it was."

"What do you mean? Count Guiccioli got along quite well with his wife's lover."

"I'm sure he found Byron much more attractive than his wife."

"You mean he was gay?" asked Rose, lapsing into Holiday Inn banter.

"I mean that his physical attraction to the Countess would have had its day. Afterward, how could her charms compare to conversation with Byron?"

"Byron seemed to prefer her charms."

"*Byron,*" said David.

"Sex fed his art."

"And he spent a lifetime biting the hands that fed him."

Rose poured more wine for both of them. "Still, the Venetians had the right idea. They made order out of the chaos of emotions."

"They were bored and rich and restless. They played games."

"I'm not talking about *them* personally. I'm talking about the chaos of emotion."

He looked at her quizzically. "You want a lover, Rose?"

"What if I said I did?"

"I'd say we'd talk it out."

"And if I still wanted one?"

"I'd say good-bye."

"I'd hate to lose you," she said.

He hardly listened to the wine talking. "We've had a bit of a disappointment."

"Oh?"

"You fortified?"

"In vino veritas."

He took out two letters from the inside of his jacket.

"Oh shit," Rose groaned.

Dear Ms. Addis:

We've now had readings on your novel *Monkey Man* and I'm sorry to have to report that we won't be offering on the manuscript. I do agree with you that it's much better than the other manuscripts I have seen from you in the past. It reads quickly and smoothly and the writing is clean and spare. However, I had trouble feeling for and believing in the characters. They were too remote and detached from the reader and thus it became difficult to really lose oneself in the novel.

This is, of course, only one opinion and I do thank you for letting me consider it. I hope you'll be able to place the novel with a sympathetic editor soon.

All good wishes.

Dear Rose Addis:

I'm afraid your manuscript *Monkey Man* isn't one that we can ask to take on. We are, however, pleased that you have sent it to us.

We are returning it with best wishes.

"Those idiots!" Rose said. "Those fucking idiots! David, this is terrible. It's worse than I ever thought. These people can't read!"

"You've written a fine book."

"And there's a good chance it will never be published."

"It'll rise."

"Shit rises, David. Shit rises."

"Maybe this wasn't the time to tell you."

"It has got to be better than discussing lovers and one-night stands."

"Rose, calm down."

She looked around at Locke-Ober's. The wooden paneling like that of her grandparents' dining room. The hushed decorum of the waiters, raising the silver lids of their serving dishes as if food were something far exalted and removed from one's digestive tract.

"You know, when I was a kid, I believed Einstein should be allowed in here in those funny little trunks he used to wear in the summertime and without combing his hair."

"And now?"

"Wait! And I also used to think anyone in her right mind would be thrilled to fuck Einstein."

She saw Reggie lifting her grandmother onto the pot and she found herself laughing.

"I don't like this place," she said. "I think I'm going to throw up."

But she didn't. She took Bufferin through the night and woke up early. David was still asleep. She watched him tenderly, wondering how he put up with her. In the morning she always felt as close to him as blood. "My provision's for life's waking part," the worldly Bishop Blougram had said to chaotic Gigadibs. It was perhaps her favorite poem of Browning's. "And when night overtakes me, down I lie,/Sleep, dream a little, and get done with it./The sooner the better, to begin afresh."

By the morning light lives are built and work accomplished. Precious things are fed by a good night's sleep.

Once she said to Kenny, "Some night we should sign in somewhere just to sleep." But for them there was only the night. The next day they were always exhausted. Rose left good for nothing, Kenny to another day.

Rose put on her robe and went down the stairs to her study. It was a front room and its windows overlooked Bunker Hill in Charlestown. She could see the bronze statue of Colonel Prescott, the sword long since broken off in his hand. Still, he was game to

charge, though the statue seemed a green ghost of himself. Stiff
and eerie, like Donna Anna's father rolled out at the Met, calling
DON GIOVANNI!!!

Colonel Prescott didn't sing. The sculptor was W. W. Story.
An American. His father was Justice Story, who has a street
named after him in Cambridge. W.W. had been a lawyer. They
still assign Story on torts. He'd gone to Rome to study art and
became a lifelong friend of Robert Browning's.

As good a reason as any to buy a house.

A web of coincidences that led to a feeling of hope. The way
Ellen Diamond picked a horse.

Etta's oriental floored Rose's study. There were hanging plants
that David saw to, a wall of bookshelves, and in front of the windows a long teak desk. The morning light came in, spotting
things.

Rose walked to her desk. Reread the letters David placed there,
before looking out the window.

She felt light-headed and light-hearted. Tomorrow was Easter.
This was a pastel day.

She didn't like Boston the way she had when she was an undergraduate. Yet there was no denying the special effect of a Boston
spring. Everything was against it. Then one day it was there.

The hell with lovers, the hell with letters!

When David woke, Rose had already been out shopping and
was now in the kitchen. She had brought home bunches of daffodils. "When a daffodil I see/Hanging down its head at me . . ."
She rarely bought flowers other than her yearly pussy willows.

"What are you up to?"

"I was just getting things ready. I was waiting for you. Want to
dye Easter eggs?"

They worked at the kitchen table, using the concentration they
brought to everything. David gave her a few tips on applying
wax.

She loved dipping an egg in dark purple and then raising it to
find it lighter than one would expect, pastel.

"My grandfather used to do this for us in the back of his store.

And my father, he once won a huge chocolate Easter egg. It was hollow. You'd look into it and there was a rabbit inside and jelly beans, a white fence, an entire scene. Things like that used to freak me out when I was a kid. They never made sense to me. They were made especially for kids. But I always knew they were make-believe."

In the afternoon they took a long walk on the Common.

They held hands.

"It's okay, David. Don't worry about me or *Monkey Man*. As long as we have each other, things will work out."

"That's for sure," he said.

Neither mentioned Locke-Ober's in the clear light of day.

Later she'd remember that day. The peace it brought and the hope. The buoyancy Boston can sometimes bring, like *An Afternoon on the Grande Jatte.*

"Hello, Rose," her mother said over the phone at ten o'clock that night. Ten o'clock! While David and she were in his study reading.

Then she heard the other voice. Her father on the extension, "Hello, Rose."

"Oh my God," she said into the receiver, "Nana's dead."

Etta Addis had not left her favorite a message. She had slipped away.

Rose never found her again. Though every April she waited.

Something was in the coffin.

"God," Rose said to Janet sadly, "why did they let them make her up like that?"

"Don't she look beautiful! beautiful!" wailed Lilly. "Don't look a thing like her," she said.

"I got her the best," Ray said. After the coffin was closed he went up to it. "Nothing but the best, like she would have wanted."

"Why girls! I'm so sorry!" Mrs. Roth, in the hall, looked up at them from her wheelchair, her balls of flesh dangling. "You've come for her things?"

"To talk with you, first."

"You want to talk? Better in the room then. I hate to stay there alone after what happened."

"It must have been hard on you," Rose said.

"I haven't slept. Even worse than when she was screaming." Janet wheeled her in. Nana's bed was stiff and white.

They fixed Mrs. Roth's wheelchair so that the sun did not hurt her eyes, and they sat facing her, the empty bed, and the glass doors that led to the day.

"I shouldn't have told her not to bang her silverware," Janet said. "I thought she had to get used to things. That she had time. Mrs. Roth, how did she die?"

She died institutionalized. Ancient Jews and black attendants were savvy, the truth elusive, inside knowledge hushed up.

"She went peacefully," Raymond and Ellen said.

What else would they be told?

"How did she die?" Mrs. Roth answered. "What goes on in this place. I've seen it all now. Rose, tell me, what do I do with it all?"

"Tell us what goes on here," Rose said.

"What's there to tell?" Mrs. Roth paused. "Do you believe in God, girls? Of course, I had a very Orthodox upbringing. But I doubt that there is anything more than this. Do you think I'll burn in hell for saying it out loud?"

The Hebrew Home and Hospital Complex was tokenly nondenominational. The Polack who had the room next door was visited daily by a priest. Mrs. Roth was convinced that they were both anti-Semites. "Here comes the Jews, here comes the Jews," she yelled at juice time. Mrs. Roth kept an ear well tuned, meantime absorbing bits of alien theology.

"Do Orthodox Jews burn in hell?" Rose asked.

"Hell! Heaven! After what I saw the other night, I doubt it all."

"And they told my parents Nana died peacefully!" Janet raged.

"But she did, girls. I should go like her when my time comes!"

"So, how did it happen?" Rose asked calmly.

"She yelled like hell for the aides. They came pretty quick — for them. 'Let down the sides of the bed, let down the sides of the bed! I want to walk to the toilet.' That was her all over. A proud woman. Always thinking she could walk. You should have heard the back-and-forth till finally they got her on the bedpan.

"Once they left, she was quiet. Till I begin to hear a noise. Funny noise. I think to myself, could this be the death rattle? A few minutes later I hear her say, clear as day, 'Bedpan.' Then nothing. When the aides came back I said, 'You'd better check Mrs. Addis. I think she's dead.' "

Rose and Janet looked at each other.

"Bedpan," Janet said.

"Where did she go?" Mrs. Roth asked. "We're taught the soul leaves the body. The windows were locked. The doors were closed. One minute alive, one minute dead."

"Funny," Rose said, "I felt the same. I thought if she were to die I'd feel it, but she just left."

"Hah! Sunday I tried to tell that to my son. I'll tell you the truth, girls, he's a brilliant man in his own line. No one can touch him there. You wouldn't dare to offer an opinion. But in life, I'll tell you, here" — she slammed her fist to her heart — "he doesn't see the complexities. Things escape him. He's not like you girls. You girls," said Mrs. Roth, pounding her heart, "you girls have it here. Of course you don't tell your children everything, but, still, there are things they should know that will not take explaining."

Janet remembered seeing the son's hat on Mrs. Roth's bed. A black hat she thought was her father's, like the one Rose wrote about in *Monkey Man,* till she saw it was new, ample, prosperous-looking, no pathos to it, cut and dried. Funny, she had said to Rose, you hit it exactly as it is. When Daddy puts on his little black hat, and stoops to kiss Nana, he looks like a little old Jew from Delancey Street, though God knows he had anything he wanted in the days Mrs. Roth's son had been wearing his cousin's clothes.

When Mrs. Roth's son put on his hat, he lent credulity to the astonishing fact that in 1976 he could make money in millinery. He backed out the door, with a furtive wave to his mother, on his way to Detroit.

Shmegegge.

"Girls, I want you to know something it's better they don't know." She motioned to the hall, where her cronies were congregating for the two-thirty snack. "You don't want them to get something on you." She paused. "I'm not so much younger than your grandmother."

"No!"

"Yes, girls. I'm eighty-eight. Mrs. Addis couldn't have been much more than that."

Actually, it was difficult to believe that the shrewd, bitchy, intelligent, and lovely Mrs. Roth was that old. But at the Hebrew Home and Hospital Complex, where the "children" could be retired in Miami and the "grandchildren" into second marriages (or new friends), it was often impossible to distinguish between the visitors and the ambulatory patients. Age took on a new level of relativity. When Janet brought Laura along with her, Laura would roll her great-grandmother fast down the halls, with a rousing yell all the way.

"Yes, I imagine we were almost the same age," said Mrs. Roth, who only three nights before had witnessed the whole procedure, including tagging, by which one leaves the place. Suddenly a worried look crossed her face. "Aren't they coming in? They must think I'm down the other hall. Roll me out, girls, will you? Otherwise I'm going to miss my juice."

"I'll get it for you," Janet volunteered.

"No, you girls have a closet to clear out."

"Wouldn't you like to stay?" Rose asked. "Nana had such nice things. Maybe you'd take something to remember her by."

"Oh, my God, I wouldn't dare!" she exclaimed. "Imagine what your grandmother would say! She'd come right back after me, I bet! Now come on, roll me out quick, girls, or I'll lose my turn."

"So Nana's prophecy came true!" said Rose after unlocking her grandmother's closet.

Most of the good things had disappeared already, and what was sent to the laundry that week would never come back.

As they took the clothes out of the closet, the procession began.

Black aides, white aides, nurses.

Pious and greedy, they came to say their grandmother had been a sweet person and to look shamelessly into the open closet.

Suddenly Rose and Janet were fighting for their grandmother's life.

No! to the aide who wanted to "buy" the polka-dot dress.

No! to the nurse who wanted the "pattern" for the white knit shawl.

No! No! No!

They stuffed glasses and corsets and stained dresses — suddenly all the good clothes were spotted and old — into shopping bags that swelled like their tempers.

They fought human nature and ended up with three bags of clothes.

"Did you find everything, girls?" Mrs. Roth asked enigmatically.

"Just about."

Mrs. Roth nodded abstractedly. She knew the score.

"Do you want us to take you to the patio for a while? It's beautiful out," Janet offered.

"Haven't I talked enough for one day? I must kill them off. The one before ended up carted off to the hospital."

From the private room the Polack yelled for a bedpan. Janet went in to see what she could do.

"Let her yell," Mrs. Roth said when she returned. "If you listen to every little kvetch, they'll all drive you crazy. And that one. When the priest came, she said, 'Mrs. Addis is dead. Can you pray for her soul, Father? She couldn't have last rites, because she's *Jewish.*' Rubbing it in like that! She deserves what she gets!"

From the Polack's room another yell. Rose said, "I'd better go and see if I can find Reggie."

"She'll be okay," Mrs. Roth answered, putting a hand on Rose's arm. "She can wait. Let her wait for the bedpan like everyone else. It's nothing. Let her learn her turn."

"Why is she in bed today, anyway?" Janet asked, as the shouting increased.

Caught, Mrs. Roth paused, torn between guilt and delight. The sisters, holding their bags of spoils, waited.

Mrs. Roth beamed in triumph. "Diarrhea, the skunk!"

❧   ❧   ❧

In Christ Hospital, propped up in bed, with no mother to visit him while Ellen was at work, Raymond spent a lot of time away from the small TV, staring at the walls.

The two Roses came to him often. His grandmother offering him chocolate. His grandmother looking in the crystal ball the way Charley feigned amazement when Janet went immediately gin with the cards stacked by him. Telling little Raymond's future was an event. The beautiful old witch loved him too much to realize the consequences of the fact that the future she pretended to see for him was a lie. A week before he entered the hospital, he drove Rose to the airport.

"Daddy, do you want me to go to Greystone with you some week soon to see Helen?"

Pause. "Truthfully, Rose, no."

"No?"

He told her, "I'm not up to it. I don't want to see her."

His daughter knew he meant forever.

"Now that he's got he*rrrr* off his mind, he can think about himself," said Ellen. She meant Etta. People didn't exactly die for Ellen. Her father went to sleep. Her mother entered fully into oblivion. Her mother-in-law finally developed a sense of decency.

In the world view she developed for her daughters, she trapped herself. *What did I know, I really used to believe people were good.*

Her confines were her comfort. She got home every night before dark. Pulled down the blinds, put on her radio, and knitted.

Once Raymond was dead, she went to Vegas for the first time on a junket with brother Lenny. There were Diamonds big in the casinos there.

She went with the action. Blackjack. Everything had to move fast. "It's so relaxing, getting out of the world."

It was out of the world to her, her world.

She never saw her similarity to all the other women at the track, at the casinos. Cotton underwear, synthetic pants suits, plastic pocketbooks. They would have all agreed with her that anything expensive you bought was a plot of salespeople against you. She read the right side of a menu first and stopped at the decent prices. The important things in life money couldn't buy. Like getting hot, like luck.

"Gamblers," she'd say to her daughters with disdain.

"You're a gambler too," Rose said.

"Me? I put aside exactly as much as I'm willing to lose."

"That certainly doesn't make you any less a gambler."

"Come to Las Vegas with me if you want to see gamblers!" said Ellen.

"What are you then?" asked Rose.

"I'm a mother. As silly as it might sound to you. As long as I know my girls are happy, I'm content."

"Oh your girls are very happy, Mother, rest content."

"Well, you ought to be, that's for sure. With that big handsome wonderful husband of yours. And Janet, what a doll she's got. The way he takes care of Laura."

"It's just like winning an Exacta, seeing such contentment all around you."

"Honestly, Rose, sometimes I think your father was right. Don't be so smart."

"*Me* smart? *You're* the smart one. When was the last time you let anyone tell you anything?"

"I don't follow the fashions. I don't have a lot of crazy friends I let sway me. I know right from wrong."

"You're a brick, Ma." Brick wall.

Not Raymond.

On the heart floor. He looked past the elevated TV to the wall. He stared the way Rose stared when she wrote.

He thought of Alsatian Rose. Though in life Rose had been calm, breathing in the effect of her magic on others, she was different in death. Glowering through stained glass. Avoiding her namesake. For once she was gone, Raymond, her favorite, was dismissed and what Rose had was passed on to a stranger.

To a girl. No woman. For where were the children to raise?

Where was the Central Avenue full of merchants to dangle? Rose Addis Willner tried to have her heart do her will, balancing a husband, a lover. There will be a tumble. Alsatian Rose won't tell her. Rose complained to her father: "She rarely says a thing."

She hasn't time. She's busy in Raymond's room. Blending into clean light green. Raymond can trace her colors on the wall.

Just as he can find Charley. Sawdust. A hot summer night's drizzle and Charley once more hoses the grass. Like the mother he once saw in white roses, Charley stays.

Etta wasn't like that. All his mother's things were left in other people's living rooms, closets, dressers.

Her spirit was somewhere far, far away, staring at nothing. As Ray could. As his daughter Rose could.

Raymond listened to himself breathing. The phone rang. He could have answered it quickly. He figured who it was. But for a while, as good as he was feeling, he let it cry for him.

"Hi, Daddy."

"Hi, Rose."

"How you feeling today?"

"Like after this phone call, maybe I'll take a walk."

Not a trace of sarcasm. Before she learned to talk Rose had responded to the timbre of the voice she heard once more over the phone. "You sound fantastic, Daddy."

"Well, I'm feeling pretty good."

"It's wonderful."

"Imagine. Wheat!"

"Incredible."

That's what young Young had taken him off at Christ Hospital. He was allergic to the staff of life. It had been killing him. Leave it to Raymond.

Rose said, "Listen, I want to see you. Saturday night we're booked, so I thought of taking the shuttle down on Sunday."

"Don't bother."

"It's half-fare on the weekends."

"Do me a favor. Stay home. You have things to do. I'm feeling fine. No use your killing yourself for me. You'll see me when I'm home."

"Well . . . You're sounding so good. Funny, I've never seen you when you've been in the hospital."

And she never would.

"He's been eating shit all his life," Ellen said to Rose. They were in the health food store on Central Avenue, the Avenue where Charley once shot craps. A thin young man with a beard ran it. "You should hear him talk," Ellen said.

"This is my daughter," she said to the young man. "Rose, just listen to him, he *knows* something about nutrition."

His knowledge was self-evident to the young man. He rode above it. He must have been about ten years younger than Rose, about twenty-five or twenty-six. Be it with the help of pot, macrobiotic diet, or meditation, he seemed, like many of his generation, to exist in levitation beyond the world.

Rose did not know how to reach him, whereas Ellen, who kept up with the columns and the radio talk shows, burst upon him like a wave, following him as he floated to the shelves containing products without wheat. His distance did not offend her. She broke through the generation gap without a blink. Just as she sat in the vast apartment Janet shared with her lover almost feeling at home.

For these were the new ideas.

Once there were old ideas.

Now there were new ideas.

The world still ran by ideas.

Grist to the wheatless mill of this Platonist.

Rose looked at her mother, who was excited that her husband was still alive. Ellen was still beautiful. Blue-eyed, blond-haired, petite and buxom, she didn't look her age any more than Rose looked hers. She looked at a distance like a woman who should have had lovers.

But if you stepped up close to her, you could almost hear the motorized aura that kept them off.

As she spoke to the young man, she rushed about the shelves, picking and choosing under his tutelage. There was a nervous intensity about her that never stood still.

"Relax," Kenny had said to Rose last night at the Ramada. Damn it! Rose thought this morning in the health food store.

As the young man rang up Ellen's purchases, Rose gave communication a try. "Listen, maybe you know something about this. My father said that while he was in the hospital he was served scrambled eggs that were as light as can be but contained no butter. I tried scrambling some on Teflon, but he swears that's not it. Do you know how they may have been made?"

Oh God, thought Rose as the young man bent his gaze down upon her.

He was absolultely right to make no further acknowledgment. What was there to say?

"There'll always be a Cheap Sam's!" Rose said later in Cheap Sam's. Now this was reassuring.

Everything in Raymond's diet had to be measured. She went among the rows of utensils. She treated her father to a one-cup and a two-cup measure.

"It's still nice here on Central Avenue," Ellen said as they headed to the car. It was still white.

"He's been eating shit all his life," Ellen said behind the steering wheel. "Now things will change."

The eggs, Rose thought. Her father was eternally restricted from crumb buns.

Not only wheat, but "Sugar!" Ellen cried out these days as an expletive more explosive than "Shit!"

Sugar? You had to be crazy once you read up on what it does to you.

Her granddaughter's generation. Laura sitting in front of the TV, phone to one ear, Twinkies in her mouth. Her young brain being picked clean.

"It makes me *sick*," said Ellen.

Eggs, thought Rose.

She remembered the Sunday many years ago, she was six or seven, when her father looked up from the Sunday *Times* crossword puzzle and said, "Ellen, 'seasonal worker.' It goes all the way across." Those were the really magical words, the ones that went all the way across.

Sometimes she and her mother helped with the puzzle. But her father surpassed them, surpassed the world. He could do the Double-Crostic alone.

In the car Rose wondered what went wrong in the life of a man who could do the Double-Crostic.

Her mother couldn't figure out the seasonal worker.

I will, thought Rose. She went to the couch and he pointed out the long row of blocks with a few filled-in letters.

"You gonna try, Rose?"

She squinted her eyes. Where would it come from, this answer he needed and she was determined to supply?

Where *did* it come from?

Ten minutes, fifteen minutes. Then the flash on that early summer day.

"Department store Santa or department store Claus," said Rose.

Raymond lifted his eyes from the puzzle and looked past her to his wife.

D	E	P	A	R	T	M	E	N	T	S	T	O	R	E	S	A	N	T	A

Eggs that are soft and fluffy without a bit of butter.

David was a good cook. She called him, but he couldn't figure it out.

"It's the phenobarb talking," said Ellen.

"I never got there in the morning, but I can have them checked out," said Kenny.

"God, they were wonderful eggs," Raymond reminisced. He actually did a slurp, like Charley.

Rose had gone through cookbooks. Nothing. How could they be so good? They must have been making them up in huge batches. They must have kept them on a steam table before they were served, like the awful ones years ago at B.U.

"Steam!" Rose cried out in the car.

"What?"

"That's it! Do you have a double boiler at home?"

"You mean one pot that fits into another?"

"Yes."

"Sure."

"I think I can make those eggs."

Raymond hung around the entrance to the windowless stand-up kitchen. He did not look as good as his voice had been over the phone, but he did seem to be feeling better.

Or was he?

"You see," Rose said. "They must make them over a steam table."

"Yeah, they do."

"Why didn't you tell me before?"

"I didn't know. Someone . . . Kenny went over and checked. But what has that to do about the price of tea in China?"

"Everything."

"Ray, come sit down until Rose finishes," Ellen called.

"Let him stand, Mother*rrr*."

She slid the beaten eggs into the pot. It took ages. Carefully, she stirred them when they began to congeal.

By this time Raymond had given up his vigil and was sitting at the dining table, waiting.

"Da Dum!!!" Rose said finally, bringing over the plate of very yellow eggs. "They were very yellow," he had said. He lifted a forkful. He opened his mouth. Put in the forkful. Chewed.

He nodded his head. "Delicious."

"And they're easy! You can do them yourself when Ma's at work. They take a little time, but there's nothing to it." He ate them slowly, along with a bit of semolina. Semolina cost a fortune at the health food store. But Rose showed them you could buy it loose from the Italian grocer for next to nothing.

"When David and I are in Italy next month, we can pick you up a few cases of wheatless pasta."

"Don't do me any favors," Raymond said. But the tone had changed. It chilled her.

She looked at his bloodless face.

He staggered out of the straight-backed chair and went to his chair and sat down.

"What's wrong, Daddy?"

"This has been happening lately after he eats, once in a while," Ellen said. "I think it's those damn phenobarbs. They've taken him off everything else that's eating away at his kidneys. Why not phenobarb too!"

Ray sat in his chair with his eyes closed and his head bobbing from side to side, the way Etta's had right after the stroke at Christ Hospital.

After this phone call maybe I'll take a walk.

Daddy!

Here was the audience for his life, but Raymond wasn't putting on a show. He was beyond the effects of his illness. His eyes flickered open and toward a heaven he couldn't see. Then closed. And his head rocked.

"Ray!" Ellen screamed.

"Maybe we should call Young."

"Too bad," Ellen said, "that you had to see this."

"How long has it been going on?"

"Since he got out of the hospital. It's hard for him to eat." They sat there watching him.

Rose saw her father at sixty, a youngster at the Hebrew Home and Hospital Complex.

Out of himself.

"What time is it?

"What time is it?"

Mrs. Maisel calling beyond the reach of his lost connections.

"It was the most awful moment of my life," she told David.

"Now don't be a Cassandra," David said.

"Who's a Cassandra? I'm telling you a fact. My father, if he's *lucky,* is going to die!"

David smiled at her in compassion.

"You don't believe people die, do you, David? Any more than you believe in sin."

"What are you talking about? Talk sense, Rose. Your father recuperated from that spell after dinner."

"His heart cannot maintain the stress of eating an egg. Young thinks it's wheat and kidneys. I think it's what it has always been, his heart."

"So you know better than Young. I'm in good company."

"I know my father."

David ignored her. When things happened, he took them as facts. But *before,* he refused to look at what led up to them. Maybe you had to roll around in shit like Kenny, or be born to a family like Rose's, to see.

She grabbed the calendar from her desk and pointed to the third week in July. "Where will we be then? London, Rome? Maybe they won't be able to get in touch with me. I can't bear it."

"So you let him go to Europe alone," Ray said.

"It's only a month," Rose answered.

It was early morning for Ray, Saturday about eleven. The eastern exposure blended him into the summer light.

"Europe you can have. The one place I would have liked to see is Egypt," said Ray. "The Pyramids, the Sphinx —"

"The Arabs," supplied Ellen. Leave it to him.

Janet had bought him a coffee-table book on Egypt that he never opened. Looked at her as if she were crazy, bringing him a book.

"I saw America," Raymond said. "More than I can say for you, sister. I saw the Mississippi when it was dry."

"Well *I,*" said Rose, "I'm going to one of the biggest manmade lakes in the East, which is very wet, and I'm going to begin a new book."

"All alone," said Ellen. "Too bad Janet's away." It was Roger's country house on Charter Lake.

"I enjoy being alone. I don't get enough of it."

"I bet," Ray said.

"I don't know what you have to say to that character," said Ellen. She meant Kenny, who was driving her up.

"He's a good talker; he's Irish," said Rose.

"He's an overgrown delivery boy," said Ellen. "I'll never understand what either you or your father see in him. Who do you think he is, Jimmy Breslin?"

"Well, Mothe*rrrr*, how else do you suggest I get to Connecti-cut?"

"I don't know why you don't take your father's car. I don't trust that VW they leave up there anyway. It's a wreck."

"I'm going to walk most of the time, don't worry. And I could never drive a car that big."

Two excuses. One too many.

It was exhilarating. It kept her mind busy.

She was nervous, drawn, underweight.

She wanted to talk with her father. 1976. They were teaching courses in the university on dying, and Rose couldn't ask her father if he wanted to talk about it.

It.

Raymond stared at the puffy, pink flesh around his elbow. The diet seemed to be healing his psoriasis. He touched his elbow with his free hand. Not to scratch. Curiously, the way a child would. He was far away. Would he come back?

The doorbell rang.

Rose jumped up too fast.

"You want some coffee?" Ellen asked, looking up from her knitting. Kenny was a big man. When he was in a room there was no denying him.

"Kenny drinks tea!"

So there! is the way Rose talked to her mother. Kenny drinks tea, so there!

Kenny sat down on the couch and looked up at Rose absolutely noncommittally. He turned to Ellen. "Less caffeine."

"Ray," Kenny said, "I feel naked without bringing you a box of crumb buns."

"Crumb buns!" Ellen hissed. "Sugar!"

"Yes, Mrs. Addis. Too much sugar's no good for you."

"Any's too much. There you have him sitting right in front of you. One thing about his mother, she was a good cook. But would he eat? No, no, not him. Anything to goad her. Spite her, spite himself. He's been eating shit all his life."

"He's not the only one, Mrs. Addis."

"For Chrissake, call her Ellen," Rose growled from the kitchen. "You sound like you're courting me!"

"May I call you Ellen, Mrs. Addis, so as not to compromise your daughter?"

"Call me anything that doesn't compromise her. Raymond, for God's sake, don't scratch!"

Ray looked up from his elbow, blank-eyed. He talked through tight lips, not out of venom; it was difficult to talk. "I'm not scratching."

Rose brought Kenny a cup of tea. She sat on the opposite end of the couch from him, looking directly at her father.

"Good tea," said Kenny.

"You have directions?" asked Ellen.

"We'll get there," said Kenny.

"I bet," said Ray.

"Oh, shit!" said Rose. Then she screamed: "Why can't we say something real to each other?"

Raymond looked at his daughter with an intensity that surpassed his prowess. The look went as far back as the first time they saw each other, but without her smile and without his surge of hope.

It was a triumph of the Addis will that, though their eyes swam in their sockets, neither cried.

"What is there to say?" Ray asked slowly. "You tell me, Rose, what is there to say?"

Good-bye Daddy.

Good-bye Rose.

❧   ❧   ❧

She sat naked on the blanket, her flesh dappled by sunlight through the trees. She stretched her legs out and looked at them, then at her thin arms, small breasts, her belly button — cutchy, cutchy coo!!! — she could still see Charley's finger flying around her baby belly and then landing in her navel. Only Kenny could touch her there without her flinching. Now a few stray black hairs surrounded it. She looked at her bush. She had to shave her inner thighs to wear her bikini underwear. She spent money on bikini underwear.

Sometimes in Boston, late at night, when David was asleep, she'd open her legs to a hand mirror. "Cozza," is what the Italians called cunt. The black seashell opening to the moist black-rimmed fire-red mussel. Cunt. Raw, primitive, inexorably intricate. It's a man's world. This intricacy crying out for the least ambiguous of nature's creations, a hard prick. Holding her mirror, she'd slink down on the couch, and masturbate. It never ceased to amaze her that she still masturbated. Though now of course there were how-to-do-it books and talk shows on how masturbation, self-love, is good for you. You could buy a vibrator. You could use one. Your partner could use one on you. She was an old-fashioned girl. "Fatto a mano" was on the label she'd buy.

This body of hers was parts. Parts to be shaved, parts that were too thin, parts that were flabby. Black hair, black bush, supple form, pale white skin. She saw her sensuality in a full-length mirror fleetingly, she saw it in Kenny's eyes.

But she didn't believe it. She didn't hold on to it. Hers was a trapeze act, all the parts rather artlessly swinging on the mind.

She watched Kenny swim. Soon he would come out of the water and walk past the trees to her. The comparison for Kenny was the Greek athlete, the male nude. She forced such images from her mind. She wouldn't have it! No, she wouldn't lay the Winkelmann trip on Kenny. When she fucked Kenny, she was fucking Kenny, and *not* the Dying Gaul.

He was Kenny.

And he wasn't enough.

David was probably in a library now. Drawn to the Continent by a grant, drawn to life by her alchemy.

He was David.

And he wasn't enough.

She thought of her father, drawn to death. She thought of herself, drawn to the suburban compromise. It wasn't at all Venetian. She thought of the three books she couldn't sell. The fourth one she would begin, because of the third. Because in the world of shmegegges, in the world of her own inadequacies, she had written *Monkey Man,* she had done something good.

Nothing came together. Parts askew. Desperately clinging to the swinging trapeze.

"Kenny!" she called out, cupping her hands to her lips. And he heard. And he swam toward shore. A parody of their relationship. She was the one who had to call. If you want me, whistle. She was the one who whistled.

He came to her wet and naked. As if there were tears dripping off his body, rolling off the hairs of his chest and legs, off his pubic hair and his prick. He is beautiful, she thought, and he is very worried about me. That's what you get from the Irish, she couldn't help thinking. Beauty and sentimentality.

She had told him her father was dying. So he took this risk. Took two weeks off on the sly while his wife and kids were in Florida. He wouldn't do that for his pleasure. He was afraid of hell.

He knew she was a witch. She scared him. She was the love of his life. But society had drawn a circle round him thrice. Society saved him.

He reached her. Dripping, he straddled her, distributing his weight on his knees and sitting on her stomach.

"You're cold!" she said.

"Warm me up!" He stroked her face.

"I'm colder. I'm frozen inside."

"Shit, Rose. Shit," he said. He couldn't say shit to his wife. He said shit a lot to his Jewish girl. He changed his position gracefully. When he made love to her there was no discontinuity.

He went down on her, opened her legs, pressed his head inside her thighs as comfortably as if his head were lying on her lap. His lips found her lips. He mouthed her. He used his tongue. He was a good cop. He had patience. And determination. He'd eat her. She'd come.

You could get arrested for doing what they were doing there. Cunnilingus on an inlet of a lake. A lake on which Rose was known.

When she moaned he took her spasms with his tongue.

Having warmed her heart he moved up on her. Kissed her. He wanted her to taste herself on his tongue. Evidence. Eat your heart, taste my devotion.

When he came in her mouth, he liked to taste that too. But this was not a day of special favors. This was lifesaving. This was pleasure on duty.

He felt her extrafragile and tremulous in his arms. He could not get this close to her without catching her spirit.

Her intensity, her need, her pain. Her relentless incompletion.

You can see too much. There were cases he couldn't take without his mental blinders. He rarely solved them, but he saw them through.

Whereas Rose took a good look at whatever came her way. Not only that; what wasn't there she searched for.

He entered her. "You're not cold, Rosy." She hadn't borne his children, or hers. She was tight and endless.

"Oh, Kenny."

"You're more than warm, you're fire."

"Sweetheart, how many uses you find for that tongue."

That was more like her.

She was on her trapeze.

He was doing his balancing act.

He penetrated deeper and deeper. He had been wet from water, now he sweated. His equipment might be unambiguous. But inside Rose it quested. It almost came in contact with the sibyl. Closer and closer, so near — almost, almost in contact, until he grew delirious of balance. Surrendered. Came.

"I wish," he whispered, rolling on his back and looking up through the trees.

"What do you wish?"

"What can't be."

It's funny, she thought that night as the sun was going down and Kenny was preparing the barbecue. She loved to watch him do things. He was so damn competent. As was David. All the step-by-step mechanical things in life. That men mastered. So did liberated women. She passed them over. If her car got stuck in the Boston snow, all she had to do was wait. A man would come over. For many of the practical things in life she was a slack bow waiting for a straight arrow.

She had known this man since she was fifteen. For five years on and off he'd been her lover.

She came onto the patio with the steak. She looked to the sloping lawn and down it to the lake.

"My father told me, when I first saw the ocean, I opened my arms and walked in. I've always loved the water. If I could pick my death, I'd drown."

Kenny looked up at her. He took the platter with the steak. She went back in to bring out the service for the table.

Tablecloth, dishes, silverware, candles. Like a dinner party in Boston. When the intellectual couples, straight and gay, sat round and discussed food with the passionate intensity Ellen Diamond gave to the possible approach of cold, rainy, or snowy weather.

The way a table should be set for a lover.

The stars were out. And the incense kept the mosquitoes at bay. They ate slowly. Neither was a big eater. Rose had bought a very good red wine.

"I'm enjoying this," she told Kenny. "Why is it that everything is filled with such surprises? Would George Eliot leave her father's bedside? Never! She stayed, she nursed him till the end. My father is dying. And I *want* to be here. I want this time with you. I didn't think I'd feel like that."

"It's not unusual," Kenny said. "It's the principle behind an Irish wake. The closer you come to death, the harder you want to live. Or a really gruesome murder. Once a really bad one even made me want my wife."

She giggled. "Must have been awful."

"It really was."

"What makes you want me?"

He looked at her. "Trying not to, maybe. Thinking of my wife and kids."

"That's flattering."

"It's a small part of the truth."

"You really are romantic."

He sat back and laughed into the night.

"What's funny?" She was smiling too.

"Oh, I don't know. You. Me. Us. The lake. You're a glutton, Rosy, and you don't know it."

"For punishment."

"Hell, no. Someday you'll see it. When poor old Dave and me are far, far behind you. And my blessings to you. For life, Rosy. For life."

Ray called her the next day, before she called him. While the market was open.

"You know that Westcott Development that I bought for you and Janet? It's way up all week. I think I'll sell."

"While you're making a profit? Don't be ridiculous. Wait a while. It'll go down."

"Don't be so smart. I got a feeling I wanta sell. I'll have them send you the check."

"Okay, Daddy. No kidding. That's really swell. I'll deposit it." The sisters. Add it to the twenty thousand he switched over to them before Etta died. The secret fear he refused to talk over with any lawyer. No facts. Just fear. That the state would demand most of everything for Helen.

They had stood in line in the bank of Renaissance marble among the workers of Jersey City on a Friday afternoon. He had picked, of course, the worst time to make a withdrawal. He in his coat and his little black hat, looking as if he'd swoon before he got to a teller. Rose heard the man behind her, rough skinned, in green mechanic's overalls, maybe as old as her father. "She wanders out right down the road in the middle of the night without her nightgown. And it's taking all we have to keep her in." Everyone in line with a mother to pay for.

"Maybe I'll take a little from both accounts."

"No, Daddy. If you're going to do it, do it right. Erase one."

"Ah, I don't know."

Somehow he had the stamina to make it to the window. When he completed his transaction he turned to her with a malicious smile.

"Here you go," he said. "Twenty thousand."

"I thought it was twenty-two."

"I know what I'm doing, sister. Listen to me. I left two in."

"Ah, shit! Then why did you bother at all! It's easier to trace this way."

"Let 'em try."

On the phone, Ray said, "It's the last thing I'm in. I even got out of the utilities. I just have a feeling . . . I'm hot."

"It makes sense to sell while the market's good. Remember Joe Kennedy: only a sucker waits for top dollar."

"So why don't I wait?"

She laughed it off, because she knew why. "That's what I said and you got mad. I thought you were allergic to a profit."

"Hey, Rose. I tried calling Kenny. No chance he decided to take a Friday off and drop up there for a swim?"

She paused for a moment. The pain was so intense she got dizzy. She was not the type to do it, but she felt faint. "Hold on, Daddy."

She was afraid Kenny had gone down to the landing dock to check out the boat. But he was still on the patio. In his shorts. Drinking tea.

"It's my father, Kenny . . ." Kenny looked startled. "I mean on the phone. He wants to talk with you."

She sat in his chair and put her hand against the cup, which was still warmed by the tea.

He wasn't gone long. He did one of his cop tricks. Snuck up behind her noiselessly. Put his hands over her eyes. She wasn't a bit jolted. Setting his cup down, she put her hands over his.

Kenny looked down toward the lake. "He didn't have much to say."

"No," she said, pressing his fingers hard so that she could almost see them in her darkness. "Just good-bye."

*

Raymond Addis entered the hospital just after midnight on Monday morning and was dying when Ellen called Rose at 6:00 A.M.

"Massive Heart Failure," Ellen said. She said it kindly, definitively, and with amazement. "Don't drive the VW when you're distracted. I'll send Moe for you."

"Don't worry. I have a friend here who'll drive me in."

"He was hot," she said to Kenny on the way. "His stocks were high. He had his hunches. I said he'd never outlive his mother by more than three months. I think I'm going to be hot too. Today is three months to the day."

"He told me to take care of you."

She put her head back. "That's the world he came from. Everyone caring for everyone else. The blind leading the blind. Him, my mother — neither had any idea of how to care for themselves. Me neither. Janet's the only one who's giving herself a chance."

No make-up, Rose thought next.

She remembered nothing else of the trip.

Raymond Addis died while they were driving, a little less than eight hours after entering Christ Hospital. Young Dr. Young said he'd never forget it. Hardly able to breathe and in pain, Ray looked up at young Young administering, and winked. Less than a day in the hospital. His corpse had to wait at the funeral home for the coroner.

The apartment was full of Diamonds. Janet had not yet returned from the coast. All that was needed was Ray distributing Cracker Jack. "I want to see him," Rose called above the noise into the phone. "What do you mean, he's not ready? I *want* to see him before he's 'ready.' I want to see my father *now* . . . Now wait, Mr. Fox. Let's get this straight. Do I or do I not have the legal right to see my father? . . . I'll be right there."

The undertaker's young assistant, decked out like a corpse, looked at her as if she were mad. The Diamonds themselves had seemed to part like the Red Sea in the living room at the Jersey Towers when she told them her intention.

At the funeral parlor, the young man asked, as if he were mimicking someone much older: "Are you absolutely certain?" She had a sudden stab of fear. How bad was it going to be?

"I want to see him. You see," she found herself explaining, "it's very important to him and to me. My father would have wanted me to see him dead."

The young man backed away. "I'll lead you down." Two floors.

She walked in alone. She insisted. Raymond was on a table, under a sheet that left his shoulders bare. His head was propped up by a wooden wedge that held his neck. His head was tilted toward her. If he were alive, he would have been quite uncomfortable.

This is what they were trying to save her from?

She walked over to him and touched his bare shoulder. "Now it's happened, Daddy." His eyes were slightly open, as was his mouth.

It was hard to believe he wasn't looking at her. That he couldn't see.

Back in the upstairs office, she asked, "Where's Mr. Fox?"

The assistant got him on the phone.

"You saw him, Mrs. Willner?"

"Yes, Mr. Fox."

"You feel better now?"

"Yes."

"Then you did the right thing."

Jesus H. Christ, she thought. "Look, Mr. Fox. His color's not bad. He looks all right. I can understand with my grandmother. After all, she was a very old lady and a stroke's not a pretty thing. But the family would have rather seen her dead than looking like Joan Crawford. This time: *no make-up.* Okay?"

"I think we can manage fine without it, if that is your wish."

She had gained credibility and respect. Without taking a course or obtaining a license, she had passed into the underworld and visited the dead.

When Raymond was finally laid out, Janet, Roger, Laura, Ellen, and Rose went to view him before people arrived. The visitors' book outside his room, however, had already been signed by Kenny. There was a huge bouquet of flowers by the coffin. Why shouldn't there be flowers for the Jews?

They approached Raymond.

"Oh my God!" wailed Rose, overtaken by the final surprise. The morning of her rationality was gone. She threw herself across the coffin. She could hear her handbag scratch the metal as she cried.

Raymond couldn't help her. His eyes and mouth were either waxed or pinned shut. Without make-up, and comfortably composed, the plain truth was on his face.

With life gone, gone too were asthma, psoriasis, hiatus hernia, angina, heart damage. He no longer looked like a man who'd say, I'll throw everything out the window, who'd say, If you're so smart sell your books.

Without pain, and without make-up to disguise its absence, Raymond at sixty looked young again.

Rose wrote the elegy Rabbi Freemantle delivered. She ended it with a Biblical thrust at the shmegegges that Raymond would have appreciated:

> I returned, and saw under the sun, that the race is not to the swift, nor the battle to the strong, neither yet bread to the wise, nor yet riches to men of understanding, nor yet favor to men of skill; but time and chance happeneth to them all.

⚜ ⚜ ⚜

From outside, looking in through the glass doors to the lake house, the sisters could see Ellen Diamond at the bridge table they had set up for her, working on the scrapbook. David was on the couch under the light, reading. Roger was in the bedroom on the phone, doing business. Laura was up the road with friends.

It was October 1977. David and Rose had driven down from Boston.

Ellen had told the sisters it was too cold to go out.

They walked down the lawn to the boat landing. The stars were out.

"Monkey Man has been keeping her from her knitting," Janet said. Almost in perverse tribute to the life Raymond Addis had lived, all the reviews were good. "Raves," Ellen said, bemused. "If only your father could have lived to see this."

He had died four months before *Monkey Man* was accepted for publication. Would it have mattered to Raymond Addis, the man who knew about X and Y chromosomes, that, though his wife had borne daughters, one of them would carry on his name? Be a Popcorn. I'll-tell-him-when-he-comes-in.

It sure would have mattered to Etta Addis. When Rose typed up a draft, she often felt she was playing the piano.

It sure mattered to Rose.

Could Raymond Addis have lived to see this, Rose wondered. It was almost as if his death released her from the bondage of his vision of his failure. He had to work out his destiny before she could work out hers.

It was almost as if Alsatian Rose were batting around with nothing better to do, the publication was such a fluke.

Her book had been picked up by a young editor, right from the slush pile of unsolicited manuscripts. It became a minor Cinderella story in publishing because it never ever happened anymore. An editor picks up a book by someone no one has ever heard of, reads it, and knows that it is good.

The young editor's vision should have been a clue to her destiny. For her life had been a weaving drawn from the house on Clifton Avenue. Her mentor had been Zeno Beni, who'd never understand her book. That old life was passing. "You were born with an old head," Jennifer Potash would soon tell her. Her future would be her youth.

The book came on the marketplace with the greatest stigma the publishing world can offer. It was that dirty word, "literary." Literature was becoming less and less what the publishing industry was more and more about.

So her success, such as it was, was unusual in that it made everybody happy. It proved that something that never happened anymore can happen. But it didn't fool Rose. She knew other books as good got buried. Hard work, dogged persistence, talent, yes. But the better you are, the more you need a witch with $50,-000 in the bank. If quality is your only consideration, you damn well better be struck by luck.

And run with it.

Rose was wearing dungarees and a heavy turtleneck sweater with a Chinese jacket over it that David had bought her in Petticoat Lane. Her hair was long and well groomed. She had it professionally blow-dried every week this fall for the photographers. Notice the pictures on the first books of women authors and compare them with later works. There's an uncanny drive at first to look impeccable. Not interesting, deep, thoughtful, prophetic, as much as pretty. First date.

And Rose had been besieged by photographers. Even Kenny blew his cool when he opened his *Time* magazine and saw her musing coyly out at him. He *called.* "Jesus Christ, Rosy. Imagine your picture in *Time!*" Excited as Laura would be at finding her in the *Encyclopedia Britannica Year Book.* Authoress on the grass.

Down at the pier Rose thought of the commotion. In these first months what she had always suspected about success was coming true. It's much easier than failure. People smile on it. They are drawn to it. So they are not exactly being what Raymond would call phony when they smile at you. And for Rose it was not unpleasant to smile back.

New York. From Jersey all you saw was the outline. Where were the pushy people? Everyone spoke just above a whisper. You had to strain to hear. And at the fanciest lunches they ordered wine not by the bottle but by the glass, like hicks.

Publishing was all new to Rose. Just not having her messages intercepted by secretaries seemed worth the twelve years' work. Just knowing that she could take bland pleasantness without tasting the bitter herbs, without her father's sneer, freed something in her. The acceptance of her book had come over her as death had come to Raymond. Granting her peace.

For a while.

It was a state she'd remember later, that what she had worked for all her life actually tasted sweet then. And that she and David had a time when they shared it.

"How does it feel?" Janet asked her down by the lake.

"Right," Rose answered. After a pause she added, "Not to mention strange."

The sisters were silent by the water. Tomorrow a double unveiling. On Monday Rose would be on *Today*. Roger would tape it for replay. Their father would never see it; Etta would not be glued to her set.

The Addis plot was in a choice location in the cemetery. On the hill overlooking the meadowlands that had become the Meadowlands Sports Complex. Trotters at night. Around it were the stones bearing the names of her grandparents' friends. The people who had come to her grandparents' parties and card games and who had eaten Etta's meals and drunk whiskey with a little water, thank you. She remembered the joke when they purchased their fashionable plots. Someday they would all be playing poker together again.

It was a spacious, well-kept cemetery, nothing like the cities of the dead one sometimes passed in New York.

Rabbi Freemantle walked by her side. At Etta's funeral he said Etta Addis had welcomed him into the community, had never failed to give. He remembered her sweet smile. At her father's funeral he said he had married Ray and Ellen.

He was an old man himself now, tall and forgetful. His delivery was British, as if he as well as his wife should have been on the stage. He always seemed distant, as if he were wondering, as Rose was, how a man of God could have lasted a lifetime among the Jews of Jersey City.

This was the cream of his congregation, spread out over the well-kept hills and vales. The crowd who had once had money and followed the crowd. The crowd who had lived in a city.

Each family had a well-wrought headstone governing its plot. Each plot crawled with ivy.

Their own simple white headstone said ADDIS. Now three of the four front graves were filled. The two newest looked raw.

Mother and son lay next to each other, a cloth over their markers. 1976. April and July. Three months to a day.

The immediate family was early. For this was Ellen's occasion, and for her, only early was on time. They hung around. Rose noticed that even Charley's plot looked bare. Why were these three graves different from the others?

"Mother," Rose asked, "What happened to the ivy?"

Etta had planted ivy like her friends.

"I decided on grass."

Over Charley's grave, the ivy had been uprooted, and a meager yellowish lawn had been laid.

"But Mother, *everyone* has ivy."

"They're still following each other like sheep. Sixty dollars more a plot, for what? To keep up with the Joneses? Not your father or me."

Laura went over and put a rose on Charley's stone.

"Janet," Rose whispered, "we're the only ones with grass."

Janet looked at her uncomprehendingly. "So what?"

"Don't you remember the poem you wrote about Nana in therapy?

XII

My grandmother
grooms
her mother's grave
by mail
$8 a year.
It's been 65 years
that she's in the
old section of
Brooklyn's crowded yard
coldly collecting tribute
from her little girl.

"So what?"

"Nana would have died."

"She did."

Rose remembered her grandmother next door at Clifton Avenue, cotton dipped in milk, each leaf rubbed till it shone. Dark jade-green ivy.

Standing on the top of the hill, Rose was shocked at her rage. Here, in the muted hush, the Addis plot would stand a disharmonious and fairly unsightly sermon on Addis individuality and the transience of things.

"Laura," the rabbi said. "You see the rocks on the headstone? Take them off dear." He turned to Rose. "The old superstition, that stones keep off the evil spirits. I hate to see it."

Rose was jolted out of her anger.

"I thought Conservative Jews still do that."

"Yes," he explained. Suddenly he was talking to her as a confidant, the way some people do to an author. "But, of course, my schooling, our congregation, is Reform."

"Reform?!"

"Don't forget. The people in your grandmother's crowd were somewhat old-fashioned and set in their thinking. I had to go very, very slow."

"Hey, Ma," Rose whispered. "Did you know the temple was Reform?"

Ellen Diamond wiped her eyes with Kleenex. "Don't talk nonsense now, Rose." Then she asked, "How does it look?"

"What?"

"The grass. Is it okay?"

Rose saw that her mother was as shaky as if Etta Addis were standing over her, keys jangling, noticing Ellen's table was set all wrong for guests.

Things, forms. What did it matter? For Ellen Diamond Addis it was the thought that counts. She'd remember the dead in her own way.

Under grass or ivy, all there was were bones. And bones didn't matter. She'd never been to the churches of Italy and seen hipbones and fingerbones encased. *Disgusting.*

For Rose too under grass or ivy or in reliquaries all that remained were bones. People who had once acted out their destinies. People like her grandmother and father. People like the

great saints. All that remained of body was bone. All that remained of human endeavor was memory encased in the world.

Bring on the books, the movies, the TV specials, the pilgrim shrines. Stud the gold reliquaries with semiprecious stones.
Uproot the weak carpet of grass and smother the Addises with
ivy!

Rose looked out over the cemetery as far as she could see, and
then to the Addises' strangely bohemian plot. What was she to
say? Under her feet were Charles, Etta, Ray. By her side was her
mother.

"It's not the way I would have done it," she said softly. "But
you've done it your way. So you stick by it."

"Oh look!" said Laura.

Cars were arriving below. Relatives started streaming up the
hill. There in the vanguard, arthritic, almost blind, Lilly struggled
against the help her daughter offered. "Where's Rose?" she cried
like the Oracle of Delphi as she stumbled against the rabbi.

"Here, Aunt Lilly."

"Boy, good for you! Who wants to be a sack of potatoes?
You've done yourself up swell. Right from the beginning I knew
you were special. God knows I could have been a writer if I had
had the time. You know —" she articulated to the group she
couldn't see — "she always looked at you like she was questioning
every word you'd say. She'd squint her eyes and tilt her head right
from the very first day."

"Aunt Lilly," said Janet, "come sit. We've set up a chair for
you."

"*I* can stand."

"Isn't it too much for you?" inquired the rabbi.

"At my age it's a pleasure. When do I get a Sunday out?"

Rose walked over to David. Unconsciously she straightened her
hair. "Greet some of these people, will you? I have a feeling
they're confused and think it's my unveiling."

A crowd gathered and the rabbi established a hush. The service
was short, just as Ellen required.

The plaques in the ground were unveiled. In loyalty, the sisters
had kept their grandmother under ninety.

ETTA — Loving mother, 1887–1976.

RAYMOND — Devoted father and son, 1916–1976.

Laura went over with the roses for Ray and Etta.

"Rabbi, will you come back to the house with us?" Rose asked.

"No, dear, I must hurry."

Rose walked close to the stones. But she wasn't allowed her deepest thoughts on the shining October day.

People came up to her, kissed her, shook her hand. Many brought clippings of her reviews that they had saved. They were her relatives whom she saw only at weddings, funerals, and Bar Mitzvahs. And they were smiling. In some mysterious way they were part of her, and she had done them all proud, down to the little cousins now suburbanites in Livingston.

It was not a celebration of memory; it was a celebration.

Rose found herself caught up in the tide. Some people couldn't come back to the house. They were determined to speak with her now.

Her father came back to her. The look of disapproval when anyone cried at a funeral, the look of disapproval when everyone made jokes and small talk and ate a lot on the days they sat for the dead.

Her father, in the front seat of the limousine that drove them from Etta Addis's burial, turns around to her once more: "Not one friend," he says again, mysteriously triumphant. "Did you see who came, Rose? I didn't have one friend there."

"David," Rose whispers at the unveiling, "I'm not going to get a chance to do it unnoticed. Please, sweetheart, please put some rocks back on the headstone."

"Really, Rose?"

"Please."

David picked up rocks. Rose watched them, big and pinkish, gleaming in the sun. In her heart of hearts she prayed that they had their own power. David fended off the evil spirits for her while the small crowd pushed Rose so that her feet were planted on top of Etta's and Raymond's grave.

❧ ❧ ❧

The waiting room was filled with small objects, bird's-eye views of miniature rooms, primitive paintings, and glaring masks. The glass-covered bookcases contained the works of Freud and Jung. Rose eyed the volumes of Harry Stack Sullivan's work. A subtle music filled the air, and so did the smell of incense. Rose sat down. She tried to make a Raymond Addis–like distinction. Forms she appreciated, but she was suspicious of symbols. People can interpret the life out of life as well as art.

She picked up a leaflet announcing the spring program of the Jung Institute. Glancing over it, she felt like bolting. This was as humiliating as if she had suddenly decided to take sensitivity training at *est*.

Jung! He told James Joyce his schizophrenic daughter was just like him, but without the art to put madness in order. Lucia. Light. Joyce lived years in Italy. Lucia Joyce. Joyce probably spent in Switzerland consulting Jung what the Addises spent on Helen. Portrait of the Artist As a Father.

Harry Stack Sullivan. The only psychiatrist Rose ever read who she felt came close to what must be the instincts of schizophrenia. *Schizophrenia as a Human Process.* He was alive when Helen got sick. But Sullivan wasn't for the girls. Sullivan and his dog. Sullivan was for the boys.

The door opened and Jennifer Potash walked in.

Rose had been warned. Take your time in choosing. The wrong analyst can be worse than none.

At her consulation uptown she knew what she wanted.

A woman.

About my own age.

No Viennese accent.

Someone I can call by her first name.

An American.

Please God, an American.

Jennifer was wearing a Gypsy outfit, an exotic cream-colored blouse and blooming red pantaloons. Her eyes were as big as a mask's, but they were limpid as a lake. She had long dark hair that she, like Rose, was letting go to its gray. She was a stunning woman.

The large room of her apartment that she used as an office overlooked Fifth Avenue and was again full of primitive objects, the shrink's collector's eye. An eye that David had. Too exotic for Etta. Alien to the instincts of Rose. Except that she always enjoyed being in other people's atmospheres.

Rose sat in the deep black chair. Next to it a table with a marble ashtray big as a slice from a tree trunk, enough to hold the multitudinous butts of anxiety.

Jennifer sat in her chair across the way. Put her feet on a Haitian stool and smiled.

"I'm a mess," Rose said.

Jennifer looked interested.

"I wrote a book. It came out to a fairly big success. I had already begun another. Then I ran dry. Suddenly I looked down at what I had to say about a character. I looked at what I had to say and I realized my point of view hadn't changed in over fifteen years. I'm thirty-seven years old and emotionally I'm lucky if I'm twenty."

"What's that I hear in your voice?" Jennifer asked. She put her hand to her throat.

"I know. It sounds like a sob."

"It sounds like pain."

Seventy bucks every fifty minutes. Alsatian Rose died with money in the bank. The price of witchcraft has always been high.

"I have a husband and a lover. I bet you eighty percent of the women in America would give their eye teeth to be like me."

"Conservative estimate."

"Give or take. And I'm dying inside. I'm drying up. I try to explain it to David — my husband. But he's been so good to me, how much of my problems can I expect him to take? So I told him I needed some time alone. I came down from Boston and sublet a place from a friend. My sister wanted me to stay with her. But I really do want to be alone.

"And with my father gone, Kenny — he's my lover — doesn't know I'm here. I guess I wear well. After all these years, it's he who has started to call me. He knows he's losing me and suddenly it's not as easy as he thought it would be. But it's as hard for me as I knew it would be, that's for sure. But something's wrong, something's wrong with my whole setup. It's as if for all I've done, I've never lived on my own or for myself. Oh, shit! This sounds like the Perils of Pauline! You know, Jennifer, order and control have character, uniqueness. Pain, chaos — in a way, if it really hurts, it's trite."

"Have you had any dreams lately?"

"I dreamed I was back on Clifton Avenue. Along the alleyway that bordered my grandparent's side of the house, there were chickens nesting. I was sent out by my mother and father to gather eggs. Some weren't yet formed. I left them. Those that were I put into my dungaree pockets, which is no way to carry eggs. As soon as I got them into our side of the house they started to break. I should have had a basket; I know that. But I'm a city girl. Why did they send me out to gather eggs?"

"It doesn't sound very practical of them. Were your parents impractical people?"

"My parents!"

"Tell me a little about them."

"My father is dead. My mother wouldn't like me to talk about her. Listen Jennifer, what do you think? Do you think I need therapy?"

"Therapy? I'd say you'd be cheating yourself if you didn't go into analysis. That quiver in your voice. I have a feeling you know a lot more than you think you do about what's causing it. We should try to get to it."

"What's the difference between therapy and analysis?"

"Analysis tries to get to the root; therapy, to patch things up."

"Do I really need this?" Rose demanded at the next session. "I know it's normal to have a hostile reaction and I'm sure having it!"

Today Jennifer's hair is pulled back. She wears a long black velvet skirt and a blouse closed high on the neck by a cameo.

"I don't encounter that reaction too often. I don't think it's so normal. Very few people I've seen have had it."

"It's a lot of money to sit around talking about my family and my dreams. It'll take you a year to learn half of what I already know about my family and their effect on me.

"And *dreams!*" Rose continued. "Maybe it's different if you're not a writer. It comes as a surprise that things can mean other things. But I'm a writer. I deal with this shit every day. I don't want to be analyzed! I don't even have the time. Maybe I'll be back in Boston in a month. Patch me up!"

Jennifer paused for a moment, still confident, like Raymond over a hard word for a puzzle, yet concerned.

"Well, the past. What we're interested in there is how it affects the present. I don't give a damn for it for its own sake either. We can enter the present more directly. No problem there. But the dreams —"

"I know. Saying I don't want to spend my time talking about my dreams to a shrink is like you telling me the novel is dead."

"Kind of. I really don't see how I can work without dreams. Again, it's what they say about the present, that I'm interested in."

"Well, maybe some dreams," Rose allowed, "but predominantly I'd like to talk about now, about the present."

"You see," Jennifer answered, "I really don't know much about you. I have to start somewhere. I picked up your book in paperback. I was planning to read it this weekend. And maybe, if you don't want to talk too much about the past, you might write me a short autobiography. If you want to go fast, I've got to have something to go on."

A SHORT AUTOBIOGRAPHY
by Rose Addis

My name is Rose Addis. I was born on 19 November 1940 in Jersey City. I lived with my parents next door to my father's parents in a big stucco duplex on Clifton Avenue. It was one of the biggest houses in the city. My sister, Janet, to whom I've always been very close, was born in 1944.

My father was a sickly man of a morose temperament. His sister was a pianist who went insane. He was always afraid this would happen to me as well. He used his considerable intelligence badly, to torture himself at the loss he saw all around him, rather than to build a life for himself. My mother was a very repressed woman whose sexuality turned into nervous energy. She made a strict dichotomy between men with the right values and men to whom she might have been sexually attracted. Though this appalls me, I'm much the same way. I rarely reach orgasm.

I admired my grandmother Etta Addis very much. She is the only person I believe ever loved me because I'm me. I replaced her daughter, Helen, in her life and she made a big fuss over me. I never thought myself as beautiful as she did. She saw a lot in me. The way an artist might make much of an object. This did not bother me. I am an artist. I respected even the inhuman in her artist's nature.

I thought my grandfather's loving nature was a fraud. Once as a child I danced wildly. I was in my own world. Oblivious, as my father would say. My grandfather saw Helen and slapped me hard across the face. I saw a weakness in him that no one else did.

I knew my father had vision and insight — his grandmother, who favored him, was a witch. He could not express what he saw. From the earliest age I knew I wanted to talk for him. To redeem him. I always wanted to be a writer. I always believed I would have something to say.

I was also always afraid I'd go nuts like Helen. Men particularly had a bad effect on me. I was afraid if I unleashed my passion there was no end to what I could do or what harm could come to me. I had a miserable affair with a madman named Carl and married a very supportive man soon after.

David built me an atmosphere in which I could work. Often I thought I was George Eliot being nurtured by George Henry Lewes. For years I wrote in absolute obscurity with the absolute support of David. Without him, I don't think I could have done it. Looking back, remembering the rejections and the disappointments and the *odds* against success, I don't know how I did it.

Then, right after my grandmother's and father's deaths — I

sometimes feel my father had to work out his destiny before I could mine — a book I wrote with him as prototype, *Monkey Man,* was accepted for publication.

My life up to then, even now, is my writing. I believe in my novels; they are better than I am.

My success made me happy. I had always wanted to be what my father called a Popcorn. The best thing about it is that, though failure is difficult, success is easy. I took it all with a Raymond Addis grain of salt, but I took it. For a while, being an Addis, I wondered if previously I actually hadn't been courting failure.

I believe in friendship, destiny, and the human heart. I would also like to fuck myself blue in the face.

Sometimes I still think I could give up everything for Kenny. I'm a mess.

I wonder what my father would say if he could see me writing off the top of my head to a shrink. The problem of his generation was that "Doctor" meant "King." They never could get over the fact that doctors were jerks like everyone else. They blamed it on the profession. Yet they called doctors "Doctor."

I call you Jennifer. I don't expect you're a miracle worker; I imagine my great-grandmother would do just as well as you. But I will try to take what you can give. I will pay your profession's exorbitant fee and hope that I can come to some knowledge of the darker parts of me.

I am thirty-seven years old. I have had a relatively good life. Excellent health (as long as you have your health, said my mother), energy, husband, lover. I have even written a good book. But it is not enough.

Why isn't there a ceremony for middle age, something between "the marriage" and "the funeral"? Maybe it would be called "the option" and you don't have to come dressed special for it; it would be come-as-you-are. But there are no ceremonies in society for maturity. Ceremonies bring you in, marry you off, and lay you out. Cradle to grave. With a big penalty in the middle if you learn to think, to feel, to want to act. "Get it over with," as my mother would say. I PROTEST!

The voices in the house on Clifton Avenue say, What? Shame on you. Use your common sense, know when you're well off. Hey! Maybe that's why my father liked Kenny. Maybe he thought he was the man who would help to keep me down.

The voices of my sister and my friends say, Go ahead! In the long run, what you discover will be better for David as well as you. You've played it safe too long. But they have all been analyzed and speak the new language.

I cannot fall back on traditional values, because I believe they are dead. All that nostalgia about roots. All that guilt. My heart used to be in shackles.

All I can do is go ahead. I'm doing things. People read what I have to say. I'm a good professional. The first in my family to make it, I am in the world.

It is not enough. I want to know myself. To be myself. To stand for myself.

I want more.